Long, hot days lead to

Exotic SUMMER NIGHTS

Escape to romance!

Biting the Apple
by Jo Leigh

Sweeter Than Wine
by Cathy Yardley

Back to You
by Sarah Mayberry

Forgotten Lover
by Emilie Rose

Trouble in Paradise
by Jill Marie Landis

Exotic SUMMER NIGHTS

JO LEIGH
CATHY YARDLEY
SARAH MAYBERRY
EMILIE ROSE
JILL MARIE LANDIS

All the characters in this book have no existence outside the imagination of the author, and have no relation whatsoever to anyone bearing the same name or names. They are not even distantly inspired by any individual known or unknown to the author, and all the incidents are pure invention.

Harlequin Mills & Boon Limited, Eton House,
18-24 Paradise Road, Richmond, Surrey TW9 1SR

ISBN: 978 0 263 87538 6

025-0709

Harlequin Mills & Boon policy is to use papers that are natural, renewable and recyclable products and made from wood grown in sustainable forests. The logging and manufacturing processes conform to the legal environmental regulations of the country of origin.

Printed and bound in Spain
by Litografia Rosés S.A., Barcelona

Jo Leigh has written more than forty books for Mills & Boon. She lives in Nevada with her three enormous cats, Zeke, Coco, and Molly. Her daily blog is available at www.joleigh.com

Want more Jo Leigh?
Have Mercy is out now in Mills & Boon® Blaze®!

Cathy Yardley needs to get out more. When not writing, she is probably cruising the internet, sleeping or watching D-list movies and adding to her unnatural mental store of character-actor trivia. She can hum along with all the theme songs on Cartoon Network and is learning Japanese from anime. Her family is considering performing an intervention for her addiction to pop culture. For those similarly addicted, drop her a line at cathy@cathyyardley.com

Sarah Mayberry picked up a love of romance novels from both her grandmothers, and has submitted manuscripts to Harlequin many times over the years. She credits the invaluable story-structuring experience she learned as a script-writer on *Neighbours* as the key to her eventual success – along with the patience of her fantastic editor, Wanda. Sarah loves to read romance and fantasy novels, go to the movies, sew and cook for her friends. She has also become a recent convert to Pilates, which she knows she should do more often.

Emilie Rose lives in her native North Carolina with her four sons and two adopted mutts. Her love for romance novels developed when she was twelve years old and her mother hid them under sofa cushions each time Emilie entered the room. Who wouldn't be curious and sneak a peek? Writing is her third (and hopefully her last) career. She has managed a medical office and ran a home day-care, neither of which offers half as much satisfaction as plotting happy endings. Letters can be mailed to Emilie at PO Box 20145, Raleigh, NC, 27619, USA or via e-mail to EmilieRoseC@aol.com

Don't miss Emilie Rose's latest book,
Wed by Deception, available from Mills & Boon®
Desire™ this month!

Born in a small town on the Wabash River in Indiana, **Jill Marie Landis** became a California transplant at the age of ten. She fell in love with the Pacific Ocean and life at the beach. Married for thirty-seven years to her college sweetheart, Jill Marie now lives with her husband in Hawaii. When she's not writing or sitting on the sand reading, she enjoys visiting family and friends, raising orchids, dancing the hula and quilting – but not all at once.

Biting the Apple

JO LEIGH

To Marsha,
for thinking of me

CHAPTER ONE

WITH GRAVEL CRUNCHING beneath her boots, Trish Avalon focused on the scent of blooming acacias as she walked to her listing mailbox at the edge of her driveway. The mesquite trees her grandfather had planted years ago gave her shade from the warm spring sun and hid most of the barren landscape surrounding the ranch.

Some ranch. There were no cattle, no horses, no crops. Just the big old house filled with memories and ache. Since her mother's recent passing, Trish had been getting the place ready for sale. It wasn't a quick job, given that her folks had been pack rats. Neat pack rats, she'd give them that, but neither one ever threw a darn thing away.

Just this morning she'd found a stash of mementos from her childhood. Baby shoes, clothes, toys. Report cards and gym trophies she hadn't thought about in years.

The packing would have gone faster if she hadn't taken that job at the drugstore. It was worth it, though, as she hadn't had to dip into her savings. The only thing she hoarded was money. Money that would get her out of Briscoe, Texas, and into New York City.

She pulled the large stack of mail from the box and closed its rusty mouth, swearing as she did each day that she'd grease the hinges. But then she'd walk inside and by the time she finished with the mail, something else would catch her attention and she wouldn't remember about the mailbox until she opened it the next time.

Once back at the house, she went straight to the big oak dining table where she dropped the stack of mail and then to the kitchen for more coffee.

Armed with the hazelnut brew she liked, Trish sat down to face the seemingly unending task of taking care of her parents' affairs. Her father had died a year ago next month, and her mother had taken sick shortly thereafter. Most everything had been set aside in Trish's life at that point—including her newspaper job in Dallas.

But soon, she'd have the place ready for the market, and the proceeds, if the house sold, would be another big step toward her dream. Unfortunately the real-estate market in Briscoe was about as brisk as the bone-dry Briscoe river.

Bills, social security, advertisements, catalogs, a sip of coffee, more catalogs—then her heart went wild as she looked at the big white envelope that had been forwarded from Dallas. It had one fancy word in the upper left corner—Hush.

There was no address underneath because none was needed. There was only one Hush, at least for Trish. Hush hotel in Manhattan. The sexy, sophisticated, expensive, unbelievably hip Hush hotel, which, just under a year ago, had launched a contest to debut their brand-new wedding services.

Trish, who never let an opportunity pass her by, had entered the contest with a video essay. But she couldn't have won, could she? No. Impossible. No one from Briscoe ever won a thing. Not the lottery, not the spelling bee, not even one football championship, ever.

Still, she couldn't stop her hands from shaking as she opened the envelope. There were a bunch of brochures, but her gaze was firmly on the letter. And there it was. The word that made the rest of the universe fade away.

Congratulations!

She'd won. *She'd* won.

Her gaze shot up to top of the page, just to make sure it was really, truly Trish Avalon they'd written to, not some other woman.

She smiled as she read the full letter. The judges, including the incredible Piper Devon who owned the hotel, had selected her video out of thousands of entries. Thousands! Two first-class tickets to JFK airport, then a penthouse suite in Hush. Eight other tickets would be hers to give to family and friends, although those would be coach. There would be a wedding dress created exclusively for her by one of the world's top designers. Flowers. A wedding dinner catered by the hotel's chef. A week's exclusive use of a hotel limousine. Spa treatments. A makeover.

Wedding pictures and a video by someone she'd never heard of, but who apparently was quite famous. Free meals. Free drinks. Free tickets to a Broadway show. Free everything a girl could want for that special, special day.

It was all perfect, extraordinary. Unbelievable. A week in New York. A whole week, free of charge, where she'd be able to go to every single newspaper and magazine and personally hand in her résumé. She'd be able to meet with editors face-to-face. To show them her clippings, her enthusiasm, her determination.

She was being handed her entire future in a silver-wrapped package, special delivery, no postage due. Nothing would ever be the same. Nothing.

All she had to do was one tiny thing. She'd have to get engaged.

BY THE TIME Mark Reynolds got back to the house, he felt like he'd been ridden hard and put away wet. Working the ranch did that to a man, and even though it ached where Gypsy had stepped on his foot, he still wouldn't trade it for anything.

He threw his hat on the coatrack then stretched his neck as he headed for his dad's office. Mark stood at the door as he watched his old man type at his computer, his bifocals perched on the end of his nose, his music, classical as always, playing softly in the background.

Mark didn't say anything. He knew better than to

disturb his father when he was writing. It had shocked the hell out of Mark when his father had decided to turn the running of the ranch over to his sons. He wanted no more to do with it after a lifetime of working sunrise to sunset. The ranch was worth something now, a lot actually. The horses Bill Reynolds had bred had become champion stock, but Bill had had enough. He wanted to write his life story, then he wanted to write a book about Briscoe, then some fiction, just to change things up.

Mark, as the oldest, had happily taken over, glad that his father had found something that gave him satisfaction. It was difficult to understand, though. Mark loved the ranch. He liked the hard work, the toughness of the country, the breeding program. He, like his father, had found his calling.

His kid brother, Chris, on the other hand…

Chris wasn't home from school yet, or at least not home from practice. The boy still bitched like hell when he had to come home each evening to chores, but Mark felt responsible for turning Chris into a man to be proud of, and a large part of that was teaching him to take his responsibilities seriously.

Leaving his dad to his typing, Mark went to the kitchen. He stood by the sink for a long time, trying to get the grime from underneath his fingernails. He needed to put some dinner together, too. Chris would eat crap all night if left to his own devices, and Dad forgot to eat if he wasn't reminded, so even though Mark didn't like to cook, he'd learned how. He wasn't going to win any prizes, but he wasn't hopeless, either.

As he dried his hands, he saw the light flashing on the answering machine. Only one message. The second he heard the voice, he knew who it was. What he couldn't figure out was why Trish Avalon wanted not just to see him, but to spring for dinner tomorrow night at the Blue Cloud, the best restaurant in Briscoe.

He played the message once more, trying to buy a clue, but she just sounded like Trish.

He went to the coffeemaker on the counter, poured himself a mug from this morning's pot, then stuck it in the microwave. As the seconds ticked away, he thought about the last time he'd seen Trish. It had been at her mother's funeral. Despite the six years that had passed since they'd been an item, he still had feelings for her. Not the kind he'd had back then, but he considered her a friend. They'd had a long talk that night, after all the other mourners had gone home, about what it was to lose a parent so early in life.

The conversation and her tears had flowed freely, but that was the last time he'd talked to her.

She was probably lonely, that's all. Come right down to it, he was pretty lonely himself. He might love the ranch, but his bed was still empty at the end of the day.

He picked up the phone and dialed her number.

THE BLUE CLOUD wasn't half as woo-woo as the name sounded. It was actually a very nice restaurant that would have been happier and more appreciated in Austin, but Trish was pleased it was in the middle of what was laughingly referred to as downtown Briscoe.

Mark had gotten there early and she joined him just as the waitress, Jennifer, put down his beer. Trish ordered a white wine, then took a moment to look at the guy who'd been her very first love.

He'd gotten better after high school, and he'd been a major babe then. Of course, they'd known each other since first-grade and it had taken a summer apart and a major influx of hormones for her to see Mark as anything but the kid who sometimes let her see his math homework.

Once the discovery was made, however, she had a whole new appreciation for what the ranching life could do for a man's body. He was everything a cowboy should be—tall, lean of hips, broad of shoulders. His eyes were as blue as the Texas sky and his hands… She sighed as her gaze settled on those amazing hands. Long fingers, kind of rough, but always clean. A person wouldn't guess they could be gentle, but they were.

"Hey, is something wrong?"

She looked up, embarrassed that she'd gone into the ozone while he was sitting across the table from her. Usually she did that in the privacy of her bedroom, but she just smiled. "Not a thing."

"So why the dinner? Is everything going all right over at your mom's place?"

"I'm still packing. I swear, I don't understand how

two sensible people could get so attached to *things*. They didn't get rid of anything."

"I remember. But they probably just thought they were being frugal."

"Yeah, well, there's frugal and then there's nuts."

"Your folks weren't nuts."

She sighed as Jennifer came back with her wine.

"You two ready to order?"

"I'll have the rib eye," Mark said.

Trish, like Mark and all the other locals, no longer had to study the menu. The special was always printed on the chalkboard out front. The rest of the menu never did seem to change. "I'll have the salmon."

"Good enough." Jennifer, who'd been a couple of years behind them at school, saved her best smile for Mark, but then that wasn't anything unusual, either.

Mark was the most eligible bachelor in Briscoe, but he was also the most reclusive. Not that he was mysterious or even shy. He just did the work of three men, which didn't leave much time for socializing. It had been an issue between them in high school—she couldn't imagine what it was like now. Trish wasn't sure, but she didn't think he'd gone out with anyone, at least not seriously, since they'd broken up at the end of their senior year.

"So why did you ask me here?"

"Yeah, well, it's gonna take a bit of explaining."

"But you're not in trouble."

"No. Unless you call being stuck in Briscoe trouble."

Mark gave her a grin that took her straight to the back of his '74 pickup after the game. Any game. They always ended up on Tripper Road, under the big trees, making out with such desperation. She could still remember the butterflies she always got whenever Mark touched her. She just hoped he thought of her as kindly. "I have a favor to ask you."

"Go ahead."

She'd worn a white T-shirt to dinner, after an hour of debate, one that was low cut and showed off her boobs. Then she'd chosen her skinny jeans, the ones she had to lie down in to zip up. Along with her high-heeled boots, she was about as sexy as she could get, which wasn't saying a whole lot. Her boobs had decided long ago to give up trying to grow, and her waist was more like a boy's than it should have been. She wasn't butt-ugly or anything, but she was no beauty. She'd never been all that clear why Mark had liked her back in the day. She'd just learned to accept it for the miracle it was, and move on.

But tonight, for this particular favor, she'd wanted to be a knockout. It didn't seem fair that he could look so handsome in his everyday clothes, and she'd had to spend half a day getting ready.

"Trish? The favor?"

"Right. Okay, well, you know how I've been trying to save up to move to New York."

"Yeah, I know."

"Of course you do. I just wanted to reiterate that my dream hasn't changed one bit since forever.

Getting the job in Dallas just made me want it more. I need to be in New York, Mark. I belong there."

"How do you know that when you've never been?"

"I feel it. I always have. If I didn't know better, I'd swear I had New York in my blood."

Mark shook his head slowly, his dark hair shaggy and sexy as all get-out. "I know you mean it, but I don't get it. I thought you liked that job in Dallas."

"It was fine, honest. But writing community news for a Dallas suburb paper isn't quite the same as writing for the *New York Times.*"

"You could apply at the *Dallas Morning News.*"

"Mark, no matter how much art and culture Dallas has, it'll never be New York."

"It's a long way to go for your dreams."

"It's not the moon. New York is just a few hours away these days."

"It's likely to be as strange as the moon."

"Maybe, but then maybe it will be everything I've dreamed of. Everything I've worked for."

He gave her a considered nod. "How can I help?"

"I'm really glad you asked," she said. She swallowed once, then looked him straight in the eye. "I need you to be my fiancé."

CHAPTER TWO

"YOUR WHAT?"

"My fiancé. Intended. You know," Trish said, "fiancé."

Mark looked at her for a long minute waiting for the punch line. Only Trish didn't even crack a smile. "What the hell are you talking about?"

"Okay, there's this hotel in Manhattan, it's called Hush, and they're starting this brand-new wedding service called Weddings by Desire and to promote it they had this big contest where they asked everyone to send in a videotape of why they should be the winner and when I was in Dallas I used the video equipment at the paper and made my own tape, which I sent in." She took a breath, but only one. "I never expected to win, of course, because nobody I've ever known has won anything, well, not anything important so I wasn't expecting anything but then today I got a package in the mail forwarded from Dallas and I won."

He waited to see if there was more. Trish took a sip of her drink then stared at him expectantly, as if she hadn't just said the craziest thing he'd ever heard from a grown woman's mouth. "Were you engaged when you made your videotape?"

"I didn't think I'd win, so, well, that didn't seem to be important. At the time."

"If you didn't expect to win, why did you—"

"I enter everything. No, that's not true. I don't enter for trips to Hawaii or Paris or for anything I couldn't sell, but the prize was a week, Mark. A whole week in New York. First-class airfare. A hotel suite. A limousine. Everything I'll need to get my dream job. I figure I'll send out résumés first, then do the follow-up interviews when I actually get there."

"You've figured that out, have you?"

"I know, it doesn't seem like enough time, but it is, because if I get a second interview I'll just stay there. I'll find a cheap hotel and I won't eat much. I've got enough saved to do that. Just not enough to do it all."

He took a big swig of his beer, questions tumbling all over themselves in his brain. The first was, "Why do you need me?"

"The prize is a wedding. A big wedding at the hotel. They're doing everything, too, including eight coach tickets for friends and family to come attend the nuptials."

The questions now all had exclamation points attached. "For real? A real wedding? With a preacher and a license and all that?"

"Well," she said, drawing out the word as she stared

at her hand on her wineglass. "Yeah, it would mean getting married, but only for a little while."

"How little?"

"A couple of weeks, max. Then we'll get it annulled, and voilà."

"Trish, honey. You're nuts."

"I know. But I also know this is a once-in-a-lifetime thing. If I don't go, I'll regret it forever. I'll always wonder."

"You never expected to win, so don't you have an alternative plan?"

"Sure," she said, but he could tell she'd lost interest in Plan B the second she'd opened that envelope. "Although it'll take me a long, long time to save up enough money to go."

He was surprised to find Jennifer next to the table waiting for them to move their arms for their dinner plates. Normally he could smell a nice rib eye from across the room, but Trish had found the ultimate distraction in her little request.

"Thanks," he said.

"Sure thing, Mark. You want anything else? Steak sauce? Another beer?"

"I'll be needing another beer, Jennifer. Thank you."

Trish didn't say a word. Nor did she look at her plate or have more to drink. She just stared at him and damned if he didn't feel like Scrooge on Christmas morning. But come on. *Married?*

"When's the last time you took a vacation, Mark Reynolds?"

"I'll admit," he said, cutting into his dinner, "it's been a while, but I can assure you, if I was to go on a vacation, the last place I would go is New York."

"They have interesting things in New York. Even you could fill up seven measly days."

He chewed on her proposition along with his steak, wanting to help a friend out, but damn. He would suffer through a week of New York if he had to, but getting married? She'd think he was an old-fashioned idiot if he told her how much the idea of a sham marriage bothered him. Unlike most folks in the country who traded in wives like returnable pop bottles, he actually believed in the institution. There'd been a time, a long time, when he'd figured he and Trish would be heading down that very road. It had been her New York dreams that had split them up.

He'd felt like hell about that for a good year after they graduated, but then he'd mellowed. No, he hadn't found anyone that he'd liked quite as much as he'd liked Trish, but then he hadn't really looked, had he?

He glanced up from his steak into eyes that used to haunt him. Sometimes still did.

"If there was anyone else to ask, I would."

"What about Dallas? You didn't meet any guys there?"

"Not any I could trust. Not like you."

Trust how? To not take advantage of her in the fancy suite? He wasn't so sure about that. They'd never had a problem between the sheets. In fact, the notion of sharing a suite was the only tempting thing about her favor. But he had a feeling she'd need him more for hand-holding than anything else. He admired her spirit, and if anyone could get a job at a big New York paper in a week, it would be Trish. Even so, the odds were pretty damn slim.

Hell, maybe he should go. He didn't love the idea, and he hadn't loved Trish for a long time, but he liked her and he'd feel like hell if she crashed and burned with some joker who didn't understand that her dreams had carried her through all life's hardships. Failing in New York was going to send her into a tailspin.

On the other hand—

"Oh, thank God," Trish said, then she dug into her dinner as if she hadn't eaten in a week.

"Wait a minute. I never said—"

"Oh, honey, I could see it the moment you decided to say yes. Of course I knew you would. And trust me. I'll make sure you have the best time ever."

He let out a long, slow breath. "Chris is going to have to agree to take on the ranch. Dad's going to have to pitch in, too."

"Oh, no." Trish shook her head, making her hair shimmer. "They'll be coming to New York, too. Well, for three days. Free airfare, free hotel. It's going to be wonderful for both of them. Imagine, Chris getting his first real taste of a big city. Your father going to the heart of publishing country."

Mark frowned. "The ranch—"

"Mark Reynolds," Trish said, putting down her silverware. “Just because you’re not happy unless you’re spending every waking second working on that ranch is no reason to punish your family. It’s a wonderful opportunity for both of them. You can always get Nate and Tom to take over for a few days. Heaven knows they can both use the work.”

“But—”

“Please, Mark. I’m convinced this is the opportunity of a lifetime and not just for me. I’m going to ask Ellen, Penny Foster and a couple of friends from Dallas to come along. And you could ask Darryl, right? He’s always up for a lark.”

Mark took another bite of steak as he tried to think of a nice way to back out of the whole deal. But what she said about his dad, about Chris, made him give her a very reluctant nod. Maybe it wasn’t the worst thing in the world to show his family a good time. And the ranch wouldn’t fall apart in a week.

Trish smiled delightedly. “We leave in three weeks. On the fourth. Bring that nice suit you wore to Mamma’s funeral, okay? And those good shirts you got in Austin.”

“I’m not your husband yet. And even when I am, I won’t be, so don’t you start up.”

She gave him a look that made him think of his happiest days. Days that had been filled with her laughter, her sweet scent.

“You’re surely going to heaven for this, sweet Mark. It’s honestly the kindest, most thoughtful—”

“Yeah, yeah,” he said, interrupting the flow of bull. “I’m a freakin’ saint.”

Her mouth opened wide, and so did her eyes. "I hope not. Did I mention that the Hush hotel suites all come complete with a cabinet full of toys? And I'm not talking about jump ropes."

It took him a full minute for that tidbit to gel, for his imagination to go from a slow walk to a full gallop. It didn't help much that Trish was laughing loud enough to make everyone in the place look their way. Or that he was blushing hot enough to start a bonfire.

HIS SECOND THOUGHTS started the moment he stepped out of the restaurant. They didn't let up all the way home, and after he'd done his final chores he had a list a mile long of why it was a stupid idea and how he wasn't going to do it, no sir.

As he finished brushing his teeth he made the mistake of remembering something he'd tried to forget. The way Trish looked in the wee hours of the morning. Her slim body naked and tan, her dark hair wild and curly on the pillow. That mouth of hers slightly open as if ready for his kiss.

"Shit," he said as he crawled into his empty bed. "Nothing but trouble with a capital T."

BY THE TIME they were ready to take off for the airport, Trish had listened patiently to each and every one of Mark's doubts and complaints. She'd tried her best to appear thoughtful. Concerned. But she knew in her heart that he'd never back out. Not for anything.

If only Mark wasn't so damned in love with

Briscoe. She'd tried to tell him there was a great big world out there, but he'd never wanted to hear it.

That's what made this trip so special. It wasn't just about her dream, although that was huge. It was also about getting Mark to step outside his comfort zone. Who knows, maybe he'd even like New York. Maybe…

No, she couldn't go there. Her destiny was in the Big Apple, but she had no doubt that Mark wasn't meant for that particular city. Maybe Austin or even Dallas, but he'd be miserable living in Manhattan.

They'd been right to break it off after high school. Yes, they had been best friends as well as lovers, but being a best friend meant supporting each other, no matter what the dream. Mark wanted his ranch to prosper. He wanted Briscoe to prosper, and she had no doubt that in the years to come, he'd be a strong influence in all areas of the county's interests. That's why he'd bought the property across from the courthouse and was part owner of the general store. He had a stake in Briscoe.

Mark had plans, all right. None of which appealed to her, unfortunately.

She was meant for the big city. She didn't even care if she had to start out writing obituaries or as a research assistant. Eventually, just as Mark would have his prize ranch, she'd have her prize job. Investigative reporter for the *New York Times*. It might take years, but all things worth having were worth waiting for.

CHAPTER THREE

AFTER THE BELLMAN LEFT. After the concierge left. After they'd been shown how to work the high-definition TV, the remotes that opened and shut everything, including the drapes, and after they'd been informed that the champagne, and everything else in the incredibly well-stocked minibar was theirs for the taking, Mark stood before the open armoire not quite believing his own eyes.

"I told you I wasn't talkin' jump ropes," Trish said from behind him.

"Uh-huh."

"Did you look at the itinerary?"

"Nope."

"Mark? Are you okay?"

He blinked. "I recognize a few things," he said. "I know where they go and what they do. But I swear to God, Trish, there are things in here that frankly scare the hell out of me."

She laughed as she put her arm around his shoulders. "Don't sweat it, sweetie. Just consider it part of the New York experience. Something to tell Darryl while you two are having a cold one."

He looked at her, not surprised in the least that she was in such a good mood despite their horrible travel day. It had taken forever to get through the airport. First-class was nice, but he'd never been comfortable flying. Add to that his serious misgivings about this whole deal, and he'd had better days.

Not so, Trish. She was giddy with wonder and excitement. He just wished he could enjoy her happiness more. He'd never thought of her as foolish, and no, he didn't know for a fact that this whole trip was an exercise in foolishness. Maybe she would get her dream job. He wanted that for her, despite the fact that her success would mean he'd probably never see her again.

"You have to admit, this is one damn fine hotel room," she said. "I'm going to take a bath in that huge tub tonight, when it's dark and I can see all the city lights."

"Uh-huh."

"We have dinner reservations at Amuse Bouche at seven."

"Uh— Amuse what?"

"Amuse Bouche. It means a delight for the mouth. Like a tiny appetizer. Jeez, you don't get out much, do you?"

He turned toward her to give her a look. She dismissed him with a laugh. "I had to look it up. It's supposed to be a fabulous restaurant."

"That gives us two hours?"

"Yep."

He headed back into the living room, away from the giant bed and the scary armoire. The couch seemed big enough, but he wondered if it opened into a bed. Nope.

"Not a chance," Trish said. She was standing in the bedroom doorway, her arms crossed over her chest. She looked pretty, despite the time change and the jet lag. "You're not sleeping on the couch."

"Well, I'm not gonna let you—"

"I have no intention of sleeping anywhere but the bed. Did you see the size of that sucker? We could sleep four in there, easy. We'll share."

He took a step back as the thought, the idea, the picture of them in bed together combined with all that stuff in the armoire hit him a low and powerful blow. "Uh…"

She smiled as if she was fully aware of the effect her casual comment was having on his body and mind, but then she took pity on him. "Relax. We're not going to do a thing that makes either of us uncomfortable. This is supposed to be a vacation. The kind with no worries. We'll make it work, okay?"

Mark sat down on the couch, not all that sure they could make it work. Yes, he'd known they were going to share a suite, but he hadn't let himself think about the sleeping part. He'd made sure not to have expectations, and more than that, he didn't want Trish thinking she was obliged. He just wished he hadn't taken a look in that armoire.

What the hell had happened to him? Used to be, especially when he and Trish were together, he didn't need an excuse to get her into bed. Or permission. Or a bed.

He wasn't even that old. Okay, twenty-five wasn't seventeen, but hell, why had his thoughts centered around not taking advantage of her? She was a grown woman. She could make her own decisions, be they to share a bed or move halfway across the country to find some kind of magical dream job that would probably end up making her miserable.

"Mark?"

He looked up to find Trish standing right in front of him. "Yeah?"

"Are you okay?"

"Jet lag."

"Uh-huh."

He tried to smile.

"Why don't you go on and use that incredible shower, then take a nap. I'll make sure you don't sleep too long."

"What about you?"

"I can't stand it. I have to get out there. I have to see at least some of the city before I go nuts."

"Good idea. Wouldn't want you to go nuts."

She bent over and kissed him on the cheek, but she didn't stand up right away. Instead with her soft perfume giving him a gentle nudge and her long brown hair tickling his ear she whispered, "Thank you, Mark. You're my hero."

TRISH GOT IN the elevator and found herself next to a very famous rock star. Not that she could remember his name, but she knew she'd seen him on the cover of magazines. She'd had no idea that he was that skinny. Whoa, dude had no ass, but he did have hair plugs.

Boy howdy, was this not Briscoe.

At the lobby, the rock star pulled out a cigarette and a lighter, closing his fist tightly around them before stepping out. There were no paparazzi waiting, only the beautiful deco lobby and the artwork that was sexy and sophisticated at the same time.

As Trish walked toward the door, she paused at the bar, which wasn't terribly busy at five-thirty, but those who were there were dressed as if they'd stepped out of the pages of a fashion magazine.

Trish had thought she looked nice for the trip. Dark jeans, white blouse, her best leather boots. Those girls, those women, made her feel like the hick she was. But was determined not to be.

She headed for her first real walk in New York, and the moment she stepped outside a frisson skittered through her body. If she'd had a hat, she probably would have done the whole Mary Tyler Moore thing. Instead she smiled. Grinned like a loon. Not one of the hurrying pedestrians spared her a second look, which was just what she expected.

Someday soon she'd be like them. Walking fast, eyes straight ahead, important things, stories, interviews, just ahead. She'd be on her way to the little corner market where she'd pick up a quick salad and maybe some wine, then to her apartment. It would be tiny, and she'd probably have a roommate, someone she'd met at the paper, and it would be three floors up, but she'd love it. Because it would be The Road, and she'd have made it happen. She'd be out of Briscoe and she'd never look back.

Her head turned then, and looked straight up the hotel building, its brownstone exterior giving no hint to the glamour inside. Or the man in the honeymoon suite.

She'd miss him. But that was nothing new. She'd been missing Mark for years.

She headed down the street, staring into store windows, gasping at landmarks. She had no idea where she was going even though she'd been perusing maps of Manhattan since the day she'd opened the letter from Hush.

She hadn't quite counted on so much of her time being taken by the wedding plans. Or the fact that the entire event, not just the wedding itself, would be followed by the press.

That last bit wasn't so bad. In fact, she planned on making some friends during the next week, and who knows what could happen from there?

It was still light outside and there was a nice breeze lifting her hair from her neck. The scent of hot dogs, of fresh baked bread, of trash and perfume and apples, made her deliriously happy, helping her find the rhythm of the city, to walk fearlessly across streets even when the light was still red.

Why, why did Mark dislike big cities so much?

He'd only been to Dallas that one time, and besides, Dallas was in Texas, so that didn't count.

Tomorrow, she'd find the time to take him out. Straight to the Chrysler Building. No one could look at that building and not fall in love. With New York. And then she'd take him to eat. Not at some fancy restaurant but to Papaya King for a hot dog. Mark loved dogs, and everything she'd read about Papaya King said they were the best.

Just thinking about it made her walk faster, made everything around her seem glamorous and fascinating. Or maybe everything was already wonderful, but the idea of sharing it with Mark…

She slowed as she passed a man lying on the sidewalk. He wore a heavy, filthy coat and his hair was matted and thick on his head. A brimming trash bag sat next to him, his filth-encrusted hand resting on it possessively. His shoes didn't match.

No one saw him. No one even broke stride.

She supposed that after a while, after she'd lived in the big city for a few months, it wouldn't faze her, either. She wasn't quite sure how to feel about that.

MARK WAS DRESSED when she got back to the suite. His hair, dark brown and shiny, had been combed a little too neatly, his jaw was shaved smooth and his eyes, a mix of green and blue that changed with the weather, looked bright and dark as he stood in front of the floor-to-ceiling windows.

"You look nice," she said.

He looked down at his pressed jeans, his polished boots and his cowboy shirt, the one that had the blue piping. His shoulders lifted in a modest shrug, which she knew for a fact was true. He didn't think he was anything special, not in the looks department. How a smart man could be so dumb was a mystery. She thought of that rock star in the elevator. On his best day he couldn't have held a candle to Mark. Every girl in Briscoe had swooned over him, but back in the day, he'd only had eyes for her.

She hadn't been the prettiest girl in their small high school. Not a cheerleader or class president or anything fancy. Just the editor of the school paper and at graduation, she'd been the valedictorian. Even so, Mark had always told her she looked great. He'd even called her beautiful once. That had been quite a night.

"Did you like it?"

"It's pretty amazing."

"I imagine it is." He walked over to the minibar and pulled out a beer. "You think I should?"

"I have to shower and change, so sure. It won't interfere with dinner."

"I was thinking about taking a look at that high-def TV."

"Have at it."

He grinned the smile that had made her melt. "I figure after tonight, I won't have time to do much TV watching. Did you get a look at that schedule?"

"We'll find time. I promise." She met him as he walked toward the couch and touched his arm. She'd meant to kiss him. Nothing big, nothing that would shake things up, but she felt suddenly shy and awkward.

She'd talked so big just an hour ago. Now she realized just how much of that was bluff. The toys in that armoire scared her to pieces. The only walk on the wild side she'd taken was to get herself a mail-order vibrator. "I won't be long," she said, hoping he didn't hear the slight crack in her voice.

"Take your time. There's like fifty channels of ESPN."

"Be still my heart."

He grinned. "You're gonna love that shower."

"I intend to love every minute of this miracle."

Mark looked out the window and whispered the same words. On his tongue it sounded like a joke.

CHAPTER FOUR

BY THE TIME TRISH came out of the bedroom, Mark had lost interest in the baseball game despite the fact he could see the individual blades of grass growing on the field. He couldn't stop thinking about after dinner. After dinner when they came back here. To the bedroom.

The last time he'd made love with Trish had been prom night. They'd gone to a real nice bed-and-breakfast over in Calloway. The rest of the class had gone to El Paso. But that night, for them, had been as painful as it was sweet. They had decided that they wouldn't sleep together again, or even hang out over the summer. Trish was convinced their relationship was like an addiction and the only way to end it was cold turkey.

It had been the worst summer he'd ever spent. Getting over Trish had been brutal. He'd thrown himself into working the ranch. Each day he'd get up with the sun then wear himself out so hard that he could barely eat dinner at sunset. He'd fall into bed, exhausted, only to dream about her.

It had taken a long time to cure himself of his addiction to her. Did he want to go through that mess again? What if Trish was like heroin? What if one night was all it would take to pull him back in?

The bedroom door opened, and there she was looking fresh and pretty as a bluebonnet. She'd left her hair down the way he liked it best. The dress she wore was tight in just the right places, and the purple, well, she'd always looked good in purple.

"You look beautiful," he said.

She reacted the way she had since day one. Her head tilted down and to the side, her cheeks pinked up and she whispered a "thanks" that she didn't believe.

He'd never understood why she felt so shy about her looks. She wasn't the most traditional beauty out there, but he liked that. He didn't want a cookie-cutter gal. He wanted—

He stood up, stopping himself before he took that thought too far. "We're gonna be late if we don't get out of here now."

Trish went to the door. "Let's hit it."

As he walked her to the elevator, he fought hard not to touch her, then remembered they were supposed to be engaged so wouldn't not touching her look suspicious? Well, he could wait until they were in the lobby, then it was a short walk to the restaurant, and that would take care of things for the short-term.

He still had no idea what he was going to do about after dinner.

"Hey," he said, "knowing you, you've looked up what's what at this restaurant."

She nodded. "I have."

"What should I order?"

"I don't think there's a thing on there you wouldn't like. They even have big, thick steaks. And onion rings."

"Okay, then. With a name like Amuse Bouche, I was afraid they were gonna force-feed me couscous."

The elevator arrived, empty.

"Have you ever had couscous?"

"No."

"Then how do you know you won't like it?"

"Same way you knew you'd love New York."

She smiled at him, and instead of giving him a jab for being a smart-ass, there was a sudden tenderness in her eyes that made him check out the elevator buttons.

He breathed again when they stopped on the twelfth floor to let in a couple of very tall, thin women. By the time they reached the lobby, they'd picked up four more passengers, men who seemed very interested in the skinny chicks. He didn't get it. But then, he didn't get most of what passed for the modern world. Not that he didn't keep up, at least to some degree. He read the big news magazines, subscribed to newsfeeds along with his grain and cattle reports. But he'd been one step behind his whole life. It wasn't going to change anytime soon.

Bucking up, he took Trish's hand as they headed for dinner. Damn if it didn't feel as natural as breathing.

She was just right. They fit together. That's why it had been so hard when they were torn apart.

"I'm nervous," she said. "It's just dinner, and I've been to really great restaurants in Dallas, but my stomach is all jittery."

"You're gonna be the classiest woman in the place," he said. "And I'll try hard not to spit on the floor or get into a brawl."

Her laughter lightened everything. "Yeah, that's just what I was worried about." She bumped his shoulder with her own.

"Anyway, tonight's just about food. The hard part starts tomorrow."

"I know," she said. "I have to sit down with that itinerary first thing and figure out when I can make some appointments. And I want to take you out. There's so much to see."

"We'll find the time," he said, although he'd already seen enough of Manhattan on his ride from the airport. Thousands of people, thousands of cars, taxis, buses, no one paying a bit of attention to any of the others, just racing to get where they were going.

The door to Amuse Bouche was high and elegant, the room itself a smooth mix of sleek and rich. There were flowers and screens and there wasn't anyone seated who wasn't dressed to the nines.

He gave his name to a woman in a short skirt, and that changed everything. The woman's eyes widened, there was a signal to someone behind her, then they were taken to a table in a private corner. A table set for four.

Once he'd held Trish's chair, another woman joined

them. She, like so many of the women he'd seen at the hotel, was slender, attractive and put together as if she was prepared to be on television. Her blond hair was pulled up on top of her head, she wore pearls around her neck and a blue suit. Despite all that, she looked young, in her early twenties. Although maybe she just had real good New York doctors.

He stood as introductions were made. Gwen Holmes was her name, and she was the new director of Weddings by Desire.

"I'm not going to intrude for long, I promise," she said. Then she turned to the hostess. "You can bring the champagne now, Lilly."

Mark held the chair for Gwen Holmes, then he sat opposite Trish. She seemed as surprised as he felt.

"I wanted to go over the schedule for tomorrow. Answer questions. Prepare you a little."

"Prepare us for what?" he asked.

"There will be cameras. Quite a few of them, in fact."

"Where?"

"Pretty much everywhere," Gwen said. "As much as I'd love to tell you we're throwing this shindig because we're just sweetie pies, the truth is, we're launching a very expensive enterprise and you're our major promotion. Your pictures are going to be in lots of magazines, on television, maybe on billboards. First thing tomorrow, we'll be signing releases. You're going to sign away all rights to your images, and for the event itself. That was in our letter, but I wanted to bring it up one more time. It can be intimidating."

The champagne arrived, and Mark hoped Trish liked the stuff more than he did. He was a man of simple tastes. Beer. Home. A good truck. A good—

"We understand," Trish said, "and believe me, this is the most exciting thing in the world. For both of us."

Her gaze met his, and she lifted her glass toward him, more to agree on the conspiracy than to celebrate their upcoming nuptials.

"There's no problem with the releases," Trish continued as she turned to look at Gwen.

"Great. Then, after we get all that boring stuff out of the way, we'll be off to Harry Winston to pick out the rings."

Mark put his glass down as he checked up on Trish. Rings were something concrete. They stood for a lot, and he knew for a fact Trish took great stock in that particular symbol. Sure enough, color came up on her cheeks and she turned away from him.

He'd had a suspicion that all this wasn't as casual as she'd like him to believe, and this proved it.

TRISH SMILED as Gwen said her goodbyes, but the smile faded as she turned back to Mark. He'd been mostly quiet as Gwen had covered all they had to do tomorrow. It would be one of their busiest days. Fittings for both of them after the rings, which they'd been told would take an hour, and that they would need to pick the rings from those taken out of the case. They were lovely rings, she'd assured them, all of them worth a great deal of money. But they weren't to window-shop.

It all seemed so real now. She was going to marry Mark. They would be husband and wife. Only, not for keeps.

Her guilt punched her square in the stomach. These very nice people were spending a great deal of money on a sham. When she knew they were alone, she leaned toward Mark. "Maybe this wasn't such a good idea," she said. "Maybe we should back out now, before they spend any more money on us."

The candle on the table made Mark's eyes seem green tonight. He was everything safe and comfortable, and yet she felt the censure in his gaze. Or maybe that was her own guilt she was staring at.

"You have to make that decision, Trish. I'm here for you. Not for them. I'm sure they're going to get everything they'd hoped for. Great publicity for their new service. For what it's worth, I don't think they'll give one damn about us after we're gone. They'll be moving on to the next publicity stunt."

"Okay, let's take them out of the equation. Am I doing something despicable? The truth now."

"No, it's not despicable. It's not the single most noble gesture I've ever seen, but I know you're not doing it to screw them."

"I'm going to send the rings back," she said, hating this. Not an hour ago, she'd been so pleased with herself. She'd been nothing but thrilled that she'd come up with this glorious plan, and now she doubted everything.

"I'll do whatever you like, Trish. I'll even pay for the tickets home. It's your call."

She sipped the champagne, amazed that she liked it so much. It was probably hugely expensive. Yet another thing that wasn't really her.

On the other hand, this was it. Her shot. So she'd used some ingenuity, that wasn't a bad thing was it? Mark was right—Weddings by Desire was going to get everything they'd hoped for out of this stunt. What happened after didn't matter. They hadn't stipulated how long the marriage had to last.

"Trish?"

She jerked, realizing the waiter was standing next to the table holding a menu out to her. "Sorry," she said.

"No problem. Take your time."

They were alone again in a snap, but neither of them opened the menus.

"Honey, what do you want?"

He'd called her honey. He hadn't done that in a long time, and the word shimmied up her spine and landed in a part of her heart she had ignored since—

"It's okay to want what you want," he said. "It's okay to go after it with everything you've got. Just don't kid yourself about what you're doing and why."

"But what do you think?"

"You're asking the wrong guy. I've found my place. I don't know what I'd be willing to do if that was taken from me. I do know I'd go far. Real far."

She nodded even though she wasn't completely convinced. Although something told her this was the kind of go-getter attitude that would make her a great reporter.

"You're right about one thing," he said.

"What's that?"

"The steak and onion rings sound perfect."

She smiled as she opened her own menu. She read each item, not skipping anything, even the soups, which were her least favorite. It all sounded incredible. In fact, everything about this place was incredible.

Her gaze moved up to look at Mark once more. It still broke her heart that they couldn't find some way to make it work. The one thing he'd always been clear about was that he wanted to marry someone who would love the ranch as much as he did. That wasn't her.

She would order the sea urchin panna cotta and the wild striped bass. She'd finish this champagne. And she wouldn't think about what they were going to do in the suite until they hit the elevator.

Yeah, right.

CHAPTER FIVE

HE WASN'T THE ONLY ONE worried about the next few hours. Mark watched Trish play with her dessert, some custard thing with chocolate cutouts that, if she were back home, she'd have finished in record time.

He'd tried to lighten things up, and for a while, it had worked. The food was about the best he'd ever had, and it always cracked him up to hear Trish moan each time she took a bite. It wasn't quite the same as her moaning in the bedroom, but close.

And the bedroom was close now, too. Unless she changed her mind about an early night and decided to go off into the city. Half of him wanted her to do just that. The upper half.

"This is how I want to die," she said.

"Huh?"

"I want to eat this until I explode. I want this to be the last thing to touch my tongue."

"I'm glad you like it."

"Are you sure you don't want a taste?"

He laughed. "Look at you."

Confused, she did. Then she smiled as she saw that her left arm was on the table, shielding her dessert from any possible encroachment. “Well, I was going to suggest you order your own.”

He leaned back, enjoying this. Her. “Order another. Order two.”

She shook her head. “If I wasn’t getting that fitting tomorrow…”

“I have to wear a tuxedo, huh?”

“Yep.”

“They’re not gonna try and do a makeover or anything, right? I won’t have to meet those *Queer Eye* guys?”

“Sweetie, there’s nothing those boys could do to make you prettier than you are right now.”

He lifted an eyebrow. “All right, what favor do you need now?”

“I’m not buttering you up. You know perfectly well how gorgeous you are, so don’t even try to pretend.”

“Gorgeous?” He rolled his eyes. “How much of that champagne did you drink?”

“Enough. And, sadly, I’ve had enough of dessert, too.”

Her plate was empty. Not even a crumb left as evidence. “I’m sure they could whip you up another in no time.”

“Get me out of here before I sin,” she said, pushing her plate toward the middle of the table.

“What are we supposed to do about the bill?”

“It’s on Hush, but I think we need to leave the tip.”

“Okay,” he said, pushing his chair back. “How much?”

"Except for the champagne," Trish said, lowering her voice, "I got a rough estimate. I'd say fifty bucks."

He winced as he realized that fifty was just tip money, but put the bills on the table. This was New York, after all. He'd expected no less.

THE ELEVATOR RIDE had been brief, the walk to the suite was over before she could blink, and now they were standing in the living room, and she didn't know what the hell to do.

Mark brushed her shoulder as he went to the giant window. "Get a load of this," he said.

Was she really so stressed over the sleeping arrangements that she'd forgotten to look at the city? She joined him, staring out across an ocean of lights. None of the movies or pictures she'd seen had come close to this view. It took her breath straight away. She had to turn a bit, but there it was—her favorite building in the whole world, the Chrysler Building. It was stunning at night. The stuff of dreams.

"I can see where a person could grow to like this view," Mark said.

"Really?"

He nodded. "It's really something. It almost makes up for the lack of stars."

"The stars are there."

"I know, but it would still be tough to lay back and stare up into a pale, empty sky."

"We're on top of the world, Mark. Can't that come close?"

He reached out and took her hand in his. "Don't let me spoil your fun. This is what you've always wanted. A shot at the biggest city in the world. A chance to kick ass with the big kids."

"You're right. And you know what?"

"What?"

"I haven't a clue what I'm doing."

"All great stories start that way, didn't you know?"

She looked at him instead of at the skyline. "How can you have so much confidence in me?"

"I've known you since we were six."

"And you've seen most of the bonehead things I've done since then."

"Everybody does bonehead things. You don't let them stop you."

She lifted his hand to her lips. "Thank you."

"You have to stop saying that. We're friends. This is what friends do."

"Bullshit. I have other friends. They aren't here."

"You were just too chicken to ask them."

"Yeah. They were all too smart to fall for my line of bull."

"Hey, weren't you supposed to be soaking in that great big tub?"

"Why, yes," she said, dropping his hand, suddenly afraid she'd made him uncomfortable. "I do believe it's calling."

"I'm gonna tackle that TV set again," he said.

"You don't need to use the bathroom?"

"I can wait. You soak as long as you want."

She nodded, then headed toward the bedroom. Once there, she got all her bathroom goodies together, then got out the slinky pink nightie she'd bought just before they'd left. But after a long study, she put it back in the drawer and took her old sleep T, the one she'd had forever, and carried that with her.

Mark didn't know it, but the shirt used to belong to him. She'd stolen it from his mother's clothesline and hadn't felt an ounce of guilt. It was the most comfortable thing she owned, and she needed all the comfort she could muster tonight.

Give her a few years in this city, and she'd wager she wouldn't have a moment of doubt.

As she turned on the water in the tub, she wondered if that was a good thing or a bad thing.

MARK CLICKED OFF his cell phone, wondering what he was going to find when he got back home. His father had said everything was fine, that Chris was doing his chores and that the horses were well cared for. That Nate and Tom were happy to have the work. But in these last few years, his father's idea of taking care of the ranch and Mark's own had become real different.

Used to be, his dad was all over every aspect of the ranch, and there wasn't one detail that was left to chance. Then he'd gotten that idea about writing and suddenly the little things hadn't meant so much.

They still mattered to Mark.

Not that he didn't want his father to be happy, to do

what he wanted to with his life, but things sure would have been a lot easier with all three men on board.

Finally, after a good couple of years of internal battles, Mark had made peace with the fact that he could only control one person—himself.

He looked at the bedroom door, wishing again that things could have worked out with Trish. She was so many things he wanted in a wife, in a partner. But she hated Briscoe and the ranching life.

With a sigh, he closed his eyes and leaned his head back on the cool leather couch. The muffled sounds of a soccer game were just indistinct enough to ignore. He smiled as he thought about Trish eating dessert.

HE WOKE WITH A START as the bedroom door opened. It took him a few seconds to get his bearings, but then he saw her, saw what she had on and whatever willpower he'd had dissolved in a heartbeat.

She had on his old T-shirt. The one that had gone missing years ago. He'd shrugged off the loss because it was just an old thing, nothing special. It was special now.

"How was your bath?"

"Incredible."

"I'm glad."

"You can get in there now. Sorry I took so long."

He clicked off the television and put the remote on the couch. When he stood, he thought about her in the bathtub, her slick wet skin, the way her breasts would bead at the nipple. He nodded at her. "So that's where that old thing got to."

She smiled shyly, then ineffectually tugged the shirt down her thighs. "I was young."

"It looks a hell of a lot better on you than it did on me."

She headed his way and he couldn't help his wandering gaze. Barefoot, she didn't make a sound as she walked. He probably wouldn't have heard her anyway, not with the way his heart was pounding. Her legs were amazing. He could have watched her walk around the world. And the T-shirt, faded blue, short, a picture of a local rock band he hadn't thought of in years barely perceptible after a thousand washes, was just thin enough that he could make out the soft shimmy of her breasts.

She'd pinned her hair up on top of her head in some kind of wonderful mess. All the makeup from earlier had been banished, leaving her pure and sweet.

They were only inches apart now, and his hand went to the curve of her neck. The touch was like the very first touch. Softness beyond belief that made him curse his callused fingers. "Beautiful," he whispered.

The way she looked at him then stole the rest of his breath.

"Tell you what," she said, kind of breathless herself. "Let's not think about anything but right here, right now."

He tried to tell her that was fine with him, but his words got stuck as he looked at her mouth.

"There are so many things I've forgotten," she said. "But I haven't forgotten one thing about you. Not the way you kiss, or the way you touch me. I—"

He couldn't stand it one more minute. His lips came down on hers for a kiss that filled a long-empty well. Slowly, slowly, he remembered her. Her taste. The way she teased him with the tip of her tongue. How it felt like honey and velvet, how it made him ache to taste every single inch of her.

She moaned, and his already hardening cock stiffened more. And when she pulled him close against her, with just that old worn T-shirt between them, he ached that old familiar ache.

With a strength he didn't know he possessed he pulled away from her. "I'd better…"

She nodded. "Right."

"So, I'll see you…?"

"Yeah."

He left quickly, before he threw her on the couch. Despite the insistence behind his fiy, he needed to be a gentleman, at least on the outside.

The bathroom made him laugh out loud. Her stuff was on every counter. Makeup stuff, hair stuff, more makeup, lotions. Good God, he had no idea she used all this goop. But, being a lady, she'd left him about ten square inches near the sink where his small black case looked lost in a forest of girly gewgaws.

It was tempting to brush his teeth and run, but he forced himself to get into the shower, which was some damn fine shower. He even washed his hair. Then he dried off, brushed his teeth, checked himself out in case he'd forgotten something vital.

With a big white towel around his waist, he headed for the door, his step slowing as he got closer. A sudden shot of nerves filled him with questions, mostly about what the hell he thought he was doing.

Then he opened the door, stepped into the bedroom. Looked at the woman on the bed.

There were no questions left. No doubts. Not even a single thought. Just need.

CHAPTER SIX

HOLY CRAP.

Trish swallowed hard as she watched Mark walk toward the bed, his towel slung low on his hips, his chest worthy of magazine covers, his hair slicked back and his face, oh man, his face was the sexiest thing she'd ever seen. Mostly because he was looking at her as if she was the sexiest thing *he'd* ever seen.

She was glad she'd put the condoms on the night table. Glad she hadn't worn a thing under her T-shirt. Grateful beyond words for winning a prize that let her be with Mark.

He got to the side of the bed and his gaze moved slowly from her toes to her eyes. The hunger was in him. In her. As she struggled to breathe she remembered being with him in all kinds of sensory detail. Her body tingled with anticipation.

When he let the towel drop, the old memories vanished. Nothing existed except this moment. His unbelievable body. The way his slow grin made her shiver.

"I think I'll take back that T-shirt now," he said, his voice thick and low.

She sat, then rose up on her knees. With him watching every gesture, she took the hem of the T-shirt in her hands and lifted.

Slowly.

His eyes were something to behold as he followed her hands. Inch by inch, she exposed her body to him. Over her hips, her tummy. A hesitation just below her breasts. Then up. Hard nipples, goose bumps everywhere. Quickly now over her head.

She tossed the shirt off the side of the bed and dared him with a smile.

He put one knee, then the next on the bed. Close. His heat touched her first, then his rough fingers skimmed her breasts. Gently, with a patience she didn't share, he painted her skin. Down her sides, across her belly, a whisper across her thighs.

All the while he looked into her eyes. A connection, one she'd thought lost forever, reestablished itself between them. Her first lover. The only one who'd ever mattered.

"I want—"

"I know," she said. There was time enough for everything, but not enough hours in the world to do all she wanted with him. So much to taste, to feel.

He moved closer and his sweet peppermint breath brushed her lips and they parted. His kiss, when it finally came, made her knees weak. Made her want to cry.

He pulled her into his arms, and even though it was awkward, her still on her knees and all, when she got there, it was home. It was the best place. Better than a hundred New Yorks.

For a long time, she kissed him back as her hands learned his body all over again. He'd changed. He'd always been well built, beautiful in fact, but now his shoulders were so broad, so perfectly muscled. His ass, well, against all reason, that had gotten better, too.

She felt him hard and ready against her hip, her tummy, but that would be the delicious dessert after her banquet of touch, of taste, of scent. God, he smelled like her dreams. Nothing on earth smelled exactly like Mark. She had carried the scent through the years, through the distances that separated them.

He pulled away from her lips but only to lay her down on the soft sheets. She looked up at him as he reached behind, admiring his chest. The dark hair that ran from his breastbone in a V all the way down past his flat belly where it met the hair around his erection.

Without conscious thought, she reached out to touch him there. Even before her fingers met flesh, he jumped in anticipation. He hissed through clenched teeth as she ran her finger down his length. A groan as she took him fully in hand.

She looked up to watch as his head fell back, as his chest swelled with held breath all from the slow pump of her hand.

No one fit her like Mark. No one made her feel like this. How many nights had she wondered if she'd ever feel like this again?

"Honey, you have to let me go."

"Why?"

"Because it's gonna be over before it's even begun."

She released him, embarrassed to admit she'd thought he meant something completely different. But no mind. He was moving again, coming to meet her on the bed, his head joining hers on the pillow.

"This is looking like trouble," he whispered as he ran his hand down her arm.

"No troubles tonight. Nothing but wonderful."

"Right," he said. "Nothing but you."

She traced his lips with her fingertip. "I've missed you."

He nodded as his hand went from the safety of her hip to the heat between her legs.

She gasped. Trembled. Without her consent, her eyes closed.

As the waves of sensation swept her away, she forgot that this was a game, a time outside of time.

And then she forgot she wasn't really his.

MORNING CAME with a phone call. Mark struggled to find the damn thing on the nightstand and when he finally got it up to his ear, his greeting was less than cordial.

It was Gwen, from last night, and she set them off in a world of hurry. A room service call first, then showers, then dressing. Trish doing that voodoo stuff with the makeup and the hair, so when she walked out of the bathroom she looked so good he wanted to go straight back to bed.

A cup of coffee and a Danish later, and it was time to run. First, to the fittings, where he lost Trish and found himself standing on a pedestal as a man took every kind of measurement it was possible to take. No, that's not true. No one wanted to know his hat size.

He had to try on a bunch of different tuxedo jackets as three women eyed him like a side of beef. They picked the winner, then it was a few more measurements then away to a room full of cameras and microphones.

He was seated on a tan wing chair facing an identical chair that was filled with one reporter after another. They all asked the same questions, even if they worded them differently.

"How did you and Trish meet?"

"In kindergarten. We were both six."

"When did you fall in love?"

"That would be in high school."

"What's Briscoe like?"

And on and on. What surprised him was that he didn't have to lie but a couple of times. He wasn't thrilled about the wedding. He hadn't proposed to Trish. So on those two, he became a shy cowboy and hemmed and hawed, and they moved on. He just kept waiting for it to be over.

That took another two hours.

THE FITTING was finally over and Trish felt as if her feet were going to explode. They'd put her in heels that were just small enough to hurt after the first five minutes, then made her try on a bunch of dresses, all of them more gorgeous than she could believe, and when they finally chose the winning number (a strapless gown with a shirred satin bodice, a full tulle skirt and a little flower on the waist) that made her feel as if she were the most beautiful bride in the world as well as the biggest fraud.

Despite standing in front of a huge three-way mirror, she managed to not quite look at herself as she was tugged and measured and photographed.

All the while, her thoughts kept slipping back to the night. To Mark. To how he'd taken her to the moon and the stars and how she'd never wanted to come back.

It was never going to work between them, so why did she continue to torture herself over it? A New York kind of gal would do exactly what she was doing only without the regret. Without the guilt. And definitely without the wishful thinking.

Tomorrow morning was her first interview. It was with the *New York Post,* and while she would prefer to write for the *Times,* she wasn't going to bitch if she nailed it. The *Post* would be a huge coup, and instead of daydreaming about a cowboy that couldn't be hers, she should be rehearsing her interview answers.

She wasn't stupid. She knew she would have serious competition, but dammit, she also knew she was good. Her enthusiasm was unlimited, her willingness to work hard was a given, and no one, no one could want it more than she did.

"Arms up."

She lifted. They fitted. One thing for sure, these women weren't shy. One of them physically reached inside the gown and moved her boob. Now that was what she was talking about.

She wanted to be a boob-mover. Not literally, of course, but still. She wanted to face her tasks without sentimentality. Without concern for anything but getting the job done perfectly.

"Arms down."

She relaxed, only to be scolded for slouching.

"How much longer, do you think?"

"Not too long now."

That from seamstress number two. There had been no names asked, none given. Everyone in the room seemed focused and too busy for such pleasantries.

Trish kept her mouth shut and did as they asked, but she couldn't help thinking that if this had really been her wedding, she'd have wondered if she was missing out on something pretty darned important.

HARRY WINSTON was next, but first, more photographs. Not at the wedding gown shop but back at the hotel. On the roof. In a garden that was one of the most beautiful Trish had ever seen.

They'd put up a tent thingy right next to the elevator and when she walked inside it, she saw three racks of clothes—two women's, one men's. Most of the clothes were casual and Western. Jeans, boots and hats, but when she got closer, she saw they weren't the kind of Western she could buy in Briscoe. These were fashion pieces with big designer names on them. They were all her size, and she wondered if it would be incredibly gauche to ask if she could keep them.

Yeah, probably.

Along with Gwen, a stylist named Ricky was there and the first thing he did was put every ounce of his attention on Mark.

"Well, this is going to be a much more pleasant afternoon than I'd imagined. Turn around, big boy."

Mark gave her the Evil Look of Death as he turned for the man, and Trish thought of his makeover phobia. If she had to step in, she would.

"Let's go with the jeans you're wearing, and..." He drew the word out as he riffled through the men's shirts. He pulled out four, all of them similarly cut with not that much ornamentation. "The boots are fine." Ricky narrowed his gaze. "Did you bring your own hat, cowboy?"

The muscle in Mark's jaw twitched. "It's in the room."

"Well, hurry up and get it. I have a feeling I'll like it better than the ones I brought."

Mark obeyed, getting out of the tent as if it were on fire.

Trish wondered if he'd come back. But she didn't have long to ponder Mark's troubles. Ricky descended on her with an eye toward making her into someone else.

"Those jeans do nothing for your behind, honey." He pulled a couple of dark pairs off the rack. "These should help. And that blouse is too big. You want something that will hug your curves. Show a little hoochie."

She wasn't sure what hoochie he meant, but she was sure she'd find out.

What really got to her was when he told her to change. Not behind a curtain, either. He wanted her to change right there in the middle of the tent.

"This is show business, honey. And believe me, you don't have a thing I haven't seen before."

"Well, I haven't shown it before, so you just turn your butt around."

With raised eyebrows, he looked at Gwen then back at her. But he turned.

She put on a Western shirt that was two sizes too small, a pair of jeans that cut off her circulation and boots that made her poor feet squeal.

The hoochie, it turned out, was boob cleavage and lots of it. So much, she had to wonder if the pictures they were taking would end up in *Playboy.*

But she just let Ricky do his thing. Thankfully he didn't stick his hand down her blouse. But that was the only thing to be thankful for.

Until Mark came back.

He wasn't wearing his cowboy hat. Instead he'd put on the hat he'd bought for his cousin Dill. Who was eight.

She laughed so hard she almost busted a button.

Ricky was not amused.

CHAPTER SEVEN

HARRY WINSTON WAS ONE hell of a jewelry store. After walking through the most intricate wrought-iron and gold-plated gate Mark had ever seen to a foyer so fancy it had a chandelier that was covered with flowers and gold and then the black and gold carpet, not to mention the cases of jewels that had to be worth more millions than he could ever imagine, he, Trish, Gwen and about a half dozen reporters were led into a private room.

Grateful to be sitting down so he had less chance of breaking something that would cost the ranch, Mark sat back as the jeweler, a really well dressed woman with white hair and a huge rock on her hand, pulled out a large velvet box. There were half a dozen engagement rings, all with matching his-and-hers wedding bands.

Mark didn't know all that much about diamonds, but he knew big. These were big diamonds. No cubic zirconium in this place. Just the real thing. Diamonds in gold, in white gold, in platinum. Round ones, ovals, pears, squares.

But the thing that captured his attention wasn't the glitter on velvet, it was Trish.

He knew right away that this was going to be tough for her. Some mysterious female gene had been switched on. Her face, always pretty, now seemed somehow softer, more vulnerable. It wouldn't shock him if he saw a tear or two—no, wait. Her jaw clenched, she sniffed away the sentiment, and steeled her shoulders. She was not going to be carried away by diamond dreams. This was not the real thing, and she best not forget it.

He hoped, for her sake, she could carry it off. Him? He was screwed.

Last night had taken him straight to the bad place. Or was it the good place? Whatever. He just knew that saying goodbye to Trish was going to be hard as hell. Harder than the last time, because this time, he knew it wasn't going to be easy to replace her. Easy? It was impossible.

"Each of these exquisite pieces are original designs by our master craftsmen. The diamonds are all GIA certified, one carat or greater, VVS1, which means there are only minute inclusions, and, as you can see, they vary in color and cut. Feel free to try them on, and ask any questions you may have."

Trish nodded as her gaze toyed with staring directly at the diamonds. Finally her hand reached out, hovered for a few seconds, then plucked one of the rings from the velvet.

If he wasn't mistaken, she trembled just a bit as she slipped the thing on. When it was home, she looked at him.

He wanted to take her out of this place. Not because she was cheating, but because she deserved so much more. Not an advertising ploy, not a cubic zirconium marriage. Hell, even if it was to someone else, Trish should have the real deal.

"What do you think?" she asked.

He tore himself away from her gaze to look at her hand. It seemed small, pale. Her nails weren't done up and there was a tiny mole just below and to the right of her thumb.

Before he could stop himself he leaned over and took her in a kiss. He wanted her to know, to understand that this, the dress, the photographs, the jewelry meant nothing. They were all so much dust. But that shy blush, the way she'd offered her long, warm neck to his lips. The sounds she made when she was *almost* there.

At the sound of a discreetly cleared throat, he pulled away from her, hoping she'd gotten his message. Hoping he wasn't going to want to stop breathing when she said goodbye.

HOURS LATER, after more photos, more wardrobe changes, more makeup lessons and just more, they were finally back at the hotel, alone in the room. Her, Mark and the ring. Rings. One stunningly beautiful one-carat round brilliant in a platinum four-pronged setting that looked better than anything she'd ever had on her hand.

All she wanted to do was take it off. Bury it in one of those rosebushes on the roof.

She was in the bathroom, sitting on the edge of the tub. Wondering what Mark was doing out there. Expecting things? Of course he was. Why wouldn't he? Last night had been amazing. Sonnets could have been written about last night.

Such a huge mistake.

Not just the sex or the ring but the whole thing. What had she been thinking? She could have hired someone to be her fiancé. It would have been clean, neat. She would have sent the rings back a couple of weeks after the annulment, and voilà. No harm, no foul. Weddings by Desire would have gotten their money's worth, she would have gotten her job and no one would have been hurt. Especially not her.

She rocked back, thinking about the kiss at Harry Winston. Mark had caught her completely by surprise, and while it had been the sweetest gesture ever, it had made her heart hurt so badly she'd nearly…

In truth, she hadn't been on the verge of running. Her feet hadn't moved, she hadn't tried to take the ring off. She'd felt bad, that's all. And for none of the right reasons.

Why had she asked Mark to do this for her? What had she expected would happen? Had she chosen him simply because she knew she could get him to agree? Or had she wanted things to change between them?

Did she still love Mark?

A soft tap on the door reminded her that the suite only had the one bathroom. "I'll be right out."

"Okay, thanks."

She went to the sink and looked at her face. After all they'd done to her today, makeup-wise, she wasn't surprised to find her skin blotchy and her eyes red-rimmed. Nice.

After a few splashes of cool water, she dried off and met Mark in the bedroom. "It's all yours."

"Actually, I'm set, I was just worried that something was wrong."

"Just tired. Anxious about tomorrow."

"The *Post,* huh?" He was sitting on the bed, his legs crossed at the ankles, a couple of the big pillows behind his back.

All she wanted to do was curl up next to him. Feel those strong arms around her shoulders. Hear his heartbeat beneath that cowboy shirt. Instead she went to one of the chairs by the window. "It's not the *Times,* but fantastic, nonetheless. I think I'd be a pretty good fit there."

"They're gonna love you."

"I just need to give them the right impression. I learned a lot from interviewing at the Dallas paper. If I'm on my game, I truly think I have a shot."

"Then let's make sure you're on your game. How about room service tonight, then an early bedtime. You need the rest."

She had to swallow a sudden rush of tears. That alone proved that she was way too tired. "I promised to take you around the city tonight."

"The city will still be there."

"Let's look at the menu, then."

He nodded, and his eyes told her he knew she was a lot more than exhausted. She didn't have to make a decision about making love because he'd done it for her. For *her.* Was it any wonder she had these…feelings?

Maybe it was still love. But love wasn't always enough, was it?

HE'D GONE to the top-floor pool and had a swim, had breakfast, read the paper, paced the room, tried to watch TV, then paced some more and still Trish hadn't gotten back from her interview.

He hoped it had gone well for her, that the people at the *Post* were smart enough to see that she was a once-in-a-lifetime find. Of course, her success would mean…

He put the brakes on his thoughts. Even if it didn't work out with the *Post,* Trish was still going to move out of Briscoe. So why not wish her the best?

He'd thought a lot about last night. He hadn't gotten much sleep despite his exhaustion. He'd wanted so badly to touch her. To make love with her. But he'd kept his hands to himself. Literally. After he knew she was soundly asleep, he'd taken a second shower. It had been quick because he'd been hard and ready from the moment he'd seen her in that old T-shirt.

Even that hadn't stopped the ache. Maybe it had just been too long since he'd been so attracted to a woman. But probably it was because she was Trish.

He crossed the room to the minibar but nothing had

changed since the last time he'd rooted through the contents. Just as he shut the fridge door, the suite door opened. He knew instantly that the interview hadn't gone well.

"Hey," she said, her accent, which she'd worked hard to lose, was clear in that one word. That only happened when her guard was down.

"Hey."

She dropped her purse on one of the end tables followed by her jacket. She looked cool and professional even without it. A pale green silky blouse and dark green pants gave her the sophistication she aimed for without all that morose black New York women seemed to like so much.

"Well, that sucked."

He joined her, choosing the leather club chair across from her so he could see her face. "What happened?"

"I waited along with a half dozen other eager young hicks. Filled out forms. Waited some more. Then we were all brought into this conference room where a junior, junior assistant, some guy named Frank who I swear was maybe seventeen, asked each of us where we'd graduated, where we'd worked and why we should get the job. The job, mind you, was as a research toady. Nothing glamorous, lousy pay. We had about a minute to answer. Frank didn't even listen. He told us we'd be contacted if they wanted us to move to the next level. That was it."

"Did he say when you'd be contacted?"

"No. And I won't be. I was about as invisible as I could be. The only shot I had was to get into a dialog with someone."

"Sounds to me like you have an even chance with everyone else there."

"Not really. There were two people that had a lot more experience. The rest of us were just hicks from nowhere."

"I'm sorry it wasn't better, but hell, it's only one interview. You have the *Times* and that other paper, right?"

She nodded. "Right. Well, I'd better get it in gear." She looked at her watch, the one that had belonged to her mother. "Gwen will be calling any minute, and I've got to get something to eat."

"Want me to call room service?"

She thought about it for a moment. "Nope. I think I'd like to get out of the hotel. I'll call Gwen instead and find out the schedule. After that, I want to find a real New York deli. I'm in the mood for a bagel and a schmear."

He laughed, hearing her say that with her Briscoe accent in full gear. "Oy," he said.

Trish smiled. "I don't think we can pass, bubba."

He crossed over to the couch and gave her a kiss on the cheek. "No, I don't think we can."

When he started to move away, Trish caught his arm, met his gaze. "Thanks for the support."

"I want the best for you. I always have."

She opened her mouth, but didn't speak. Instead

she let him go and ducked under his arm in her haste to get to the bedroom.

He watched the closed door for a long while. Wishing…

CHAPTER EIGHT

THE NIGHT STRETCHED before Trish like a giant red carpet to the city. After another round of wedding interviews and a lunch that was great, but wasn't the deli she'd longed for, she, Mark and the engagement ring were finally on their own.

"What do you want to see first?"

Mark leaned back on his heels as he watched the traffic roll by on Madison Avenue. "Darlin', I have no clue."

"Well, haven't you ever wanted to see anything in New York? Rockefeller Center? Times Square? The Rainbow Room?"

He looked at her then and his slow smile pulled her right back to their first year of high school. Mark had been just Mark since they were six. Nothing special, not the most annoying of the local boys, but a bit of a show-off. Then she'd gone to Briscoe High wearing a sassy short skirt and a twelve dollar blouse from Nordstrom's Rack. Not to mention Clinique eye makeup and lip gloss. She'd thought she was so hot, eggs would fry on her butt.

She'd walked into first period English and neighbor Mark turned in his chair. His gaze had roamed from her Payless Shoes to her Glamour Cuts hair, and he'd smiled. *That* smile.

It was all over but the formal announcements.

Here she was on the brink of her brand-new life, ready to take on Manhattan and still, as always, her heart skipped two beats, the butterflies swam in her tummy and she just plain melted. The disappointment from the nonexistent newspaper interview had transformed itself into a fierce desire to show them. Her confusion about roping Mark into the extravaganza of this wedding had become muted as he'd so clearly gotten into the spirit of the fun during the wedding chores.

If only she wasn't so drawn to him. If she'd met someone else, or if he'd done some horrible thing to her. But no. He was still that boy that had made her sigh in Mrs. Carrel's first-period class.

"How about we walk a while. I've been sitting too much. I'm getting used to it."

She pointed past his shoulder. "That way is Times Square."

"Times Square it is."

He turned, reached back and took her hand in his. "Give me the nickel tour," he said.

"I don't know enough about the city to do that."

"Sure you do. Tell me what you love about it. What draws you here above all other places."

They walked at a leisurely pace, which seemed slow compared to those rushing past them. Everyone seemed to be late for something. Trish, on the other hand, wanted the world to slow, to stop. Holding Mark's hand, thinking about how to explain her love for the city. It was heaven.

"Well?"

"Movies," she said. "Woody Allen had a large part in my first stirrings of love for New York. But he wasn't the only one. Every time I saw pictures of Manhattan I got all excited. It was as if I'd already been there, as if it was where I belonged, if I could only get there."

"I think you'd have to go pretty far to find a place less like Briscoe."

"That had something to do with it," she said. They stopped at a crosswalk and marveled at the games the pedestrians played, daring taxicabs and black limos to run them down like bowling pins.

"I don't mind traveling," he said, "but it's getting home that I like the best."

She shoved his shoulder with her own. "Liar. You hate leaving your ranch."

Mark shook his head. "I don't hate it, but I do worry. Dad has other interests these days, and we both know that if Chris could, he'd spend all day playing video games."

"How's your dad's book coming?"

"I have no idea. He won't let me read it till it's done."

"Still. Good for him. It's really never too late, is it? Not for the big dreams." They slowed their pace as they waded through a crowd of people exiting a tour bus. As she caught sight of all the cameras around all those necks, she mentally kicked herself for not bringing hers along.

"I suppose you're right," Mark said. "It's weird, though, that I never knew he wanted to write. He never said anything."

"He probably told your mom." She looked over at Mark and was surprised at the sadness she saw there. "What's wrong?"

"Nothing."

"Mark, it's me."

He smiled at her. "I thought my father would love the ranch until he kicked the bucket."

"I'm sure he does love the ranch."

"Not so's you'd notice."

"Now he has you. He trusts you to take care of things."

"But—" He loosened his grip on her hand but she just held on more tightly.

"But what? The man's worked hard his whole life. He deserves a chance to branch out. Not everyone is like you, Mark, not even your hero."

"My hero?"

"I know how much you care about your dad. How you've tried to model yourself after him. It's a great compliment to him that you've turned out so well. But don't begrudge him because he did his job."

Mark shook his head as they stopped at the corner of Times Square. For a long time, he just looked at the lights, at the giant TV screens and the Broadway marquees. He seemed awfully interested in the pizza joint across the street, and Trish realized she was hungry, too. But pizza wasn't on her menu.

"Come on," she said, tugging on his hand. "I want to take you to dinner."

Trish had memorized the address, but had no idea how far the place was from where they were, so they hailed a cab. It took about twenty-five minutes to arrive, and after she paid the driver, they got out at East 86th Street. At Papaya King. Supposedly one of the best hot dog joints in the world.

"This is where we're having dinner?" he asked, grinning to beat the band.

"I also know how you feel about hot dogs."

Mark looked at the joint, which was really just a big old hot dog stand painted brilliant greens and yellows. There was a line, of course, but everyone in it seemed to be in a pretty happy mood, a good sign.

OF COURSE TRISH had brought him to eat hot dogs in New York. He'd loved dogs since childhood, and he was the nutcase at barbecues who passed up the sirloin steaks and even the Texas beef ribs only to eat a half dozen hot dogs, complete with mustard, relish and onions. As everyone liked to tell him so often, it was a sickness.

She dragged him into the line and she was so tickled with herself she was practically hopping from foot to foot. Damn, she was adorable when she got like this. It was one of the things he liked most about

Trish, that she could be such an unabashed kid. She didn't give a damn what anyone else thought. Even the cliques of Briscoe, which were downright evil.

He was helpless, of course. He had to kiss her. And when he did, not even hot dogs stood a chance. He pulled her into his arms and in front of God and all the people in line, he made sure she was well and truly kissed.

She fell into him, as if her bones had gone soft. He was all too eager to hold her. To keep her close. To taste her and feel her.

But the hot dog line would wait for no man or woman. They broke it up and moved along, but he didn't let go of her. His arm was around her waist and hers was around his. It was just like old times when she slipped her hand into his back pocket.

He enjoyed his Papaya King hot dogs and his mango pineapple juice. But it was nothing compared to how much he enjoyed the company.

"WHAT WERE YOUR responsibilities at the *Star-Telegram?*"

Trish stopped herself from adjusting her jacket again and looked squarely at Tom Finster, the man interviewing her at the *New York Times.* "I was an editorial assistant for the Lifestyle editor. I was responsible for compiling column material for weddings, birth announcements, the calendar of events and the obituaries. I also wrote some feature articles, which you'll see in my portfolio."

He had the portfolio in front of him. Open. But he didn't even glance at it. Or her. Mostly he was watching his computer monitor.

"What makes you think you're right for the *Times?*"

"I've studied the paper for years. I know each section well, I know the styles and points of view of all your columnists. I've done my homework about the city, about the paper and about the people. I've got an old-fashioned work ethic, and I believe in doing the best possible job no matter what the task. I'm accurate, I know about the printing cycles, and I'm not afraid of hard work."

"Uh-huh," he said, showing no more interest in her than he would a pesky fly on the window pane.

It was nothing less than torture. Her dreams smashing against indifference and shattering into a million tiny pieces. He wasn't going to hire her. It wouldn't have mattered what she'd said, either.

She knew the newspapers in New York were competitive, but she'd never have guessed she'd have been so outclassed. Her old boss at the *Star* had tried to warn her, but had she listened? She was so sure she could convince these people to take a chance on her….

It didn't mean she was going to quit. There were smaller papers in the city. If she had to, she'd apply at each one. Somehow, she'd find a way to stay here, to keep the dream going.

Only the dream had lost its vibrancy. It had turned from color to black and white, and at the moment, she wasn't sure she had it in her to repaint.

Finster typed for a moment, then turned to her. "You have a nice résumé, but I'll be honest with you. To get into this paper, you'd need a lot more experience. Go back to Dallas and get some years under your belt. Get your feet wet in the national and international sections."

Trish sat straighter. "I appreciate your honesty, Mr. Finster. You've given me a strong direction and that means a lot."

He actually smiled. "This is the most competitive market on the planet. Good isn't enough. Excellent isn't, either. You have to walk in here a star."

She stood and held out her hand. "I'll be back."

"I bet you will," he said as he gave her back her portfolio.

She headed out of the old building, debating stealing a little more time to get a good look at the offices, at the bullpen, but she was needed back at Hush. The final wedding dress fitting was today, and then they were going to tape some TV promos. Gwen had nearly had a heart attack when she found out Trish would miss two hours.

At least Mr. Finster had turned out to be a mensch. She grinned. A mensch. She wondered if there was another soul in Briscoe, Texas, who knew the word, let alone what it meant. No, she was meant for bigger things. If it took a few more years to get there, so be it.

But on her way back to the hotel, the city looked different to her. The color here had changed, too. Or maybe it was just that her eyes had lost their stars.

MARK TRIED TO KEEP his mind on the reporter and not worry so much about Trish's interview, but it was tough. The woman, name of Patty, was from some tabloid, something he'd never heard of. She was dressed in some weird outfit that he supposed was the height of fashion, but man it looked uncomfortable. Especially the shoes. Those heels had to be at least four inches tall.

"One last question?"

Mark nodded. "Whatever you need, ma'am."

Patty smiled at him as if he were some kind of treat she got out of a cereal box. "You are just the most adorable man. Anyway, tell me a little more about your first trip to New York. What's the most exciting thing you've seen?"

He didn't have to give that one much thought. "The look on Trish's face when she put on the engagement ring."

Patty sighed. "One thing's for sure. They certainly picked the couple who were most in love. It gives me hope. Of course, finding a guy like you in New York is damn near impossible."

"Why's that? I'm not all that different, even if I do come from Texas."

She laughed, then, and he wasn't such a hick that he didn't get the joke. She didn't even bother to explain. All she did was pat him on the shoulder as she teetered out of the bar in her high-heeled shoes.

CHAPTER NINE

"WHAT AREN'T YOU TELLING ME?"

Trish looked away knowing it was stupid and useless to try to fool Mark. He above all people knew when she was upset. He read her so well. No one, not even her own mother, had ever been as attuned to her. Sometimes, she loved that. Right now, not really.

"Talk to me, girl."

They were finally back in the suite after a very, very long day. It was just past midnight, and they both needed to get a good night's sleep.

Tomorrow was the wedding.

Mark's Dad and his brother had come in yesterday along with Darryl and Trish's friends. Not that they'd had a moment to talk, but Hush was certainly treating them well.

"Is it about tomorrow?"

"Partly," she said, resigned to spilling all the beans. If she was going to talk, she might as well have something to wet her throat. She went to the fridge and pulled out a diet soda for her and held up a beer for him.

"I'll take a soda, if there's one that's not that diet crap."

She got him his favorite and went back into the living room. Her gaze skidded to the panoramic view of the city and for the very first time, it didn't make her breath catch.

"Alrighty then," he said, leaning back in the club chair. "Which part about tomorrow is making you so upset?"

"Just the wedding part," she said, only partly kidding.

"I know. It's a big deal," he said, as if he hadn't caught that it was a joke.

Okay, so maybe it wasn't a joke. Maybe she just wanted it to be.

Mark popped the top of his soda. "You know, I've come to the conclusion that we were the perfect two people to have won this prize."

She paused with her drink halfway to her mouth. "Oh?"

He nodded. Took a swig of pop. "We've given them more than they had any reason to expect. We haven't complained, we've been forthright in all the interviews. Hell, you think a young couple who were truly in this for the wedding would have been so accommodating? Couldn't happen."

"Why on earth not?"

"Because getting married for keeps is a very emotional experience. It's for life. It matters. No matter what, you're signing on to go the distance with that one other person. That ring has to be significant, and that doesn't come with a hefty price tag. No matter how beautiful those rings were, they weren't from the heart."

As if she'd been kicked out of her chair by a giant boot, she was on her feet, soda sloshing out of her can, finger pointed straight at his face. "You know what? You're stubborn as a mule, Mark Reynolds. Even when it makes sense to get some damn help on your ranch, help that wouldn't hurt your bottom line a bit, you dig your heels in and work until you get sick. How many times have you had pneumonia?"

He opened his mouth, but she just stepped closer. "You think everyone who doesn't think like you do is not just wrong, but stupid. Don't even try to deny it, because I've been with you after a night at the Renegade, and you've sliced and diced those good ol' boys into mincemeat."

Again, he opened his mouth.

"You never give your brother a break. He's a kid, dammit, and he has a right to choose his own life. Sure he can help on the ranch, it's good for him to have the discipline, but don't discount his dreams. He has a right to them, too."

"Are you finished?"

"I'm not sure yet."

"Let me know," he said, as calm as you please.

She wanted to yell some more, and the truth was there was more to yell about. Mark was no saint, and he was no angel. He brooded and was quick to leap on other people's mistakes.

But he was also the most amazing man in the whole damn world.

She burst into tears, great big wet tears, and she ran into the bedroom, slamming the door shut behind her.

A minute later, she heard him open it. Shocking, because she was still wailing like a banshee. She should have locked the damn door.

He sat on the edge of the bed. Quietly. Patiently. She didn't want him to see her like this. Not because she was crying, but because she could feel all that TV makeup running down her cheeks.

Oh, the hell with that. He'd seen her look her worst. She'd seen him, too. They'd been through it all together. No, not all.

"You need some tissues?"

She sniffed and nodded. The bed rose a little, then dipped when he came back. She held her hand out and he stuffed it. Several minutes later, she finished mopping up her face, and while she knew her eyes were swollen and her skin a perfect mess, she faced him.

"I'm not ready," she said.

"For what?"

"For New York. For the *Times* or the *Post* or any of them. I'm a small-town girl with a dream too big for my britches."

"Not forever. You'll get the experience and then you'll come back."

She shifted on the bed until she was sitting closer to Mark. "I don't know if I want to," she said, her voice an embarrassed whisper.

His hand touched hers. “It’s okay. You get to change your dreams, Trish. You have a right to do that.”

“I just don’t know what I want,” she said. “It’s always been so clear. All of it. The job, the apartment, the travel. I’d dreamed it in every detail. And now, all I feel like is the biggest fool in the whole world. I screwed up, Mark. So, so badly.”

He stood and pulled her up with him. “Let’s you and I go to bed. You tell me every little thing that’s got you worried. In the morning, things will be a lot clearer.”

She nodded, drained of every bit of energy, and headed to the bathroom. She needed a shower. She needed to sleep. She wished she were anywhere but here.

SLEEP WOULDN’T COME. Trish had no idea what time it was, but it was way late. She was going to look like crap tomorrow, which was just perfect.

She looked over at Mark in the moonlight. He’d been asleep for a while. Of course, that was her fault, too. He’d wanted to talk. She tried, but in the end, she just couldn’t. She’d already confessed to being a fool. She hadn’t the strength to fill in the details.

So, what now? What next?

She fiddled with her engagement ring. Her fake engagement ring. Tomorrow she would add a fake wedding band and sign fake wedding papers, and kiss her fake husband in front of hundreds of strangers.

Did it get any better than this?

She laughed at her own joke because really what were her options? She couldn't stop the proceedings at this stage of the game. That truly would be unethical, even beyond her shaky moral code.

She didn't used to have the shakes when it came to stuff like this. She used to be proud of her accomplishments and her behavior.

Not only had her dreams gone up in smoke, but her self-image was way too close to the ashes.

Mark turned over, and she got real quiet, afraid she would wake him with her screaming thoughts. Too late. His head came up from the pillow.

"Go back to sleep," she whispered.

He shook his head, then scooted closer. "You need something?" he asked, his voice all growly. "Water?"

"No. I'm fine."

"Somehow I doubt that."

With a sigh, she met him halfway on the bed, resting her head on his chest. "I'm so screwed."

He laughed, but in a nice way. "There's nothing you can do about any of it tonight, Trish. You might as well get some rest."

"I've tried. It's hopeless."

There was a long stretch of silence where the only thing she heard was his breathing. Then his hand pushed back the hair from her forehead in the gentlest caress. "Maybe I can help."

For a moment she thought he was going to sing her a lullaby or something. He disabused that notion as he pulled her up to meet him in a kiss.

She hesitated, but not for long. He hadn't been sleeping so long that he had morning breath, but she had the feeling she wouldn't have cared if he had. She needed this. Needed him.

He couldn't hate her too much if he could kiss her like this, could he? Maybe he wasn't embarrassed for her. Or filled with pity.

No, she was the only one feeling those things.

"Hush," he whispered, pulling away only a smidgen. "Don't you worry about a thing, honey. I've got you."

Touching his naked chest, feeling the warmth of his skin and his comfort, she fell into his embrace leaving behind her doubts and fears and judgments.

True to his word, he never once let her go. With a slow tenderness, he made love to her. With her. So thoroughly that there wasn't an inch of her body that didn't thrum with pleasure. From her lips to her toes, he showed her how he felt about her. Despite everything.

He whispered the words that had come to be theirs alone. Words that on another man's tongue would have sounded absurd. But theirs was a shared history of silliness, of sounds whose familiarity made them special.

Even though that old T-shirt was on the ground somewhere outside the bed, she felt wrapped in him no matter where his hands were. No matter how his teasing tongue made her plead.

When it was time to catch her breath, to cool her body down after the most perfect climax ever, he was still there.

"You still with me?" he said, his voice low and intimate.

"Uh-huh."

"Good, because there's something I want you to think about. You remember when we were growing up, there was the Briscoe County newspaper?"

She nodded against his chest. "It was what, four pages?"

"On a good day. But anyway, Jeb Smith still has all the equipment in storage. It's pretty dated, but it wouldn't take all that much to get the paper up and running again, especially now that computers can do so much of the work.

"Maybe, instead of going back to Dallas, you could consider becoming a publisher. Briscoe County has grown. There's lots of folks who could use a weekly paper. And if you were the publisher, you could make that paper into anything you wanted it to be. That would give you lots of experience, wouldn't it? I mean, you could write the stories, do the copy editing, editorialize, all of it. And when you're ready, you could come back and have something real and fine to show these New Yorkers. Anyway, it's something to think about, right? An option."

"Right," she said. "An option."

He kissed the top of her head. "Go to sleep. There's plenty of time to decide what you're going to do."

She nodded again, her body limp and so tired she could barely move her head. But her thoughts? A whole different story.

CHAPTER TEN

THE ROOFTOP GARDEN at Hush had been transformed. The flowers bloomed in a sea of brilliant colors and fragrances. In the center of the roof Weddings by Desire had gone all out to create a magical space. There was a rose-covered arbor, a string quartet, champagne at the ready and chairs and room for everyone, including the press. The decorations were all pastel and soft and blended with the flowers seamlessly.

Trish wasn't able to enjoy the scenery for long, however. Gwen hurried her away into the bridal room, adjacent to the swimming pool. Hush had taken equal care there, providing the bride-to-be and the wedding party with ample space to dress, do makeup and hair—there was even a gorgeous chaise for the bride to rest on, should the need arise.

Trish would have preferred a bed and about six more hours of sleep, but her adrenaline was sufficient to keep her awake. That and the espressos she was sucking down.

She was led to the beauty station where two women and a man were at the ready. One for hair, one for makeup, one for nails. Sinking down in the barber chair, Trish tried to relax. She had an entire hour scheduled here, then it was on with the dress, then on with the show.

The team situated themselves so they could all work at once, and Trish gave herself over to the primping. But instead of the calming meditation she'd meant to do, she thought again about what came next. Not just here, at Hush, either. She knew this was a defining moment. That what she decided here would determine the course of the rest of her life.

MARK DIDN'T HAVE TO BE at the hotel for another forty-five minutes, so he let the waiter pour him another cup of coffee. His father, his brother and his best friend Darryl had joined him for breakfast in a little coffee shop two doors down from Hush.

"So what do you think?" he asked.

His father shrugged. "It's a good place to visit, but I wouldn't want to live here."

Mark turned to Chris.

"I like it. There's so effin' much to do here. All night long, man. I saw a Chinese restaurant that's open until five in the morning. Jeez."

"It ain't bad," Darryl said. "But I miss home."

Mark sipped his coffee, debating the wisdom of finishing the last Danish. Better not.

"So," his Dad said, "this wedding thing. You and Trish. It's all for show."

"That's right. But we can't tell anyone that."

"You have your license, right? And there's going to be a real justice of the peace up there?"

"The marriage will be legitimate. Just short-lived."

"Why's that again?"

Mark sighed. "Dad, I told you. Trish wants to live here. In the city. She wants to work for a major paper. I can't wait to get back to the ranch."

"That's fine and dandy, but pretty inconsequential. Do you love her?"

Mark did not want to have this conversation. It was hard enough to face the day feeling the way he did. "Can we talk about something else? Please?"

"Sure, we can talk about anything you like. But the problem isn't going away. You need to tell her."

"What, that she needs to give up her dreams and become a rancher? She hates Briscoe. She hates ranching. It's not gonna happen."

"How do you know, if you don't ask her?"

"She knows her options." Including the one he'd offered up last night. Not that he would tell his father, but he'd pulled out the only ace he'd had. That Briscoe paper idea had been his last, desperate plea. Trish hadn't brought it up once this morning. Not a word. It was time to let it go.

"I see her point," Chris said. "If I didn't have to, I wouldn't go back to the ranch. Not a chance."

It hurt to hear his brother's words, but they weren't a surprise. Mark remembered what Trish had said about allowing Chris to have his own dreams. "What do you want?" he asked. "Is there something specific? After college, I mean?"

Chris looked startled. "Well, yeah."

Even their father was paying attention now.

"I want to fly."

"Fly what?"

Chris's cheeks were flushed and he looked as if he was exposing a dirty secret. "Helicopters. I want to join the Air Force and get my license. And when I get out of the service, I want to be a life flight pilot for a hospital."

Mark sat back in his chair, dumbfounded. "How long have you been thinking about this?"

"Since I was twelve."

"Why didn't you say anything?"

He gave Mark a look that was like a punch in the stomach. "You didn't want to hear it. I know you love the ranch, dude, but it's not for me. It never has been."

"Yeah," Mark said quietly. "It doesn't have to be for you. I'd still prefer you go to college."

Chris nodded. "I'm planning on it."

Mark got the check from the center of the table. He left the money along with a New York-size tip. "I've got to get ready. See you guys up on the roof. And, Darryl, don't you dare have a beer until the wedding's over."

"Jeez, man. I may be a hick, but I'm not a dummy."

Mark hit his friend on the back of the head, but he smiled as he did it.

"Still time to tell her you love her," his dad said.

"Dad, she knows."

"Does she? Really?"

Mark didn't answer. But he pondered the question all the way back to the suite.

THE STRING QUARTET started playing the wedding march, and it was all Trish could do not to throw up. She was standing at the edge of the garden, Gwen at her side. From here, she could see it all. The gorgeous decorations, the stunning flowers, her friends Stephanie and Larissa from Dallas, Penny who she'd known since third-grade and her maid of honor, Ellen. Across the aisle sat Mark's dad and Chris. Even Darryl looked good in his tux. And, of course, the media. There were three television cameras, a whole gaggle of photographers and reporters. Piper Devon, Hush's famous owner, was there, too, looking stunning in a pale pink dress.

It was someone's dream wedding. Just not hers.

It should have been. Mark, in his perfect tuxedo complete with a rose in the lapel, was everything she'd ever wanted in a husband. Best friend, confidant, lover. But the life he could offer her, had offered her…what of that? Was it possible for her to find happiness, the forever kind, in Briscoe? Could she find the satisfaction she'd yearned for on a horse ranch? Running a newspaper that would be more focused on the grain reports than the situation in Washington?

Gwen touched her arm. It was her cue, and she had rehearsed this moment enough that she knew just how slow to walk, just how hard to smile.

If only her heart wasn't breaking into a million

pieces. If only the ring on her finger meant what it was supposed to mean, instead of a glittery, brilliant lie.

Each step brought her closer to the shambles her life had become. She'd finally, early this morning in the fabulous shower, come to terms with the end of her dream. New York wasn't for her. Not now. Maybe never.

So what would she put in its place?

Dallas, where she could get her old job back, where she could continue to learn and develop as a journalist? Where she could start dating again, looking to find a man like Mark?

She felt the cameras on her, heard the delicate strings as they wafted over the garden. The justice of the peace looked serene and happy in his best Sunday suit. Everyone around her seemed so pleased. So thrilled to be part of this momentous occasion.

Even Mark. God, the way he looked at her! Despite every one of her sins, her conceits, her schemes, everything about him, especially his eyes, spoke of his love for her.

Too quickly, she was at his side. He smiled at her and with great care, lifted the veil from her eyes.

The justice cleared his throat. "Dearly beloved—"

"Wait."

Mark looked at her sharply. The justice seemed insulted. And she could feel Gwen's panic from five feet away.

"Wait," she said again because she had to. The veil had been lifted, all right, and with a clarity that made the rooftop shimmer, she turned to Mark. “We need to talk.”

He nodded once, took her hand and led her back down the aisle. All the way to the quietest part of the garden. All the way past the furious clicking of cameras.

The quartet had stalled, but by the time they were alone, they were playing Pachelbel’s Canon.

“What’s wrong, honey?”

“Everything,” she said, not at all sure how to go about this. “You’ve been… I…”

“Take your time. There’s no rush.”

She took a deep breath. “Do you love me?”

He nodded. “I have since that first day of high school.”

“Do you love me enough not to resent me when there’s so much to be done on the ranch? When you’re out there in the middle of winter and I’m away on a story? Do you love me that much?”

“Someone told me once that I was as stubborn as a mule. That I could hire help when I needed it. I think that piece of advice was worth taking.”

“You’ve always wanted someone by your side. A helpmate.”

“That’s true. But help comes in a bunch of different ways.”

“You have to be sure about this, cowboy, because what I’m saying here is that I love you. I love you so much it would be a sin against everything that’s holy to walk away. But I’d rather cut off my own arm than give you a life of resentment and disappointment.”

His slow smile—*that* slow smile—changed everything. "Honey, you're who I choose. Is that clear enough?"

She smiled right back. "Wow. That's very, very clear."

"Are you gonna be okay with the Briscoe County paper?"

"Yeah. I am. As long as you're there. As long as we can be together."

He looked over his shoulder at the stunned and impatient crowd, then back into her eyes. "Trish Avalon, will you be my wife? For keeps?"

She flung her arms around his neck, whacking him in the head with her bouquet. After a kiss that made her toes curl and her heart happy, she met his gaze and said, "I do."

* * * *

Sweeter Than Wine

CATHY YARDLEY

CHAPTER ONE

CHAD MCFEE'S PHONE VIBRATED in the pocket of his black Hugo Boss suit. The call display showed the name of his sister, Violet. He glanced around. There were several other people in the lawyer's office, all chatting amongst themselves—mostly older people, and a few of his cousins. Walking out into the hallway, Chad answered the phone. "Hello?"

"So, what'd you get?"

He rolled his eyes. "Vi, this isn't a good time. Besides, they haven't even read the will yet. And that question is tacky."

Violet made a rude noise. "Great-Uncle Charles was ancient, and you know it. It's not like any of us were that close."

At three years younger than he was, his "kid" sister was twenty-seven. Neither of them were children. Still, she could be pretty childish when she felt like it. "He obviously felt close enough to me to leave me something," Chad said, feeling a little badly that he hadn't been closer to the older man after whom he was named. That didn't stop him from being curious as to what Great-Uncle Charles had left for him. A small, guilty part of him hoped that it was money. Great-Uncle Charles had been wealthy, and considering the McFees were one of the wealthiest families on the West Coast, that was saying something.

"I'll bet he left you something dumb and sentimental. Like a pocket watch," Violet said, bursting his bubble and bringing him back to reality.

"Probably," Chad admitted.

"Mom and Dad hope it's money," Violet added. "Especially after your little indie movie fiasco."

Chad growled. "That was six months ago. Aren't they going to let that go?"

"You nearly wiped out your trust fund with that, you know. Did you really think they were just going to laugh it off?"

"I've still got some money," he said. "Not that it's any of your business. Or theirs, really."

"It is if you keep getting money from them," Violet pointed out.

"You're the one who keeps getting them to pay for your stuff," Chad said defensively, hating that she was dragging him into this conversation. She loved stirring up drama. He suspected it was just out of sheer boredom, like when she couldn't find a friend to go shopping with her or she'd broken up with her latest boyfriend du jour. "Didn't they pay for your birthday party in Hong Kong? And your car?"

"Yeah, but they don't care about stuff like that," she laughed. "The McFees are supposed to spend money and enjoy themselves. Besides, people like hearing about the latest things I've bought." Violet paused a beat. "At least I don't embarrass them by throwing money at little projects that keep failing. How many 'business ventures' have you been in, anyway?"

He shut his eyes and counted to ten. "Don't you have a club to go to or something? Some fashion show to attend? Or someone *else* to annoy?"

She laughed again. "No comeback for that one, huh?"

"I'm hanging up now."

"Mom and Dad are going to want to talk to you when you're done. That's all I was calling to say."

"Wonderful." Chad rubbed at his temples. He was starting to get a huge headache. "Fine. Message delivered. Beat it."

"Bye." She hung up, and he shut off his phone. He'd call when the whole thing was over, but he wasn't looking forward to it.

At least I don't embarrass them by throwing money at little projects that keep failing.

He walked back into the lawyer's office and sat down, arms crossed. He loved his family, and they did have a point about his last few investments. But he was getting sick of being considered the black sheep of the McFee Empire simply because he'd taken a few chances. They hadn't always been a multi million-dollar family, he consoled himself. If his great-great-grandfather McFee hadn't hit it rich in gold and turned it into a string of very successful restaurants and then frozen foods, his parents would be broke, too. It took risks to make it big. He just hadn't picked the right risks, that was all.

Chad looked around the room. His cousins were in one corner, looking like they were arguing amongst themselves. They were all in their thirties and forties, wearing chic black clothing and matching stern expressions. There were also a few people who looked like businessmen—Great-Uncle Charles was known for being on the board of directors for several corporations.

Finally, the lawyer stood up and began the reading of the will. The bulk of the fortune went to Great-Uncle Charles's children, who looked moderately happy at their share of the pie, although they still glared at one another. Chad imagined they would probably get their own lawyers to squabble out the details. It was a sizable fortune, so he guessed he couldn't blame them, and they *were* brothers and sisters. Hell, he'd considered hitting Violet with a lawsuit or two, just because she annoyed him so much. He thought back to his phone conversation with her. They'd never really gotten into rough-and-tumble fights when they were younger, but they'd fought fairly intently. That hadn't changed a lot as they got older, though they still spoke often.

"And to my great-nephew and namesake, Charles 'Chad' McFee…"

Chad shook his head to clear his thoughts, and then focused on what the reedy lawyer standing at the podium had to say. Everyone else seemed curious to see what he was doing there.

Violet was probably right, he thought, trying to squash hope. He was probably getting a pocket watch, or some antique paperweight.

The lawyer adjusted his glasses and read directly from the will. "'I know that we haven't been that close, all things considered, over the past few years.'"

Chad felt a pang. He'd been busy, but he really should've spent a little more time visiting the guy. A little late now, he thought with remorse, and for a second his eagerness to find out what he'd inherited was eclipsed by guilt.

"'The McFee fortune is large, but some things are more important than money. I learned that the hard way. And, if what your parents have been telling me is accurate, so are you.'"

The cousins chuckled maliciously at that little commentary, and Chad scrunched down in his seat a little. *Good grief,* he thought. *Am I supposed to be getting lectures on my spending habits from beyond the grave, now?*

He was probably getting a calculator, at this rate. Or maybe an *Investing for Dummies* book. *Yuk yuk, isn't that hysterical?* The family would be talking about it for years.

"'So to you, great-nephew, I am giving one of my favorite possessions,'" the lawyer continued, clearing his throat. "'You are now owner of the Honey Ridge Vineyard, in Napa.'"

Chad blinked, not sure that he'd heard that one right. A vineyard? He hadn't even known Great-Uncle

Charles liked wine, much less owned something as frivolous as a vineyard!

"'It has been a joy for me, in my old age,'" the lawyer said, and his voice warmed, as if Great-Uncle Charles himself was channeling through the thin old man. "'I give it to you with only one stipulation—that you allow the current vineyard team to finish out one last vintage, should you decide to sell it. They're good people who work hard, and they deserve that much.'"

There was a murmur that went through the small crowd at that point. Everything up to that point had been given away with no strings attached, so this seemed odd.

The lawyer was obviously skimming ahead, because he cleared his throat with even more gusto, as if hesitant to continue. Finally, he said, "'I give this to you because I know, of all the family, you will understand and honor my dying request…instead of bringing lawyers into it and trying to have it all your way.'"

Ooh. Chad glanced over at the cousins, who were now looking guilty and scowling instead of looking smug. *Score one, Great-Uncle Charles!*

The rest of the will reading was short and to the point—various items and knickknacks. When it was done, one of his cousins, Eldridge, came over.

"I can't believe he gave you the vineyard," Eldridge said without preamble.

"Me neither," Chad said, honestly enough. "I didn't even know he had a vineyard."

"He bought it about ten years ago, after Mom died," Eldridge said. "He was a bit silly about it, to be honest. It was sort of a retirement hobby, I think."

Chad was curious. His great-uncle hadn't seemed the type to have hobbies, considering he'd kept making money right up to the day he died. He didn't think the man had ever retired.

"Anyway, too bad you can't sell it right away," Eldridge said. "Unless you're planning on keeping it?"

"I just found out about this," Chad pointed out. "I have no idea what I'm planning on doing with it."

"It's a money-loser." Eldridge waved his hand dismissively. "You'll want to ditch it, first chance."

Chad nodded, eager to get home at this point. "Uh, okay," he said, then put out his hand. "I'm so sorry for your loss."

Eldridge looked nonplussed for a moment, then shook his hand. "Thanks," he mumbled, sounding a little choked up, then quickly walked away.

Chad sighed. There might be more to life than money, he thought as he grabbed his coat. But money was a lot easier for his family to deal with.

LEILA FAIRMONT HAD DONE a lot for Honey Ridge Vineyard. She'd stayed up countless nights, working heaters to make sure the grapes didn't freeze during frosts. She'd contacted the best agriculturalists in the business during the blight that struck some of their prize Merlot grapes, year before last. She'd supervised the business, farming and winemaking aspects of the entire enterprise since she was twenty-five years old, now nearly four years. She couldn't feel closer to the vineyard if it were her own child.

Still, she'd never gone up to a total stranger's house and introduced herself before.

She had gotten news from Charles McFee's lawyer that the vineyard had been given to his nephew, Chad McFee. She'd never met Chad. For that matter, she'd barely met Charles. He was responsible for the continued survival of Honey Ridge, though, and for that, she was very fond of the man, who had seemed very old and very, very serious on the occasions he'd visited the vineyard. Charles McFee had been an old-school, tweed-and-pinstripe business type, who apparently had developed a passion for being a vineyard owner late in life. He'd given them tons of money and never balked at costs or disasters. He had been a true patron, and he'd let Leila, and her parents before her, run the place as their own.

She drove through the unfamiliar streets of San Francisco, feeling frustration at herself for getting lost—and even more frustration at being nervous. If Charles were anything like his uncle, he was a quiet, stuffy, pleasant sort of investor. He probably had the same wire-rim glasses, though not as thick, and his idea of a good time was checking out stock prices while sitting in the bathtub. The image made her giggle.

Leila found the condo, finally, in a nice neighborhood in Nob Hill. He likely had a gorgeous view. He was also obviously very rich. The trick here was going to be convincing him that Honey Ridge was, indeed, a good investment.

She parked her beat-up van on the hill and got out, straightening her very best business suit and praying for strength. Honey Ridge had been in financial straits for the past two years, and only love had kept Charles McFee giving money to the cause. She couldn't thank the man enough for his patience. Her parents had been head vintners of Honey Ridge since she was a child, and when they left to start a new vineyard in Australia, Leila had begged them to intercede on her behalf. Even though twenty-five was an unbelievably young age for a head winemaker, she had grown up on wine and had studied winemaking in college. She'd done everything necessary to one day run the vineyard she'd fallen in love with. Charles McFee had taken a chance on her, based on her parents' recommendation.

Now, the vineyard was recovering slowly, first from blight, then from last year's drought, which had hit all the independent vineyards hard. She just needed another year or two to bring it around.

If only Charles hadn't died!

Still, she thought, as she walked up the concrete stairs that led to the front door of the condo, the man had been ninety if he were a day. It was selfish of her to expect him to hang on just to bail her out.

She rang the bell and, after a moment, a puzzled voice came over the intercom. "Yes?"

"Mr. McFee?"

Another pause. "Yes. Who is this?"

"My name is Leila Fairmont. I'm from Honey Ridge Vineyards—"

"I'm not interested in buying anything today," he said quickly.

"Well, you're already the owner," she said, with a little chuckle. He thought she was some kind of door-to-door solicitor! "I'm so sorry to be barging in unannounced like this, but I left you several messages, and I was hoping for just a few minutes of your time."

A slightly longer pause. Then, "Yes, of course. Leila Fairmont. Give me a second, I'll get you."

She smiled. He was probably in the middle of some business plan or something, she thought with a grin, and didn't want to be disturbed. She took a deep breath, standing up straight, and held her slim briefcase in front of her. She knew she looked the picture of professionalism. Now, to just…

He opened the door, and Leila couldn't help it—her mouth fell open.

He looked like a frat guy. He was wearing a pair of sweats and a tank top that left little of his body to the imagination. His arms were chiseled and nicely muscular, without being obnoxious or overly bulky. His waist was slim, and she'd bet anything his stomach was ironing-board flat, probably rippled with muscle. His hair was a rich reddish-brown, and it was tousled and mussed in a way that had nothing to do with artistic sculpting gel. It just looked…

Sexy. Natural, just-got-out-of-bed sexy.

Her mouth went dry. "Mr. McFee?" she croaked in disbelief. "*Chad* McFee?"

"You must be Leila Fairmont," he said, as if it were the most natural thing in the world for him to greet her this way. He opened the door, gesturing her in. "I've been meaning to call you. I'm sorry I didn't sooner—things have been a little crazy. I just got back from a birthday party, actually."

"Oh?" She couldn't help it. She sneaked a quick look at his butt as he walked into his living room. Was *nothing* on this man less than perfect? When he turned, she made a show of glancing at her watch, to make sure that he didn't catch her scoping him out. It was four o'clock in the afternoon.

Had he been out all night, then?

"Have a seat," he said, gesturing to two huge gray leather couches. "I'll just be a second. I need to get a cup of coffee. And an aspirin." He laughed. "Can I get you anything?"

She shook her head, sitting on the couch, feeling dismayed. She was expecting a tweedy business nerd, not some party-hearty poster boy!

And certainly not a sexy one.

Chad came back out with his coffee. "Sorry. Jet lag always hits me this way," he said, by way of explanation.

"Jet lag?" She couldn't track what he was saying. That wasn't a good sign. "I thought you'd just been to a party."

"Yup. It was in Ibiza. Spain," he clarified, taking a long sip of the coffee. "Ah, that's the stuff. So you're from the vineyard I inherited. How's it going?"

She blinked, thrown by…well, everything. "It's going okay," she said guardedly.

"Well, that's good."

Leila sat there a minute, staring at him as he smiled at her sleepily. Maybe this was a bad idea. Maybe he'd just be like Charles—keep writing the checks and stay out of her way. Anybody who just jetted off to Spain for a birthday party had to be doing okay financially.

"How's the harvest coming?" he asked.

"Uh…well, it's only July," she said. "We're planning on harvesting in September this year. That's a little early, but I want to have the time to age the Merlots, which we're famous for, and experiment with some blends."

She stopped as she saw his eyes glaze over. Now, he was the one who wasn't tracking.

Apparently, he didn't know anything about wine at all.

"Anyway," she said, feeling stupid for deciding she had to meet the new owner, "I just wanted to see who our new investor was, and answer any questions you might have about, er, the vineyard. But I see this is probably an inconvenient time for you. Anytime you'd like to come by Honey Ridge, though, I'd be more than happy to give you a tour."

She was staring full into his face when she said it,

which she realized was probably a mistake. He was looking sleepy, so his amber-brown eyes were low lidded, like he'd just come out of bed…or he was still in it, and wouldn't mind company. His slow smile was sinfully handsome.

"That could be nice," he said, and his voice was low, rubbing over her skin like raw silk.

"Um. Yes," she said, fidgeting with her briefcase. "Right. So, no questions?"

He frowned for a moment, thoughtful. "Actually, yes, as long as you're here. How's the vineyard doing financially?"

Leila blinked. Then she opened her briefcase and got out the little presentation she'd meant to go through, back when she'd assumed Chad was Mr. Tweedy Nerd. "Here is a snapshot of our financial picture, as well as our plans for future expansion and growth."

He reached over, his fingertips inadvertently brushing against hers as he collected the slim report. She shivered, and felt like an even bigger idiot. Leila watched as he breezed through the pages.

"Hmm," he said. "Well. This will take me a little time to go over, but I appreciate you having it pulled together so neatly."

She wondered if he'd really read it, or if he'd chuck it into a desk somewhere. A house this big, a guy this rich, had to have some huge mahogany desk, even if he just used it to play video games or seduce women with by saying, *Let me show you my study*.

Her mind flashed a picture of how he might seduce her—and how big that mahogany desk might be, with two people on it—for just a moment before she stopped herself. *Knock that off. He's the new owner, you idiot!*

"Well, I guess I'll be going," she said, standing up quickly and putting out her hand. "I appreciate you taking the time to meet with me, Mr. McFee."

"Call me Chad," he said easily, with that quicksilver smile. "And Ms. Fairmont?"

"Call me Leila," she said, to be fair.

"Leila," he said. She'd never heard anyone say her name the way he did. Man, did she have to get out of there! "I think it's only fair to warn you that I am very serious about my investments. I'm going to take you up on that offer of yours."

"Which offer would that be?" she squeaked, then cleared her throat with a frown.

That smile turned lethally sexy. "I'll be out for a tour, at the very least," he said. "But I think I'd like to really investigate what makes your vineyard tick. I mean, I'm the owner, right? I shouldn't be in the dark about it. I have a ton to learn, I'm sure."

"Uh…" This wasn't going the way she'd planned. At all.

"And I'm sure you'll show me," he said confidently. "Can I count on you?"

"Er…all right," she said uncertainly. "I mean, of course. Of course, you're welcome to come anytime you like."

He smiled and shook her hand, his palm warm and solid over hers. "I'm looking forward to it," he all but purred.

She took her hand back, still feeling his warmth on it, and then fled with a nod and a hasty goodbye.

Going back to her van, Leila was surprised to find herself trembling a little. Instead of a kindly old man, she had a young man to deal with now. A rich, jet-setting, socialite guy, sexy as all get out, who might or might not have intentions of being hands-on when it came to her vineyard. Which gave her two sources of concern.

One: how was she going to convince a guy who knew nothing about wine not to just barge in because he was bored…and how was she going to convince him not to drop them when he got bored of this new toy?

And two: more disturbingly, as she thought of his smile and his handshake…just how hands-on was her new boss planning on being?

"CHAD, WHAT ARE YOU thinking about?"

"Hmm?" Chad looked over the family dinner table toward his mother, who had asked the question. "Sorry, what?"

"You're so distracted lately," his mother noticed. "Anything going on? Some girl maybe?"

"As long as it's not another investment," his father muttered, from the far end of the table, causing his sister Violet to smirk. Chad was surprised to see Violet there, actually. She'd been at some resort for the past week, or so her tan seemed to suggest.

"So which is it, Chad? A girl, or an investment?" his mother continued, in her gently relentless way.

A bit of both.

Leila Fairmont had dropped by his house a few days before. He couldn't get her off of his mind, and he wasn't sure why. She was cute, of course—honey blonde, five-six, with a trim body that had curves in the right places without suggesting any kind of surgical enhancement. But while she was cute, she wasn't what he'd consider beautiful. He'd seen enough porcelain-perfect near-model socialites to know the difference. But there was something about her—fidgeting with that leather briefcase of hers, or tugging on her business skirt—that seemed adorable. That, and the fact that she was obviously concerned about her livelihood, the vineyard.

"I think I'm going to be gone for the summer," he ventured carefully.

"Really?" His father looked up from his beef stroganoff at that point. "You know we're going to the lodge in Scotland. Are you going to be in Europe? You should swing by if you are."

"You'd better not be in Mazatlan," Violet said sourly. "I don't want to keep running into you at parties."

He sighed. If he'd realized his family was going to be out of the country, he might've kept his mouth shut and saved himself the trouble. But he'd already put his foot in it, and now they were all expecting him to break the news.

"Actually, I'll still be in the country. I just won't be around my condo, that's all," he clarified.

"Oh. Well," his father said, and turned his attention back to eating his dinner.

"That sounds good," his mother said, frowning at her husband. "Where will you be then, darling? On your friend's yacht? That was lovely, as I remember."

"Ah, no," Chad said. "Actually, I think I'll be out in Napa for a while."

"Napa? That's nice," she enthused. "I haven't been in wine country for…well, years now. At least, not in the United States." She turned back to Chad's father. "Do you remember when we spent those months in France, at that château right by that charming little vineyard—"

"Vineyard," his father said, and Chad could see the wheels turn and the connection finally click. "Your great-uncle Charles's vineyard. Don't tell me you're actually going to stop by and see the damned thing."

"It's my vineyard now, actually, Dad," he said, keeping his voice mild and eating his own dinner.

"You *are* selling the thing, though, right?" His father made it sound like a leper colony. "You're getting rid of it as soon as possible."

"Part of the provision of the will," Chad said quickly, trying to head off his father's tirade, "was that the current vineyard team gets to finish out this harvest, and bottle it. I can't sell it until then."

"You probably could," his father grumped. "If you'd just let me call our lawyer..."

"Dad," Chad warned.

His father sighed. "Your uncle knew he had a sucker in you," he finally said. "So, what exactly are you going to check out at this little vineyard of yours?"

"I don't know," Chad admitted. He hadn't planned on looking at it, in all honesty. He had just planned on waiting until he got the okay that the last bottle was finished, and then he was planning on dumping the whole thing on a Realtor or something. But then, he hadn't met Leila. "I've always liked wine."

"Yeah," Violet snorted. "*Drinking* it."

Chad ignored that little jab. "So I thought I'd see what sort of wine cellar they have, what the grounds are like, stuff like that. Get a sense of the place," he said. "If I'm going to know what it's worth to sell, I ought to check it over."

He figured that was what it would take to placate his father, and he was right...for the moment, anyway. His father simply harrumphed and went back to eating, giving his son a baleful stare every few minutes.

Chad got the feeling he wasn't going to be getting off that lightly, but he was glad for the reprieve. He spent the rest of the evening listening to Violet spin stories about her rich friends and their various feuds and gossip. His father tuned that out, too, although his mother was able to keep up, even adding little bons mots of her own from her older social circle. "Just try not to give them anything nasty to write about in those social columns, Violet," his mother concluded. "The way I keep reading about those Hilton girls…it breaks your heart, it really does. It's just embarrassing. And then to turn around and hear they think they're making their own money!"

Chad frowned. "Don't they have a clothing line or something?"

He shouldn't have. His father took the opportunity to pounce. "They might be embarrassments, but when they put their money into something, at least they're successful at it."

"Dear," his mother warned. "Please. Not at the dinner table."

"I just want our son to realize that I keep having to hear about his little hobbies every time I go to the gym or the yacht club," his father replied. "Violet might be burning through her trust fund and going to every soiree in the Western hemisphere, but kids your age, in your social circle…who isn't expecting that?"

Chad rolled his eyes. "You're still mad about the movie not making money, huh?"

"All of it, Chad," his father growled.

Violet stopped looking smug when she realized her father wasn't just doing his usual posturing—he was well and truly steamed, and he was about to unleash it. She sat up in her chair, her eyes darting toward the door. "Um…excuse me," she said, and fled.

"First there was your little Internet business, that you shelled out half your bank account for," his father said.

"That was just before the bust," Chad argued. "I wasn't the only one who got burned."

His father held up a hand for silence. "Then there was your real estate brainstorm."

Chad squirmed. He'd gotten taken for a lot of money, from a friend of a friend who had conned a bunch of them. "That was a mistake," Chad admitted. "But it did teach me to be much more careful about research and who to invest in."

"Then, there were those cars…that cruise ship… and finally a movie. What the hell do you know from movies?" His father shook his head. "You just meet these people, and they're so happy, and you think it'll be so much fun that you dive in without thinking. Dammit, Chad!"

He crossed his arms. "I know I've been overenthusiastic," Chad said. "But dammit, Dad, what am I supposed to do? Get a job over at the family company?"

"Lord, no," his father said, with an undertone of *Lord knows what damage you'd wreak if I let you go there!* Chad felt his chest burn with humiliation. "If you just keep your spending reasonable, you don't have to work. Ever. Do you know how many people would love to be in the position you're in?"

Chad clenched his jaw. He knew it was unreasonable. He knew that he could just sit in the lap of luxury and cruise for the rest of his life, if he wanted to, just as his father had said. The thing was, he was bored—bored with parties, bored with traveling, bored with the same old thing. He knew it was pathetic, the old "bird in a gilded cage" dodge. But when he invested…he supposed the closest thing to what he experienced would be gambling, but it wasn't just the risk. It was feeling like a *part* of something.

Unfortunately, the things he kept choosing to be a part of were usually stuff his friends pulled together, and while they meant well, they usually had the attention span of a gnat. He'd learned, the hard way, that the next time he invested in something, he was going to not only know everything about it, he was going to develop it himself.

"Just remember what I said, son," his father said, finally concluding his lecture. "Stop trying to be something you're not. Just…I don't know. Buy a car or something. And knock off trying to be Mr. Tycoon, okay?"

Chad swallowed his humiliation and pushed away his plate. "Thanks for dinner," he said in a monotone.

His mother looked thankful that the discussion was over. "Would you like some dessert?"

Chad shook his head. He'd had enough for one family dinner.

"Well then, have a fun time in Napa," she sang out brightly. "We'll call you as soon as we come back in September, okay?"

CHAPTER TWO

THAT FRIDAY, at noon, Leila gathered her motley crew of vineyard workers and assorted staff to meet their new owner. She paced awkwardly in the courtyard, feeling nerves course through her. Most of them were due to the fact that Mr. "Call Me Chad" McFee had probably read her report on the state of the vineyard by now, or at least, there was the possibility he could have…and by this point, he might've decided to simply sell the place, which was probably the most logical conclusion. For all she knew, he'd called to tell her he'd be showing up to "inspect" the place as a final courtesy, before pulling her aside and dropping the ax personally. It didn't seem likely, but weirder things had happened.

Of course, on a purely personal level, she admitted that at least part of her nervousness had nothing to do with the vineyard…and everything to do with seeing Chad again, for whatever reason.

If that wasn't stupid, she didn't know what was.

Leila glanced at her watch. She could deal with droughts and blight—hadn't she had to face them both, in the past two lousy seasons? She'd even face a swarm of locusts, if it came to that. But this was her last chance at bringing back the vineyard she'd grown up with. Her last chance at making her parents proud.

She might not have had a lot of boyfriends, but she did know that they could be distracting. And a man as distracting as Chad McFee was one disaster she really had to be wary of.

She was still thinking this when he walked up to her. She jumped, startled, when he tapped her shoulder.

"Sorry," he said with a roguish smile. "Didn't mean to scare you."

"Surprised me, that's all," she quickly corrected, even though her heart was still trip-hammering a mile a minute. "Let me get the gang all assembled. I told most of them this morning that you'd be stopping by to check us out. I mean, to check out the vineyard."

Shut up, you're babbling. In an effort to get back her bearings and what was left of her dignity, she rang the community bell, a deep, resounding bell that she'd gotten in college, from an Asian monastery. The gong rattled her rib cage, but it also got all the farmhands in, which was the point. Pretty soon a throng of people were gathered in the "courtyard," the grassy area beneath an almond tree by the main house.

"Well, here he is," she said, by way of introduction. "Chad McFee, our new owner, and Charles McFee's… great-nephew, was it?"

He nodded.

They stared at Chad. Chad looked back at them,

and she could sense him squirming under their attention.

"Um, perhaps you'd like to say a few words?" she prompted, wishing this could be easier. Charles hadn't ever addressed the vineyard, but then, he was content to deal with Leila, and before her, Leila's parents. He'd never wanted to "check things out" the way Chad did.

"Sure," Chad said, shrugging, and he smiled at the crowd. People smiled back, friendly, but Leila knew them enough to read their expressions. In his white T-shirt and jeans, and his sneakers, he looked like just plain folks. But his T-shirt was obviously expensive, not something you bought in a three-pack at a discount store. Same with his jeans, some name brand that probably cost hundreds. And the sneakers—white leather with black-and-red trim, and an expensive logo. They were a dead giveaway.

"Er, hi," he started, waving. It was just this side of shy, sort of goofy. Utterly disarming. "Glad to meet you all."

There was an echo of responding greeting, murmurs and waves.

"I have to admit something," he said, shifting his weight nervously from one foot to the other.

Leila felt her heart clench. *Oh, please don't tell them you're thinking of selling the place.* She'd considered the possibility, but thinking the worst and actually witnessing it were two completely different horrors.

"I am not a winemaker. At all. Or is that vintner? Isn't that what you guys are called?" Chad looked at Leila for clarification.

Leila nodded, feeling a little relief seep into her system.

"All I know about wine is how much I usually pay per bottle," he continued, with a nervous chuckle. They didn't laugh in response, causing him to clear his throat awkwardly. "So I want to see exactly what goes on at a vineyard, and what it's like to work here. I'm in your hands completely, blank slate, totally at your disposal. Whatever you tell me to do, I'll do, until I learn what goes on here. Does that sound fair?"

It was charming, Leila thought.

It was also, unfortunately, probably the worst thing he could have said.

Julio, the head of farming, had a wicked smile in his eyes that did not register in the rest of his impassive expression. "Well, the best way to learn about winemaking," he said, in a voice that sounded much older than his thirty-four years, "is to start from the ground up."

"That's what I had in mind," Chad said enthusiastically. "So, what's the ground, metaphorically speaking?"

The man had no idea what he was asking for. "Uh, Julio," Leila interrupted, "Chad isn't really…I mean, he shouldn't be doing hard labor."

Julio shrugged innocently. "The man said he wanted to learn, Leila. I'm just trying to help him out."

She knew where that would lead. Chad would be doing the roughest, crappiest manual labor that needed doing. Call it hazing.

If Chad had any lingering thoughts of getting rid of Honey Ridge, a day full of the torture that Julio and his crew would dish out might be the deciding factor in tipping the scale toward ditching the vineyard completely.

"I think what Chad means is more of an overview," she countered, frowning intently, trying to will Julio to read her mind. *Please, don't screw with him.* "He ought to learn, yes, but—"

"If I may?" Chad interrupted.

She turned, surprised at the tinge of anger in his voice. "Yes, of course."

"Chad here knows exactly what he means," he said, in a way that clearly illustrated what he thought of being referred to as if he wasn't there. Leila felt her cheeks heat with a blush of embarrassment. "You don't need to coddle me. Sure, I haven't worked on a farm, but I'm in good shape, and I'm not completely useless." His words had a particular bite on that last word.

"I never meant…"

"If it'll help me learn what it's like to work here, and what goes into our product, then what the hell. Bring it on," Chad said fearlessly. "I'm sure I can handle it."

Oy. She felt a tinge of worry. *I'm sure I can handle it* were famous last words. *Infamous* last words. Right up there with *How bad could it get?*

"Well, then. We're getting ready for harvest and for bottling," she said, shifting her voice back to business. "This year, we're getting the Cabernet and the Pinot Noir in by end of September, gang."

There was a loud chorus of grumbling at that announcement, quickly diverting attention from their new owner/whipping boy.

"What's the rush?" Vince, one of the farmhands, complained.

"We got nailed with that frost last year, and it took out half our crop," Leila reminded him, the pain of the loss still fresh. "That's not going to happen again this year. This year, more than ever, we're going to get the vintage perfect, got it?"

"Yes, ma'am," Vince drawled.

"That was just a fluke, sweetie," Marisol, Julio's mother and a part-time cook at Honey Ridge, said with concern. "Things happen that you can't control, especially with wine. You know that."

Leila sighed. Marisol was the closest thing she had to a mother here in Napa, since her own had moved to Australia. "I know, Marisol. But…" She glanced at Chad, not sure how much to divulge. "Well, I want to make sure the things we can control go perfectly."

Marisol nodded, although she still didn't look convinced.

"Okay, enough gabbing. You guys know what to do," she said, knowing that was true.

"Come with me, Chad," Julio said, his voice equal

parts amusement and a wickedness that Leila didn't trust. "We'll get you started on something easy."

She saw Chad disappear toward the vats, and went to Marisol, who wordlessly hugged her.

"I miss my parents all of a sudden," Leila said against Marisol's shoulder.

"I'm sure they miss you, too," Marisol answered. "You know, you could've just gone with them. I hear that vineyard they're running is really coming along."

"You know what this place means to me," Leila said. "And they fought to convince Charles I was good enough to run it, even though I was young. I couldn't leave."

Marisol just shook her head. "I'm going to make some lunch," she said. "Tell that new owner of ours that he's welcome to a bite. I imagine he'll be starving after a few hours with Julio."

Leila smiled weakly as Marisol disappeared into the house. Then she turned toward the vats, but saw that Chad was already out and headed toward the fields. This time, he had a pitchfork and a wheelbarrow.

He also had his shirt off, she noticed. Her mouth went dry.

He wasn't kidding when he'd said he was in shape. He had a lean physique that was cut out of marble. *Gorgeously golden, tanned marble,* she thought, knowing she shouldn't stare, but she was somehow unable to stop herself. She knew he was good-looking. She'd done some belated research on him, and seen photos of him online. She'd even seen him in sweats. But she realized none of that did him justice, now that she was seeing him, literally, in the *flesh.*

As if sensing her gaze, he glanced over at her, shooting her a quick "what, me worry?" grin before disappearing into the rows of grapevines.

Leila blushed and quickly turned back to the house. She needed to get this under control. She couldn't afford to lose focus. A gorgeous new owner with a killer smile was not on her list of things to do.

At least she wouldn't have to worry about the attraction tonight, she thought grimly. The guys were going to work him for hours. If his muscles could stand it, that would be one thing. But without his shirt, she was fairly certain that by dinnertime, he'd be burned scarlet as a lobster. In fact, if today went as badly as she feared, she might not be seeing him at dinner. Or after. Or possibly ever.

BY THAT EVENING, Chad was tired. No—he was exhausted. Actually, he couldn't even come up with a word to describe adequately how physically wrung out he felt. In the course of his "orientation" they'd been true to their word, giving him no deferential treatment. He'd polished the stainless-steel vats that held the wine, he'd "punched" down the frothy mixture of fruit pulp and grape skins that rose to the top of the vats, he'd swept the cellars. He'd even picked a few grapes by hand, although he was bad enough that they stopped him almost immediately. They hadn't been vindictive, which was good. He even suspected they were being tolerant, since he was no doubt slower at the menial tasks than any of the experienced staff. And they weren't being mean. He was grateful that Julio had sent him to the main house to get some sunscreen and forced him to take water breaks, or else he would probably be suffering from heat stroke. Julio hadn't even commented on Chad's obvious stupidity, but instead had merely suggested that keeping a shirt on might be a better plan. The rest of the crew only grinned a little. For the most part, though, they'd offered helpful advice, and accepted him with a good-spiritedness that he'd never experienced before.

When he'd "checked out" his other investments, and asked to learn about them, he now realized he'd been humored, pampered and, for the most part, snowed. They didn't want an owner getting involved and mucking things up, so at the movie, they'd let him hang out in the actor's trailer (right then, he should've known that with their budget, getting the guy a trailer was a costly mistake) and look through the camera lens. And the real estate stuff was so dodgy, he'd never even seen the site. These guys apparently had no qualms about letting him really learn what it was they did. And they loved it. Chad could tell that immediately. They wanted him to love it, too.

Of course, if his father wanted him to sell… He shook his head. They would all be out of a job if he sold the place, he realized. And with the little disasters Leila had mentioned, this place was not doing well financially. He'd do better, personally, if he just sold the place—the land itself was more valuable than the grapes.

It was more than he wanted to think about. In fact, all he wanted to do right now was drive back to his hotel, order room service and soak in a hot shower for an hour or so. Of course, that would require standing. Chad wondered absently if the hotel had a suite with a Jacuzzi tub.

As he was walking past the main farm house, headed for his car, he saw that a picnic of sorts had been set out on a few tables, on a grassy patch by the cabernet vines. The vintners and farm hands were putting out food from the kitchen, and Julio was pouring red wine out of their bottles and into funny-shaped glass pitchers.

"Hey, Chad," Julio said, grinning and still continuing the slow wine transfer. "I meant to ask you… would you like to stay for supper?"

"Uh…" Chad thought of his aching muscles. "I don't want to impose," he said instead.

"You're the new owner," Julio answered. "You can impose all you want. Besides, we do this every other week or so, especially during harvest. Nobody wants to go home and cook after a long day." Julio had finished pouring, and he held up the empty wine bottle displaying a competitor's wine label. "Also, it's still business. Sort of. We try different wines to see what the other guys are doing."

Chad noticed that, while the other workers looked

busy arranging food, they were obviously listening for his reply.

It would probably be rude not to stay, Chad thought. And he'd probably look like a wimp if he bowed out. Or he might look like he wasn't interested in the vineyard—which he was, more than he'd even expected to be. He really did want to learn.

But if you get close to these people, and you wind up selling the place anyway…

He sighed to himself. His life had been a lot less complicated, just a few weeks ago.

Just then, Leila emerged from the house with a platter of vegetable crudités and three kinds of dip. "Oh, Chad," she said, her violet eyes opening wide. "I didn't know you were still here. I thought you'd be long gone by now." Then her cheeks went rosy, as if she realized that what she said could be considered rude. "I mean, you put in a long day. I figured…I thought you'd want to go sleep or something."

"Julio asked if I wanted to stay for your picnic," Chad said, smiling. He wasn't sure what flustered her so much around him, but he had a few guesses, and it was cute as well as sexy.

"Oh," she said. "Um…of course you should stay. We should get to know our new owner, right?"

He grinned, a slow, inviting grin that he knew she couldn't mistake for anything else.

She nearly dropped the platter. Recovering, she put it safely on a table and muttered, "I'll go get more food," then dashed back to the house.

He turned back. "I'm staying," he told Julio. *Oh hell yeah, I'm staying.*

Vineyard or not, he knew he'd never have gotten this personally involved in one of his investments if it hadn't been for Leila Fairmont.

Chad noticed that Julio was no longer smiling at him, but instead was giving him a thorough, almost disapproving, once-over. Chad suddenly wondered if maybe Leila and Julio were an item. Or if Leila and *anybody* were an item. He hadn't seen a ring, and hadn't gotten the impression that she was involved with anyone, but he'd been wrong before. He should probably be more careful until he knew, one way or the other.

Leila came back out and walked over to him, still giving off that vibe of tension—and awareness. "I'll be honest," he said. "I'm pretty whacked, so I can't stay too long."

She smiled, and Julio lightened up a little. Chad relaxed a little, too. He watched as Leila poured herself a glass of red and took a few slow sips, closing her eyes.

Damn, she's pretty.

Deciding to make the best of things, Chad changed the subject. He pointed to the decanter she'd poured her wine from. "What's that all about?"

"You see how wide the base is? That's to help the red wine breathe. It increases the surface area, so more air can touch more wine. Pouring it from bottle to decanter helps mix air into it, too."

"Seems like a lot of trouble," he said.

Her warm, gentle smile hit him like a fist in the stomach. "Hey Julio, what is this? The Jordan Cabernet?" At Julio's nod, she continued, "Do we have any still in the bottle?"

Julio grabbed a still-corked bottle out of a box and handed it to her. Chad watched as she deftly removed the cork and poured him a small amount in an empty glass.

"Taste this," she said, "and tell me what you think."

He drank it, aware more than ever of the scrutiny of the people around him. "It's nice," he ventured. "Better than most of the wine I drink, I guess."

Actually, it didn't taste much different than the wine he drank at almost every party his friends gave.

Leila didn't laugh, although Chad could've sworn Julio snickered. Instead, she took his empty glass, and poured from the open, "breathing" decanter. "Now, try this," she said, staring at him with interest.

He was momentarily sidetracked by her intensity, but forced himself to focus. He took a tentative sip, wondering what the joke was. Then he blinked in surprise. It was as if the taste of the wine took up all the room in his mouth. His brain scrambled to process it.

"This is the same stuff?"

Now several people did laugh, but it was a happy sound, Chad noticed. Like when introducing a friend to your favorite restaurant, and being happy he liked it. Leila's smile was like liquid sunshine. "Pretty cool, huh?" she asked, with a wink.

Another farmhand, Ted, walked up, a little hesitant. "You should try that with the food. It complements the flavors unbelievably."

"Thanks," Chad said, feeling a little foolish. Now that he thought about it, he *was* hungry. Probably from doing the first hard labor of his life, he thought with a grin. He went for a chunk of Gouda cheese.

"You don't want that," Ted said immediately.

"Why not?"

Julio stepped in again, with a glass of white wine. "Cheese takes the edge off of terrible wine. Something about the cheese-making process, I don't know. But if you've got a really lousy vintage, eat a chunk of cheese with it, and it tastes less sour." He grinned. "That's why you see all those pictures in France, with a peasant drinking out of a jug, holding a big old hunk of cheese."

Leila grinned. "And that's why they usually serve it at wine tastings. So your taste buds get psyched out and you won't realize the wine's not that great." She crossed her arms, looking smug. "We never serve cheese at our tastings."

"Of course we don't," Chad said feeling a little foolish, but also intrigued. "So why do you have cheese here?"

"Some of our competitors put out some real 'cheese-worthies,' so we put it out to save our taste buds," she explained, eliciting an appreciative laugh.

Chad nodded. There was a lot to learn…and after a full day of hard work, his brain felt as slow and achy as his body. He liked the atmosphere, liked the education—but hated feeling like the slow kid, the obvious idiot.

"So you didn't know anything about wine before you got the vineyard?" Ted asked innocently.

"Well, not the process, but I've had plenty of wine," he said, with a laugh.

"What's been your favorite?" Julio asked.

Chad saw his chance. "Well, I don't have a favorite," he said, trying to sound worldly, "but I've had the 'sixty-eight Chateau Vincente Bordeaux."

He tossed that out with quiet pride, knowing that the stuff cost nearly nine hundred dollars a bottle. He knew this because his friend Lester had pointed it out when he'd poured it at his dinner party. And since they were all connoisseurs here, from the looks of it, he figured that *they'd* know. He'd been around good wine, all right!

"When'd you have it?" Julio asked.

When? "Uh…a year ago, I think," Chad said. This wasn't the impressed and awed reaction he was going for.

"Too bad," Leila said, taking another sip of wine, shaking her head slightly. "I hope you didn't pay too much for it. That wine peaked four years ago." At his blank look, she added, "It would be slowly turning to vinegar, and the taste would be way off."

"I…a friend bought it, actually," Chad said.

"Do you know some people actually paid six hundred dollars a bottle for it, back in the day?" Julio said, with a chuckle. "Amateurs. Just because a wine's expensive doesn't mean it's good."

Chad thought about Lester's nine-hundred-dollar boast, and decided to keep silent. He'd made a big enough fool of himself for one day.

Leila smiled at him gently. He couldn't win, he thought. He just couldn't win.

"I guess I'll be driving back to the hotel now," he said, wishing she would smile at him with admiration instead of tolerant amusement.

"So soon? You haven't eaten anything."

"That's fine," he said tightly. "I think I've had enough for one day."

"I'll walk you," she said, and followed him to his car. "How are you feeling?"

"Tired." He realized she looked concerned, so he added, "But it's a good tired."

"Don't let it bother you."

He didn't make the jump in logic. "Don't let what bother me?"

"Not knowing about wine," she said. "Nobody's born knowing. You'll pick it up."

"Oh." Chad squirmed. "I just don't like feeling slow, that's all. Especially since I own the place now."

She put a hand on his arm as he reached for his car door. Her palm felt warm, warmer than even the heat of the day. "You're a fast learner, I can tell," she said. "If you want, I can go over some stuff with you privately, so you don't have to feel embarrassed in front of the whole gang."

He was about to say no, since that would actually make him feel even more foolish—and she was the last person he wanted to look foolish in front of. But then it occurred to him. Private lessons. Maybe, just maybe, that was the best way to find out more about not only wine, but his favorite vintner.

"Okay," he said. "How about over dinner?"

"Dinner?" she asked, her voice sounding stunned.

"Yeah. Maybe tomorrow night?" He thought about his aching muscles. If they hurt like this now, by tomorrow, he'd barely be able to walk, much less…

Much less what? What were you planning on doing with her?

"Not tomorrow night," he amended. "How about next Tuesday?" He grimaced as a spasm of pain rippled his back. "I should be feeling human again."

She made a smile of sympathy. "Sure thing," she said, and he felt a little guilty. "Next Tuesday. I'll make dinner here, and go over wine stuff."

"Sounds good."

He had a date—of sorts, he thought, as he got into his car and drove away.

He shook his head. Apparently, he was just complicating his life now for the hell of it. But from what he'd seen of Leila…

He smiled. She might be worth the headache. But he'd still better see just how salvageable this new vineyard of his was, or he'd be hurting the very people he was getting to like.

CHAPTER THREE

"YOU KNOW, he's not that bad," Julio said. "Except for the whole, you know, not-knowing-anything-about-wine thing."

Leila grimaced, leaning against an oak barrel they'd just finished sealing. "If it weren't for a bunch of bankers and insurance salesman and other novices that didn't know squat about winemaking, California wouldn't even have the kind of wineries and vineyards it has today."

"I know that," Julio said with a gentle grin. "Your parents taught me that, same as they did you, remember?"

"Yeah, well," she said, realizing that he was just teasing. "He's just self-conscious, that's all. You should've heard his voice when he said he couldn't come in today. I'll bet he couldn't even walk."

Julio nodded, leaning against another barrel. "I'll bet. He might not know much about wine, but the guy's kind of a nut when it comes to enthusiasm. I've never seen anything like yesterday, with him trying to do all the chores we piled on him."

"Yeah, why *did* you guys haze him so hard?" she asked, crossing her arms.

"Didn't mean to," Julio said. "He just wouldn't say no, so it became kind of a test, I guess. And most of us could do the stuff. He was just too stubborn."

"Well, you might've been more careful, is all I'm saying." Leila could still hear the pain and, worse, the embarrassment in Chad's call this morning. "He needs time."

Julio shot her a sly look. "Really? You're not this careful with most of our new hires. Got a thing for him?"

She could feel her cheeks heating and quickly turned to another barrel so Julio wouldn't notice. "I'm just saying, this is the guy who's going to be cutting our checks," she pointed out. "We might not want to cripple him."

"You've got a point there," Julio admitted. "Think he's going to sell the place?"

Now Julio's voice took on a note of concern. He'd been there as long as Leila had been. They'd grown up together. She'd lived in the farmhouse since she was six, and he'd been born just a few miles away—Marisol still owned the house. More importantly, Julio had a wife and two kids to think of.

For Leila, this place was a dream come true…a way to prove herself as a master vintner, a way to justify her parents' faith. For the others, it was a living…and that was way more important. *Just one more reason I can't let this vineyard fail,* she thought, worry gnawing at her stomach.

"I don't know," Leila said honestly. "He genuinely

likes the place, which I think is a good start. We just have to convince him that it's worth saving."

"Now, now, don't get stressed about it," Julio said. "I know you. I can hear the gears grinding in your head from here."

Leila smiled weakly. "I keep trying to think of what else we can do. The Merlot was great last year—even if we lost half the crop. And we're still bottling some of the best wine in the valley," she said, with defensive pride.

"Nobody's saying we're not," Julio soothed. "Nobody blamed you for the blight or the drought or the frost. Things just happen. That's nature, you know?"

"I know," she said, "but…"

"No buts," Julio said sternly. "You're like my kid sister, you know that. Everybody who's worked here knows how hard you work. But they also know that…" He paused, clearing his throat.

"Know what?" she asked, curious.

Julio took a deep breath and motioned her to sit down. She sat on a barrel, waiting for his reply. "We all love wine here," he said slowly.

"Well, duh." She rolled her eyes.

"But you're getting a little mental about it," he said, and put up his hands defensively when she made an irate squawk of disbelief. "Hey! Don't tell me you're not obsessed, *chica.* When was the last time you had a date?"

"What does that have to do with the price of tea in

China?" Leila said impatiently. "I work hard. And where would I meet somebody anyway?"

"We have friends. People try to set you up all the time. My wife's tried to set you up three different times in the past year alone," Julio pointed out.

"I hate blind dates," Leila moaned. "And your wife just sort of sprang them on me. At family gatherings, no less!"

"Okay, Angelina's not very subtle," Julio agreed. "But if you don't like the people we're coming up with, why not Internet date or something?"

"What's with the sudden interest in my love life?" Leila crossed her arms, feeling even more vulnerable.

"You're unbalanced, Leila," he said. "Girl cannot live on wine alone."

Leila sighed. "Listen, when I get the guarantee that we've got financial backing, when I *know* that Honey Ridge is going to be okay…then I'll date. I'll see whoever you want, I'll set up a profile online. I'll take out a billboard. But until then…" She struggled to find the right words. "If Honey Ridge goes under, and I feel I didn't do absolutely everything I could to try to save it, I think it would wreck me, Julio. It would be beyond awful. I just can't face the thought."

Julio sighed. "You take things too seriously," he said. "You always did."

"I know," she said.

"It's amazing your wine is as good as it is, actually," Julio added.

Leila frowned. "Thanks a lot," she said, hurt.

"No, you're phenomenal. Don't even try to pretend you have self-doubt," Julio scoffed. "But to be a good winemaker, you've got to have a sense of fun. Risk. Adventure," he said, waving his hand flamboyantly. "Otherwise, you go all corporate, and it tastes… awful."

She nodded. She knew exactly what he meant.

"So maybe," he said persuasively, "if you spiced up your love life, your wine would be even better, huh?"

She stared at him. "You sneak. You're trying to get me to agree to dating just to save the vineyard."

"I'm saying if you're serious," Julio said piously, "you'll consider all options."

"What, I should 'take one for the team' to improve my vintages?" Leila asked, laughing with bewilderment.

"Of course not," Julio said. "But hey, if something comes up that stirs your interest, why not see where it goes? It could only help the wine, after all."

"Oh, yeah," Leila laughed. "And where exactly am I supposed to find some handsome, sexy guy who…"

She suddenly stopped laughing as Chad's face popped into her mind, like a blinding flash of clarity. She gasped.

"You keep thinking about it," Julio said drily, "and tell me if you come up with anything."

"I *couldn't*," Leila whispered, scandalized. She glanced around to see if anybody else could hear them. "He's the owner, for pity's sake! He could decide to sell the place tomorrow, for all we know! And even if he didn't…I have to work with the guy! What are you—crazy?"

"I can't help but notice that none of your reasons include that you're not attracted to him," Julio said.

Leila's blush could've toasted marshmallows, she felt quite sure. "That's such a dumb idea, I can't even…I won't even acknowledge it," she muttered.

"I'm not saying marry the guy," Julio said. "I'm not even saying sleep with the guy, honestly. You're probably right about that. But he's obviously interested in you, and you've had your hormones in deep freeze for so long they probably don't even remember what to do."

He had a point there, Leila thought, biting her lip.

"Wine's romantic. Flirt a little, play a little, loosen up. You don't have to be so tense all the time. It wouldn't kill you to think about something other than work."

"Don't you have to check soil or something?" Leila asked.

Julio laughed. "Just think about what I said." With that parting shot, he went back to the vineyards.

She sighed heavily. The thing was, she didn't know how to just play. There was too much to think of, too many things that could go wrong. Too many ways that everything could go to hell in a handcart, with her at the wheel.

And playing with somebody like Chad McFee?

Well, that was playing with fire.

IT WAS AROUND TWO-THIRTY when Chad picked up his cell phone, dialing the number he knew by heart.

Renaldo picked up the phone. “Hey there, Chad,” he said, his voice as casual as if he were talking to a friend. “How’s it going? And please tell me you don’t need a huge amount of money for some new project of yours. I’m a financial adviser, not a miracle worker.”

“Ah, but you’ve worked so many miracles,” Chad said, chuckling even though he meant it. Renaldo had been his financial adviser since he was fifteen years old, strangely enough—when his father had given him ten thousand dollars and told him to learn about the stock market.

“Well, what is it this time?” Renaldo said, with a long-suffering sigh. “Ostrich farm in Bakersfield? Ski resort in Idaho? And please tell me it’s something you’ll actually let me research this time,” he added with a note of disapproval. In some ways, Renaldo was harder on him than his own father was. “I told you, if you keep making these wild agreements, you’re going to blow through your trust fund like a class-five tornado.”

“This isn’t really my fault,” Chad protested, only to get cut off by Renaldo’s snort of disbelief. “I…*ow*.” He winced as he stretched too far to get his glass of water, causing his arm muscles to scream.

“What was that? You hurt yourself?”

“Actually, yes. I’ve been working.” Chad groaned as he sat down on the corner of his hotel bed.

“Working?” Renaldo said the word as if he couldn’t recognize it. “Doing what?”

He sighed. "Remember that vineyard I inherited?"

"Well, yes…" There was a long pause. "You're actually…wait a minute. What exactly are you doing there? I thought you'd go take a peek, grab some bottles of wine, play lord of the manor."

"Not this time. Not even close," Chad grumbled. "I told them I wanted to understand the vineyard from the ground up."

"So, what, did they make you tour the entire place or something?"

"This week, I'm a cellar rat," Chad informed him.

"You mean, you're doing actual *physical* labor?"

He closed his eyes, rubbing his temple with his free hand. "If I didn't know better, man," he said, "I'd swear you were laughing at me."

"Just with delight," Renaldo said. "A cellar rat. My God. That's brilliant. So what menial chores have you been learning?"

"I've punched vats, I've cleaned, I've hung grapes. I've harvested grapes, for that matter," he said. "They're really careful here. Nothing automatic—nothing that gets trampled. Costs more, but it's worth it—you can taste the difference, since there's no fungus or mustiness that creeps in when you have flat-dried grapes or grapes that have been crushed too early by a harvester." He rattled off everything he'd gleaned from his talk with Julio and Ted.

Another pause. "You even sound like a vintner," Renaldo said, and his tone was more admiring. "And you've spent how much this week?"

"Not a dime…unless you count the cost of maintaining the vineyard, I guess," Chad said. "I haven't been drawing a salary or anything."

He thought briefly about Leila. He wondered how much the vineyard paid her. It couldn't possibly be that much—with the expenses, he knew, they didn't make much profit.

Still, it's better than selling the vineyard and firing her, since then she's not going to make anything at all.

"Well, I am happy for you," Renaldo said. "So, other than making my day—since I'm going to be laughing my butt off at you for at least the next hour—what did you need from me?"

"Actually," Chad said, unsure how to broach the subject. "I wanted you to do me a favor this week. I need you to run some numbers."

"That's what you're paying my retainer for—that, and being your on-call shrink," Renaldo joked. "Numbers for what?"

Chad took a deep breath. "I want you to run some profit-and-loss numbers on Honey Ridge."

Renaldo let out a low whistle. "It's not great, from what I recall," he said slowly. "But don't worry—when it gets bought out, the company buying it isn't going to care about profitability. They'll be buying it for the land, to expand. And I'll make sure you get a good price, don't even sweat it. You should be ahead, even after the indie movie disaster. That's got to be a comfort."

"That, er, wasn't what I meant," Chad said. "I meant….how bad would it be if I, you know, kept it?"

The pause this time was so long, Chad wondered if his cell phone had cut out. "Hello? Renaldo, you still there?"

"I'm sorry, I want to make sure I heard that right." Renaldo's voice was tight. "Did you just ask me to run numbers in case you wanted to *keep* the vineyard?"

"That's right," Chad said stoutly. "I know. I know it seems crazy."

"More than seems," Renaldo said. "You don't know anything about wine. Damn it, I didn't even know you *drank* wine. So, what, after a week of hard manual labor you've decided to become a man of the land? You're going to chuck your hard partying ways, and become a farmer?"

"Vintner," Chad said, noticing the sullen edge in his own voice.

"Come on, Chad. I'm sure you're having fun, but let's be reasonable."

"Are you kidding?" Chad spit out. "I'm not having fun! I've been working my butt off! The people here are great. I don't know if you'd understand, but they're all incredible. They love what they do. They work hard, and they all work together. And everybody knows why they're here, and what they need to do, and they all pitch in…"

And he'd been part of it. Through his weird deal with Leila, he'd been allowed to become a small part of the Honey Ridge family. He knew people by name. The work itself was grueling, yeah, but at the end of the day he still felt better than he did any day at his family's companies. Hell, most of the time, he knew that people at his family's companies didn't even want him there. They were just humoring him because he was an heir, not because he could contribute anything valuable.

"I see," Renaldo said. "Is this guilt, then? Because you're going to be putting these people out of business?"

Chad let out a breath. "Yeah, that's part of it. A big part of it."

"Well. I have to say, it's nice to see this side of you." Renaldo managed to not sound patronizing about it. At least, not much. "But you've got to be reasonable. It's amazing that Honey Ridge has stayed alive this long. Your uncle Charles threw a lot of money at it, which helped. And it was starting to turn a corner, but some bad stuff happened. I'll need to look at it. Bottom line—it's a brutal time to be an independent vineyard, Chad, and they have to know that. If it weren't you putting them out of business, it'd be somebody else. They're grown-ups, they know the score."

Somehow, that didn't make Chad feel better. Especially when he remembered Leila's face when she talked about Honey Ridge, what it meant to her. When he remembered all the faces out there in the courtyard, looking at him expectantly.

"Just do me the favor, and run the numbers, okay?" Chad said, and it came out a little more belligerent than he meant it to.

"It's futile, but if looking at the actual numbers will help, then okay, I'll run the numbers," Renaldo said. "It sounds like this place is really affecting you."

Chad closed his eyes, and pictured the vineyard in the setting sun, just before he'd driven off. Leila had been walking slowly toward the house, back in from the grapes. She'd paused to smell a rose from one of the thorny bushes that grew at the end of a row of grapes. She hadn't even looked back at his car, he remembered. She'd looked beautiful, and completely at home.

"Yes," Chad said. "This place is definitely affecting me."

THE FOLLOWING TUESDAY, Leila waited on the porch of the yellow farmhouse, watching as various farm hands and winemakers got into their cars and drove home. She had finished checking the Cabernet blend that afternoon, and then she'd knocked off early, an uncharacteristic gesture. She was still remembering what Julio had told her.

Relax. Play a little.

Flirt.

She was supposed to see Chad tonight, and teach him about wine and winemaking. She was even making dinner, a simple stew in the Crock-Pot and fresh-baked bread, thanks to Marisol. When she'd come in from the fields, she'd taken one look at herself and winced. Of course, Chad had already seen her like this and she wasn't trying to dress up, or anything. But there was no sense in both of them sitting there grungy, was there? Besides, she felt dirty, and her palms had purplish-red stains from the grapes. She would just get a little cleaned up, since she had the time before he showed up. If he even remembered—for the rest of last week, and even yesterday, he'd gone home as soon as work was over.

Two hours later, she was scrubbed clean and smelled like lavender and mimosa, thanks to the lotion she had smoothed on her skin. She usually didn't have the time or the patience, but she was running early, Leila justified to herself. Besides, it was relaxing, and Julio had told her to relax.

It'll make the wine better, she told herself. She'd do a lot to improve the wine. Ask anybody.

She saw Chad, walking in from the vines with Julio. He was wearing jeans, the same expensive type he'd been wearing that first day, but now they were marked with dirt and wine stains. His black T-shirt had a dusting on it, as well, and his hair was ruffled by the wind. He should've looked grubby, but Leila got the feeling there was no way this man could look anything less than…

Delicious, her mind supplied. She suppressed it.

Chad was listening intently to Julio. "So when there's a mutation in the grape vines," Leila heard Julio explaining, as they got closer to the house, "it changes the flavor ever so slightly. Same with the environment. We call the mutated grape vines 'clones,' and—"

Julio broke off lecturing when he saw Leila. He grinned, taking in her appearance. Not that she'd done anything special. She was just wearing clean jeans and a soft periwinkle tank top that was more feminine than what she usually wore. And her hair was up. No big deal, she assured herself, crossing her arms.

"Looks like you guys worked hard today," Leila said, struggling to keep her voice light and easy.

She knew exactly when Chad focused in on her. He seemed to drink her in with intensity, studying her from the crown of her head to the toes of her slip-on shoes. She looked down at the plank boards beneath her feet, feeling warm.

"You look nice," Chad said, and she smiled in response.

"I should get going," Julio said. "My wife's waiting for me, and the kids start school soon…you know how that goes."

Leila nodded, feeling a little wistfulness at the picture of Julio's domestic bliss—marriage, family. *Something other than work*. She cleared her throat. "Tell Angelina I said hi, and the kids, too." Then she looked over at Chad. "You mentioned that you wanted to learn more about wine. I made some dinner, if you want." Then, when she saw Julio's eyes gleam, she quickly added, "But if you're tired, it can wait. And it sounds like you've done a ton today."

"No, no," Chad quickly assured her. He didn't notice Julio's little smirk as he walked away. At least, Leila hoped he hadn't. "Thanks for remembering."

She shrugged, nerves making her want to fidget. "Come on in. Welcome to my house."

She could feel his presence as he followed her in, large and warm. Her heart beat a little more rapidly. "Julio and the gang tell me you've been working really hard," Leila said. "They're impressed."

"Didn't think I had it in me, huh?"

She could hear the edge of bitterness in his voice, surprising her, and she quickly shook her head. "Even experienced farmhands have trouble keeping up with a fully operational vineyard and winery, if they've worked in other types of crops," she said. "You've picked things up very quickly. Especially for someone outside the business."

He nodded, the bitterness evaporating as he accepted the compliment. "It's fun." His voice suggested that even he was surprised at that statement. "I enjoy it. A lot."

She started to lead him into the kitchen, but stopped when she realized he was lingering in her living room. "What's wrong?"

"I guess I never put it together that you actually live here," he said, as he took in the overstuffed couch in front of her fireplace, the wrought-iron wine rack, and the stained-glass lamps. "It's nice."

"Thanks. It's the head winemaker's house—just another one of the perks of the job. My family became head winemakers when I was little, so I've lived in this house a long, long time."

Chad accompanied her to the kitchen, where the scent of the herbed beef stew wafted in the air, interwoven with the fresh, yeasty smell of newly baked sourdough bread. They both laughed when his stomach growled.

"There's plenty," she said, putting everything out on her rustic maple kitchen table. "Please. Dig in."

Leila poured them both a glass of the Honey Ridge Merlot and, as requested, he dug in.

"So…you've been here about a week and a half," she said slowly. "What do you think?"

She had to wait for an answer, since he had taken a huge bite of stew and was slathering butter on the still-warm bread. "This is heaven," he answered instead, then sighed. "Sorry. What was that?"

"I asked what you think of the vineyard," she repeated.

"It's fantastic."

Leila waited for him to expand on the thought. Instead, Chad continued to shovel in stew as if he hadn't had food in a month.

She smiled at his obvious relish. "What do you think of the wine?"

He took a gulp, then sighed. "I'm probably not enjoying it as much as I should. I can't remember ever being this hungry," he said, by way of apology.

"It's the work," she said, chuckling a little, "and the fresh air."

She let him finish the bowl of stew and bread in relative silence, keeping the talk light. Then, she asked him if he wanted to sit in the living room and finish the wine he'd barely touched.

He settled on the couch with the wine. She started

a fire in the living room, then sat on the couch, careful to sit on the other end.

"I really appreciate the opportunity to learn, and to work hands on here, Leila," Chad said, and he really did sound grateful. "I had no idea it would be like this."

"Like what?" Leila asked, thinking that his tone sounded promising.

"Absorbing." He took a slow, considered sip from his glass. "Wow. This is really great."

She smiled. "Our Merlot. The movie *Sideways* makes it sound like Merlot is for rubes, but there are some nice vintages out there."

"And this is one of them," he said enthusiastically, taking another sip. "Am I doing this right?"

She nodded. "I like to smell the wine first." She put her nose in the glass and took a deep breath. "Then, you swirl the wine around—check the color, see if it clings to the glass."

"Okay." He followed her instruction.

"Then, take a sip, keep it on your tongue, and take a deep breath," she said. "Let the air flow over your tongue. The taste of a wine is just as much about the aroma as the actual flavor."

He did as she directed, his eyes closed as he almost frowned in concentration. It made him look like a harsh dreamer. After a long moment, he finally opened his eyes, smiling at her.

"It tastes good, but I don't know what I'm looking for."

"All that matters is that you enjoy it," she said.

"You'll develop a palate in time. It takes a while, but if you really love it, you'll begin to taste all kinds of things you didn't realize before. Honey, violet, fruit, smoke…it's going to open up a whole new world for you."

"Wow." Chad shifted his weight a little, getting more comfortable. "You know, I've never seen anyone with as much passion for anything as you have for wine."

She shifted a little too, and then realized that the gap between them had closed—not a lot, but enough. She swallowed, hard.

"In fact," he added, leaning ever so slightly closer to her, "I've never met anyone quite like you, period, Leila."

She took a deep breath. He looked so serious and sounded so good.

Her mind emitted one quick alert but was drowned out by the overwhelming sensations she was experiencing. She leaned forward. She could smell the musky scent of him, like freshly turned earth and an expensive, spicy cologne. She could smell the Merlot on his breath. His breathing quickened, matching her own.

She kissed him…first, just a slow brush against his lips, like an accident, a test. Then she held her breath and went for it, kissing him with intensity.

Leila wasn't sure if she moved to close the gap, or if he pulled her closer, but she was practically in his lap, his strong arms banded around her like steel. Not that she was trying to escape. If anything, it was as if she was trying to melt into him, meld with him, become one person. She hadn't been kissed like this in a long time. Hadn't kissed anyone like this in…well, ever.

She pulled away after what felt like a long time—or the blink of an eye. She'd lost all sense of time. No. She'd lost all *sense.*

"I'm sorry," she said quickly, edging back fast enough to hit the arm of her couch sharply. "I shouldn't have…that was my fault."

"Shh," he said, pursuing her, moving toward her end of the couch and reaching for her. "I'm not sorry at all. I've wanted you since I first saw you. I still want you." Chad stroked her shoulders. "I want you, now."

She blinked. She'd just kissed him, and enjoyed it. But he seemed to be talking about a lot more than kissing.

Relax. Play a little. Flirt.

She could do those things. But what he was asking for, she couldn't do casually. Especially not in light of who he was. What he was.

You don't sleep with the owner.

"I, uh…wait a second," she said, dodging his lips when he moved in for another kiss. Even as part of her body desperately wanted it, she forced herself to stand up and walk to the far side of the room. "This is too fast. I'm sorry," she repeated.

He frowned. "I'll go slow, don't worry. It's okay,

Leila," he said softly, as if he were talking to a frightened animal. "Don't overthink it. It's no big deal."

"Which part is no big deal?" she asked quietly. "The part where I kiss the new owner of my vineyard, and my employer—or the part where we would've slept together?" She shook her head. "Either way, it seems like a pretty big deal to me. To anybody else who was looking at this from a business standpoint, it would seem like a major mistake. In fact, it'd look downright dumb."

"I wasn't being dumb," Chad growled in frustration. "Listen, it's not like I go around sleeping with people whose companies I invest in, you know."

"So you agree this was a bad idea," she said quickly.

"I wasn't just learning about the vineyard to sleep with you," he said. "This isn't just some *hobby*."

"I'm really, really sorry." She bit her lip. "You'd better go. I really am…"

"Don't apologize again," he snapped. "Thanks for a lovely dinner. I'll see myself out."

She watched as he closed the door with some force and drove away. Her body ached, but her head ached more.

She should've known better, Leila told herself bitterly. Now, instead of loosening up, she'd only made things worse.

"CHAD! BACK FROM the wilds of Napa!"

Chad took in Lester's shouted toast with a wan

smile. He had driven into the city because he knew Lester would be having one of his parties, Tuesday or not. Lester always had a party going. If you wanted to have a good time, Lester was your hookup for good, old-fashioned, drunken debauchery. There was nothing serious about Lester, except his pursuit of a good time.

He'd understand what "no big deal" meant, Chad thought with asperity.

He was still stinging from his little dinner with Leila. He'd kissed her. No, she'd kissed *him.* And now she was acting as if she'd committed treason, and the fact that he wanted to sleep with her was also tantamount to some horrible crime. What the hell was her problem, anyway? He didn't make a habit of it. He told the truth: he'd never slept with anybody he'd invested money with.

Granted, they were all men. But he wouldn't have, anyway. He took his investments seriously. Of course, getting involved with her did create some issues, and she probably had a point.

But she'd pushed away from him like he was a leper, and treated him as though he should've known better and he hadn't thought things through. As if he didn't understand what it meant to be in business. That rankled him more than anything.

Lester introduced him around to the gang of partygoers. Most of the women were "Lester specials"… cookie-cutter gorgeous, with perfect bodies and porcelain faces with identical chiseled cheekbones. The best that plastic surgery could deliver, he realized, wondering how long he'd been this cynical. The one thing that all that sculpted perfection couldn't erase was the calculating looks in their eyes: the ones that seemed to absorb his clothes, his stature, and somehow extrapolate his bank balance and his possibility for marriage.

Maybe *that* was why Leila's reaction seemed so out of line for him, he thought bitterly. He was used to a more transactional type of relationship—you wanted something; she wanted something, an exchange was made. Leila wanted something from him, namely Honey Ridge. And it had to be obvious that he wanted something.

Namely, her.

But did you really want things to go that way? His conscience pricked him mercilessly. *From what you know of her, did you honestly think that's how she wanted things to go?*

If you did—man, she's right. You are *dumb.*

"I've got the full bar going tonight, buddy," Lester said, obviously noticing Chad's unusual reticence and trying to cheer him up. "And, of course, I've got wines too…now that you're Mr. Vineyard."

"Don't call me that," Chad said absently, knowing that it only emphasized the fraud he felt like. Then curiosity got the better of him. "What kind of wine do you have?"

"Let's see," Lester said, snapping his fingers at the busy bartender and causing Chad's embarrassment level to inch up a tad. "Barkeep! What sort of wine have you got open?"

The bartender smiled politely, although his eyes seemed full of disdain. "Red or white?"

"Red," Chad said quickly, and Lester nodded imperiously in agreement.

The bartender addressed Chad from then on, ignoring Lester completely. "We've got a Beaujolais, a Cabernet, and a Syrah," the man said in a dry monotone.

"Any of them local?" Chad asked.

The bartender's eyebrows went up. "The Syrah is from Napa. From the Far Niente vineyard."

"Do you recommend it?" Chad asked, but Lester interrupted.

"Is that the expensive one I ordered?"

"No, sir," the bartender said, and Chad could almost hear the man's teeth clenching. "That would be the Beaujolais. It's French."

"Go for it, Chad," Lester said, giving him a gentle nudge. "Nothing but the best, to buck up my buddy."

"Actually," Chad said, "I'd rather go with the Syrah."

Lester looked at him. "What, you've got something against French wine?" He paused. "Or just expensive? I told you, I'm covering all this."

Chad shook his head. "Just because it's expensive doesn't mean it's any damned good, Les," he said, with a little laugh. "If I learned anything this week, it's that."

"Well—" and Lester sounded irritated "—obviously *somebody* thinks it's good, if it drove the price up."

Chad shrugged, feeling like an idiot as the bartender handed him the glass. "I'm still learning," he conceded.

Lester was still talking when Chad took the glass, taking a deep breath, just as Leila had shown him. He then swirled it around. It had a good color, he thought—that deep garnet tone, clinging slightly to the crystal. Then he took a sip. It was okay. "Has this had any time to breathe?" he asked.

The bartender shook his head. "You might want to let it sit a minute," he said, with obvious approval.

Lester had finally shut up, as Chad swirled the wine around in his glass, trying to get the air to mix in. "You're not kidding with all of this," Lester said.

"Kidding with what?"

"You're keeping the damned thing," Lester crowed. "You *are* Mr. Vineyard!"

"Why are you riding me about this?" Chad asked irritably. "So I like wine. I've always liked wine."

"Yeah, but you weren't a poster child for pretension." Lester crossed his arms. "You used to order a few bottles—of the *expensive* stuff—and get plastered. Just like the rest of us," Lester said, gesturing to the rest of the party. "You used to have *fun.* What happened?"

Chad surveyed the party. The place was chock-full of the usual suspects—other socialites, hangers-on, trust-fund kids and the nouveau riche alike. They were all staring, circling like sharks. There was none of the camaraderie Chad had felt in the short time he'd spent at Honey Ridge. Granted, then, he'd felt like an outsider—and a wine idiot. But at least he could sense that the people there genuinely *liked* each other.

These people didn't necessarily hate each other, but again, it was transactional. Mutual back-scratching. People of the same station, with the same mind-set, getting drunk, escaping from whatever in their lives wasn't worth facing.

Am I like these people?

Was that what he was doing? Spending money, trying to be a "part" of something?

He didn't know why he was judging them. He only knew that, like the picnic, he no longer felt he fit in. And what was worse, he wasn't sure that he *wanted* to fit in anymore…at least, not with these people.

Chad sighed, turning to Lester. "I don't know what happened," he said, feeling completely at a loss.

Lester shook his head. "You had a bad break. You're running low on money, and your family's giving you grief," he said, and for a change, he actually kept his voice respectfully low. "That's enough to rattle anybody. I was there once."

"Really?" To his knowledge, Lester had been rolling in money all his life. His family had invented something crucial, like the fluorescent lightbulb or something, and consequently Lester had never had to work a day in his life.

"Yup. When I graduated from college, and I was bumming around Europe, my parents cut me off. Said that I was just drifting, and that I needed to get some direction. Told me to stop wasting my time and their money."

Chad knew what that felt like. His last family dinner was still burned in his mind. "Then what happened?" he asked with interest.

Lester shrugged. "I sold my cars and a bunch of the stock that was in my name, and just laid low for a while. After six months of being incommunicado, they freaked out and I got in their good graces again," he said, with a touch of pride. "I figured it was just a bluff, and I was right. They might have thought they wanted me to stop drifting, but they don't want you to disappear completely. It worked like a charm."

Chad suddenly had a sour taste in his mouth, and it had nothing to do with his glass of Syrah. "Really," he said, unsure of what other comment he could make.

"Sure, it gets boring partying sometimes," Lester said shrewdly. "Are all these people my friends? Probably not. But what the hell else are you going to do? I don't give a damn about working."

"But you invested in that movie, just like I did," Chad protested. "And that real estate thing…"

"I already apologized for that," Lester said, rolling his eyes. "But besides, that's not really working. That's like…I don't know. Roulette or poker. That's just something to do."

Chad looked down at the bloodred wine in his

glass. His thoughts, again, turned to Honey Ridge. For Leila or Julio or any of them, the vineyard wasn't just something to do.

Which part of this is "no big deal" for you, Chad?

Lester clapped a hand on his shoulder. "You know what? Screw the wine." He took Chad's glass and put it down on the bar. "Your problem is you're thinking too much. Bartender! Get me four rounds of shots. The nastier the better."

The bartender looked at the half-full glass of wine, and Chad could've sworn the man shot him a disappointed look.

"It was very good," Chad said. "Too good to get plastered on."

He nodded but still looked disgusted. "Vodka or whiskey?" he asked in the same monotone he'd used with Lester.

Chad sighed. "Better make it vodka."

He only hoped that, after he drank himself into a stupor, he'd be able to forget all his feelings of discontent…and the conversation he'd just had with Lester.

CHAPTER FOUR

THE NEXT MORNING, Leila was still roiling with embarrassment over what she was euphemistically calling "The Incident."

So she'd planned on having a little harmless fun, teach a little about wine, and maybe stir her hormones up a bit. Instead, she'd wound up pouncing on the guy, who then saw it as an invitation to go to bed with him and, from a certain standpoint, she wasn't sure she could blame him. Not that she thought she should have slept with him, or regretted not sleeping with him.

At least, I don't entirely *regret not sleeping with him.* She was human enough to admit that, after over a year of celibacy, her body had complained mightily when she'd denied it what was so close at hand. And it was her body's reaction that caused her to slightly regret what she'd done to Chad. She hated the term "tease," but after a kiss like that, and then going cold on him…

Well, she never should've kissed him in the first place, and that was that. Today, she was going to apologize, throw herself on his mercy, and pray that the two of them could just put the whole ugly "Incident" behind them. Especially if it in any way weighted his decision on whether or not to keep Honey Ridge. She'd like to think that he wasn't so petty, that he wasn't here simply because he was attracted to her. That he wouldn't just up and sell the place because she wouldn't give in to temptation.

Of course, that didn't mean he wouldn't decide to sell Honey Ridge for reasons that had nothing to do with her. She winced. At least the painful humiliation of The Incident had taken the edge off her worries, and the dull ache that was the thought of losing Honey Ridge.

She heard the roar of the engine of Chad's sleek silver car as it zoomed toward the parking area, kicking up a dust trail in its wake. She glanced at her watch—nearly noon, she realized. She wasn't about to chastise him for being late, and she hoped that Julio did not give him grief. She wondered if he was as hesitant to come in as she'd been.

This is ridiculous, she chided herself. She hadn't committed murder, after all. So she'd kissed him and wanted him, and then stopped them both. So what? They were not teenagers. They were grown, mature adults, and there was absolutely no reason they couldn't hold a civilized conversation. She'd clear the air, get it out of the way and apologize.

Then, just maybe, ask him point-blank if he's thinking of selling the vineyard.

Her stomach trembled with nerves, but she straightened her shoulders and walked over to where he'd just parked, waiting for him to open the door. He emerged, looking somewhat worse for wear. He had a day's growth of beard, making him look scruffy. It would have made him look rakish, she thought with a private grin, if it weren't accompanied by very bloodshot eyes.

The man was obviously hungover.

"Morning, Chad," Leila murmured. Getting drunk—she hadn't thought of that. Or rather, she'd thought of it but then decided against it, precisely because she hadn't wanted to feel the way Chad was obviously feeling this morning. She still suffered the occasional sore head after friends' wine bashes, and she knew the price of overindulgence. She felt sympathy for him, especially since he still winced at her deliberate whisper.

"Yeah, yeah, I'm here," he said.

"You didn't have to come in, you know," she said, still in the lowest voice possible. "No offense, but you look awful."

"That's funny, I feel awful," he growled sardonically. "But I said I wanted to learn, and I wanted to work. So I'm here, dammit. If you've got a problem, take it up with the *owner*."

She felt her stomach knot. Apparently, the civilized-conversation theory wasn't going to work this morning. He was angry, and he was going to be rude.

"I was going to tell you I was sorry for last night," she said, crossing her arms in front of her and frowning. "But you're not making it easy."

"Didn't I tell you I don't want you to keep apologizing?" Chad slammed his car door shut, then gripped his temples for a moment.

Serves you right, she thought vindictively.

"So what do you want from me?" she asked sharply, and then immediately regretted it when he looked at her with surprise.

"You know exactly what I wanted from you," he said, in a low voice that was both sexy and angry. "But what you don't seem to understand is, what I wanted had nothing to do with business. And if you didn't want to do something, you didn't have to. Period."

Leila swallowed hard against the lump in her throat. "I know you wouldn't force me to do anything," she said, hating that she'd made him feel like such a beast. "But…you've got to admit, Chad, sleeping together would not be the greatest decision on our part. I mean, we've still got the whole vineyard issue to deal with."

"What 'whole vineyard issue' are we talking about?" he snapped irritably. "The fact that I'm the owner? Is that what the problem is? Because you don't want to sleep with your boss?"

Now, her temper leaped to the fore, and all the anxiety that had been churning around since she'd found out Charles had died spilled out of her in a torrent. "The problem is," she shot back, "I have no idea when or if you're going to get rid of the vineyard I've worked so hard for. I don't know if you're going to decide to keep it on a whim, or sell it tomorrow just because you want the cash. *I don't know you.* And I've been walking on eggshells, trying to make sure you're happy and that you enjoy yourself here in the hopes that you're not going to just scrap Honey Ridge like some toy you're bored with!"

The words were loud enough to almost echo, and in the dusty area in front of the house, they were like two gunslingers, staring at each other with narrowed eyes and shallow breaths. He'd started the challenge, she'd answered it. There wasn't any backing down.

"So, what you're telling me," Chad said, his voice lazy even though his eyes were brightly intense, "is that last night was just another example of you trying to keep me happy, so I'd keep Honey Ridge?"

It took her a second to puzzle out his insinuation, but when she did, she gasped with shock. "I did not try to seduce you to keep the vineyard!"

"Well, if you did," he drawled back, "you didn't do a very good job of it."

She felt tears stinging at the corners of her eyes, and stood up even straighter, staring at him with an almost tangible violence. "So, because I didn't seduce you, you're going to sell, is that it?"

"What I feel about you has nothing to do with this damned vineyard," he said, taking a step closer to her. "Can't you understand that?"

"Well, what I feel for you has nothing to do with it, either," Leila countered, not backing down. She looked up into his eyes.

He finally showed a ghost of a smile. "Now we're getting somewhere."

She put a hand on his chest, stopping him from leaning any closer. "But no matter how I feel, or how you feel," she said softly, "the vineyard's *still there*. I can't just pretend it doesn't matter to me. I can't ignore that I might lose it, and that you are the one making that decision."

Chad took a step back, his eyes widening. "You can't possibly ask me just to keep it to make you feel better," he said. "I can't do that."

She felt ice pierce her chest. "No, I couldn't ask you to," she said sorrowfully. "So where does that leave us? Nowhere. We can't get involved as long as Honey Ridge is in limbo, Chad. It wouldn't be right."

He grimaced. "You're making it harder than it needs to be."

"I'm just telling the truth. Everybody knows that the place could shut down any day, on your command. Can you see how stressful that makes everything? If I slept with you, and then you had to shut the place down tomorrow—I don't know. I wouldn't want to blame you," she said honestly, "but some part of me would feel betrayed. That's lousy, I know."

His eyes blazed. "You'd think it was personal."

"No. I wouldn't think it was personal for you." She said, looked down at the ground for a second. "But what I'm saying is I know it would be personal for me."

Chad was silent for a moment, and when she looked up, she could see the muscles in his jaw clenching. He was still angry, although it was a contained anger.

"Well, here's one thing that might help you sleep at night, for at least the next month or so. When I inherited Honey Ridge, one of the stipulations of the will was that I could not sell the place until you guys bottled one last vintage. No matter what else happens—" and he put particular emphasis on that phrase "—you'll get to finish out the season. I can't make any promises after that, but at least you know you're not out of a job tomorrow, and neither is anybody else."

"So...we have until September?" she asked, feeling bleak. There wasn't much hope, not much at all.

"Yeah," he said, and stalked away, toward the vats. "You've got till September."

"Well, we'll do what we have to do," she said, almost to herself.

"Do that," Chad shot back, even though the statement hadn't been directed at him. "I certainly plan to."

With that, Leila felt her stomach drop. He was going to sell Honey Ridge. Maybe he'd had no intention of even trying to see if it was worth saving. Maybe he was just killing time, and she was one of the diversions. Maybe it was all some big gag.

The tears that had been looming suddenly hit her in a storm, and she disappeared back into the house. At least, she thought, he didn't see her cry.

THAT NIGHT, after cleaning the cellars and helping Julio close the oak barrels that now held the Cabernets, Chad made his way slowly toward the farmhouse. He'd saved cleaning the cellars for last, waiting until everyone else had gone home for the night. He'd had a full day (well, a half day) to think about what had happened the night before and what had happened when he came in that morning. He hadn't meant to be that brutally honest with Leila, nor had he meant to imply that he'd be getting rid of the vineyard, or that he would've sold the place already if it weren't for Great-Uncle Charles's will. It was a stupid, emotional act on his part, pure pettiness. He didn't like the idea of Leila kissing him simply out of fear of reprisal, or because she was so desperate to save her vineyard that she would give herself up for it, physically if need be. He didn't like being accused of being a dumb businessman who thought emotionally more than he thought practically—one who might just toss a moneymaker on a whim, simply because he was bored with it.

Or one who might keep it, just because he was unbelievably attracted to the head winemaker.

He waited until Julio left, after admonishing him 'not to work too hard,' and then Chad made his way to the farmhouse.

He had to apologize.

He had to make sure Leila was all right.

As he walked toward the farmhouse, he saw that the light in the kitchen was burning. The fireplace was lit, as well. He could smell the rich smoke from the chimney, and the front window glowed with cheery, red-tinged warmth. He knew Leila was home.

Chad hoped she'd let him in, and hear him out.

He knocked on the door. It took a while, and he was starting to lose hope, but eventually she opened it.

She was wearing faded jeans with the right leg torn at the knee—not an artistic, store-bought tear, but one that obviously came from hard work. She also wore a beat-up flannel shirt in a burgundy-and-brown pattern, and her tawny blond hair was up in a ponytail. She didn't look as polished or pulled together as she had last night, when she'd kissed him, he noticed. He could see the smudges beneath her eyes, making her look weary. She was either exhausted, or she'd been crying. Possibly both. Either way, he felt horribly guilty.

"Chad," she said, and her voice was monotone, lacking its usual warmth and openness. "I wasn't expecting to see you here."

"We need to talk," he said. "About this morning. And last night," he added, then sighed. "We need to get things straightened out."

Leila paused, chewing at her full lower lip for a second in a way that would've been sensually distracting if it weren't for the obvious apprehension in her eyes. Finally, after a long pause, she nodded.

"Come in," she said, then walked down the hallway. He closed the door behind him and followed her.

He walked past the living room, noticing that, unlike last night, it was in disarray. Books were piled up on the floor, leaving the built-in bookcases barren. There were a few cardboard boxes leaning against the wall, waiting to be assembled. "What's all this?" he asked, as he followed her toward the kitchen.

"I'm getting ready to move," she said, and the twist of guilt in his guts knotted a degree tighter. "I figured I'd start with stuff I wasn't using—the books, the artwork, stuff like this. Then kitchen items and linens, then clothes. It shouldn't take me that long. I'll probably have to arrange for movers for my furniture, though," she said, and it was as if she were trying to get the whole process straight in her head, explaining it to herself rather than to him.

He felt cornered. "Leila, I didn't say I was going to sell the vineyard. I just said it was an option," he protested. "And nothing's happening till September, and nothing's happening immediately. Besides, I had a headache that could've killed a rhino this morning and I was in a wretched bad mood, and I took it out on you. I had no right to do that."

"You didn't say anything that wasn't true, though," she replied, taking a ceramic mug off the counter. "Did you want some tea?"

He shook his head, then stood closer to her, waiting until she stopped avoiding his eyes, to make sure he got his point across.

"I spent last night at my friend Lester's house—although 'friend' is a loose term for us, I figured out," he said, slowly and gently. "I used to party with his crowd all the time. We did all sorts of things together—crazy trips, big spending. Investments."

She nodded, but she looked puzzled.

Chad sighed. "I haven't had what people would call a 'real job.' I inherited all my money," he explained. "I have a trust fund. My parents funnel money to me from the family accounts."

"Chad, why are you telling me this?" Her voice was soothing.

"Because I want you to understand," he said. "I've made a lot of bad investments over the years. I haven't come up with a single winner, and I'm starting to realize that it was because I played at it. I didn't have any real passion for it. I just went in with other people. I had fun, I dabbled, but they were bound to fail because I didn't care. Not the way you do, about Honey Ridge." He sighed. "Not the way I'm learning to care about this place."

She sighed. "It's only been two weeks."

"I know that," he said, and he gritted his teeth with frustration at himself. "I know. It's too soon to know for sure. And I don't know anything about the winemaking business. So I can't just say I'll keep it, especially when I haven't run all the numbers."

He was quiet for a moment. Then, he was surprised—no, shocked—when Leila placed a gentle hand on his shoulder.

"I didn't know you were beating yourself up so badly about this," she said. "I didn't think past what the place meant to me. I didn't think at all about what this decision meant to you."

It was maybe the kindest thing anybody had ever said to him. Chad couldn't help it. He leaned his head down against her shoulder. After a moment, he felt her fingertips brush against the hair at the nape of his neck, and he enfolded her in a hug that wasn't sexual, but merely comforting—both giving, and receiving, support.

"I didn't want you to think that I was just making this a hobby because I was bored with my life," he said. "I don't know why, or how, but this place matters to me. *You* matter to me, for different reasons. And I feel that one wrong move, and I'm going to ruin everything."

She made a little sympathetic noise, holding him tighter. "You're not going to ruin everything," she said. "It was unfair of me to put that much pressure on you. You're going to do what you feel is right, just like I am. You're not hurtful. I know that and I shouldn't have reacted the way I did."

He inhaled deeply, breathing her in—earthy tones from her work in the vineyard, the subtle aroma of wine and smoke from the fireplace, and her own scent, a woodsy floral combination that was more intoxicating than any wine. They stood like that for a moment, and Chad savored it.

Then, deliberately, he stepped away from her and walked to the far end of the kitchen.

"You weren't wrong, not completely," he said. "It would be complicated if we were to…get involved."

She nodded, but he could've sworn he saw regret on her face, as well.

"It's not final death overtime yet," he said. "I have my financial advisor running numbers. If it's at all viable to keep Honey Ridge going, then that's what I'll do. Not just for you," he added. "For me, because I really do enjoy it. I'm not just saying that."

"I know." Her eyes were luminescent. "You can tell by how you're learning."

He took a deep breath and stuffed his hands in his pockets. "So. Where does that leave us?" he finally asked. "I don't want to make any more mistakes or have any more fights like that one."

Leila nodded vehemently. "Amen to that."

"Hands off, that's a given," he said, almost to himself, and with a real sense of loss. Because if the news was bad, he'd have to sell the vineyard, and he knew what that would mean to her. No way would she want to get together with the man who had destroyed her livelihood and sold her childhood home out from under her. At the same time, if he kept the vineyard, he'd still be her boss. Where would that leave them?

"Maybe we should cancel the private lessons, too," she said tentatively.

His sense of loss doubled. He had enjoyed spending time with her…not just simply from a sensual standpoint, but because she was good company. Granted, he'd only spent the one night purely alone with her…

A flash of what had happened in just that short time hit him. "Good idea," he agreed.

"But we can still hang out when there are other people present," Leila amended, causing him to smile.

"Good," he said. "I'd like that."

"Actually," she said, "toward the end of the season, there's usually a big winemakers' party at a nearby resort. A lot of the little indies show up there. You might find it fun, if you want to come with me."

Like a date? Chad squashed the question as soon as it leaped to mind. "That sounds great," he said. "I'm glad we talked."

He held out a hand, and she took it…a handshake, to seal their agreement. Her hand was soft and warm in his.

He would've given up half his fortune to be with her the way he wanted to, he thought. But if he screwed this up with her, he got the feeling that he'd be losing a lot more than an inheritance. He wasn't sure what that was, but it was bigger than anything he'd experienced, and it confused the hell out of him.

With that, he said, "Good night, Leila," and let himself out the door.

THREE WEEKS LATER, Leila and her crew had finished bottling most of the vintages. She'd hurried, even though part of her wanted to drag her feet. She didn't want to get caught by an early frost again, which was the whole reason she was finishing early. But she now knew that Charles's will only protected the vineyard until they bottled this final harvest. Soon, Chad would have every right to sell the property and collect his money, if he chose to do so.

She'd spent a good amount of time with Chad in the past three weeks, always observing their agreement. She'd had dinner with Chad, Julio, his wife and Marisol, and they'd had a wonderful long conversation about Honey Ridge's history and legacy, as well as wine in general. There were still picnics every week, and she talked with him then. And they'd worked together. He tried to absorb everything, like the world's most eager student. It was fun to discuss stuff with him, to watch as he grew and learned, and got more and more enthusiastic.

If they happened to go into the wine cellar and walked a little too close to each other, it was her own stupid fault that her heart raced ever so slightly. And if he walked her to her porch, always with other people around...well, it wasn't against the law to daydream.

And if the nights were getting progressively longer, and she was having trouble sleeping...

Leila shook her head. She didn't want to think about it. September was already coming up like a freight train, with the possibility of losing Honey Ridge and everything that entailed.

Including never seeing Chad McFee again.

She needed balance and equilibrium. She needed a reminder of what she was in all this for.

She went to the farmhouse and picked up the phone, gripping the receiver more tightly than she needed to. She heard the phone ring, and heard a familiar voice answer: "Hello?"

"Hi, Mom," Leila said, feeling a wave of relief and comfort just hearing her voice.

"Leila, dear! This is a surprise!" Her mother was bright and cheerful, just the way Leila had always remembered. "We've been so busy, and I've been meaning to call, but I haven't had more than a minute to shoot off an e-mail, you know that. Spring and all, and the time difference…but I'm rambling. How are you?"

"I'm…" Leila thought about how to word it. "Hanging in there."

"Oh, my," her mother said. "What's wrong? I can hear it in your voice."

"You got my e-mail, saying that Charles McFee died, right?"

Her mother clucked sympathetically. "A pity. He was a good man, and he believed in the vineyard. We couldn't have asked for a better patron. Still, I'm sure at his age…well, he wasn't surprised. He was getting tired those last years we knew him. You mentioned that he passed the vineyard on. How's that going?"

Leila sighed. "His great-nephew Chad has taken the place over," she said carefully, "but I'm not sure he'll keep it. He may sell. It hasn't been making money the past few years, after all."

"I know that tone, too," her mother said. "You're blaming yourself, and you should stop it. Force majeure, my dear…acts of God. You didn't cause the drought or the frost."

"Yes, but it was always in the black when you and

Dad were running the place," Leila said, feeling childish and whiny but unable to help herself.

"Leila, love," her mother said patiently, "you're a winemaker. You know that a vintage depends on a million different variables. You can plan for some things and you can fix some things, but so much of it is pure, blind, random luck."

"It's frustrating," Leila admitted. "I wanted to do so much with this place. Especially after you and Dad fought to get me the job. I just…I feel like such a failure."

There. She'd said it. Somehow, saying it loosened the lump of lead that had been weighing down her chest, and she wiped at the tears that escaped from her eyes.

"It is frustrating," her mother soothed. "But it's also what makes winemaking so exciting. That's why it's art, instead of just work."

"I know that," Leila snuffled.

"Yes, but you've never really applied it," her mother gently corrected her. "Not at Honey Ridge, and not in your life, from what I've noticed. It's always amazed me how stubbornly focused you can get when you want something." She chuckled. "You get that from your father, you know."

"How is he doing?" Leila said, feeling a little better.

"He's out in the pouring rain, checking on the grapes. You know your dad."

"And how are you doing?"

Her mother gave a sigh of contentment. "Australia was one of the best moves we could've made. It was a huge change, and it took a lot of getting used to, but it's been a blast, as your father would say. I swear, it's like he's twenty years younger," she said. "I guess you're never too old for a new adventure. He thinks that a little risk improves the wine."

Leila thought about the last time she'd used that argument: *I'm just doing this to improve the wine.* Then she'd kissed Chad, and…well, that hadn't turned out so hot.

"A little risk could also turn the wine cheese-worthy," Leila pointed out.

"Glass half-full, sweetie," her mother reminded her. "You'll get through this. Just don't worry about things that are out of your hands. If Honey Ridge's time is up, then it's up. You don't have to sacrifice your whole life. Just learn from it, take the experiences, and move on."

"Yes, Mom."

"When your father gets in, I can have him call you."

"No, I just needed to hear your voice," Leila said. "I'll call again in two weeks. I love you."

"I love you too, sweetie."

Leila hung up the phone, then looked out the window. Chad was working with the other laborers, joking with Ted and Julio about something. He looked like a completely different person lately. He was livelier now, more comfortable in his own skin. When she'd first met him, he'd struck her as a frat boy, a rich guy who was completely clueless. Now, he seemed more mature. Like a wine that had breathed, he'd come into his own, somehow, and was expanding and turning more complicated every second she knew him. He seemed more like *himself*, even if she hadn't known him more than a month and a half.

You need to take more risks, Leila.

Julio had been right, and so had her mother. Leila had been so careful, so rigidly inflexible, that she hadn't made any room in her life for experimentation. She'd been so intent on succeeding, she hadn't wanted to actually *live,* or take the chance of making a fool of herself, of making a mistake. She was so afraid of losing what she had that she was damaging the very thing she had set out to create. She wanted everything perfect.

That was no way to make wine—and it was no way to live.

She was tired of controlling things. She was tired of fighting the attraction. She might never see Chad McFee again after a week from now; she might never work in Napa again, for all she knew.

But one thing she did know was, if she was going to have one regret in life, it wasn't going to be that she had the chance to feel the love of a wonderful man, if only for a night…and that she'd watched that chance pass her by.

CHAPTER FIVE

LEILA SMOOTHED down the skirt on her little black dress. She had her hair up in a chignon, with tendrils escaping to tickle at the back of her neck, and she was wearing makeup. She was also wearing her "CGM's" as Julio's wife Angelina called them…her "come get me" stilettos, with tiny bows at the heels.

She knew what Chad's reaction was when she was just wearing jeans. She couldn't wait to see how he'd feel about her when she was all dressed up and really *trying* to get his attention. She wasn't sure if she was going to seduce him outright, but she knew that the party was just a pretense, a reason for her to be with him alone—and a reason for her to look like this, while she was alone with him.

She got the feeling that they'd make the rounds, say hello, mingle a little…and then she'd gently make sure he took her back to the farmhouse. She'd offer him some wine, and they'd see where it went from there.

Leila glanced in a mirror in the resort lobby, one last check. She watched as her own plum-painted lips curved into a wicked, thoughtful smile. They'd just see how the night shook out.

She walked back to Chad, who had checked their coats, trying her best to look sexy and not totter in her heels. "So, here we are," she said, taking a deep breath before looping an arm through his. "Your first winemaker party."

"You look right at home," he said, and he gave her an intense perusal that suggested more than he was saying. His smile was evocative, and she felt warmth hit her right in the pit of her stomach. "You look amazing, actually. The shoes are great, but the dress…"

"Not a lot of call for cocktail dresses at the vineyard," she said, deliberately letting her body brush against his as she dodged another knot of people who were crowding the hallway. She leaned a little closer to him, to be heard. "You clean up pretty well, yourself."

Leila could feel the muscles tense beneath her hand, and for a moment, she felt his breath brush against her neck. She shivered.

"I don't mind dressing up when the occasion calls for it," Chad murmured, stroking her arm. "But I've learned that I prefer a more quiet, private life lately. Like at Honey Ridge."

She smiled. His voice had such an endearing mix of heat and ruefulness. "I would've thought you'd miss the high-society party thing," she said.

"Well, the last party I went to seemed to cure me of that," he said. He hadn't gone into many details about that night, but she got the feeling it had been a turning point for him. She did know that it was the last time she'd seen him hungover. "So no, I don't miss the party life at all."

"I'm glad," she whispered.

"Besides," he said, as he brushed a stray curl away from her jaw with his fingertips, causing all her nerve endings to jump to attention, "I'd rather spend time with people I genuinely care about…and who genuinely care about me."

For a second, it was as if they were the only two people in the place. Then someone jostled them, and her chest bumped against his. She could feel her cheeks heating with a blush.

Wait till you get home, at least!

Chad cleared his throat. "Want a glass of wine?" he asked. "I mean, I guess that's why we're here, right?"

She nodded, then led him toward the crowded bar. She felt tongue-tied and her heart was still skipping from their contact.

"And maybe," he whispered, and she could feel the heat of his breath against the nape of her neck, "maybe we could duck out early."

The words were music to her ears, but before she could turn and answer, another voice interrupted them.

"Leila Fairmont, where *have* you been hiding yourself?"

Leila sighed, then smiled as a portly, silver-bearded man walked over, clapping her on the shoulder. "Bernard," she greeted him. "How's it going?"

"My dear, I've just bottled a Muscat that would shame any dessert on earth," he enthused, his eyes gleaming. "But don't get me sidetracked. I heard that ancient patron of yours finally got out of the business—in a manner of speaking. What's going on over at Honey Ridge? There's been talk."

She clenched her jaw and stepped back so Chad was included in the conversation. "I should introduce you to the new owner," she said. "Chad McFee, this is Bernard Schwartz, of Nocturne Vineyards."

"Pleased to meet you," Bernard said cordially, his eyes shrewd. "It's a great place, Honey Ridge. They put out one of the best Merlots in the Valley."

"I know," Chad said easily.

"Maniac or tourist?"

Chad blinked. Leila shook her head. "He's asking if you've owned a vineyard before, or if you're new to the business," she said, frowning at Bernard. "This is his first vineyard, Bernard. Be nice."

"No offense intended, honestly," Bernard said. "I'm sorry, I have a chronic case of foot-in-mouth disease. Thankfully, *I* own a vineyard. So I can usually blame it on being plowed."

To Leila's relief, Chad grinned. "That's a perk I hadn't even thought of," he said.

"Trust me, you'll love it. It's hand-to-mouth, especially as an indie, but it's completely addictive. You won't know how you lived any other way after a year or so." Bernard's grin was wide. "Well, this is something we ought to toast. What have you had tonight?"

"We just got here," Chad said. "Should we be trying your Muscat?"

"You can taste some of that later," Bernard said. "Work up to it. It's a dessert wine, after all."

"I didn't know that," Chad admitted.

Bernard's eyes widened. "I see. You really are new to this." He put a heavy hand on Chad's shoulder, his eyes gleaming. "Let's introduce you around."

Leila sighed. So much for the idea of ducking out early. Bernard was practically a social director. Before the night was over, Chad was going to know every single person at the party.

An hour later, as she'd predicted, Chad was ensconced in the "old boys network" of vintners. Leila knew most of the men, after years of being in the business. Bernard pulled her aside.

"Seriously, are you all right?" he asked.

She glanced to make sure Chad wasn't listening. He wasn't—he was learning about the blight that had nearly destroyed all the vineyards in the 1980s, from an old vintner who had started out as a musician in L.A. "I'm hanging in there," she said.

"There's talk that one of the corporate wineries has an eye on your land." Leila's stomach clenched. "You know how much the land is worth, and all. And Chad's new at this. Does he plan on staying with it?"

"I don't know." She felt numb. "I hope so. He seems to really enjoy learning about the wine, the vineyard, the whole nine yards."

"And you two don't exactly look like business associates, if you don't mind me saying," Bernard said.

She wasn't sure if she minded or not, so she just shrugged. "One thing at a time," she said, causing Bernard to laugh.

"He just needs to get bit by the bug," Bernard reassured her. "Do you remember the first time you could tell the difference between a Syrah and a Cab? Or the first time you made a really stellar wine? It's pure adrenaline."

Leila smiled, closing her eyes…remembering. "I could tell the difference when I was thirteen," she admitted. "And I remember the smell of our first really phenomenal Merlot, the taste of it."

"There you go," he said. "Get the guy hooked on that, and he'll never leave."

She gave Bernard a little hug in gratitude, and then walked over to where Chad was sitting. He had a few bulb-shaped glasses in front of them, each with only a little bit of wine. He twirled the ruby liquid in one, then let it slide up the side to watch if the wine clung or not. He put his nose in, inhaling deeply. Then he took a slow sip.

"Wow," he said, after a long moment.

The crowd of men and women around him crowed triumphantly. "You see? Nothing to it," the ancient musician, Simon, said with approval. "You look like an old pro."

"What are you drinking?" Leila asked.

He scooted over on the bench, and she sat next to

him as he proffered the glass. She took a sip. It was full-bodied, with hints of raspberry and black cherry and smoke. "Pinot Noir," she said. "Nice. Yours, Simon?"

Simon nodded. "Yup. I was just telling your man here about the clones we've been grafting."

She looked over nervously at Chad, to see how he liked being referred to as "her man."

He didn't even seem to notice, more intent on the conversation. "So, it took you five years to get the balance right?"

"It's a million different elements," another winemaker, a woman named Sylvie, piped in. "There's nature, there's environment, there's the pressing and how you manipulate it once it's off the vine, there's the aging. There's just plain, blind, dumb luck, to boot. It's a lot like gambling."

"It's a work of art," Bernard rumbled, and they toasted each other, smiling broadly. They weren't drunk…not even close, at least not on wine. They were drunk on the process.

Chad was right there with them, looking mesmerized.

"You doing all right?" she whispered, under cover of the raucous laughter. "Still want to leave early?"

"Actually, this is really interesting," he admitted, and he looked at her with a combination of embarrassment and helpless happiness. "Do you mind if we stay a bit?"

Leila thought about why she'd wanted to take him

out of here…her plans for him later, at the farmhouse. But when she saw the genuine fascination in his eyes, she realized that as much as she wanted him, she loved this side of him. She loved that he was as interested in what she did as she was. And if he wanted to learn more, why would she take that away?

She sighed softly, just to herself. Besides, the night wasn't over yet.

"I love wine," she said, and it was the simple truth. "And I'm glad you love it, too. Don't worry. We can stay as long as you want."

Later that night, Chad drove Leila back to the farmhouse. He was feeling a warm glow, not so much from the wine he'd imbibed, but from the company. Over the course of three hours, he'd had sips of several different kinds of wine. But he felt he'd learned enough for a college course or two. Of course, he'd never been that interested in any of the college courses he'd taken, way back when, so it probably wasn't a good comparison.

He was riveted by wine.

He looked over to see Leila's face, traced by the bright moonlight, looking like an angel. She didn't catch his glance, but instead watched the landscape, transfixed by the beauty of the vineyards and the softly rolling hills.

He might be riveted by wine, he thought. But he was obsessed with Leila Fairmont.

"You looked like you had a good time tonight," Leila said, not breaking away from the view.

"I did," he said honestly, paying attention to the road. Then he shot another glance her way. "Didn't you?"

"I've been to a million of those parties," she said, causing him a moment's worry—maybe he'd spent way too long there. But her next remark comforted him. "I would have had an okay time, but having you there made it special. You made everything new, and seeing how enthusiastic you've become about wine, in such a short period of time, is just incredible. You probably don't realize just how much you've picked up this month."

This month. Which brought to mind the fact that his self-imposed deadline was fast approaching. His parents and Renaldo were starting to get antsy, too.

He pushed that out of his mind, focused on Leila instead, which wasn't that hard. "I haven't had this much fun in years."

"It shows," she replied.

They were quiet for a moment. "My only regret," he said slowly, "was that I guess I kept you out way too long. But you looked gorgeous. You wouldn't want to waste that outfit just staying at home, right?"

He was trying for a light, teasing tone, and still glancing over occasionally to check on her. So he inadvertently caught the look, shot through with fire and wicked amusement, that she sent his way at the question.

"If you had been at the house with me," she said in a low, husky voice, "believe me, it wouldn't have been wasted."

His stomach clenched into a ball of desire, causing the rest of his systems to go haywire.

She wanted him.

Well, he knew that, just as much as she knew he wanted her. But she wanted him *tonight*. Hell, she wanted him *now*.

And from the sounds of it, she meant to have him. Tonight. Now.

Chad swallowed hard.

"You okay?" she asked, still sounding amused. "Or was I too forward?"

"Well, you might want to save statements like that for when I'm *not* driving," he said in a choked voice.

Leila chuckled, a sinfully sensual sound. "We're almost home," she replied. "I figured it was enough time."

He looked—they were on the border of the property. They'd be at the farmhouse in a matter of minutes.

He wanted her, she wanted him. He shouldn't let it get more complicated than that.

The only problem was, his conscience muttered with its implacable logic, they might have one incredible night, but there would still be all kinds of problems in the morning. Namely, the fact that he might have to sell the place, put her friends out of work, put *her* out of a job and out of her home. She might want him now, but how could she not look at him like some kind of monster if he did all that *and* slept with her too?

Of course, maybe you don't have to sell. You don't even want *to sell.*

He blinked, shocked temporarily out of his lust-soaked recriminations. That wasn't his conscience. That was another inner voice entirely.

You haven't gotten the numbers from Renaldo. You'd love to be with Leila, sure, but you also love the life. You love vineyards. You're enjoying yourself even when you're working. Why screw everything up?

"Chad? Are you okay?"

"Huh?" He noticed that Leila's voice no longer had the sexy, raspy, full-of-longing tone it had. She sounded concerned.

"You've got this faraway look, and we've been parked for a few minutes," she said, her violet eyes dark with worry. "I didn't mean to shock you, or anything. I was just kidding around."

She thought she'd done something wrong. He swallowed, hard. He'd never met someone so fiery, so sweet, so…so *amazing* as Leila, in his whole life. He hated that he had to meet her this way. But maybe, just maybe, everything could work out after all.

He leaned over the stick shift of his now shut-off car, and kissed her, hard, with all the passion and confusion he was feeling. She seemed stunned by it initially, but soon enough she was matching his passion—and then raising him a level. She tasted of wine and heat, her tongue tickling his, causing him to groan. He pressed her into the leather of the passenger seat—and promptly got hit in the hip with the gearstick.

"Ouch, dammit," he said roughly, pulling away and taking a deep, uneven breath. "Okay, not in the car."

She laughed. "Then why don't you come inside?"

The words hung there, heavy with invitation. Chad thought about it…then sighed heavily.

"The thing is—we'll still have some issues hanging between us," he said slowly.

She stared at him. "I was trying not to think about that."

"I know," he said. "And ordinarily, I would ignore absolutely anything to sleep with you. I wouldn't care about tomorrow. I'd just want to make love to you for hours until we were both exhausted, and worry about the consequences later."

Her eyes lit like beacons, and her hand rubbed his thigh gently. "Okay. Okay," she murmured, her breathing going shallow. "I can live with that. That sounds good."

It took every ounce of self-control he had, and some he didn't realize he had, to put his hand on hers, slowing the maddening motion of her fingertips. "But here's the thing," he said, his voice thick with desire. "Ordinarily, tomorrow would suck, and you'd probably be hurt. But I wouldn't care, because I wouldn't be there."

He was ashamed at his own admission, and her hand paused on its own.

"I see," she said, pulling her hand away. He could feel her withdraw, both physically and emotionally.

He leaned over, stroking the petal softness of her

cheek. "I'm not proud of who I was, or what I've done. I can say this—I would be there tomorrow, for you," he said. "But that doesn't mean I want to do anything tonight that'll hurt you in the future. I want the way to be perfectly clear before we get together, because when we finally *do* get together, it's not going to be for just one night. Can you understand that?"

He held his breath, waiting for her response.

Leila stared at him, her eyes almost black in the moonlight. Then, he saw her lips curve into a smile, before she pressed a kiss on him, full of tenderness and promise.

"I understand," she said. "But how can we clear the way?"

Chad sighed raggedly. "I need to talk to my family and my accountant tomorrow," he said. "And then I'm going to see what my options are. And I am going to do everything I can to keep the vineyard."

She let out a gasp. Then, slowly, she asked, "It's not...it's not just for me, though, is it?"

"No," he said. "I care about you, more than I could've believed. And I don't want to hurt you. But I care about Honey Ridge, too, now." He sent her a smile, tinged slightly with pain at what he was turning down. "I'll find out definitively tomorrow. Can you wait one night?"

"All right," she said. "I can wait one night."

He kissed her again, and then watched as she got out of the car and went up to the house. He had never wanted anything as badly as to go up to the house with her, and have her. He knew if he so much as opened his car door, all his miraculous self-restraint would evaporate and that's exactly what he would do. But she was too damned important for him to screw this up.

He could wait one night, too, he decided.

Still, it'd be the longest night of his life.

CHAD SAT in his father's study, squirming slightly in the high-backed chair. It was sumptuous leather, but it always felt uncomfortable to him, although he supposed that had more to do with the circumstances than with the seat itself. He never sat in the thing unless he had something really important to discuss or, more to the point, something to justify. He'd sat here after each of his investments had gone down the tubes. Chad had sat here when his father had replenished his trust fund, the first time.

God, I hate this chair.

Today, though, was more important—and more painful—than all of those previous incidents combined.

He'd already spoken to Renaldo this morning, and the verdict was not good.

"Hey, Renaldo," he'd answered his phone, still churning with joy and frustration from the night before. He wanted Leila; he wanted Honey Ridge; he had a definite vision of what he wanted his future to be. He could not remember feeling more impassioned, more happy.

"We need to talk," Renaldo had said. "Chad, you can't keep the vineyard."

Chad had been driving, and he'd gripped his steering wheel. "Why not?"

"It's hemorrhaging money."

Chad had swallowed hard. "I know it's fallen on hard times the past two years, but that's just a fact of the business," he'd said carefully. "This year's bottling went smoothly. And even though last year's crop was small, the wine itself is remarkable."

"This isn't about the wine," Renaldo had countered. "This is about the vineyard itself. It won't survive another year on its own without some serious cash influx. It won't even survive through Christmas at this rate. The collectors are circling, and you haven't given them any money yet. It's overextended. Charles knew that, but Charles had boatloads of money to throw at it. You don't. Your trust fund—even when it was at its peak—isn't enough to bail Honey Ridge out of the hole it's in. And it certainly isn't enough to keep it operational for another year or two, which it would definitely need to help you recoup your losses." Renaldo's voice had been melancholy but firm. "You'd be committing financial suicide, Chad. I can't advise you to do this."

"But…" He'd felt happiness seep from him like blood from a wound.

"At least the sale of the land will more than cover the losses." Renaldo had tried to comfort him. "You'll come out ahead—not a lot, but enough. That land is valuable, more than the vineyard. You'll be all right. It'll replenish what you lost on the movie, probably."

He'd winced. "It's more than the money, Renaldo."

Renaldo had sighed. "Well, unless you can think of a way to suddenly get a few more millions to throw at this, I don't know what to tell you."

After hanging up, Chad had thought about the dilemma, and the only solution he could come up with had led him here…to his father's study, to the dreaded chair.

He imagined police interrogation room furniture was more comfortable.

His father walked in, looking the same as always—vaguely stressed and harried. Even though he'd just come back from a European vacation, even though he was wearing a polo shirt and a pair of khakis, he looked like he had just stepped out of a boardroom, where he'd received bad news. Chad had no idea how his father managed it, since he didn't even work anymore. Hell, he hadn't worked since he was thirty-seven.

"I'm a little surprised that you wanted to meet with me, son." His father sat in the position of authority behind the broad bird's-eye maple desk that dominated the room. "What's going on?"

Chad took a deep breath. This was the painful part. "I need your help."

His father's eyes widened. "What mess are you in now?"

He gritted his teeth. "It's not a mess. It's a business proposition."

Now his father's eyes shut. "Oh, God," he muttered. "Tell me this isn't another one of your cockamamy investments, Chad. I warned you. I told you before we left that you needed to stop all this nonsense!"

Chad took out his small leather portfolio, containing the numbers he'd pulled together from Leila and Renaldo. "I am asking for you to put money into a business venture," he said. "I'm not asking you to bail me out. I'm asking on behalf of Honey Ridge Vineyards. And I'm not asking you to do it blindly. I've brought research, that shows you why they need the money—why *we* need the money," he corrected, "and how we'll be able to not only pay back your interest, but get you some return on it in the future. This isn't charity. It's business."

His father now stared at him as if he'd never seen him before. "Are you kidding?" he finally asked, bewildered.

"Dad, I know that I've been an idiot and a flake in the past," Chad said, grinding out the admission painfully. "But I also know that I was just playing at business then. You were right about that."

His father looked gratified at Chad's acknowledgment. "So what makes this different? You were only there, what, two months! Tops!"

"I love wine, Dad," Chad said, then grimaced when his father chuckled dismissively. "Not just drinking it. I learned about the whole process. I worked, actually did physical labor. I fell in love."

Now his father scowled at him. "Should've known there was a woman involved in this whole fiasco."

Chad felt his anger bubble at that one, but he shook his head. "I fell in love with *wine*, Dad. And with winemaking."

He'd also fallen in love with Leila, improbably enough. But he was not about to bring her into this—not to face his father's derision. Chad was going to do that on his own.

"Well, I hope you two are very happy together," his father said. "Because I'm not investing a damned dime in your vineyard."

Chad felt his stomach clench. "If you just front us some money, not even the whole investment," Chad said, trying not to plead, "I can reimburse you in the next six months. I just need time to get the vineyard back on its feet. In the next six months, I could get my friends to put the money in, set up my own investment collective. I could pay you back."

"You don't get it, do you?" his father said. "I don't care about your vineyard, and I don't care about the money. *I don't want you to keep throwing yourself into these damned foolish business dreams!*"

Chad stared at his father, aghast.

"Do you know how embarrassing it is, for you, for all of us, when you keep failing?" His father hit the surface of his desk with a balled fist. "I've tried to spare you that, but you keep ignoring me, doing your own thing, falling flat on your face. Well, I've warned and I've talked, and I'm sick of it."

Chad felt his chest burn like acid. "I see." He loaded up his portfolio. His father had been a long shot, anyway, but he'd hoped that, by showing how serious he was, he might relent.

"You're going to try anyway, aren't you?" his father said. "What's your next move? You don't even have one, do you?"

"I'll try my friends," Chad said, wincing at the thought of Lester as one of the vineyard's patrons. "And if that doesn't work, I'll figure out something."

"You don't get it at all," his father said. "You don't know what it's like to be broke, to not have this endless flow of money…to actually *struggle* for something. You think I'm just going to be there to bail you out forever."

"That's not it at all." *You've never struggled for anything, either. You were born into money, same as me!*

"Well, son of mine," his father said, "welcome to the real world."

"I'll make this work," Chad said, stubbornly. "I just wanted to come to you first."

"This isn't about the vineyard," his father snapped. "This is about you. I'm cutting you off. Your trust fund is gone. You're on your own."

Chad sat there a moment, in shock. He had wondered if his father would help, but he hadn't anticipated this.

"So whatever money you've got, you'd better hold on to it, because that's all she wrote," his father said smugly. "You want to know what it's like? You want to ignore your family and go your own way? Well, then, here's your chance."

Chad forced himself to stand up, even though he felt numb. "All right," he said slowly.

"Do you understand? You're cut off!"

"I get it," Chad repeated. And he didn't listen to the rest of his father's tirade as he walked out the door.

He was on his own. His trust fund was gone. He had some possessions, but he had no money, nothing to offer Honey Ridge—or Leila, for that matter, he thought absently. His friends would probably give a little, out of charity, but they would not want to continue to hang out with him. He knew them well enough for that.

He was in a corner.

He thought about Renaldo's assessment. *You'll be able to cover your losses with the sale.*

He was going to have to sell Honey Ridge, he thought, the pain of the realization circling out of him in waves.

And he was going to have to tell Leila. Tonight.

CHAPTER SIX

LEILA SAT IN HER LIVING ROOM, waiting for Chad.

She'd spent the afternoon bottling the last of the year's wines. Each vintage seemed to hold some crucial part of her, some essence of her spirit, if that wasn't too melodramatic a way to put it. After all, there was something of her spirit in every bottle that left the place. But this was different. It would be interesting to see, in a few years, how this year's harvest had fared, whether it would be one of Honey Ridge's best years, or one of its worst.

At the end of the day, though, once it was in the bottle, one couldn't control what happened next. One had to simply hope for the best, and plan for the next vintage.

That was what she was doing, she thought, as she smoothed the skirt of her dusty-rose sundress around her legs. It was all out of her hands now, no point in worrying over something she couldn't control. She could only enjoy what she had, and make the most of it.

She heard the roar of Chad's car and was on her feet before she realized it, heading for the front door and standing on the porch.

She'd always remember the moment afterward… standing on the old porch, her hands on the railing, polished glass-smooth by years of rough hands rubbing over it. Watching Chad step out of his car, his hair tousled by the early autumn breeze. The grape leaves were turning colors, and in the sunset the hills looked aflame. It was one of the most breathtaking things she'd ever seen.

He walked toward her with purpose, almost stern, and then he walked up the steps.

"I missed you," he said simply, and then kissed her, taking her breath away in an entirely different way. She clutched at his shoulders, marveling at their strength, wondering why she'd bothered fighting their attraction for so long.

After a long moment, Leila pulled away, panting slightly, feeling light-headed. Then she looked in his eyes.

They were filled with darkness, and a hint of despair, and while a part of her quavered at the sight of it, the rest of her knew instinctively not to question. He'd get to it, in time. Right now, he needed to sit down. He needed comfort.

"Come in," she said breathlessly. "I've got some wine you might want to try."

He nodded, letting her lead him into the living room and pour him a glass of Syrah. He took a sip, but she knew he wasn't tasting it, wasn't savoring it. He was playing out something in his mind—bracing himself. Just as she was, she realized.

Instead of waiting for him, she sat down next to him, kissing him tenderly, tasting the Syrah on his tongue. Then she stroked the hair on the nape of his neck, tracing her fingers down his neck. "It's all right," she murmured. "It's okay. It's going to be fine."

That seemed to surprise Chad, and he allowed her to take him into her arms, rubbing his shoulders. "How did you know?"

"I just had to look at you," Leila said.

He was silent for a moment, board-stiff, with waves of pain coming off him, and her heart ached for him. "I tried," he said finally. "I wanted to keep Honey Ridge. I had no idea how much money we were losing."

She closed her eyes. She hadn't either—not really. She'd always been more about the grapes and the wine than the ledgers and margins. "So there's no hope?" she said, wanting to be clear.

"I'm selling the vineyard," he said, and he choked on the words. "I am so sorry, Leila. I am so very, very sorry."

"I knew you'd have to," she said, even though she hadn't wanted to believe it. "And it's all right."

"How can you say that?" he said, pulling away from her, studying her face. His looked harsher—older, she realized, in some intangible way. "I know how much this place means to you! I couldn't believe how much this place means to *me*, in just a few months, and you've lived here most of your life! You've always wanted this. So how, exactly, can you look me in the eye and tell me that this is 'all right'?"

He was furious, not at her, but at himself, at the whole situation. Still, his words stabbed, pointing out everything she'd railed against herself. This was what she'd wanted her whole life. This was what she'd dreamed of and planned for, since she was a child. And it was going away.

And yet it really was going to be all right.

"You know," she said, trying to figure out a way to put it in words, "there's a lot that can go wrong in a season. Frost. Drought. Fire. Bugs. You name it, we've had it."

Chad stared at her, obviously not getting it.

"But you still do it," she said, kissing him on the cheek, "because you love it. And when something happens, you just say 'it'll be better next season.' And you *keep* going."

He leaned into her, and she took comfort in his heat, in his arms around her.

"So you're saying," he said, his voice muffled against her neck, "that it's good that I'm dumping the place, since with the frost, fire, bugs and whatnot, it's a real lemon?"

He surprised a laugh out of her. "You idiot," she said, but realized he wasn't serious—he was just trying to take some of the pain out of the situation by joking. But she wasn't ready to joke, not yet. "I'm saying," she said clearly, framing his face in her hands as he held her hips loosely, "that when you love something, you just find another way."

He smiled. "I can't believe I found you. I can't believe what you mean to me. I think I might be falling in love with you."

Leila couldn't swallow. She could barely breathe. She could only stare at him.

"I know it's sudden," he said, his voice ragged. "And I know I don't have a chance, with all of this. But I thought you should know."

How long had it been since she'd heard those words from a man? And how long had it been since she had felt like this?

She couldn't answer immediately. Instead, she wordlessly took his hand, leading him up to her bedroom. The covers were turned down. She'd known, no matter what else happened, it would come down to this.

Chad paused in the doorway, staring at her. "It's more than this," he said solemnly. "You know that."

She nodded, still silent. Then she reached to the back of her dress, unzipping it slowly and letting it drop to the floor. She hadn't worn underwear, so nothing was impeding his vision. It had been years since she'd stood, naked and vulnerable, in front of a man in this way.

He looked at her almost reverently. Then he reached for her, with infinite gentleness, stroking her skin, murmuring tender words against the crown of her head as he kissed her.

After some artless fumbling on both their parts, they managed to get his clothes off, too, and slowly made their way to the bed. It was as if they were both nervous, as if it were equally important to both of them, and neither wanted to make a mistake. But soon, his hands smoothing over her bare skin caused her blood to heat and her breathing to go shallow. Her gentle stroking motions turned more ferocious, grasping, wanting. He grew more insistent, kissing her with a furious fire, molding the white-hot planes of his body against hers.

In the moment before he eased into her, she couldn't think of anything about her past, about her future, about what she'd wanted. She didn't care about the vineyard or the wine in the cellar or anything. Her only thoughts were of him, and of how she felt at that instant.

"*Chad*," Leila said, in a rippling murmur, as he moved inside her. She clung to him, clawing her nails down his back. This was perfect, she thought, before all thought fled altogether. This was fiercely, utterly *right.*

They moved against each other with tender passion, and when it was over, she still clutched him to her, as if she couldn't bear to be more than a heartbeat away.

"I might be falling in love with you, too," she murmured, and only by the sudden tightness of his arms around her did she know he'd heard what she said.

That didn't change things. He was selling Honey Ridge. They were both moving, and more than likely moving on.

But she'd had her one night, her last vintage. It was perfect. And if it was all she ever got—so be it.

CHAPTER SEVEN

"HEY, CHAD! Man, did you miss out in Machu Picchu. What a scene!"

Chad sipped at his wine—a little indie out of Oregon, a red blend. It had promise, but it also had some sourness, he noted, and jotted down the observation in a notebook he'd purchased. Then he looked up to address Lester, who was standing beside him in the crowded San Francisco restaurant. "Hey, Les."

"Where the hell have you been hiding yourself?" Lester's eyes gleamed. "We haven't seen you in ages. And I've got a party coming up."

"I can't make it," Chad said quickly, taking another sip, "but thanks anyway."

"What, are you a monk now?"

Actually, Chad thought with a humorless grin, he was. "Just busy."

"Doing what?"

"Selling my vineyard," he said. Even after three months, it still hurt. "Escrow just closed. It's out of my hands now."

"All right! Finally, you'll be back in the black," Lester said, all but rubbing his hands together. "Which is good, because the Christmas party I've got coming up—you won't believe it. You've heard of that ice hotel they set up in Sweden, right?"

"I told you, I'm busy."

"Sounds like you're not busy anymore," Lester said practically. "You sold the place." Then his eyes narrowed perceptively. "Wait, wait, don't tell me. You've got a girl, huh?"

That did cause Chad to wince. "Not at the moment."

And it was true. After their one night, after telling her he was in love with her, Leila had woken him up the next morning, presented him with a cup of the best coffee he'd ever tasted—and then told him that they probably shouldn't see each other again.

"Why not?" he'd asked, stunned to the point of numbness. "I thought you said that you wouldn't hold it against me! I didn't want to sell the vineyard. I just...I *have* to!"

"I know," she'd said, caressing his face, her eyes wet with tears. "But that doesn't stop what has to happen. I have to find a new place to live. I have to get another job. I have to make choices with my life." She'd paused, and she'd gotten that practical tilt to her chin that he loved—or at least, that he'd loved before that moment. "And so do you."

"You can move in with me."

"I'm sure I could, but I need to work with grapes. You live in the city. That's a hell of a commute."

"I could get a place out here," he'd said, with the

desperation of a man arguing against a death sentence. "It wouldn't be that hard."

"I care about you. That hasn't changed." She'd sat next to him. "But I need to get my life sorted out. You can understand that."

"So where does that leave me?"

Leila had stared at him then. "You tell me, Chad. Where does that leave you? What do you want to do now? You can't have the vineyard. And you've got a bunch of financial stuff you're going to need to think of, from what you've just told me. What's your next move?" Her eyes had been expressive. "What do you *want?*"

He'd been pushed off balance. He hadn't thought beyond that. He'd thought the vineyard was the answer to all of his problems, just as he'd thought Leila was a part of that solution. But when one part of the solution failed, it seemed, all of it did.

He still loved Leila, and he hadn't been with anyone since her. But when she'd taken a flight to Australia to visit her parents, he hadn't protested. He still called her but respected her need for space.

True to his word, his father had cut off his trust fund. He'd gone over all the money he had in his personal account, the worth of his condo, and the money he'd make on the sale of the vineyard. He had made some hard decisions.

His days of "playing" were over.

"I'm waiting for someone, Lester," he said, seeing Renaldo entering the restaurant, scanning for him. "But it's been nice catching up."

Lester simply shook his head, walking away. Chad shook Renaldo's hand. "Thanks for making the time to meet."

"Thanks for not calling me at home anymore," Renaldo said. "How are you doing?"

"Hanging in," Chad said. "Listen, I also wanted to thank you for handling the vineyard sale."

"No problem," Renaldo answered. "You got top dollar. Any idea what you want to do with the money? I can put you on to some good investments."

"I've been doing some research, myself," Chad said slowly. "And I've drawn up a plan."

"Really? This *is* news."

Chad didn't laugh, even though he knew Renaldo meant him to. "I'm thinking real estate."

"Okay. Any idea where?"

"California's getting a little too expensive," Chad said. "I was thinking of Oregon."

"Oregon? What's in Oregon that's got you so interested?"

Chad pulled a manila folder out of the briefcase that he hadn't carried for years. He handed it to Renaldo, who opened it, scanning its contents quickly. Then Renaldo looked up at him, surprised.

"Are you sure about this?"

"There are a lot of good wines coming out of Oregon right now," he said. "I know where I can get some quality used equipment cheap. And I've got a guy helping me out as far as scouting the location. He assures me the land's worth it."

"A guy?" Renaldo's voice was skeptical.

"Not one of my old party cronies. Julio Escobar," Chad said. "He was head of the farmlands at Honey Ridge. He's given it the seal of approval. I don't know if I can afford to hire him, but I trust his recommendations."

"Well," Renaldo said, nonplussed. "Well. You know, it wouldn't be a slam dunk."

"I don't expect this to happen overnight," Chad said soberly. "I have the business background, and I've been running some numbers—how long it would take us to be profitable, what it would take to cover payroll, the whole nine yards." He pulled out another manila folder, passing that to Renaldo. "I'd appreciate your help looking it over, though."

"You really have been working," Renaldo said. "Damn, this is comprehensive. You seem to know what you're talking about."

"I know."

Renaldo looked at him for a second, then cleared his throat. "Can I ask you a question for a second? Not as your financial advisor, but as your friend."

Chad nodded. He'd always thought of Renaldo as both, anyway…or else he never would've called him so late at night.

"Is this for you?" Renaldo asked quietly. "Or is this for the girl?"

Chad sighed deeply. "I've asked myself the same question," he said.

"And…?" Renaldo prompted.

"It's for me," he said, and he knew that the truth rang in every word. "I miss her, and I love her, and I won't deny that I'd like to have her with me. But when I worked at the vineyard, for the first time in my life, I loved what I did. I felt like a whole person. I don't think that what you do defines you, or anything like that, but I do know that not doing anything, and wasting my life, was making me miserable. And being miserable and not myself was never going to be good enough for her. She wanted me to get my life together, and she never guaranteed anything. I see now that, the way I was, there was no way I could be with her."

"So you are doing this for her," Renaldo said, and Chad hastily shook his head.

"No. I'm doing this for me. I'm just saying she was right."

Renaldo nodded, then he sighed. "This could take a while to pull together."

"That's okay," Chad said. "My calendar's pretty empty for the foreseeable future."

"I DIDN'T KNOW it got this cold in Oregon in the winter," Julio said to Chad, shivering at the kitchen table, his large hands gripping a large mug of coffee.

"But the vines are going to be okay, right?" Chad said, pouring himself a third cup. It was January. He had been owner of the vineyard for a month. In that time, he'd managed to hire a skeleton staff, and even had a few investors. He spent most of his days planning the next year's vintage and focusing on hiring.

He spent most of his nights working himself into oblivion and trying not to focus on the fact that Leila was working in Australia and hadn't returned his calls for a week.

He missed her, with an intensity that he couldn't believe. Still, he had a life, which was more than he could say before he'd met Leila and gone to Honey Ridge, and for that, he thanked her.

"How are we coming on the head winemaker search?" Julio said suddenly.

Chad closed his eyes against the pain of it. "Still looking," he said casually. "I've got a few résumés that look pretty decent."

"It'll get easier, boss." Julio said.

"How's your mom?" Chad asked.

"She's looking forward to trying something new," Julio said, grinning. "Although if she thinks you're not feeding me properly, she may move up here."

"If she'll feed me, too, she has my blessing," Chad said, chuckling. "Go ahead, knock off early. I'm sure your family's waiting for you."

"The kids did want to play in the snow," Julio said. "Thanks, boss." He left.

Chad was alone in the large old house. He'd sold his car, trading it in for a work truck. He'd sold his place in San Francisco. He'd also ditched most of his furnishings—Scandinavian modern looked downright stupid in the relatively rustic wilds of an Oregon vineyard. Still, the place seemed large and empty.

He was in the process of starting a fire when he

heard a knock on his front door. Probably a solicitor, he thought, although his heart beat quicker, as always, as he answered it.

Leila stood there on his step, and for a moment he wondered if she were a mirage, something his heart-sick imagination had conjured up. Until he realized she was shivering.

"Are you *kidding* me with this cold?" she said, stepping in uninvited.

He closed the door behind her. "It got cold in Napa," he said inanely, still struck with disbelief that the object of his affection was currently dripping the remnants of sleet on his foyer rug.

"Not like this," she said, then stared at him for a moment, as if studying him.

Chad knew he looked nothing like he had the first time she'd seen him. He was wearing a flannel shirt and a pair of jeans, as well as a thick sweat jacket. He wore boots, for God's sake. He hadn't shaved that morning. He probably looked like a mess.

She looked the same as always—her hair tawny and wild, her violet eyes wide. She looked perfect.

"I missed you," he said in a quiet voice.

She threw herself in his arms, and he kissed her with all the passion he'd been shoring up in the months they'd been physically apart. She was tearing at the buttons of his shirt even as he went for her jacket. More by luck and chance than any sort of planning, they wound up in his bedroom, kissing each other fervently, gasping incoherent phrases of longing and love.

"Don't ever, *ever* just vanish on me again," he said, kissing her breast and making her gasp.

"I won't," she promised. "I had to fight to stay away."

"Well, don't do that, either," he warned.

"I had to know that you were doing things for yourself, not just using me as another escape," Leila said breathlessly, as she shucked off her own jeans. Lying there, deliciously naked, her eyes were still serious. "I had to *know*, Chad. I couldn't bear it if you got tired of me because I wasn't the answer to your problems."

He nodded. "I deserve that," he said, lying naked beside her and savoring the warmth of her compact little body. "I didn't know how much I had to learn until I lost Honey Ridge, and you."

"And now?"

He looked around, at his much less luxurious surroundings. "I think I can be happy here," he said.

It was the answer she was looking for, apparently, because she proceeded to make slow, sensual, thorough love to him, as if trying to erase all memories of their being apart.

Afterward, with her lying in his arms, Chad felt just as he had when he'd first come to Honey Ridge. He felt as if he'd come home.

"I hear," she said, pressing a few kisses against his chest, "that you're looking for a head winemaker."

With that, he felt a bubble of happiness. "Yup," he drawled. "Interested?"

"I could be," she said.

"You know, you'll have to turn in a résumé—*ow!*"

He laughed after she punched him in the ribs, then looked at her seriously. "I know, this place is a risk. And it's not Honey Ridge."

"It's got a good feeling to it," she said, smiling. "And I think I could be happy here, too."

He nuzzled her neck. "I'll do everything I can to make sure you are," he said.

"What do you call this place, anyway?"

Chad smiled down at her. "So far…I'm calling it Long Shot Vineyards."

"Sounds like a gamble," Leila said, then pulled him close and kissed him. "Count me in."

Back to You

SARAH MAYBERRY

A big thanks to Marsha for thinking of me for this anthology, and to Margaret for helping make the manuscript as good as it could be. None of my writing would get anywhere without the advice, support and inspiration provided by Chris, who really is my hero.

CHAPTER ONE

HE'S NOT supposed to be here.

Becky Taylor froze on the threshold of the restaurant. Across the room, Cal MacKenzie leaned against the far wall, tall and dark and gorgeous. After ten years, the unexpected sight of him stole her breath away and sent her heart hammering into overdrive.

He was supposed to be in London. He'd moved there five years ago with his new wife, and Becky hadn't had any word through the grapevine that he was back.

He had every right to attend the staff reunion—they were both ex-employees of Hannigan's Discount Emporium, a family-owned store that had paid many a student's way through college. The thing was, she wouldn't have come if she'd known he was going to be there.

Becky quickly corrected herself. Of course she would have come; staying away would have meant she still cared.

"Hey, look—Cal's here," her old friend Carolyn said behind her.

Becky forced a smile.

"How about that."

"Now it really is the old Hannigan's gang," Carolyn said.

"Yeah." Becky hoped she didn't sound as off balance as she felt.

She shot another glance across the room. This time Cal was staring back at her. He raised the beer in his hand in silent greeting, his blue eyes smiling at her.

It was a warm Sydney night in the middle of a hot Australian summer, but all the little hairs on Becky's arms stood on end. It had been a full decade since she'd last seen Cal, but he still had the same effect on her. Damn him.

Carolyn was already exchanging hugs and exclamations with the group of people nearest the door. Becky wiped her sweaty hands down the thighs of her jeans. She spotted a discreet sign for the ladies' room on the door to her left. Three steps, and she was closing the bathroom door behind her and sighing with relief.

A moment. That was all she needed. A short moment to get over the surprise.

She stared at her reflection in the mirror, unhappy with the dazed expression on her face.

He's here, get over it. It doesn't matter, it doesn't mean anything. It definitely doesn't mean anything to you.

She and Cal had gone their separate ways a long time ago. The memory of how shattered she'd felt when he called an end to their brief relationship might still make her squirm with self-consciousness, but the days of her mooning over him were long gone. She was thirty-one now, not twenty-one. She owned her own home, she drove a sleek and sexy sports car, and until recently she'd been in a live-in relationship with a successful, attractive man. She was worlds away from the girl she'd been when Cal MacKenzie had ruled her world. The only reason she'd felt that illicit surge of excitement when she'd seen his tall body standing there was because she'd been taken by surprise. He'd once meant something to her, now he didn't. End of story.

She squared her shoulders and dug out her lipstick, smoothing on a fresh coat then topping it with lip gloss. Her lips looked shiny and full when she'd finished. She fluffed her long, dark, curly hair and adjusted the hem on her red T-shirt. Determined to prove something to herself, she exited the bathroom and made a beeline for the far wall where Cal still lounged, laughing with a handful of men.

He straightened as he saw her approach. She found herself looking up into his tanned, handsome face, a hundred old memories washing through her as she noted the way his black hair still flopped over his left eye, and how his mouth still quirked up more on one side than the other when he smiled.

"Becky Taylor," he said. "Good to see you."

Before she could respond, he ducked his head and leaned close to plant a kiss on her cheek. For a few seconds she was swamped with his heat and scent.

She had to blink to clear her head as he straightened again.

"Cal MacKenzie. Aren't you in the wrong hemisphere?" she asked, amazed at how casual and light and assured her voice sounded.

"Moved home last year," he said. He placed his empty beer bottle on a nearby table and angled his body so that he cut her off from the rest of the group he'd been standing with. Almost as though he wanted her all to himself.

She pushed the stupid thought away. She didn't care if he wanted her all to himself—she didn't want him. That was the important thing.

Sliding a hand into the back pocket of her jeans, Becky cocked her head to one side.

"Still in IT?"

"Yep. Started my own consultancy with a mate, actually."

"Brave of you. It's a pretty competitive field."

"We're doing okay," he said.

She'd already noted his Hugo Boss jeans, Gucci boots and the expensive Longines watch on his wrist. She guessed he must be doing very well—but then, Cal had always been modest. Even as a young man, he'd possessed a quiet confidence and charm that had drawn people to him. Herself included.

"I hear you're with David Jones now," he said, naming Australia's most prestigious department store. "Ladies' fashion buyer, is that right?"

Had he asked after her, or had someone told him what she did for a living?

"That's right."

"I suppose that means you've been jetting around, checking out the latest fashion shows?" he asked.

"As much as I can," she said. She could brag about Paris, New York and London, but she had no need to impress Cal. He was just an old work colleague. No big deal.

"I was admiring your boots when you came in," he said, and they both glanced down at her dark red, hand-tooled Western boots. "They look like the real deal."

"They are. Straight out of Texas."

She was very aware of the way his gaze travelled back up her jeans-clad legs and over her breasts before it returned to her face. She felt a flare of excitement when she saw the desire in his eyes.

Unbidden, a handful of sense memories raced across her mind: the feel of his long, strong fingers stroking her body, the way he used to whisper in her ear as he drove her to her climax, the aching, needful fullness of his body moving inside hers.

She licked her lips and tucked her other hand into her back pocket to stop herself from reaching for him.

Then she realized what she was doing and she snapped to attention.

Pathetic. Ten years, and he cocks his little finger and you're ready to go on the spot. Too sad for words, Taylor.

"So, is your wife here?" she asked pointedly. Time to nip this flirtation—if that was what this was—in the bud.

Cal held up his left hand, displaying his ringless fingers.

"Divorced," he said. "Papers just came through. How about you?"

Divorced. He was divorced. Which meant he was free. Available.

"I'm not married," she said evasively.

"But you're living with someone, aren't you?" Cal asked.

Becky blinked. He *had* done his homework.

"Not anymore."

He looked pleased. She glanced away to break the spell he was weaving around her. She'd always found him fatally attractive. Right from the very first day when she'd looked up from reading a book in the staff room at Hannigan's and Cal had been standing in the doorway, a dark-haired god with blue eyes and a roguish smile. She'd been nineteen years old, and his innate charm had hit her like a freight train.

Even though she knew it smacked of retreat, she cast a look over her shoulder, scanning the party for an escape route.

"Look, there's Cheryl. I haven't seen her in ages," she said with relief. "I'd better go say hi or she'll kill me."

She had a smile fixed firmly in place when she turned back to him.

"Great to see you, Cal," she said.

Before he could say anything else, she turned and walked away.

CAL WATCHED her walk all the way across the room. More specifically, he watched her ass. Becky had always had a great ass—full, high, firm—and time had not altered it one iota.

God, she looked good. And she was single. He couldn't believe his luck. If he was completely honest with himself, she'd been the main reason behind his appearance at the reunion tonight. Sure, he'd wanted to catch up with a few old buddies, but it was Becky who had really drawn him. For ten years, the memory of their time together had burned bright as the hottest, most sexually satisfying time of his life. They hadn't been able to get enough of each other. He could still remember how desperate he used to be to get his hands on her smooth, creamy skin after a full shift working alongside her. More than once they'd wound up in the backseat of his car in the parking lot or in the dark corner behind the box crusher in the stock room, tearing at each other's clothes until he was inside her, giving her what they both wanted.

Was it any wonder that his thoughts had gravitated toward her now that he was a free man again?

He kept his gaze on her as she joined the group of ex-Hannigan's employees near the bar. Her hair was longer than when he'd known her. Back then, she'd kept her curls short and well-tamed, but he liked the way they cascaded around her shoulders tonight, the overhead lighting picking out rich highlights in the tumbled, dark mass. She'd put on a little weight, just enough to make her hips rounder and her breasts fuller, but her face was exactly the way he remembered it—the small, upturned nose, the full lips, the big brown eyes. She had the smoothest, clearest skin of any woman he'd ever known, and he could still recall the way he used to chase the blushes across her body when he had her naked in his bed.

Cal registered the tightness in his jeans. If he didn't stop staring, he was going to embarrass himself in a very public way. He hadn't expected to be so struck by her. When he'd hoped that she'd be here, when he'd speculated as to whether the old fire would still be there between them, he hadn't imagined anything like the heat that had ripped through him the moment he saw her. It had honestly been as though the years had fallen away and they were two kids again—two kids who desperately wanted to jump each other's bones.

Across the room, Becky laughed and brushed a stray curl away from her cheek, tucking it behind her ear. Even though he'd been staring at her shamelessly for the past few minutes, she hadn't glanced his way once.

He was forced to a reluctant conclusion—that the heat he was feeling was one-sided and only one of them was interested in bone-jumping.

It had been a long time between drinks; it had been crazy to think that there might be something left between them. Just because his thoughts had constantly drifted to her over the years, wondering what she was doing, who she was with, who was to say that hers had done the same?

Which left him standing alone at a reunion with no beer in his hand and a hard-on in his jeans. Not exactly a recipe for social success.

Forcing himself to look away, Cal shoved a hand into his pocket and rejoined the group of men he'd been hanging with before Becky entered and rocked his world off its axis.

He had the answer to the question that his body had asked when he received the invitation to the reunion—yes, Becky was still the hottest woman he'd ever known. And no, he would not be getting a chance to relive history.

A damn shame, but he would survive.

BECKY WAS so tense and wired after she got home from the reunion that her T-shirt was damp with perspiration. Nervous energy, caused by pretending that she didn't care a hoot about Cal all night. What a joke.

The truth was, she'd been painfully aware of his every move. His laugh, who he was talking to, what he ate or drank. Seeing him so unexpectedly had really thrown her for a loop.

If there was one saving grace to the whole evening, it was that she was a better actress than she'd ever given herself credit for. Despite how she'd been feeling privately, she was pretty damned sure that no one had guessed how she really felt—least of all Cal himself. She'd been cool with him every step of the way, even when he'd approached her again after dinner and spent half an hour lounging in a chair talking to her and Carolyn about old times. She'd been supremely conscious of every pass his blue-eyed gaze made over her body and her face—but not once had she allowed him to see how much his slow, lazy appraisals affected her.

Being with the Hannigan's crowd had been the perfect incentive to keep her guard up. Carolyn had been well aware of her crush on Cal all those years ago, and she'd been thrilled when Becky and Cal had finally gotten together. When it had all fallen in a heap after just a month, Carolyn had been a sympathetic and supportive friend, but Becky's pride had demanded that she keep the extent of her hurt to herself. To Carolyn and the rest of her Hannigan's colleagues, she and Cal had had a fling for a few weeks that hadn't worked out. They'd both moved on, and only Becky knew how big the hole was that Cal had left in her heart—and that was the way she wanted it to stay.

As Becky shed her sweaty clothes and stepped beneath the shower, she forced thoughts of Cal to one side. He was the past, history. She wanted to wash him off the way she was washing away the stress and tension of her evening. Down the plughole with him, and may he never blight her life again. He'd wreaked enough damage already, thank you very much.

After towelling herself dry, she slid into bed and switched the light off. Closing her eyes, she acknowledged to herself that she was pleased to have survived the evening with her dignity in tact. Willing sleep to come, she slowly relaxed her body into the mattress.

She should have known better. In the months following their breakup, dreams of Cal had tortured her endlessly. Tonight, she was revisited by them with a vengeance.

There was no narrative to her dreams, just flashes of memory twisted into new shapes by her subconscious. Images of Cal's tall, strong body naked and ready for her, the too-familiar need to be close to him pulling at her, the tearing hurt of knowing that having had her, he didn't want her anymore.

She woke panting, the sheets twisted around her legs. She growled low in her throat as she rolled from her bed and grabbed the low-dose sleeping tablets she kept in her travel kit to help conquer jet lag. Downing one with a mouthful of water, she returned to bed, smoothed out the sheets and pummelled her pillow into a new shape.

"Get out of my head," she told Cal, even though she felt a little crazy doing it.

Rolling onto her side, she stared at the darkened square of her bedroom window until the tablets kicked in and she drifted into dreamless sleep.

Tomorrow was another day—a beautiful, fresh, Cal-free day. Bring it on.

YOU'RE THIRTY-ONE, Cal. Too old for this kind of crap.

It was three in the morning, and he was standing naked in the living room of his penthouse apartment, staring out at the darkened waters of Sydney Harbour. To his left, the bridge hung like a fairy-lit coat hanger in the sky, and all around the harbor, lights twinkled in the predawn blackness.

Everyone was asleep—except for him. He was too horny to sleep. Too restless and unsettled. He should have asked Becky out tonight. He'd been waiting to get her alone before he tried his luck in case she shot him down in flames, but it had never happened. Possibly because she hadn't wanted it to happen. The jury was still out on that one. Now he wished he'd thrown caution to the winds and just asked her, witnesses or no witnesses.

He walked into the kitchen, fumbling in the dark for a brandy balloon before pouring himself an inch of the golden liquid. Back in the living room, he hit the play button on his stereo and sank into the comforting soft leather of his couch. The mellow sounds of Coldplay filled the room as he sipped at the brandy and let his mind wander.

In the twelve months that he'd been back in Australia, a lot had changed in his life. Generally he had a sense that they'd changed for the better. His marriage hadn't survived the changes, but he was becoming more and more philosophical about that. In the end, he and Natalie had wanted different things. When she'd pushed him too hard, he'd pushed back.

He liked being back in Sydney. It was such a dynamic city, full of brash confidence and energy. And the weather—it was unfair even to think of comparing the gray heaviness of a London winter with the clear blue skies of home. Then there was his company. He and his partner, Daniel Strong, had attracted an exclusive set of clients, all of them high-end, and business was booming. Hence his penthouse apartment and very nice lifestyle.

He was quietly satisfied with all that he'd achieved in his thirty-one years, give or take one divorce and a few foolish decisions here and there along the way. So why was he sitting buck-naked on his sofa, swilling brandy in the vain hope that it would send him to sleep?

Becky Taylor. She of the perfect ass and the creamy breasts and the fiery passion of yesteryear. Closing his eyes, he relived the moment when she'd walked in the door tonight and stood there in all her red-cowboy-booted glory.

To hell with it. He was going to ask her out. As soon as it was remotely close to business hours, he'd look up her number at David Jones and call her. That was the only way he was going to get any closure on this; he felt it in his bones.

As though he'd finally given his tired body what it needed to sleep, he suddenly felt gritty-eyed with weariness.

"About time," he muttered to himself as he downed the last mouthful of brandy.

First thing tomorrow, he was making his play.

"BECKY, how are you?" the deep voice asked.

Becky's fingers clenched the phone receiver and she shifted to the edge of her seat.

"Cal? How did you get my number?" she queried stupidly.

"I looked it up. I wanted to ask you something, something I should have asked you last night at the reunion."

Becky swiveled in her chair and stared out at the spectacular view she had of Sydney's Hyde Park, a swathe of oak-and-plane-tree-dotted open space that created an oasis in the middle of the city.

"Yes?" she asked cautiously.

A surge of excitement raced up her spine. She squeezed her thighs together, sending a silent signal to her body— *Not on your life, pal. Not in a million years is* that *going to happen.*

"Will you have dinner with me?"

She was holding her breath, and she let it ease out slowly. Cal was asking her out. She hadn't imagined the spark of interest in his eyes last night. He still found her attractive. He wanted to explore that attraction.

All very good reasons to say no. But she hesitated, the word on the tip of her tongue. The silence stretched between them as her mind raced. If she said no, what would he think? That she wasn't up to the temptation? Worse, that she still had feelings for him? Pride demanded that she protect herself, as it had demanded all those years ago that she walk away from their brief relationship with her head high when he told her he wasn't ready for a big commitment, that things were moving too fast for him.

"Sure. When were you thinking?" she said.

It was her turn to be on the receiving end of surprised silence. He hadn't expected her to say yes. Interesting.

"How about tomorrow night?" he suggested. "Café Sydney?"

"I love it there. Sure. Shall we say eight?"

"I'll be there."

"You'd better be, since you called me," she said.

He laughed, the sound low and deep and compelling.

"See you, Beck," he said. Then she was listening to the dial tone.

Regret kicked in immediately. Was she *insane?* She had no business going to a cosy dinner with the man who had snapped her heart in two so efficiently all those years ago. Talk about being a glutton for punishment. Why on earth would she put herself in such a precarious position, especially when it was clear that Cal wanted to sleep with her again?

She was reaching for the phone before she realized she had no way of contacting him. She didn't know the name of his business, and she was almost certain he wouldn't have a publicly listed home number. A quick check on the Internet confirmed it. She slumped back in her seat and slapped her forehead with the palm of her hand.

"Stupid," she said, just as a familiar face appeared in her office doorway.

"Oooh, self abuse. Please don't stop on my account," Gareth said, swaying his way toward her guest chair.

Gareth was her opposite number in male fashion, and so gay that one of the secretaries had jokingly dubbed him "super gay" at the office Christmas party one year. It was a badge Gareth wore with pride—literally. In the annual Gay Pride parade last March, he'd worn a cape and a skin-tight Lycra bodysuit with a specially designed SG insignia on his chest. Now, he folded his long, slender legs and rested his beautifully manicured hands on them as he waited for her to continue.

"It's not the same with someone watching," Becky told him.

"Tell me about it," he said, rolling his eyes dramatically. "This is why I always advocate video cameras—if you must share, technology makes it so much less intrusive."

Becky laughed. "Sometimes I think you have a Ph.D. in innuendo."

Gareth looked pleased. "I do try, darling. Now, tell Uncle Gareth what's wrong. You know I always offer the best advice."

It was true—for an outwardly frivolous person, he was very perceptive. Or, as he liked to put it, his "emotional IQ topped out at freakin' genius."

"Just wrestling with a ghost from the past," she said, shrugging. "An old flame asked me out to dinner, and I stupidly said yes."

Gareth's eyebrows wiggled.

"How old is the flame? And is there a spark still?"

"Ten years. And it's dead and gone. Just my pride left to rake over the coals, really."

"But he wants to reignite it?" Gareth asked, really getting into the whole fire metaphor thing.

"I guess so. I need to track down his phone number and cancel."

Gareth looked down his nose at her, and somehow she found herself telling him everything: how she'd fallen for Cal the moment she met him, how she'd found out almost straightaway that he had a girlfriend, how she'd worked alongside him for two years, the tension between them building every day. And how she and Cal had gotten together the moment he broke up with his girlfriend and fireworks had exploded between them.

"We saw each other almost every single day for a month. I utterly adored him. And then he told me that he wasn't ready for another serious relationship after coming out of three years with another woman."

"Ouch. How old were you both?"

"Twenty-one when we broke up. Intellectually, I understood where he was coming from. He was a good-looking guy, he was studying, he'd been tied down for three years. He wanted to party. But I felt like I'd been given the keys to the kingdom then had them snatched back again. I'd been in love with him for a year, and I only got to have him for a month. Not nearly long enough."

"Poor Becky," Gareth said.

"Yeah, well." She sat up a little straighter. "Anyway, it's all ancient history."

"Uh-uh. No way. You have unfinished business with this man. He cut you off before you were ready. You need to readdress the balance. You definitely can't cancel. What you have to do, Becky, my girl, is knock that man off his feet, dazzle him utterly, then walk away and leave him with his tongue hanging out and his zipper bulging. Revenge," Gareth said, eyes wide for dramatic effect.

It was a compelling argument. She loved the idea of letting Cal think he was charming her all night, only to pull the rug out from beneath him at the last minute. It would give him a small taste of his own medicine.

"You're tempted, I can tell," Gareth said. "I should warn you I have a Ph.D. in temptation, too."

"It seems a little petty," Becky said.

It was a token objection, and they both knew it. She was already imagining the look on Cal's face when she sashayed away from him. Not that she'd be able to see his reaction, not having eyes in the back of her head. But she could imagine it. Oh, yeah, she could imagine it.

"Petty, schmetty. Life hands us very few moments to be true divas, Becky. We have to grab them with both hands and hang on tight." Gareth clutched at two fistfuls of air, hauling them flamboyantly toward his thin chest.

"Okay. I'll do it," Becky said impulsively.

Gareth smiled and clapped his hands. "Girlfriend, you will *so* not regret this," he crowed.

Becky grinned back at him, feeling empowered all of a sudden. If she were a man, she'd beat her chest and give a Tarzan yell. Instead, she sat back and crossed her legs, feeling very feline and satisfied.

Yes, indulging in a little revenge fantasy was petty. But it wasn't as though anyone was going to get hurt, was it? Just Cal's ego a little, perhaps. She was certain he had plenty to spare.

"I'll need a new dress," she said.

"Oh, yes. And killer shoes. And underwear—something really slutty."

Becky raised an eyebrow.

"It's a psychological thing," Gareth said. "Trust me. He will never know it's there, but you will. You'll feel like a warrior queen."

A warrior queen. After years of feeling not good enough and discarded.

It sounded like a damned good exchange to her.

CHAPTER TWO

HER CONFIDENCE lasted until she was standing in front of her bathroom mirror the next evening, mascara wand in hand. Her whole body was shaking so much she was in serious danger of taking out an eye. She had to steady her wrist with her other hand before she could get a decent coat on.

Not a great sign.

She glanced down at her Slutty Avenger underwear. Her breasts were pushed up by a black satin-and-lace balconette bra. She wore matching panties and black garters and sheer black stockings. She was dressed to tempt and seduce. She should be feeling in control.

She *so* wasn't.

Becky reached for the deep red silk dress she and Gareth had chosen for tonight's dinner. It was part of the latest shipment of couture they'd received from Paris—a sleek, fitted, cocktail-length dress with a startlingly low back and neckline and a slit up one side. If she sat right, Cal would get an eyeful of stocking and garter. She'd practiced for ten minutes earlier in front of the mirror and was confident she had the move nailed.

She slid her feet into a pair of suede stilettos in the same deep red. They made her feet ache after about five minutes, but like the underwear, they made her feel sexier, stronger, braver than she really was.

She sprayed on perfume, hitting all her pulse points. Then she picked up her elegant clutch purse. She was ready.

She was also trembling with anticipation and nerves.

So much for being the Slutty Avenger.

She took a cab to Café Sydney. Traffic was light and she arrived early. Taking the elevator to the top floor of the heritage-listed Customs House, she veered away from the restaurant's reception desk and made her way to the ladies' room. Sitting on the closed lid of a toilet, she waited a full fifteen minutes before re-emerging.

Childish, but her knees were knocking together and she needed every bid of edge she could get.

Cal rose to his feet as the waitress led her to him. He'd scored a coveted balcony table that offered them privacy and a spectacular view of the Opera House and the Harbour Bridge.

"I was beginning to think you'd stood me up."

He had no idea how close she'd come to doing just that.

She went to flick her hair over her shoulder, then remembered she'd worn her curls in a sophisticated updo. She dropped her hand lamely to her side.

Smooth, Becky. Real smooth.

"Traffic was bad," she fibbed.

He smiled, the left side of his mouth quirking up just a little bit more than the right.

"I ordered champagne. I hope you still like it."

He looked deep into her eyes as he said it, and a fierce, hot memory rose up inside her—Cal pouring champagne over her breasts, Cal dipping his tongue into her belly button to suck out precious drops, the cold fizz of champagne bubbles tingling between her thighs.

She opened her mouth to say something sassy and clever and tantalizing.

"Yes."

His smile widened. He was wearing a charcoal shirt with French cuffs and a pair of black wool trousers. Discreet cufflinks glinted at his wrists. His hair gleamed darkly in the candlelight. His skin was tanned, and his eyes looked incredibly blue by contrast.

He was so damn sexy. She wasn't sure what it was about him that had always got to her so badly. Sure, he was good-looking, but she'd slept with other good-looking men. And yes, he was charming, but so were a lot of other guys. There was just something about the knowing, slightly naughty look in his eyes, and the ready curve of his lips, and the way he seemed so comfortable in his own skin….

He signaled the waiter and a glass of pale-yellow champagne appeared in front of her. Cal raised his.

"To old friends," he said.

She slid her fingers around the cool glass of the champagne flute.

"Friends? Hmmm."

That was what the Slutty Avenger would say, right?

He tilted his head to one side. "Okay. To old lovers."

She couldn't exactly argue with that.

She hoped like hell that her hand wouldn't shake when she lifted her glass.

"Much more accurate," she said. "I think we were too busy having sex to ever really be friends."

He laughed. "True. Maybe I should have said to great sex, in the interests of being really accurate."

She raised her glass to her mouth. Her hand was blessedly steady. The champagne tickled her tongue and tasted pleasingly dry in her throat.

"Nice."

He sat back in his chair. "So, tell me about the last ten years," he said.

She crossed her legs, but the table blocked his view of her stockings. She frowned. She hadn't thought about that minor detail when she'd practiced earlier that evening. She *so* wasn't cut out for this femme fatale business. Definitely an amateur.

"What do you want to know?"

"How did you get into fashion buying?" he asked. "You were studying economics when we were working together."

She explained that she'd dropped out of her degree in the third year and worked her way up from the shop floor, and he told her about his start-up IT company. By the time they'd given their orders and worked their way through their starters, some of the tension banding her chest had eased.

Probably the champagne had a bit to do with that. By her count, she was on her third glass by the time their mains were slid in front of them. She felt as buoyant and full of potential as the bubbles beading her glass.

"I like your hair long," he said as the waiter moved away from their table. "It suits you."

It was the first personal comment he'd made since their toast.

"I keep toying with cutting it short again, but it takes so long to grow. And the in-between stage was a bitch. I felt like a human fuzz ball for months."

"Don't cut it," he said. His gaze slid over her face before delving into the deep shadow between her breasts.

That quickly, the tension was back between them. She squeezed her thighs together under the table, aware of the heat building between them.

She eyed his body and wondered if he still had the strong tan lines he'd had as a younger man. He'd surfed and spent a lot of time in the outdoors, and she could still recall the way the rich nut-brown of his flat, muscled belly had given way to paler skin low on his hips. She could also remember how quickly she could get him hard, and the way he always stared intently into her eyes as he slid inside her, hard and hot and ready…

"I've thought about you a lot over the years," Cal said, his words an uncanny echo of her own thoughts.

He cut a slice off his porterhouse steak. "Wondered what you were doing. Who you were doing it with."

Her heart kicked against her ribs and she swallowed a huge lump of lust. All she could think about was what it would be like to be with him again. To feel his skin against hers, his breath in her ear, his body moving against hers.

Their eyes locked across the table, and she knew he was thinking the same thing.

If she was really the Slutty Avenger, she would be doing a victory dance right about now. She had him exactly where she wanted him—hot for her, putting himself on the line. All she had to do was string him along for another hour or so, then sashay away, leaving him with a hard-on and the bill.

But she wasn't the Slutty Avenger. Not by a long shot. She was practically panting, and a throbbing ache echoed her heartbeat between her thighs. She wanted him. Bad. Just as bad as when they'd both been twenty-one years old and full of raging hormones.

She stared at him, her mind working like a hamster in a wheel, trying to get a grip on the situation. He was too sexy, too tempting. She wasn't going to be able to walk away from the invitation in his eyes.

As soon as she admitted as much to herself, a strange relief flooded through her. She was going to sleep with him. She was going to run her hands over his body and let him run his hands over hers. She was going to taste his skin and welcome him inside her. They were going to revisit the past in the most physical, real way possible.

But it will just be sex. That's all. I'll take what I want from him, and I'll walk away, she promised herself. A variation on her original plan, and nothing more.

It would be even more effective this way. She'd get to have a good time, and finally put the ghosts of the past to bed. And she'd get to walk away leaving *him* wanting more.

She closed her eyes for a second, savoring the knowledge of what was to come. Then she opened them and locked eyes with him again. His blue gaze was dark and smoky with intent. They stared at each other, neither of them eating.

She smiled a slow, anticipatory smile. She felt light, as though the champagne she'd been drinking had carbonated her blood. He smiled back at her. Her breathing was shallow, her belly muscles tight. Her breasts tingled, and she didn't need to look down to know they were already hardening with desire.

"Are you hungry?" he asked, his voice a low rumble.

"Not for food," she said.

He stood in one smooth, powerful move. "Then let's get out of here."

She stood. He stepped close and took her hand, looking deeply into her eyes.

"I thought I'd exaggerated how sexy you were in my mind," he said. "I thought there was no way you could live up to my memories."

His gaze swept over her, and she felt a surge of feminine power. He wanted her as badly as she wanted him.

He turned, tugging on her hand as he pulled her toward the reception desk so he could take care of the bill. She eyed his broad shoulders as they walked, his words echoing in her mind.

He'd thought about her. And he thought she was sexy. Sexier even than his memories of her.

Triumph and relief and need coursed through her. He shot a glance across to her as he handed over his credit card. The animal need in his eyes made her forget everything sane and sensible.

No man had ever affected her quite like Cal. No man had ever gotten her as hot or made her feel as decadent and wanton and wild.

Trepidation twisted in her stomach as she remembered how she'd felt in the weeks and months after they'd parted ways all those years ago. Empty and dissatisfied and terrified that she'd never find another man who would make her feel as good.

Was she about to make a very stupid mistake? Was she willfully deluding herself that she could handle this situation, that she could handle him?

"Come on," Cal murmured near her ear as he found her hand with his again and pulled her toward the elevator.

She followed him because she wanted to and because she had to. But she wasn't completely gone. No matter what, she would not stay the night with him. She made the commitment to herself as the elevator doors closed and Cal put his arms around her from behind and pulled her back against him.

Her breath got caught somewhere between her lungs and her throat as he splayed one big hand over her belly and the other just under her breasts.

"This is a great dress," he said, the warmth of his chest pressing against her bare back. "I've been wanting to get you out of it all night."

"That was pretty much the idea," she said.

She felt the warm, gentle press of his lips on the side of her neck, followed by the wet lick of his tongue. Desire shot through her like lightning as she arched her neck to allow him greater access.

"Becky, if you had any idea what you do to me…" he murmured against her skin.

Her whole body was trembling with need and anticipation. His hands clenched the fabric of her dress as he pulled her closer. She could feel the hardness of his erection against the curve of her bottom.

This felt so good. *He* felt so good.

She twisted in his arms so that she was facing him. She rose up on the balls of her feet and kissed him, her lips opening over his, her tongue sliding inside the hot, slick darkness of his mouth to caress his tongue, to suck on it, to bite it gently, suggestively.

Cal groaned low in his chest and grabbed her butt,

dragging her closer to him and grinding his hips into hers.

"I don't think I can wait," she confessed as they broke from their kiss.

His cheekbones were dark with desire, his lips glistened from their kiss. He slapped a hand toward the buttons on the elevator wall, and the elevator stopped at the next floor.

Without a word they both stepped into the muted darkness of a four-sided balconied walkway that ran around the open space at the centre of the building. While Café Sydney occupied the top floor of Customs House, several prestigious businesses had their headquarters there. Becky figured they must have exited onto one of the commercial floors.

They walked the length of one side of the walkway until Cal found a waiting area tucked into the corner of the building. Two floor-to-ceiling walls of glass came together to offer yet another amazing view of the harbor.

Neither of them gave it so much as a glance.

Cal moved in on her with intent, his fingers sliding up her neck and into her hair as his mouth angled down on hers. His tongue was hard and demanding in her mouth as his body pressed against hers. The pins and combs holding her hair in place fell to the ground and her hair was suddenly loose about her shoulders.

"I've been wanting to do that all night, too," Cal murmured as he kissed his way across to her ear.

She gasped as his tongue traced the inner curve before plunging inside. She was so ready for him it physically hurt. She reached for the buttons of his shirt, sliding them open by feel alone as Cal continued to plunder her ear.

Then she had her hands on his chest. His skin felt hot and smooth and she pressed her palms flat against him and curled her fingers possessively into the resilient strength of his pectoral muscles. He was bigger, broader than when they'd been younger. She mapped his width with her hands, then found his nipples and began to tease them.

His hands found the zipper at the back of her dress. The hiss of it descending was a seductive whisper. Cal lifted his head from her ear to gaze at her as he pushed her dress off her shoulders. Red silk pooled at her waist and he mouthed a four-letter word as he took in the creaminess of her breasts pouring over the black satin cups of her bra.

His hands slid up her ribcage and onto her breasts, cupping them, molding them. Then he pushed the satin down beneath her breasts and his fingers found her nipples.

He pressed kisses into her neck as he teased her with his hands, squeezing gently, flicking his thumbs back and forth, shaping her with his palms.

"Everything is better than I remembered," he said against her skin, his voice rough with desire.

She was so overwhelmed by sensation and lust that she could barely think. She knew she should probably be more worried about the fact that Cal was pressing her against a thick glass window, and that anyone glancing across from one of the neighboring buildings could see them. She simply didn't care. There was only one thing on her mind—satisfaction. She wanted Cal inside her, pounding into her, giving her what she'd fantasized about in the unacknowledged, dark corners of her mind for ten years.

Her hands shook as she reached for his belt buckle. His erection strained against the zipper of his trousers, thick and powerful, a promise she was about to collect on. He sprang into her hands as she released him. So hard. So silky and yet so strong at the same time. She wrapped her fingers around him as he lowered his head to her breasts and sucked a nipple into his mouth.

She clenched her hand around him as need pierced her, arrowing through her body to where she throbbed for him. He bit her nipple, then sucked it, hard.

She was panting, and so was he. He smoothed his hands down her hips, found the hem of her dress. She moaned as he slid his hands up her stockings. Then he was caressing naked skin, and his fingers were gliding between her legs to where she needed him the most.

The firm press of his fingers against the damp satin of her panties made her moan again. He gave an appreciative sound in the back of his throat as he stroked her once, twice. Then he slid his hand inside her panties and into her slick readiness.

A shudder racked his body as he felt how wet and hot she was. She pushed his trousers and boxers down his hips, then stroked her hand up and down his shaft. Her thumb found a single bead of moisture on the plump head of his penis and she knew he was just as turned on as she was.

"Becky," he groaned against her breast.

"Yes," she said.

His thumbs hooked into the waistband of her panties and pushed down. She took over when they reached her knees, stepping out of them. Cal immediately pushed her back against the window and hooked one of her legs up over his hip. She felt the delicious pressure of his hard-on sliding between her folds. Then he slid inside her, big and hard and thick.

"Oh, boy," she panted as she stretched around him. Her memory had been holding out on her, big-time. He felt so right, so perfect inside her.

He huffed out a laugh.

"Oh, boy? Is that the best you can do?" he asked. His hands gripped her bare backside as they both savored the moment.

She stared into his eyes. "I can do a lot better than that."

She tilted her hips and started to tell him what he was doing to her, her words a whisper against his skin as she kissed his neck and his mouth and his ear and his chest. Cal's grip intensified on her butt as he began to thrust into her—long, slow, powerful strokes that pushed her closer to the edge with each penetration.

She lifted her other leg so that he had her entire weight. She hooked her ankles together behind his back, gripped his shoulders and held on for dear life as he pressed her against the glass and pounded into her with increasing urgency.

"Yes," she sobbed as her climax began to sweep her away.

Cal's mouth found hers. Her desire peaked. She opened her eyes and gazed into Cal's blue eyes as she came and came and came, her body tightening around his, her breath harsh and desperate. His lips pulled back into an animal snarl as he found his own climax, but his eyes never left hers. He stared at her the whole time that his body lost itself in hers, his fingers clutched into her backside, his thighs trembling.

For a few precious seconds afterward, he rested his forehead against hers and they simply breathed together. Then he released his grip on her butt and she slid down his body and stood on her own two feet.

Her body vibrated with satisfaction and the echo of passion. Her breasts were still wet from his kisses. Her dress was rucked up around her hips, the silk crushed.

She pushed her hair back off her forehead. Cal was busy tucking himself back into his clothes. She tugged her bra up over her breasts and slid her arms through the sleeves of her dress.

"Could you zip me?" she asked, turning her back to him.

His fingers were warm against the skin of her back as he eased the zipper along its tracks.

She wasn't about to climb into her underwear in

front of him. Instead, she bent to collect her panties and stuffed them into her evening bag. Very elegant. She was sure there was a paragraph covering just this situation in an etiquette manual somewhere, but she'd never read it.

Cal was buttoning his shirt, and she watched him slide the last button home.

Time to walk away. Time to regain the dignity she'd lost ten years ago when he'd broken her heart.

"Well, Cal, dinner was lovely," she said with what she hoped was a casual smile.

"What we ate of it, you mean," he said drily.

She shrugged a shoulder.

"Dessert was worth it." She took a step forward and pressed a kiss to the angle of his jaw. "Thanks. It was great to catch up."

He frowned as she turned away.

"Where are you going?" he asked. He sounded surprised.

"Home. Where else?"

"I thought we could go back to my place," he said.

Despite what they'd just done together, a hot rush of desire washed through her as she thought about what that would mean. More Cal. Much more.

What could it hurt? You still won't stay the night. And you'll get him out of your system once and for all.

Becky frowned. She'd been chipping away at her own resolve ever since she'd said yes to Cal's dinner invitation. She had to draw the line somewhere, or there'd be precious little of Operation Dignity left to salvage. And then she'd be back where she'd been all those years ago—left gasping and needy when Cal had had his fill of her.

"I've got an early start tomorrow," she said. "But thanks for the offer."

"Right."

She forced a smile. She had to get out of there before the word *yes* escaped her lips.

"See you round, Cal," she said.

Then she turned on her heel and walked away.

CAL STARED as Becky walked away from him once again, her high heels clicking on the tiled floor.

They'd just had stupendous, gut-wrenching sex, and she'd calmly put herself back together and said goodbye as though it was nothing special.

Not what he'd expected. Not by a long shot. But then, none of it had been. He'd known he was still attracted to her. The reunion had illustrated that in no uncertain terms. But he hadn't expected to be so hot for her that he'd abandon dinner and find the nearest dark corner to bury himself in her. He was a seasoned, experienced businessman, for Pete's sake. Not a randy kid anymore.

And he hadn't expected it to feel so good to be with her again, to touch her, taste her. She'd felt familiar, but also excitingly different, and she'd been so turned-on that he'd almost embarrassed himself before he could give her what they both wanted.

He frowned. He still couldn't believe she'd just

asked him to zip her up and then left him standing there. In the old days, Becky had been affectionate, warm. She'd never been able to get enough of him. And he'd never been able to get enough of her. All that intensity had scared the shit out of him hard on the heels of his breakup with Virginia, his long-term girlfriend. As blown away as he'd been by the sex, as much as he'd always enjoyed Becky's wit and sense of humor and sharp take on the world, he'd felt as though he was jumping feetfirst into another serious commitment. He'd been twenty years old. It had freaked him out. All his mates had been partying, seeing the world, having one-night stands. And he'd been in danger of turning into Mr. Monogamy.

He'd told Becky how he was feeling, that he wanted to pull things back, lighten up. She'd been upset. She'd cried. But then she'd pulled herself together. She'd said she understood where he was coming from. They'd worked alongside each other for a whole year after their short, tumultuous relationship had ended, work buddies who knew each other's bodies really, really well.

He'd still been hot for her. He wasn't a saint. They'd been so good together, he'd been unable to look at her without remembering. He'd even tried to score with her again on a casual basis when he'd had too much to drink at one of the Hannigan's Christmas parties. She'd turned him down. Then the next thing he knew, she'd quit, and the only contact he'd had with her was through the staff grapevine.

Cal ran a hand through his hair, then checked to make sure his fly was closed and his shirt buttoned properly. Crossing to the elevator, he punched the button and checked his watch. It was only ten. If she'd come home with him, they could have had all night.

Get over it, Cal. She didn't want anything more than what she got. Suck it up and move on.

He told himself the same thing when the urge to call her gripped him the next day. Badgering Becky with phone calls was not going to change anything.

Still, his hand hovered over the phone. He laughed at himself. He felt as though he'd regressed ten years. Time to take his own advice and get over it. They'd had a great night, a one-off. End of story.

A MONTH LATER, Cal found himself sitting in a church in the richy-rich Melbourne suburb of Toorak on a sizzling summer day, watching another former Hannigan's friend, Carolyn, walk down the aisle to marry her high-school sweetheart, Phil.

Even as he marveled at the fact that their relationship had survived the transition into adulthood and beyond, he found his gaze constantly drawn to the pew near the front of the church where Becky sat. She looked gorgeous in a dark green dress with tiny black flowers on it. Her hair was loose around her shoulders, and he spent almost as much time watching her as he did the bride and groom.

Afterward, at the reception, he arrived early in the ballroom and saw they were sitting at neighboring tables. He hesitated only a second before switching placecards with the man sitting next to her. If someone had put him on the rack and shone a light on him and demanded he tell them why he wanted to sit next to her, he would have said it was because he liked Becky. He always had. But it was also because he felt as though there was unfinished business between them. And yeah, he wanted to have her again. So sue him—sex that great didn't come along too often, in his experience.

She raised an eyebrow when she entered the ballroom a few minutes later and found him seated at her table.

"I could have sworn Carolyn said she was putting me next to Roger Lee," she said.

He gave her his best faux-innocent look, and she shook her head and laughed.

"You always were used to getting your own way," she said.

"To the victor the spoils."

He stood and held her chair out for her.

"Wow. Next thing I know, you'll be throwing your tux jacket over the nearest puddle for me," she said.

He inhaled her spicy-fresh perfume as she sank into the chair. She smelled as good as she looked. And he already knew she tasted twice as good.

"What can I say? I've picked up a little polish over the years."

She eyed his suit knowingly. "More than a little."

She reached out and rubbed the fabric of his lapel between thumb and forefinger.

"Armani, yes?"

He shrugged, quelling an adolescent surge of pride that she'd noticed his expensive threads.

"If you say so."

Her eyes brightened with amusement. "Don't tell me—you have so many designer tuxes in your wardrobe, you can't remember which one you brought down to Melbourne with you?"

He smiled back at her. "Something like that."

"Oooh. Big guy. I bet you own your own company and everything."

She laughed then, and the low huskiness of it hit him in the gut. He shifted in his chair, aware that he was rock-hard for her all over again. His gaze dipped to the swell of her breasts, outlined by the silky fabric of her dress.

"You look great," he said.

The smile was gone from her face when he looked up and their eyes locked. Something dark and hot flickered in the depths of her big brown eyes, and she swallowed visibly.

A slow smile curved his lips. He might be hard, but she was just as aware of him. He knew it the way he knew the earth wasn't flat, the way he knew cats hated dogs and dogs hated postmen.

"Where are you staying?" he asked.

"The Hyatt. You?"

"The Adelphi," he said, naming one of Melbourne's smaller, boutique hotels.

She licked her lips. He flicked his eyes toward the

bridal table where Carolyn and Phil were talking and laughing with family and friends. It was going to be a long few hours while they waited out the meal and the speeches and the dancing. Until he could get Becky alone again.

He made it to the end of the main course before sitting next to her and not touching her the way he wanted to became too much for him. He felt like a kid again, out of control. He wanted what he wanted—and he wanted it *now.*

She was talking to the person sitting on her other side, and he waited impatiently for her to turn to him.

"Want to go for a walk?" he asked.

"A walk?" She arched an eyebrow at him, a smile quirking the corner of her mouth.

"Yeah. A walk."

He found her knee under the table.

She sucked in a surprised breath.

He slowly pleated the soft fabric of her skirt beneath his fingers as he gathered it up, inch by inch. She stiffened in her chair as his hand found her silky stockinged leg.

"Tell me you're wearing garters again," he said, fascinated by the way her pupils had dilated with desire.

"Stay-ups. Garters ruin the line of this dress," she said.

He glided his hand up her thigh until he hit bare flesh. She shivered. He slid his hand higher and encountered the smoothness of her satin underwear.

"What color?" he asked quietly.

Her eyelids masked her eyes for a beat before she answered.

"Red."

"One of my favorites."

He stroked her through the satin, and she bit her lip.

"Cal," she said.

He wasn't sure if it was a plea or a warning. He knew what he wanted it to be. Leaning back in his chair, he glanced toward the entrance to the ballroom, then back toward the bridal party.

"I figure we've got about fifteen minutes before they even think about cutting the cake," he said.

She took a deep breath.

"Yes."

WHAT AM I doing? One look, one touch and I'm trailing after Cal again, looking for someplace to get hot with him. This is insane. I'm insane.

Becky knew she should pull her hand free and go back to the table and ignore Cal for the rest of the evening. She also knew she wasn't going to. She'd been dreaming about him for four weeks, ever since their dinner. She might have walked away from him, but he'd gotten under her skin.

Not like when they were kids. Definitely not like that. She'd assured herself of that fact over and over. This was purely a sex thing. But it had still driven her crazy for the past month.

As Gareth had said when she'd given him a shame-faced, bare-bones report of her evening at Café Sydney, she sucked at being the Slutty Avenger.

Right now, however, revenge was the last thing on her mind. As always with Cal, lust had short-circuited her higher brain functions. She wanted to get off. Nothing else. She was even prepared to miss dessert for the privilege.

"In here," Cal said, and he opened a door in the hallway they were traversing and pulled her into a linen cupboard.

She laughed. "You've got to be kidding," she said, looking around at the cramped space lined with shelves piled with tablecloths and napkins.

"I'd never joke about something this serious," he said.

Then he kissed her, pressing her back against the door, one hand finding her breast through her dress, his thumb teasing her nipple into hard, demanding arousal.

"You get me so hot," he said.

She couldn't speak. She was too busy gasping as his other hand slid up under her dress and inside her panties.

"Ohhh."

He grinned at her, a wicked, knowing grin.

"Spread your legs for me, baby," he said.

She did so mindlessly, watching as Cal shrugged out of his suit jacket and threw it onto a shelf behind them. Then he was on his knees, lifting her dress, tugging at her underwear.

Her knees went weak as she understood what he wanted to do. He'd always been so good with his mouth and hands. He was one of the few men she'd been with who genuinely got off on the act of pleasing a woman.

She flattened her hands against the cool wood of the door as she felt the warmth of his breath between her thighs. And then he was tasting her, his tongue by turns delicate and rough, his hands cupping her backside as he held her close.

She shuddered and bit her lip and closed her eyes. Within minutes, her orgasm washed over her with the force of a tsunami. Then Cal was unzipping his trousers, and she was gripping his big, hard erection and guiding him once more between her thighs.

"One day, we should really consider doing this in a bedroom," he said as he took her full weight and pressed her back against the doorway.

"Shut up and kiss me," she panted.

Afterward, they put themselves back together in silence. Becky slipped out of the cupboard first and made a beeline for the ladies' room. She closed her eyes briefly when she caught sight of her reflection. She looked like a woman who'd just had two orgasms in a linen cupboard—cheeks flushed, hair mussed, lipstick smeared halfway up her cheek.

"You are such an idiot."

The woman staring back at her knew it, down to her bones. She was playing with fire. And there was only one inevitable result—she was going to get burnt.

No more. No matter what it took, this had to stop now. Before she did something even more stupid than sleep with Cal.

She took a deep breath. Then she started to erase the telltale signs of their encounter.

CHAPTER THREE

THREE WEEKS LATER, Becky stepped out of the shower and reached for the towel folded neatly on the corner of the vanity. She blotted her face dry, then briskly toweled off her body. Naked, she crossed into the bedroom to find her clothes.

"Stay the night," Cal said the moment she entered the room.

He was sprawled across his bed the way she'd left him after they'd made love for the second time that evening, deliciously naked against chocolate-brown sheets.

His blue gaze followed her every move as she reached for her underwear and began to dress.

"I can't. I've got—"

"An early start at work tomorrow," Cal said drily.

It was the same excuse she'd used every time she'd seen him over the past few weeks.

"Tomorrow's Saturday, Becky," he said, propping himself up on his elbows. "That one's not going to cut it."

"I was going to say it's my nephew's birthday, and I promised my sister that I'd go over early and help her set things up."

"What, at six in the morning?"

She pulled her linen trousers over her hips.

"No, but I've got some running around to do before I get there," she said.

Cal dropped flat onto his back and crossed his arms behind his head. For a few minutes there was nothing but the sound of her clothes rustling as she finished dressing.

"Is there some kind of unspoken rule against you staying the night that I don't know about?" he asked quietly.

Yes. It's the only way I can retain control of the situation. This way, we get what we need from each other, but I can't fool myself that it's anything more than what it is.

"It's easier this way," she said.

"How? It's two in the morning. Wouldn't it be easier just to go to sleep? I promise I won't snore or steal the sheets."

He kept his tone light, but she could hear the edge beneath it. She grabbed a scrunchie from her handbag and pulled her hair into a haphazard ponytail. This conversation had been coming for a while. Perhaps they should have had it up front when he'd called her after Carolyn and Phil's wedding. That way they would have clarified the ground rules going in. She'd thought they'd been pretty obvious, but apparently they were about to get even more so.

"Are you saying you want to turn this into a relationship, Cal?" she asked bluntly.

He blinked. The surprise in his face was like a slap. Clearly, having a relationship with her had not even crossed his mind.

"I've only been divorced three months, Becky. I'm still finding my feet again, remembering what it's like to be single."

She reached for her handbag, keeping her head down as she blinked rapidly. What had she expected him to say? Yes? That he saw her as more than just a warm body? That he'd asked her to stay because he wanted to wake up and find her lying beside him, not because he wanted to have more sex with her?

Maybe. Even though she'd convinced herself that she'd gone into this with her eyes wide open.

History repeating itself.

The thought lent steel to her spine. She eyed Cal coolly.

"You're not interested in anything else," she stated for him. "And neither am I. This arrangement suits me fine, and I would have thought you'd be happy with it, too."

Cal's gaze narrowed. There was a long silence as he studied her, apparently trying to work something out.

"So this is just about sex?" he said.

"Hasn't it always been?"

She busied herself with digging her car keys from her handbag, aware she was walking a dangerous emotional line. The truth was, she was close to sitting on the edge of the bed and crying like a baby. Or like the rejected young woman she'd been all those years ago when he'd first cut her loose. Because this was what had always been at the heart of the problem of her and Cal—she loved him, while he only loved having sex with her.

Cal sat up and reached for his boxers.

"I like you, Becky," he said.

She forced a smile. "I know that. I like you, too. But let's not pretend it's anything other than what it is. We're not kids anymore, we don't need to dress it up."

"Is that why you said no to dinner tonight? Because you didn't want to dress it up?"

"Yes."

He stared at her. He was pissed, she could see it in the firm line of his mouth.

"So you're happy to screw me in fifty different ways, but you don't want to break bread with me?"

If she thought his reaction was anything more than piqued pride, she'd be jumping with joy.

"If I wanted dinner and movies and whatever else, I'd be in a relationship. And that's the last place I want to be," she lied. "I've got a lot going on at work right now. This suits me. If it doesn't suit you, then I understand. It's been fun."

Where was this calm, cool voice coming from? She felt as though someone else had taken over her body while the real Becky quivered in the corner feeling nauseous and shaky and weak.

Cal rubbed the stubble on his chin.

"So we're what? Bed buddies?"

"Yeah," she said.

"And anytime I want some action, I just call you?"

"Yep. And ditto for me. No need to ask each other to the movies or out for dinner or whatever."

"For your information, I really wanted to see that new George Clooney movie last week."

She simply raised an eyebrow at him. They'd wound up skipping the movie and going straight to bed.

"Yeah, all right, point taken," he said grudgingly.

"I'll call you in a few days," she said.

"Hang on."

Cal stood and moved close. He slid a hand behind her neck. He kissed her, his tongue slow and silky in her mouth. His face was full of promise when he raised his head.

"You could stay a little longer, couldn't you?"

She searched his eyes, trying to find something more in them than sexual hunger. She already knew he was hard again, his erection straining against the soft fabric of his underwear. It would be so easy to let things start up again, to fall back into bed with him. She gripped the cold, hard metal of her car keys, hanging on to her self-control.

"I really have to go," she said.

"Okay."

He leaned in again for one last kiss, but she turned away, pretending she hadn't noticed. She suddenly knew she couldn't handle having him touch her right now. Her skin felt as fragile as gossamer. If he touched her, she was afraid it would rupture and all her feelings would tumble onto the floor between them and he'd see the truth.

She made it to her car before hot tears spilled down her cheeks.

She loved him so much. Seeing him again, sleeping with him, had resurrected all her old feelings and then magnified them tenfold. She'd thought she could handle the situation, that she could sleep with him and prove something to herself and to him.

She'd thought she could show him that she didn't care. That he hadn't hurt her. That she hadn't felt rejected and humiliated and somehow lacking all those years ago.

But Cal had grown into a dynamic, sexy, fascinating man, so much more compelling than the young man she'd fallen in love with on the shop floor all those years ago. In bed, he was instinctive, passionate, daring. Just looking into his eyes was enough to turn her on. And he had a great sense of humor and a knowing wit that never failed to make her laugh.

He was the man of her dreams. Again.

And once again he didn't want her.

She forced herself to remember what he'd said: *I've only been divorced three months. I'm still finding my feet again, remembering what it's like to be single.*

Just like last time, only then he'd been young and full of juice and feeling trapped after three years with one girlfriend.

They were both excuses. He didn't feel the same way about her. Never had, never would. She had to face that fact now and stop kidding herself.

She hunched in on herself as her shoulders shook. Her chest ached, and she rubbed her sternum with the heel of her hand, over and over. It hurt. She loved him so much, and it physically hurt that he didn't love her back.

Even though she was an experienced, grown woman now, for a few weak moments she allowed herself to ask the old, old questions.

What's wrong with me that he doesn't love me? What don't I have that he's looking for? Aren't I beautiful enough? Clever enough? Funny enough? Am I too needy? What's wrong with me?

"God!" she moaned, disgusted with her own wallowing.

Talk about a pity party. If she was listening to a friend vomit up all this tragedy, she'd give her a swift kick in the butt and tell her that the problem wasn't with her but with Cal, or fate, or pheromones or some crazy mix of all those things that decreed that people did or didn't fall in love with each other.

She was smart, attractive, a good person. She didn't need Cal's approval or love anymore to prove that to herself. It might hurt that she'd been foolish enough to fall for him again, but just as he'd become a more compelling, nuanced, multifaceted version of the young man he'd once been, so had she become a more sophisticated, confident woman. She didn't need Cal or his love. She *wanted* it, but it was not essential to life as she knew it.

She scrubbed at her wet cheeks with her hands. No doubt she looked like a mad-ass raccoon, sitting here in her car on a darkened city street outside Cal's apartment block with mascara smearing her face.

She started her car and pulled away from the curb. A curious calm settled over her as she drove. She felt both lighter and heavier. At last she'd acknowledged the truth of her and Cal: it was never going to happen between them.

No more pretending she was just having a fling with him for old times' sake or proving something to herself or him. It was over between them, for good this time.

It wasn't until she was pulling into the driveway of her small Victorian terrace house in Woollahara that she wondered what she was going to do when Cal called her again. She'd just spelled out the rules of their involvement in no uncertain terms—sex, no strings, no commitment. How was she supposed to back out of their deal when she'd gone to so much trouble to assure him she wasn't even remotely emotionally invested in their relationship? She couldn't very well tell him the truth—that she'd finally admitted to herself that she still loved him, which made having sex with him a really bad idea since he didn't feel even remotely the same way.

Switching off her car, she rolled her eyes at her own pride. That was what had gotten her into this stupid mess in the first place, after all. Pride had made her accept that first dinner offer. And pride had made her put on that dog-and-pony show tonight in his bedroom. And now pride was squirming in her belly at the thought of turning Cal down when he next suggested they hook up, just in case he guessed how she felt.

Okay, pride *and* lust. It would be hard to say no to more of his beautiful body and clever hands. To know that she would never again hear him sigh her name against her skin as he made love to her. That she would never again be filled with the sweaty, needy, greedy desire for him that gripped her every time they saw each other.

Tough cookies.

Her jaw hardened as she let herself into her house. She could go cold turkey on the sex. And she could definitely suck up a bit of damaged pride since the only alternative was to keep sleeping with Cal in order to maintain her facade of not caring. There was no way she was doing that to herself—making love with a man she loved but who only *liked* her was not something she was signing on for, thanks. She'd never been into sadomasochism. Self-delusion, yes. But not willful self-hurt.

She'd avoid him for a week or two, then tell him that she had a big work project coming up and she wanted to concentrate on it. Or better yet, that she'd met someone. He was in no position to challenge her. They'd made no commitments to each other. And if he suspected something deeper was going on…well, she could live with that. Whatever it took to get him out of her life once and for all.

And next time there was a Hannigan's reunion, she'd ask if he was going to be there before she blithely walked in the door and was blindsided by him all over again.

Later that morning she woke to churning nausea and just made it to the bathroom in time to lose what was left of last night's dinner. She put it down to the situation with Cal, and possibly the shrimp cocktail she'd grabbed after work with Gareth before joining Cal at his place.

When she threw up Sunday morning, and then Monday morning, an impossible suspicion began to form in the back of her mind. Tuesday morning, she rinsed her mouth out after what was becoming her traditional prebreakfast barf and reached for her packet of contraceptive pills. No stray pills remained in the blister pack, which meant she hadn't forgotten to take one. Not this month, anyway. She pulled open the cabinet behind her mirror, scrabbling around to see if she'd left last month's blister pack lying around, so she could check that, too. She hadn't. She sighed. The odds of her being pregnant were incredibly slim. She'd been on the pill for over five years. Even if she *had* slipped up, her body would have to have been poised on the starting block, ready to explode into fertility at the first hint of an opportunity. What were the odds of that happening?

Then her gaze fell on the bottle of antibiotics she'd been prescribed last month for a nagging ear infection. She'd wanted to take care of it before she had to fly to Melbourne for Carolyn and Phil's wedding, she remembered.

She'd glanced at the bottle dozens of times over the last few weeks as she brushed her teeth and did her makeup and her hair, and not once had the familiar warning printed along the bottom of the label registered. But today it did. Big-time.

Warning—Antibiotics may decrease the effectiveness of birth control pills.

Her mind went blank. A rushing sound filled her head. She sat down on the closed toilet lid and stared at the towel rack.

She'd thrown up four mornings in a row. She'd also taken antibiotics, then had wild monkey sex with Cal in the linen closet at her friend's wedding.

She pressed her hands to her breasts and squeezed them gingerly. Were her boobs bigger? Unusually tender? Different in any way?

She didn't think so. She stared down at her belly. It looked the same as it always had—as though she needed to really commit to doing two-hundred sit-ups a day if she wanted killer abs like Cameron Diaz.

Was it possible that right now there was a tiny new life growing behind her belly button?

She stood. She hadn't showered or had breakfast, but she didn't care. There was a convenience store on the corner, and she knew for a fact that it had pregnancy tests because she'd often noted them when she picked up milk and pitied the poor woman who was so desperate to find out whether she was pregnant that she bought her test from the quickie mart.

Hah.

She dragged on a skirt and T-shirt, not bothering with a bra, and slid her feet into flip-flops. She slung her purse over her shoulder and slammed out her front door. Once she was in the street, she became acutely aware of the fact that at thirty-one, her breasts were not as up to going out in the world sans support as they used to be. She kept her arms crossed over her chest the whole way to the convenience store.

She couldn't be pregnant. She'd have to be the unluckiest woman in the world. She'd been taking antibiotics for five days, and she'd had sex with Cal once in that time frame. Unless he possessed some kind of supersperm, there had to be another explanation for her nausea.

There was one test left on the shelf, and she lunged at it as though a horde of other desperate women might appear at any moment. She handed over cash and was out the door again in the space of a few seconds.

She tore the pack open as she walked back home, uncaring now that her breasts bounced with every step. She rapidly scanned the instructions. All she had to do was pee on a stick. She eyed the plastic indicator window. It had better say what she wanted it to say. Otherwise…she wasn't quite sure what she would do.

Ten minutes later, she sat on the edge of her bathtub and stared at the blue cross in the indicator window.

She was pregnant.

Her head spun. She didn't want to be a single parent. She wasn't really sure if she wanted to have children at all. It was something she'd discussed on and off with Jack before they'd split up, but they'd never gotten beyond the talking stage. When they'd gone their separate ways, she'd been profoundly grateful that the only people they'd had to consider were themselves.

But now the decision to have children had been taken out of her hands. She was going to have Cal MacKenzie's baby.

She gasped as the top threatened to float off her head. She bent over, gripping her knees as she shoved her head between them. Slowly the world stopped rocking and rolling.

A thought slid into her mind. She could take care of it. She didn't even have to tell him. She didn't have to tell anyone. One trip to the clinic, and this moment, this feeling would be history.

She stood and crossed to the telephone. Punching in a number, she counted one ring, then two, then three rings before her sister answered at the other end.

"I need to talk to you. Do you have work today?"

Amy worked part-time, but Becky could never remember which days.

"No. I was actually going to come into the city and

raid your shoe department. Can't beat that staff discount."

"Amy, I think I'm pregnant." Becky closed her eyes. God, she couldn't even say it properly. "I mean, I know I am. I just did a test."

There was a moment of profound silence.

"Oh my God. This is fantastic. You know I've always wanted the kids to have cousins."

Despite how desperate she felt, Becky smiled. Amy had been hassling Becky to hurry up and pop out kids for years now. Her sister was such a natural mother, she probably couldn't comprehend that news like this might be unwelcome, not to mention downright scary to Becky.

"Well, I'm glad someone's pleased," Becky said.

There was a short pause. "I'm sorry. I'm such a doofus. I just assumed you and Jack must have gotten back together…." Her sister trailed off, waiting for Becky to fill in the gaps.

"No. I've been, um, seeing Cal MacKenzie. You know, from back in college."

"Cal MacKenzie who broke your heart? That Cal MacKenzie?"

"That's the one."

"Isn't he married?" her sister asked.

"Not anymore."

"Thank God. Sorry, but I know how you always had such a thing for him and I thought for a moment there that maybe you'd let yourself get sucked into something ugly because you couldn't say no to him."

Becky rested her forehead on her hand and closed her eyes.

"Does that mean I can come over?" she asked. She didn't like how small and sad her voice sounded, but there was precious little she could do about it.

"Of course you can! Don't be an idiot. You could come over even if you'd humped a football team's worth of married men. You know that. What time should I expect you?"

"I need to phone in sick to work. Maybe an hour?"

She didn't feel even a moment's compunction about taking a sick day. She figured finding out she was unexpectedly pregnant by her teen crush gave her the world's biggest get-out-of-jail-free card.

"How many weeks are you?" her sister asked when she opened her front door an hour later.

"Four weeks. I think. I guess I'll need to have a scan or whatever to confirm that. Is that what happens next?" Becky asked.

Her sister pulled her into a bone-crushing hug.

"You're going to keep it," Amy said. "I'm so pleased. When you said it was Cal's and you sounded so miserable about it, I wondered."

"Of course I'm keeping it. Maybe when I was a kid I wouldn't have. But there's no reason why I can't look after a baby and be a good mum now. I've got my own place, a good job. You and Mum will help out. I'll get by."

Becky hadn't realized how much had fallen together in her mind during her shower and the drive over. The first rush of panic had subsided. She was pregnant, and it was unplanned, but she could handle it. She *would* handle it.

Amy frowned. "What about Cal? Where does he fit into all of this?"

"He doesn't," Becky said firmly.

"Why not? He made half a baby, same as you. Why shouldn't he handle half the consequences?" Her sister had her hands on her hips and a martial light in her eye.

Suddenly Becky remembered that her sister had never been Cal's biggest fan.

"Because I love him desperately, and he thinks I'm just a great lay," Becky said bluntly.

Her sister opened her mouth then shut it again without saying anything.

"Exactly," Becky said. "I am not going to spend my life eating my heart out over a man who will never feel the same way toward me that I feel toward him. Been there, done that, didn't keep the T-shirt. Having this baby tie us together forever is bad enough."

Instantly she realized what she'd said. She pressed a hand to her stomach and ducked her head to address her navel. "Sorry, little guy. I didn't mean that the way it sounded."

Her sister's eyes filled with tears as she noted the small gesture. Becky shook her head adamantly.

"No. We are not going to cry, Amy. I can't afford to. I have to sort this out. I need to come up with a way to tell Cal. And I need to set everything up so that he can see that I don't need anything from him."

"You could just not tell him, if you're so worried about it," her sister said. "Thousands of women don't."

Becky instantly shook her head. It was an easy way out, but she couldn't take it.

"No. I want my baby to know who his father is. What I don't want is Cal feeling obligated or trying to take control. He can be a part of the baby's life, but not mine."

She still wasn't sure how she was going to keep the two things separate, but she would find a way. She had to.

"Good luck with that one," Amy muttered.

"What's that supposed to mean?"

"Men come over all me-Tarzan, you-Jane when they find out they've planted a seed. Trust me on this. Craig was practically pounding his chest when I found out I was pregnant with Kyle."

"That's because he loves you and you guys had been trying for ages. This is different. Cal is different. He's a newly single guy, fresh from a divorce. He's got a new company, he's making money. He just wants to have a good time. He doesn't want the commitment of a baby. He definitely doesn't want it with me."

Her sister blinked rapidly again and Becky pointed at her.

"If you make me cry, you're going to have to go inflate a dinghy or something because it's going to be a while before I stop."

Her sister hugged her close.

"I'm so sorry. I've always wanted you to have kids so you could experience how amazing it is. I just never imagined it would be like this."

Becky closed her eyes and hugged her sister back. "I know. Me either."

CAL SLID two champagne flutes onto his kitchen counter, then stole a black olive from the bowl he'd placed nearby. Sultry music played on the stereo, and a tray of antipasto sat alongside the bowl of olives and the champagne bucket. The lighting was low, he was fresh from the shower, and the harbor was putting on its usual spectacular nightly show.

For the fifth time in the last fifteen minutes, he checked his watch. Becky was late. He'd called her earlier in the week to tee up a time to see her, but he'd had to wait until Friday for her to be free. A whole week since he'd had her naked in his arms. Was it any wonder he was feeling distinctly edgy?

He ran an eye over his arrangements again, sliding the olive bowl a little more to the left to stop it crowding out the antipasto platter. He was just about to replace the plain glass champagne flutes with the cut-crystal ones he'd brought back from London when he realized what he was doing.

Fussing. Primping like an old lady expecting the vicar for tea. Or like a nervous man determined to woo a woman into bed.

Except he didn't need to do that, did he? Becky had

made that more than clear last Friday. This thing they had together was about sex and nothing else. Whenever he felt the need to get off, he didn't have to come up with the pretext of dinner or a movie or a theater show before he could get her naked. He just had to pick up the phone and she'd arrive, ready to head straight into the bedroom and get busy.

He frowned. He wasn't sure why their deal left him feeling uneasy. On the surface, it was every man's wet dream. He craved Becky's body. Several times a day he was visited with memories from their sessions together. The clench of her hands on his butt as she urged him to go harder, faster. The taste of her on his lips. The way her body shuddered and then turned soft and languid after she came. Today, he'd been sitting in a quarterly update meeting with his business partner when he'd had a flash of Becky's face as she savored him riding high inside her.

It was crazy to question the gift he'd been given—great sex with no obligations. After the way things had ended with Natalie, it was just what he needed. She'd become so clingy toward the end, so jealous and possessive. He'd lost count of the number of times she'd accused him of having an affair. He'd been working like a dog to pay for the lifestyle they'd become accustomed to—there was no way he'd had time to squeeze in a little extra on the side, even if he'd been so inclined. Perhaps if she hadn't had trouble finding a job she enjoyed in the U.K., things might have turned out differently. But she'd been restless, dissatisfied, and she'd funneled all her anxiety into their relationship. Ironically, she was the one who'd wound up having the affair. Out of boredom, she'd said. And because she'd wanted to make Cal jealous and test his love for her.

He guessed that the fact that he'd been able to walk away from his marriage with relatively few scars was evidence that perhaps he hadn't loved her as much as he'd thought he had. He'd misjudged her. He could admit that to himself now. He'd assumed Natalie's confidence was a part of her and not just a mask that she put on like the makeup she insisted on wearing every day, no matter what.

His thoughts shifted to Becky. She was the polar opposite of Natalie. Dark to Natalie's blond, and genuinely confident, a woman with a career and life of her own. She'd always had backbone. Always known what she wanted and gone for it. It was one of the things he admired about her the most.

The doorbell chimed. On his way to answer it, he adjusted the dimmer switch, brightening the room to normal levels. He picked up the remote for the stereo and killed the smoochy music, too. For some reason, he felt stupid for trying to turn their evening into anything other than what it was.

"Hey. I was getting ready to call out the search choppers," he said as he let her in.

She gave him a tight smile and slipped past him into the apartment.

He frowned. Something was wrong.

She hadn't changed out of her work clothes, for starters. She always went home to change before meeting him. She hadn't quite met his eye when he'd opened the door, either.

"Are you okay?" he asked as he joined her in the living room.

"I'm fine," she said, but he caught a flash of distress in her big brown eyes. He stepped closer and placed a hand between her shoulder blades, rubbing her back soothingly.

"You're as stiff as a board."

She shrugged a shoulder, almost as though she was trying to shake his touch off. Then she stepped forward, out of his reach. She turned to face him, her hands clenched together in front of her.

"There's no easy way to do this. I had this big speech planned, but I'm just going to say it. I was taking some antibiotics before Carolyn and Phil's wedding, and I didn't think about what that might mean. And then I started throwing up this week."

He stared at her, confused. What was she saying? That she was sick? That something was wrong with her? A wave of protectiveness and fear raced through him. He didn't want Becky to be sick. Not when he'd just found her again.

"Cal, I'm pregnant," she said.

Two very simple words, but they changed his world forever.

CHAPTER FOUR

"PREGNANT." Cal stared at her, his brain not quite putting two and two together and getting parenthood.

"As in having a baby. Our baby, to be specific."

Stupidly his first thought was for the champagne. "You won't be able to drink, then," he said.

She stared at him, and he shook his head.

"God. Sorry. I'm just…I don't know."

"It's a lot to take in." Her voice was flat, distant.

"You're on the pill, right?" he said, confused.

In the back of his mind, he was aware that there were other things he probably should be saying. Reassuring, supportive things. But he'd just been hit with the biggest surprise of his life and he didn't have a manual of political correctness on hand to guide his every move.

"Like I said, I was on antibiotics for an ear infection before Carolyn and Phil's wedding, and apparently they can affect the body's absorption of the pill in some people."

"Right."

Becky dropped her handbag onto the kitchen counter.

"I want to keep the baby, Cal," she said in a rush.

"I know having a termination is maybe the smarter thing, but I think I could be a decent mother and saying no to this baby because it's not convenient doesn't sit well with me."

Cal scrubbed his face with his hands. He felt as though his brain was filled with marshmallow. Why couldn't he think straight? He was painfully aware of Becky watching him, waiting for him to say something.

"I know this is a big shock," she said after a short silence. "The last thing you want in your life."

Cal found himself staring at Becky's stomach. In a few months time, she was going to get big and round. She'd start walking with one hand on the small of her back and the other on her belly. People would want to touch her in the street.

She was having his baby. Their baby. A baby that was half him, half her.

"When are you due?" he asked.

"Carolyn and Phil's wedding was early January, so I guess that means it will be sometime in September."

"Right." Plenty of time to get things organized. To get his head around this.

"I want you to know that I've got things covered," she said. "I've spoken to my sister and my boss at work and my mum, and I can take six months maternity leave and my sister and my mum have offered to look after the baby between them when I go back to work so he won't have to go into childcare. I own my own home, I earn a good salary, I'm looking into getting a nice safe hatchback instead of my Audi."

He frowned. "Why do I feel like we're in a job interview?"

"I'm trying to explain that you don't need to worry about anything. I'd like for the baby to know who you are, to spend time with you when he or she is older, I guess, but until then there's really no reason why this should mess with your life too much."

Cal stared at her. "You're having a baby, Becky. My baby."

"Our baby. And I know this is the last thing you need or want in your life. There's no need for you to feel trapped or anything like that."

"That's the second time you've said that," he said, his frown deepening.

"What?"

"That this is the last thing I want in my life."

"It's true, isn't it? You just got divorced three months ago. You're still finding your feet, remembering what it's like to be single again."

Why did he feel as though he'd heard those words somewhere before?

"That doesn't mean I'm not going to step up and meet my obligations. I'm thirty-one, Becky, not some kid who's going to bail at the first sign of trouble."

"I told you, you don't need to feel obligated. The baby and I are all taken care of—there's nothing for you to do."

"What if I *want* to do something? You'll need help financially, for starters."

Her full lips pressed together and her chin came up.

"I don't need your money. I told you that."

"There is no way I'm standing by and letting you shoulder the burden of bringing up our child on your own," he said.

Her lips got even thinner.

"Fine. I'll keep a record of what I spend on the baby and you can pay half. Anything else?"

"What about doctor's visits, that kind of thing? That's going to be expensive."

"I have insurance, it's covered."

"You'll need a specialist. I'll ask my brother for a recommendation." Andrew's speciality was orthopedics, but he'd know who was the best.

"I've already booked an appointment with my sister's doctor."

"Maybe we should hold off on that. My brother might know someone better."

"My sister has had four children with Dr. Martin. She trusts him, and so do I."

Her jaw was set, and her hands were crossed over her breasts. She looked the very picture of stubbornness.

"Would you like me to come to the doctor's appointment?" he asked.

"Why?"

"Why the hell do you think? To support you."

She threw her hands in the air.

"I don't need your support, Cal, and I don't want it. We're two people who happen to have good sex together, but that's it. Under any other circumstances, we'd sleep with each other until one or both of us got bored, then we'd go our separate ways. Just because this has happened shouldn't change that."

"We're a little more than two people who sleep with each other," he said. "We've known each other for more than ten years, Becky."

"No. We haven't spoken to each other for ten years. We knew each other a little when we were at university. That's it. I wouldn't even call us friends."

He'd never thought her big brown eyes could look so cold.

"Well, I consider you a friend," he said stiffly. "We worked together. We've slept with each other, I enjoy your company."

"Yeah, and when I left Hannigan's we never said another word to each other until the reunion. That's not how friends behave, Cal. Friends call each other up and drop each other e-mails every now and then. Friends are there in good times and bad. We only ever did the good times."

He shifted his feet, shoved a hand into the front pocket of his jeans.

"I thought about you. But it would have felt wrong to make contact. I was married."

She stared at him, color rising in her pale cheeks.

"Doesn't that just prove my point? It's like I said the other night. We were only ever about the sex. And just because this has happened doesn't change anything."

She slid her handbag up onto her shoulder. "I'll call

you once a month to keep you up to speed on everything during the pregnancy, and I'll send you copies of the scans or anything else that comes along. We can work out child support things closer to when the baby is due, if that's what you want to do."

She headed for the door, leaving him staring at the space where she'd been standing.

"Wait a minute," he said.

She turned on the threshold of his apartment, her face perfectly calm and composed. How could she be so together when he was reeling, trying to come to terms with the fact that his whole life had changed?

"Be honest with yourself, Cal. You're a party guy—always have been. You've got this place and a sporty car and a business that's making lots of money. I know you probably feel like you have to say and do the right thing, but I don't need anything that you have to offer. I certainly don't need you coming along for the ride out of guilt. Let's just take it as read that you're off the hook and move on, okay?"

She walked away, her stride long and sure. He stared at her back until she stepped into the elevator car.

At about the same time, he started to get angry.

Phrases from their conversation circled his mind.

This is the last thing you need or want in your life.

You're a party guy—always have been.

And his personal favorite: *Let's just take it as read that you're off the hook and move on, okay?*

Becky had walked in the door, broadsided him with

the news of her pregnancy, then bulldozed him into a corner with about a million assumptions about who he was and what he wanted. She'd subdivided her pregnancy into neatly apportioned lots, and generously agreed to allow him access to one or two of them. He could see scans. She'd give him updates. She'd like the baby to know he was its father, and for him to have contact with the child once it was old enough.

She didn't want his money or his friendship, and she certainly didn't want him holding her hand through any of it. All she'd ever wanted from him, it seemed, was what was between his legs.

We were always only about the sex.

I wouldn't even call us friends.

Out of all the things she'd said, those two last comments burned him up the most. Yeah, it pissed him off that she thought he was some feckless playboy asshole tooling around in his Porsche, more than happy to turn a blind eye to the fact that he'd gotten someone pregnant because it might cramp his style. What the hell did that say about her opinion of him, for freak's sake?

But the thing that really got his blood boiling was the way she kept rewriting history. They *had* been friends, no matter what she said. Before they'd slept with each other, they'd spent hundreds of lunch breaks and tea breaks talking in the staff room. Every staff function, they'd wound up in a corner somewhere, making each other laugh. Yes, there had been plenty of suppressed flirtation in all of those encounters, but they'd liked each other, as well as lusted after each other.

He ran his hand through his hair, then glanced around his apartment. The champagne, the food, the stereo and lighting he'd set up and then chickened out on at the last minute—it all seemed to mock him.

He'd always wanted kids someday. He and Natalie had tried for a short while when they'd first arrived in London, but his work had become so hectic that they'd both agreed the timing wasn't right. Then their relationship had started to dissolve and the idea of kids had been well and truly off the agenda.

Now he was going to be a father. And he was damned if he was going to let Becky draw a neat little box on the ground and tell him he couldn't step outside its bounds. He had rights. He wanted to be a part of his son or daughter's life.

And despite the cool look in Becky's eyes, despite the fact that she was clearly, utterly unthrilled to find herself linked with him for life, he wanted to help her. She might not be prepared to acknowledge it, but there had always been more to them than sexual attraction. There was a reason why he'd backed off all those years ago. The same reason that she'd been the first person he'd thought of when he was single again.

Grabbing his car keys, he headed for the door.

BECKY WAS still shaking by the time she let herself in her front door. Telling Cal she was pregnant had been one of the hardest things she'd ever done.

She dressed in her favorite pair of threadbare flannel pyjamas despite the heat. She needed the comfort of the familiar. If she was the kind of woman who went in for soft toys, she'd be clutching one to her chest right about now, too. Instead, she sat on the couch with her knees pulled tight to her chest.

If she could go back in time to the night of the reunion and change things, she would. She'd turn around the moment she saw Cal, and simply walk out the door. So what if her old friends and work colleagues guessed that she still had feelings for him? A bit of self-exposure was better than this.

She rested her chin on her knees and tried not to remember the things he'd said when she'd given him the news. He'd talked about meeting his obligations. He'd used the word *burden.* She scrunched her eyes tightly shut and grit her teeth.

A burden. The last thing she wanted was to be considered a burden in Cal MacKenzie's life. Not when she loved him. Not when she craved his touch and longed for the sound of his voice.

Tears burned at the back of her eyes. She swallowed them down. She hadn't cried since that night outside Cal's apartment, and she wasn't going to now. She was going to have a baby, and that child needed her to be strong and sure. From now on, every decision she made affected both of them. The days of thinking and behaving selfishly and impulsively were over.

She uncurled from her position on the couch. She felt vaguely nauseous, and she groaned. Her sister had explained that just because it was called morning sickness didn't mean it only happened in the mornings. She'd added that she'd thrown up day and night for twelve weeks with her first child, and had warned Becky that the same might happen to her. It seemed her prediction was spot-on.

"Great. All I need," Becky muttered.

The sound of someone pounding loudly on her front door made her jump on the spot. She stared down the hallway at the glossy black door, knowing who was on the other side and dreading yet another conversation with Cal.

"Becky, I know you're in there and I'm not going anywhere so you might as well let me in," he yelled.

It was past ten, and she was sure that her neighbors wouldn't appreciate her having a yelling match through her front door.

Cal glared at her as the door swung open between them.

"I didn't even have your address," he said tightly.

His hair stood up in unruly spikes as though he'd been running his fingers through it, and his cheekbones were dark with emotion. He brushed past her, inviting himself into her home.

"I had to ring Carolyn up and ask her for your address, because I don't know where the woman who is pregnant with my child lives," Cal repeated as he swung around to face her in her living room.

Becky stood in the doorway, feeling at an acute disadvantage in her baggy pyjamas when he was fully dressed.

"It's never come up before," she said.

"Because you didn't want it to come up," he said. He stabbed a finger at the air between them. "Ever since we hooked up again you've been calling the shots. You decide when we'll meet, where we'll meet, if you'll stay the night or not."

"I didn't hear you complaining." She crossed her arms over her chest. She could feel her heart hammering against her ribs, and nausea swirled in her belly.

"I have over twenty employees," he said. "People who rely on me to pay their mortgages and keep food in their kids' mouths. I ring my parents once a week and try to see them at least once a month, and I donate to a bunch of charities."

Becky shook her head. What the hell was he going on about?

"Cal—"

"I'm not an asshole, Becky. I don't spend my spare time partying with morons and driving around in my car showing the world how great I am. I was married for five years, and I was faithful for every one of them."

She stared at him. "I wasn't aware that I said you were an asshole who did any of those things."

"Yeah, you did. You said I was a party guy. That I

always have been. That's not me. Maybe for a few years when I was in my early twenties, but not anymore."

"Okay. Well, I'm sorry if I offended you. I was simply trying to make a point. This is unexpected news, not something you planned for or even remotely want. And I'm prepared to take care of everything. So it doesn't need to make too much difference in your life."

Despite her reassurances, Cal's frown only deepened.

"You're doing it again, making assumptions about who I am and what I want and how I feel."

Becky opened her mouth, then closed it without saying a word. She didn't know how to respond to him.

"What do you want, Cal?" she finally asked.

"I want to help you. I want to do this with you. I want us to start acting as if we actually like each other."

She stared at him. He had no idea what he was asking for.

She'd worked for a year with him after their breakup, and it had been hell. Every time she'd had to go to work she'd felt half-hopeful that something may have miraculously changed since she last saw him and he'd have realized what he'd thrown away. And every time she'd had to listen to him laughing and joking about what he'd done on the weekend with his buddies, the other girls he'd met, the good times he'd had. Every work shift she'd had to face the fact that having fun with his friends was more important, more valuable to Cal than what they'd shared together.

She wasn't going through all that again.

"I've told you what I want to do. I've told you I'll take care of everything. You don't have to feel that this is a burden you have to take up or a responsibility or an obligation."

"Jesus, Becky." Cal looked to the ceiling as though seeking patience. His blue eyes burned with intensity when he returned his gaze to her. "This is not a burden to me, and if you say it one more time I'm going to get really pissed. I'm thirty-one years old, and I've always wanted to have children. I want to be a part of this."

Becky shook her head, instinctively rejecting what he was saying. She couldn't handle knowing these things about Cal. She didn't want to know that he was responsible and mature, that he'd been faithful to his wife. She definitely didn't want to know that he wanted a family.

She wanted him to be a playboy, an attractive, sexy guy she'd stupidly fallen in love with, but who would never make her happy, even if he did love her in the same way that she loved him. She wanted him to be unsuitable, impossible, out of the question. Because if he wasn't, it made the fact that he didn't love her too hard to deal with. He went from being a guy who would never settle down to a guy who wanted to settle down. A guy who wanted a family. A guy who wanted all the things she wanted—but who simply didn't want them with her.

"I don't think I can do this right now," she said.

"Tough. I'm not letting you push me into a corner and tell me what's what again," Cal said. "I'm sick of hearing you tell me what you think I am, how this is the last thing I want and how I'm thrilled to be single again. You don't know me at all, Becky."

He was standing too close, and he was too big and tall for her little living room. She felt cornered, overwhelmed. He had no idea what he was doing to her, what this meant to her.

"Don't put all this on me," she said. Suddenly she felt incredibly, incandescently angry. Not just at Cal, but at life, at the unfairness of loving a man who would never love her back. And angry at herself for putting herself in this situation in the first place.

"You said those things, Cal. *You* said you'd only been divorced three months, that you were just getting used to being single again. *You* called the baby a burden, not me. So don't you dare tell me I'm putting words in your mouth."

He frowned. "You're taking it out of context."

"Really? I asked you if you wanted a relationship with me, and you told me you'd only been single for three months. What was I supposed to take from that, Cal?"

He stared at her. "Are you saying that you want to have a relationship with me?" He sounded incredulous, mystified.

Becky stared at him, at his gorgeous face and strong, lean body. Why did she have to fall in love with him all those years ago? And why couldn't she get over him now?

Suddenly she felt bone weary, utterly exhausted. There was no way she could protect herself from Cal now that she was pregnant with his baby. There was no way she could allow him access to their child and hope to quarantine him from the rest of her life. He was going to be a part of her life forever. Unattainable, but always there.

"Don't worry. I'm not going to make this any more awkward than it already is," she said. She blinked furiously and turned away. "Do you want a coffee?"

Maybe they could both calm down, sit down and hammer out some kind of arrangement.

Cal caught her arm before she'd taken two steps.

"What do you mean by awkward? What's awkward about you wanting a relationship with me?"

She tried to shrug him off. "It doesn't matter."

"Yes, it does, Becky. There's been enough unsaid bullshit between us. Say what you mean for once."

She glared at him. "Why should I? Why should I lay everything at your feet so you can pick it over and see if any of it interests you? I'm done with being rejected by you, in case you hadn't noticed."

He dropped her arm at last. "If you're talking about when we were kids, we both know the timing was wrong," he said.

Years of anger and hurt swelled inside Becky.

"You have no idea, do you? You think that just because you walked away from what we had easily, it was the same for me. I loved you, Cal MacKenzie. I worshipped the ground you walked on. I used to look forward to going to work just so I could see you. I thought you were the funniest, the smartest, the sexiest guy I'd ever met. I was so jealous of your girlfriend. And then you broke up with her, and suddenly you were mine. For four whole weeks."

She took a deep breath, distantly aware that Cal was staring at her, his face pale.

"And once you'd screwed me every which way, you dumped me like yesterday's garbage. And I realized exactly what I meant to you."

"That's not how it was," Cal said tightly. "You meant something to me."

He took a step forward, but she held up a hand, warding him off.

"I know exactly what I meant to you—hanging out with your buddies and chugging beers and having sex with nameless girls was more important to you than what we had together."

"That's not true," he said, frowning. "I thought you were fantastic, Becky. God, I was obsessed with you. I used to feel so guilty when I was with Virginia because you were all I could think about. You were the reason we broke up. When we first got together, it was so good, so intense, you blew my mind."

Nausea rolled up the back of her throat. She didn't want to hear this. Didn't want to hear Cal try to justify or explain. She shouldn't have said anything. Laying out her hurts before him was worse than pathetic. She didn't want his sympathy. She definitely didn't want his guilt.

"Stop," she said. "Don't say another word. Let's just agree that I was an idiot and you had a nice time and that history has just repeated itself."

Cal stepped forward and grabbed her shoulders. She could feel the heat from his body, smell his after-shave. Helpless tears filled her eyes. Why did he have so much power over her?

"Will you let me finish? You were never just a good time to me, Becky. Being with you was the most intense, amazing time of my life. The way I used to feel when you were lying in my arms… Like my chest wasn't big enough for my heart. When we were together, all I wanted to do was get as close to you as possible. And when we weren't together, I couldn't stop thinking about you. I picked up the phone ten times for every one time I called you."

He stared down at her, his blue eyes compelling, his face tight with intensity.

"I didn't break up with you because I didn't care, Becky. I broke up with you because I cared too much, and it scared the shit out of me. When I was with you, I thought about houses and babies and being together forever. I was twenty years old. I had no idea what to do with any of that. It freaked me out. I loved you with everything I had. That's why we broke up."

Becky blinked. Cal had loved her? All those years ago, he'd broken up with her because he'd loved her too much and he couldn't handle it?

It was such a huge twist on what she'd accepted as the truth, she could barely comprehend what he was saying.

Even as her emotions overwhelmed her, bile rose in her throat and the nausea that had been threatening all evening took control of her body.

Becky clapped a hand to her mouth, spun on her heel and raced for the bathroom. The door hit the wall with a bang as she shoved it open. Then she was on her knees, her body convulsing as she lost her dinner to the toilet bowl.

Her hair hung around her face as she retched. She was vaguely aware of Cal entering the bathroom behind her. She desperately wanted to tell him to leave her alone, but was in no state to do so. Then she felt him gently gathering her hair, holding it at the nape of her neck as her stomach rebelled yet again.

The warm weight of his hand landed in the middle of her back as the nausea retreated.

"Are you okay?" he asked quietly.

"Water would be good," she said, keeping her back to him.

Her hair fell free again as he stood and moved to the vanity. She heard the rush of water filling a glass as she reached up and pressed the flush button.

"Here."

He passed her the water and a wet towel. She rinsed

out her mouth until the acid taste was gone, then wiped her face.

Finally she turned around to look at him, shifting on the cool tile until her back was to the wall. He was crouched down beside her, a concerned look on his face. They stared at each other for a long silent moment.

"I'm guessing that was morning sickness?" he finally asked.

"Yep. According to my sister, I've got another eight weeks of it to look forward to."

She drew her knees into her chest. Cal sat down, leaning his back against the bathtub so that they were facing one another. Cal's gaze searched her face for a few long beats before he started talking.

"That night when we went out to dinner, I told you that I'd thought about you over the years. Not just about the sex, Becky. I thought about that great dirty laugh you have. And the way you always get so fired up for the underdog. And the fact that you're so strong and independent that sometimes it would drive me crazy when you wouldn't let me buy you dinner."

She smiled faintly as she remembered the running argument they'd had over her paying her own way.

"You were the only reason I went to the reunion, you know. I wanted to see you again. I wanted to know if I still felt the same kick in my gut every time I looked at you."

She eyed him across the space that separated them. "Do you?"

"Oh, yeah. Might even be worse now. Maybe I understand what I threw away all those years ago when I chickened out."

Becky held her breath. What was Cal actually saying? She'd been uncertain of him for too long to take anything he said at face value.

"When I told you I was just getting over my divorce, I wasn't saying that I wasn't interested in a relationship with you," he said. "I don't want to be one of those tragic guys who gets divorced and then marries again in a few months time because he can't stand being on his own. And you told me you weren't interested in a relationship. You told me your career was important to you. That we were about sex and nothing else."

Becky squirmed a little as she considered their conversation from his point of view. She'd been so busy protecting herself that she hadn't considered what signals she'd been sending Cal. She'd been so sure she knew the score where he was concerned.

"I thought that was how you felt," she said.

"You didn't give me a chance to say anything else. You were pretty clear that being with me was just about what happened in the bedroom."

Her gaze slid over his shoulder as heat rose into her cheeks. She felt ridiculously exposed and foolish.

"I thought you knew," she said. "I thought it was obvious how I felt and I was simply trying to hold on to a little dignity."

"Like I said, there's been a lot of unspoken bullshit between us. Me trying to find out if I threw away the best thing in my life all those years ago, and you throwing how not interested you were in my face at every turn."

Was that what she'd done? She'd thought her reaction to him, her longing, was evident in every glance she sent his way, in every gesture, in every word out of her mouth. She'd felt as though her love was written in the sky, huge and obvious.

"I've never been not interested in you, Cal," she said quietly.

"I realize that now. And I'm sorry I hurt you so much all those years ago, Becky. I wasn't ready for us. I think I knew on some level that I'd hurt you badly, but I never really admitted it to myself. That would have made it impossible for me to try to start things up with you again. And that was something that has been in the back of my mind ever since I knew my marriage was over."

Becky felt something hot and wet splash onto her hand, and she realized she was crying.

"Don't cry," he said. His face was twisted with regret. "I can't stand seeing you upset."

The gentleness in his voice fed the hope in her heart, and the tears fell faster. She was too scared to believe in what was happening between them, what they were both admitting to each other. She'd wanted this all her adult life.

"Becky," he said, and then he was in front of her, drawing her into his lap and holding her close as he pressed kisses onto the top of her head, her forehead, her wet cheeks.

"Please don't cry. I'm sorry I hurt you. And I'm sorry I didn't push harder when you started talking about us just being bed buddies. I should have told you how I felt, what I wanted straight up."

Becky clutched at the soft fabric of his shirt, feeling the warmth and the heat and the realness of him.

Cal. After all these years. Holding her so tightly, so closely that his voice vibrated through her body when he spoke.

"Tell me now," she whispered brokenly. "Tell me now what you want."

He took a deep breath, then she felt the nudge of his finger beneath her chin as he encouraged her to lift her face up. Tears sheened her eyes as she swallowed and met his gaze.

"I love you, Becky. I want to build a life with you. When you told me you were pregnant tonight, all I could think about was that of all the women in the world, you were the one I wanted this to happen with."

Becky absorbed his words into her soul, the certainty in his voice and the sincerity shining from his face filling the empty spaces that doubt had made inside her.

"Say it again," she said, lifting her hands to cup his face.

"Which bit?" he asked, the shadow of a smile on his lips.

"All of it."

He cupped her face in turn, his thumbs brushing the tears from her cheeks.

"I love you, I love you, I love you," he said.

He opened his mouth to say more, but she closed the space between them and pressed her lips to his. She could taste the salt of her own tears, and she could taste him, and her heart ached in her chest as she understood that she finally had the dream. After all these years, Cal loved her. They were going to be together the way she'd always wanted. And they'd made a baby together. A baby they'd watch grow together. Maybe there would be other babies, too.

She felt desperate to be as close to Cal as possible, and she began tearing at his clothes as their kiss deepened. He seemed to understand and share her need, and they peeled each other's clothes off between clinging, wet, soul-searing kisses, their hands caressing bare skin as it was uncovered, fingers clutching greedily.

Then her back was flat on the cool tile of the bathroom floor, and Cal's warm weight was on her. She felt the hardness of his erection between her thighs. She tilted her hips to invite him inside, and he filled her with his body.

"I love you," she said. "I love you so much, Cal."

"I love you, Becky," he said. "And this time, I'm going to make sure I get it right."

He began to move, and they locked eyes as the magic that had always existed between them began to heat their blood. She didn't look away once as he stroked into her, one hand cradling the nape of her neck as though she was the most precious thing in the world to him. Quickly her climax built, and still she held his gaze. She could see the love in him and his own passion rising. She could feel the tension in his body, and she loved him with her hands, mapping his strength, molding him to her, wanting to get as close as it was possible for two people to get.

"Becky," he breathed.

"Cal," she answered.

They came together, offering their vulnerability to each other along with their bodies.

Afterward, Cal rolled onto his side and pulled her against him as they both gasped for breath. Becky's heartbeat was still pounding in her ears when Cal turned his head to one side to look into her eyes.

"Marry me," he said, his face suddenly very serious and determined.

She stiffened, the old caution rising inside her. She opened her mouth to speak, but Cal pressed a finger to her lips.

"Before you answer, all I want to hear is what you want. Not what you're worried about or what you think is right or what you think I want. What do *you* want? What's your heart telling you right now, Becky?" he asked, his voice vibrating with intensity.

She blinked, and the last, unacknowledged puzzle-piece of her dream slid into place. It was crazy, the two of them making so many decisions so quickly. So many things could go wrong….

"Yes. My heart's saying yes."

Cal closed his eyes, and when he opened them

again she saw a world of relief and satisfaction and happiness in them.

"Like I said, this time I'm going to get it right," Cal said. Gently, he tugged her closer still and Becky rested her head on his chest, savoring the heavy thud of his heart beneath her ear.

For the first time in more than ten years, she allowed herself to experience her love for him as a blessing and not a curse. Emotion filled her, expanding her chest, her belly, warming her arms and legs. Cal loved her. He wanted to marry her. She was going to have his baby. Their baby.

Cal kissed her again, and she felt the glide of his hand as he found her belly. The palm of his hand cupped her gently, reverentially. Becky smiled against his mouth, and she felt him smile in return.

"It's going to be all right, isn't it?" she whispered.

"It's going to be more than all right," he said. "It's going to be amazing."

Looking into his eyes, Becky knew it was the truth.

EIGHT MONTHS later, Mrs. Becky MacKenzie gave birth to a five-pound, seven-ounce baby girl. She and Cal had argued over names the entire course of the pregnancy, but they both took one look at her and decided she looked exactly like a Poppy Kathleen. After an overnight stay in hospital, all three went home to the three-bedroom Californian-style bungalow that Becky and Cal had bought together near the sun and surf of Bondi Beach in Sydney's east. Poppy was mostly oblivious to proceedings, but Cal and Becky were both acutely aware of the occasion—and blissfully, achingly happy that life had handed them a second chance to get things right.

Forgotten Lover

EMILIE ROSE

To the very special friends who stick – even through the hard stuff. You know who you are.

CHAPTER ONE

"TALIA RIVERA. Where is she?" Jake asked the woman stationed at the emergency-room registration desk.

"And you are?"

If she had to ask she wasn't a fan of his show.

"Jake Larson. Someone from Grady Memorial called me and said Talia had been brought in by ambulance."

Jake tried to stifle his impatience with protocol while the hospital employee checked his ID and then her computer to verify he was the one the hospital had contacted.

"Have a seat in the waiting room, Mr. Larson. Someone will be right with you," she drawled in a thick Georgia accent.

Jake didn't have time to sit. Friday afternoons were always hectic. He had a customized Viper back in the shop awaiting the finishing touches. The owner had paid half a million for Jake's expertise and wouldn't appreciate a delay in delivery. He also had to prepare for next week's taping of *Larsonize This!* But curiosity demanded he find out why Talia had given his name as a contact when he hadn't seen her in four years.

He turned away from the desk, went through security and entered the crowded waiting area. Not in the mood to talk shop or sign autographs, he avoided making eye contact, ignored the few empty vinyl seats and found a place to stand outside the main traffic pattern.

Unwelcome but familiar smells and sounds inundated him, reminding him of a time he'd rather forget. Nothing smelled like a hospital. And then there were the moans and whimpers, almost drowned out by the blare of a TV tuned in to a soap opera. Before social services had removed him and his siblings from their parents' home when Jake was eleven, the E.R. had been the Larson family's only health-care provider.

His gaze roamed the room. There were kids everywhere. Crying ones. Dirty ones. Pale, silent ones. Shouldn't they be in a separate pediatric waiting room? Did they really need to be exposed to the drugged-out junkie muttering in the corner or the drunk heaving in the trash can?

Jake wasn't crazy about children. His years in the foster-care system had taken care of that.

But he wasn't that poor kid anymore. He made a good living customizing cars for his cash-laden clients, and his weekly TV show specializing in taking the average Joe's clunker and turning it into a one-of-a-kind collector car had made him famous and increased his business tenfold.

"Jake Larson?" a woman in a white scrub suit, her

salt-and-pepper hair scraped back from her face, called from a doorway.

Bodies perked up around him as recognition dawned. These people represented his show's target demographic, the ones who wrote the hundreds of letters that arrived each week, begging to have their ragged rides Larsonized. Any other day he'd stay and yak. Not today.

Jake moved swiftly toward the woman. "Yes."

"I'm Sue. Ms. Rivera's nurse. This way." She briskly led him down a corridor crowded with curtained-off beds and past a sign that read Red Zone. His gut turned to lead. That didn't sound good. *Red* implied urgent.

"Ms. Rivera is in the Red Zone because of her head injury," she explained, as if she'd followed his gaze. "Her CAT scan and MRI are clear, but there are gaps in her memory that concern us."

"What do you mean gaps?"

"She doesn't know where she is or what brought her to Atlanta," Sue said over her shoulder. "She has partial amnesia."

"Amnesia? Get real."

Sue stopped in her tracks, turned and nailed him with a hard stare. "Her condition is very real, Mr. Larson."

She pivoted on her squeaky rubber-soled shoes and resumed walking. The deeper they penetrated into the E.R. the more the sounds and smells of misery bombarded him with memories. Bad ones. Of broken bones and bloody gashes, of being dragged away from his crying, pleading mother.

Sue rounded a corner and abruptly pulled back a curtain. "Talia, Jake's here."

Talia. Jake jerked to a halt. She'd changed, and yet she hadn't, but his reaction to her was the same as the first time they'd met. His heart rammed against the wall of his chest like a crash-test car and his mouth dried.

Her brown eyes looked huge in her ashen face. A purple knot marred her forehead. Another swollen bruise surrounded a small cut high on her left cheekbone that had been sealed with strips of tape—the kind he kept in the garage for when he didn't have time to drop everything and dash to the doctor's for a quick stitch or two. Dark, wavy hair, longer than the short, chic style he remembered, had been tucked behind her ears and fell to her shoulders.

He found no welcome in her expression, no enmity either. No anything. "Hello, Talia."

"Hi?" Her voice was little more than a tentative whisper.

Sue stepped forward. "Talia, do you remember Jake? His name and address were on the emergency card in your wallet. We called him when you couldn't give us any other family members' names."

Talia's bottom lip wobbled almost imperceptibly before her straight white teeth pinched it still. Fear invaded her features as she searched Jake's face. She shook her head and winced. The hand not connected to an IV lifted and touched her temple beside the bruise. "I'm sorry. I don't."

The sucker punch of her words winded him. She'd *forgotten* him? *Forgotten* the nights she'd spent in his bed, in his arms, the countless times he'd lost himself in her body? *Bull—*

"You are the correct Jake Larson, aren't you?" Sue asked. "You know Talia?"

Jake inspected Talia through narrowed eyes. What game was she playing? He didn't believe the amnesia garbage for one second. That was the stuff of the soap operas playing on the waiting-room TV, not real life. "We know each other. Very well."

Or so he'd thought before she'd packed up and moved out of his condo without even the courtesy of a goodbye. He'd returned from an out-of-town business trip and found her and her belongings gone and only a brief Sorry-this-isn't-working note as an explanation. He'd tried to track her down at work, but she'd quit her job and left town. He hadn't followed.

Sue's gaze found his. "There are gaps in her memory. For example, she knows the date, her name, her home address, her son's name, and—"

"Whoa." Jake recoiled. "Her son?"

Sue nodded to a pair of chairs pushed against the white tiled wall, their plastic backs facing Talia's bed. Jake had taken the lump on them for a pile of dirty laundry. Closer inspection revealed a small child curled beneath white blankets in a makeshift bed. Jake took a cautious step closer for a better look, but all he could make out was the top of a head covered in wavy hair the same glossy dark shade as Talia's, and a fan of lashes across sleep-flushed cheeks.

Talia had a child.

"Adam is the first thing Talia asked about, but I assured her he's been thoroughly checked over by our pediatric resident and he's fine. His car seat protected him."

Jake barely registered the nurse's words. His polo shirt with the Larson Ltd. embroidered logo suddenly felt tight and scratchy. He shrugged to ease the discomfort, but couldn't shake it. Thoughts clicked like a ratchet in his head.

His?

No. They'd had rules. An agreement. And she'd left him. She wouldn't have skipped town if the boy was his, would she?

"How old is he?" he forced himself to ask through tight, numb lips.

Talia turned panicked eyes to Sue, who lifted a shoulder and said, "He's potty-trained, and judging by his teeth we're guessing he's no more than two-and-a-half. Talia's drawing a blank on Adam's age and his birthday, and he's either too young or too upset by the accident to tell us."

Two-and-a-half. Jake did the math. Too young to be his by six months. Thank God. He released the breath scalding his lungs.

Nonetheless, the uneasiness he'd experienced earlier didn't vanish. He shifted in his work boots. Wealth, success and the notoriety he'd gained since his series launched had taught him that almost everybody wanted a piece of him.

Talia had hinted about marriage before she'd left, but she'd backed off easily enough when he'd restated his intention never to get married or have kids. He'd told her then that his career would always be number one. If she'd wanted more than the no-strings affair he'd offered, she'd never let on.

But she'd left before he'd inked the TV series deal. Had she seen his face in the news, a magazine or on a calendar and decided to try again? Limelight was one hell of an aphrodisiac for some women. Or so he'd learned. But why come back now?

And if the boy wasn't his, whose was he? Had she turned to someone else soon after leaving Jake? Or had she left him for another man? Had she been two-timing him when they were together? A bitter taste filled his mouth.

"Talia was knocked unconscious," Sue interrupted his dark thoughts. "The standard protocol is to keep her overnight and repeat the MRI tomorrow morning to make sure she doesn't have a slow bleeder. You'll have to take Adam home with you."

Jake whipped his head back to the nurse. "Me? No way. What about the kid's father or Talia's?"

"Do you have a name and number for either?"

"No."

The nurse turned to Talia. "Have you remembered the names or numbers, hon?"

Talia's worry-widened eyes gave the answer before

she shook her head and winced. "I—I don't. I just can't..."

"It's okay. It'll come." The nurse patted Talia's hand and turned back to Jake. "If you don't take Adam I'll have to temporarily place him with the Department of Social Services."

Jake flinched. He wouldn't wish DSS on any kid. Sure, there were success stories, but he and his siblings had been separated and hadn't reconnected in the years since entering the system. But that had been twenty-five years ago, and he wasn't still hung up on what-could-have-beens. He'd moved on and made a success of himself and his business. Larson Ltd. was practically a household name in certain circles, thanks to syndication.

He shook his head. "There has to be somebody else."

"Please, not social services. I'll think of someone else. Just give me a minute." There was a desperate edge to Talia's voice that Jake hadn't heard before, and she gripped the bedrail so tightly her knuckles gleamed white in the fluorescent lights.

So she did remember what Jake had told her years ago. He scrutinized her pale face again, searching for another crack in her act, but her expression revealed the perfect blend of fear and bewilderment.

"We're running out of time, hon. Adam's going to wake up and get rambunctious like boys do. I'm afraid he'll get hurt." Sue looked at Jake.

He backed away mentally and physically. "I live

alone and I work too many hours to look after a kid. Find one of her friends or a coworker who can take him."

"Don't you hear her? She can't remember anyone else and calls to her home phone are picked up by an answering machine. She thinks she and Adam live alone."

"If she remembers that, why can't she remember somebody who can keep the boy?"

The lines on Sue's face deepened into a scowl, revealing her irritation with him. "Talia, we'll be right back."

The nurse indicated that Jake follow her with an imperiously pointed finger. She led him around the corner. "Look, she's from out of state, and we don't know the full scope of her injuries yet. We can't turn her loose to collapse and possibly die from a bleed in a hotel room somewhere."

Alarm traveled like ice through Jake's veins, chilling him. He didn't want Talia back in his life, but he didn't want her dead, either.

Sue continued, "Her head injury looks mild, but the partial amnesia is worrisome. It can be a sign there's more going on that we don't see yet. We can take care of her, but somebody needs to take care of Adam. He can't stay here. We're short-staffed and can't watch him. In another few hours this place will get Friday-night, payday crazy. He could get hurt or worse, some nut job could drag him out of here and we wouldn't even see it happen. We don't get to choose the quality of our patients, you know."

Jake recalled Friday nights in the E.R. all too well. Scary place for a kid.

"We're still waiting on the word from the North Carolina police. Sometimes out-of-state connections aren't as quick as we'd like."

"I'm not equipped to care for the boy." As lies went, this one was an act of desperation. As the eldest he'd been the only babysitter his younger siblings had had most days and nights while his parents worked two jobs each. But that had been decades ago. And he hadn't done such a great job. "Doesn't the hospital have a nursery for the employees?"

"We have a day care, but it's also short-staffed, has a waiting list and slew of regulations about immunizations. We can't just shove an extra child in there. Adam can tell you what he needs. He's quiet, but he talks."

Jake gritted his teeth and scoured his brain for a solution. He had to find a way out of this. "I'm not the man for the job."

"Yeah, well, until we hear differently you're the only one we got."

His gut burned as though he'd swallowed hot charcoal. "I want to talk to her doctor."

"I'll get him. But you need to think about that little boy in there, Mr. Larson. Adam's frightened and he needs someone."

Jake couldn't think about anything else. "That someone isn't me."

YOU'LL HAVE to take Adam home with you.

A shiver shook Talia. She hugged herself.

"Need another blanket, hon?" Sue bustled off without waiting for an answer, leaving Talia alone with the stony-faced Jake Larson, whose black polo shirt seemed to match his mood.

Talia didn't need a blanket. She needed her memory back. All of it. Not the spotty canvas she currently possessed.

Who was this man and why did the thought of him taking Adam send waves of fear rippling through her? She had a snapshot of Jake in her wallet along with a card bearing his name and phone number, written in her own neat handwriting. Although his hair was shorter now and the devastating smile and sexy glint in his eyes were missing, that face, with a chiseled jaw and tanned skin stretched tightly over high cheekbones, was unmistakable.

If she knew him well enough to carry his picture, why couldn't she remember him? But when they'd given her the wallet to go through, she'd looked at that photo and come up with nothing.

She bit her lip and studied Jake from his deliberately disheveled short, dark hair to his wide shoulders, muscled biceps, flat belly and lean khaki-encased hips. He was the kind of guy to turn heads and quicken pulses. Hers included. But there were no memories attached to the physical attraction.

She dampened her dry lips. How well did she know him? He'd said *very well.* But what did that mean? Had she worked for him before she moved to North Carolina? Judging by the small car embroidered on his shirt beneath the words *Larson Ltd.,* she didn't think he was a doctor, and she had a strong feeling she worked in a medical setting. Not only had she understood all the jargon being thrown at her by the hospital staff, she'd been able to read her chart when the guy who'd brought her back from MRI had left it on the bed.

But she couldn't remember her son's birthdate or if he had any allergies—two questions the staff kept asking over and over. What kind of mother was she to forget such basic, critical information?

Her gaze returned to Jake's. Something in the way his bittersweet-chocolate-colored eyes traveled over her hinted at more than just friendship. Was she dating him? Sleeping with him? Warmth rushed her skin, chasing away the goose bumps.

Was he Adam's father?

My God, you don't even know who fathered your child.

And she couldn't exactly ask Jake. She'd be humiliated and he'd be insulted.

"Thank you for coming." She didn't know what else to say. Jake's dark stare unnerved her, and she needed to fill the silence and ward off her increasing panic.

If she had her cell phone she'd have other people to call. Wouldn't she? People who might have answers to fill the Swiss cheese of her memory. People who wouldn't inspect her like bacteria on a petri dish. But neither the paramedics nor the police had found her phone at the scene of the accident. She knew she owned one, a pink one, and that she hated it and planned to replace it as soon as her contract ended.

But she couldn't recall her little boy's age. Trying had given her an excruciating headache. The doctors had offered to give her an injection to kill the pain, but they'd warned it would knock her out. She couldn't sleep. She had to watch her son and be there for him if he needed her. Gulping down the terror clawing at her throat, she glanced at the chairs where he slept in a small ball.

Adam. Her heart. Her world. Her everything.

How could she know that and not recall when or where he'd been born?

The police officer who'd come to the hospital to take her statement had told her she was lucky to be alive—a driver had turned the wrong way down an exit ramp and hit Talia's sedan head-on. He'd also said that if Adam hadn't been in the backseat he probably wouldn't have survived since the passenger side had taken most of the impact.

Talia didn't remember anything about the wreck. The last thing she recalled was searching for an exit off Interstate 85—but not which exit—and then she'd awoken in an ambulance screaming for Adam. There was nothing in between. And she had no idea why she and Adam were in Atlanta when they lived two states away.

"Why me, Talia? Why call me after almost four

years of silence?" Jake asked in a deep, gravelly voice that resurrected her goose bumps.

Four years? Not lovers then. At least not currently. And not Adam's father if the doctors were right about her son's age.

So who was Jake Larson? He wasn't the kind of man a woman would ever forget. Why couldn't she remember him? "I don't know."

Disbelief twisted his lips. "I'm not buying that."

He thought she was lying, and for once, she wished she was. "It's all I have at the moment."

And it wasn't nearly enough. How could she protect her son if she couldn't identify friend from foe?

She needed to go home. And as soon as the doctor returned she'd tell him so.

CHAPTER TWO

"WE THINK WE'RE DEALING with some kind of dissociative amnesia," the disgustingly young resident told Jake an hour later. "That's when the patient blocks out a traumatic event. Murderers often use this as a defense, claiming they can't remember the crime. Sometimes molestation or rape victims repress memories in the same way because they can't handle what was done to them."

Talia gasped and the doctor held up his hand—a hand that bore no calluses, Jake noticed. "None of those possibilities fits your profile, Talia. There are no APBs or warrants out for your arrest and no missing-person reports. Our state police checked.

"A second choice is hysterical amnesia. It's pretty rare, but it's another version of blocking out unwanted memories or something too painful to recall."

"Which do you think she has?" Jake asked, trying to pinpoint the intern and wondering why the guy didn't realize Talia had to be faking it. C'mon. Amnesia?

"We're not sure. The first isn't usually a result of trauma. The second is. So is the trauma linked or totally separate? We don't know." He shrugged his narrow shoulders and stroked his peach-skinned jaw. "Whichever she has, it is extremely important to her recovery and her mental health to let her memories return on their own. We think they will, given time, but if they don't and the lack of memories impedes her daily functioning, then we have options."

"Like?" Jake prompted, hoping the guy would come up with something to get Jake off the babysitting hook.

"Hypnosis."

More psychobabble. Didn't these people practice real medicine? Jake believed in facts. And so far he'd been told Talia's "illness" was one that couldn't be proved or disproved by tests or X-rays, which in Jake's mind meant it didn't exist.

"Mommy!" the lump under the blankets shrieked, and Jake nearly jumped out of his steel-toed boots.

"I'm here, Adam."

The child sprang up, shoved off the blankets and scrambled to the floor, riveting Jake's attention. Talia's son climbed into bed and snuggled in his mother's arms. She hugged him, closed her eyes and buried her nose in his hair. The hand she stroked over the shiny locks trembled.

The boy looked like her. Same mouth, wavy hair and honey-toned skin. His chin was more square than round like Talia's. Jake's gut twisted with something that felt a lot like regret, but was more likely hunger pains. He'd missed lunch to come here.

The kid tolerated Talia's tight hold for a few seconds and then squirmed. "Need to go potty."

Talia's eyes widened and then she bit her lip and looked at the doctor, who pointed to Jake.

Jake jerked as if zapped by a hot wire.

"C-could you take him?" Talia asked.

He frowned at the doctor, who shook his head, and then Jake scanned the E.R. for an available nurse, orderly, anybody. Everyone was knee-deep in something else. Damn. "Where is it?"

The intern/resident/whatever pointed toward the end of the hall.

"Adam, go with Jake," Talia said in a wobbly voice.

"Stranger?" the boy warbled.

Talia hesitated. Her worried eyes flicked to Jake and then back to her son. "No. Friend."

"'Kay." The boy slid from the bed and shoved his tiny warm hand into Jake's. Jake startled at the trusting gesture, and then he started walking. Fast. But he couldn't outrun the kid skipping beside him or the memories riding his back of having others depend on him.

And letting them down.

TALIA'S GAZE fixed on the tall man and small child heading down the hall. A suffocating panic rose within her. She clutched the bedrails and fought the urge to run after them. Gulping air failed to ease the choking sensation in her throat.

She forced her attention back to her doctor. "I don't

understand. Why can I remember so much, but forget the important facts?"

"The brain is powerful. It can block out things that are too painful for you to recall. My guess is there's something you don't want to remember."

Aghast, she blurted, "But I do want to remember. I *have* to remember."

"Systemized amnesia is a subcategory of dissociative amnesia. It targets one specific event or person."

Talia's gaze returned to the hallway, searching for the man she couldn't remember and the child she adored. Both had disappeared.

Did she have a reason to want to forget Jake Larson? If so, why was his name the only one in her wallet, and why was she in Atlanta where, according to the nurse, Jake lived?

Filled with a sense of desperation and frustrated by the blank screen in her mind, she said, "You mentioned hypnosis. Let's do that now."

The doctor shook his head. "First we need to give your memories time to return on their own."

"But I must have a job to return to…or family or something. I just want to replace my car and go home. Please. Sign me out."

"For your own safety I can't do that. And I wouldn't suggest making any major decisions, like purchasing a car, until we have a handle on the amnesia. I'd definitely advise you against driving home. Flying's probably not a good idea, either, because of the cabin-pressure changes."

"But I can't be trapped in Atlanta. I don't know anyone here."

"You know Mr. Larson."

Did she? The hammer in her head pounded harder.

"I need to go home," she repeated. She knew it deep inside even if she didn't know why. "We can take the train or a bus."

"And who would watch your son if something happened to you on the trip? With an injury like yours it pays to be cautious. Stay with us twenty-four hours. Take a few days to ease back into the normal activities of caring for yourself and your son, and see how it goes. If you don't have any problems by the end of the week then you can plan your trip home. Who knows? Maybe by then your memory will have returned and all of your questions might be answered."

But what if they weren't? What if a week or a month or a year from now she still had blank pages in her memory?

How could she care for her son? If she couldn't even remember his birthday, what else had she forgotten?

TRAPPED.

Jake watched the social worker walk down the hall, taking Jake's last chance of escape with her. He didn't want a houseguest. But what choice did he have unless he let Adam go to a group home? Not the place for a little kid who'd just had his cage rattled. Sure, the social worker claimed it would only be a temporary measure, but that's what they'd told Jake when they'd separated him from his brothers and sisters. Temporary had stretched into forever.

He turned his attention to the pale woman in the bed. Talia didn't look any more thrilled by the circumstances than he was. The pain and worry lines etched across her forehead and around her mouth had deepened in the past hour, but she'd repeatedly refused the medication the doctor had offered because she said she wanted to keep an eye on her kid.

The only way she'd get any relief was if Jake took the boy and left. Hell of a dilemma. Both choices sucked.

Frustrated, he stabbed a hand through his hair. "I'll take Adam tonight. And if the Raleigh police can't find anybody else by the time they release you tomorrow, I'll put you up for a couple of days."

Her expression told him she hadn't missed his reluctance. "We could go to a hotel."

"You heard what the doc said about that. Too risky."

She bit her lip and finger-combed the boy's hair. "I guess so."

Adam smiled up at her from the inflated-latex-glove balloon Jake had made him to keep him from getting antsy. The trust in the kid's eyes brought back memories Jake would just as soon forget. Memories of his younger brothers and sisters, who'd once looked at him with hero worship. "We'll come back midmorning. I have a couple of errands to run, but he can tag along."

"I—thank you." She hugged the child tightly. "Adam, you get to have a sleepover at Jake's tonight. Be good for him, okay?"

"'Kay."

And even though she forced a smile, Jake could see letting the kid go was tearing her apart.

Sympathy dampened his resentment. "He'll be fine."

She nodded carefully and her eyes filled.

He'd never seen Talia cry. He had to get out of here before the waterworks started. For the kid's sake. And his. He held out his hand. "Come on, squirt. Let's go for a ride."

"Not so fast," said the nurse. "You'll have to have a car seat before you can take him. There's a baby store one block down. We'll wait."

He had a reprieve, but only a short one.

THE KID stuck like flypaper.

From the moment Jake had jerked awake Saturday morning to find a warm little body curled against his spine instead of in the guest room where he'd left Adam, through checking Talia out of the hospital after lunch, the kid had stayed glued to Jake's side. Adam didn't say much. Jake had no idea whether that was normal for the kid or the result of the wreck, but he'd bet the boy didn't miss much, either. Those big brown eyes, so like Talia's, had followed Jake's every move.

Could Adam be only two and a half? Had to be. If anybody would know, the hospital pediatrician would. Adam wasn't telling. Jake had asked. Five times.

As soon as Jake extricated the kid from the new car seat, Adam squirmed free, bounced from the SUV and clamped one tiny hand in a vice grip around two of Jake's fingers, forcing Jake to use his free hand to open Talia's door and help her out.

She placed her hand in Jake's, and the warm contact sent shockwaves of awareness through him. He throttled back his response. No sense in repeating history. Especially a scenario that had ended badly.

"I'm sorry you had to buy a new car seat. I'll reimburse you." Talia alighted carefully, never lifting her coffee-colored gaze above his chin.

He released her the second she looked steady on her feet. "The hospital insisted. Said yours wasn't safe after the impact."

"No. I guess not." He almost hadn't returned after he left the hospital yesterday to get the car seat. Talia wasn't his responsibility anymore, and he didn't have the time or energy to deal with her or her son.

But for the sake of their past friendship, Jake had bought the seat and then taken Adam back to the shop. His office manager had watched the boy while Jake completed the delivery of the Viper.

Because he'd wanted to find some other sucker to assume responsibility for Talia and her kid, this morning he and Adam had swung by the impound lot to search Talia's wrecked car for a name, a telephone number, anything that would get him off the hook. But his plan had backfired. He hadn't found anything useful, not even her missing cell phone. And seeing the crumpled heap of metal had made him sick to his stomach. He might not want Talia back in his life, but seeing how close she and her kid had come to dying had rattled him.

He returned his attention to his unwanted guest. Talia's eyes looked huge in her pale face as she scanned his six-car garage and then his large brick house in the same wide-eyed way her son had yesterday.

So sue him. He had money and he flaunted it. His impressive house was about as far as he could get from the tiny Alabama shack he'd shared with his parents and four siblings. He'd hired a professional to turn the house into a showplace. And it looked good… even if it did feel like a pricey hotel.

Talia dampened her lips. "This doesn't look familiar."

"You've never been here."

Her shoulders sagged and her lids fluttered. With relief?

"I asked my housekeeper to swing by and leave dinner in the fridge."

Adam tugged Jake's fingers. "Kin I hab a peanut butter sammich?"

No surprise there. The boy was an eating machine. He'd asked for a sandwich for dinner last night and another for breakfast and lunch today. Cut in squares. Not triangles. Jake had forgotten how picky kids could be. And how cute. But he still didn't want one depending on him. "Sure."

"Jake."

He turned. Talia hadn't moved from beside his Escalade. She braced a hand on the door.

"I'm sorry we're being so much trouble. Thank you for taking us in and for dealing with my insurance company."

He had an ulterior motive. Dealing with the insurance company would shorten her stay as his guest. "No problem. Your car's a total loss. Nothing worth salvaging. I retrieved your luggage and personal effects. Everything's inside. The cop cleared that with you, right?"

"Yes. Thank you," she said in a quiet voice.

He nodded and headed up the herringbone-patterned brick walk. He didn't want her gratitude. He wanted her out of his life and back wherever she'd come from. But first he wanted to know why she'd had his name listed as the only emergency contact.

And why she'd left him.

After unlocking the front door, he shoved it open. The kid bolted for the kitchen.

"Adam— I'm sorry. He's not usually so forward."

"Quit apologizing."

"I'm sor—" She bit off the words when he scowled. "Look, it's obvious you don't want us here. I promise we'll get out of your way as soon as we can."

Damn. He was being an ass. But making nice was difficult when he *didn't* want her here and was almost certain she was lying about the amnesia thing. He expelled a breath. "Come in."

She stopped in his foyer and indicated the faded green scrubs the hospital had given her. “Would you mind if I showered and changed before we eat?”

Traces of blood still matted the hair by her temple. The hospital had cleaned her up only as much as necessary to tend her wounds. They’d missed a few spots. He shut down the images of her hurt, bleeding and unconscious as quickly as they formed.

“Your stuff’s in the room at the top of the stairs. First door on the right. Can you manage by yourself?”

If she needed help, he’d have to call his housekeeper to make another unscheduled Saturday visit.

“I think so.”

“There’s an intercom in the bathroom. Use it if you have to. I’d better check on the kid.” He pivoted on his heel and left her in the foyer, but walking away couldn’t prevent the memories of Talia with water beading on her long lashes and streaming over her smooth skin from forcing themselves forward.

They’d been good together. Damned good.

So why in the hell had she left him? And for whom?

He intended to find out.

JAKE LARSON clearly did not want her around.

Talia might have lost her memory, but she hadn’t lost the ability to sense when she was unwelcome. And while Jake had been patient and kind with Adam, he’d been cool to her.

What had she done to earn that frosty attitude? She wanted to know and she planned to find out.

Holding tightly to the elaborately carved banister, she descended to the foyer. Jakc's house was a testament to his success, an exquisitely decorated showplace done in neutral shades, from the richest cream to the darkest chocolate. But it was soulless. There wasn't a sign of his personality anywhere. Too bad. Clues to this man she used to know might have helped fill in some of the missing bits of her memory.

She couldn't delay facing her reluctant rescuer any longer. Adam had been bathed and tucked into bed. Getting him settled had taken her a little longer than usual because he had been excited about his morning with Jake and spending a second night in Jake's house.

Following the shaft of light through the darkened house, she located Jake's study. He sat behind a wide polished desk with a diagram of some sort spread in front of him. His concentration was so deep he hadn't noticed her.

She knocked on the open door and he jerked up his head. "Did you need something?"

"I wanted to reimburse you for the car seat." Wagging her checkbook, she entered the room filled with tobacco-colored leather and dark wooden furniture.

"Forget it."

"Jake, car seats are expensive and—"

"Do I look like I'm short on cash?"

"I wasn't implying you were. But you don't need

to bite my head off." She didn't want to argue. Her headache had subsided somewhat, but it was still nagging in the background. She'd simply leave the check where he'd find it when she went home. She sat down on the sofa facing his desk. "I was also hoping you'd tell me more about…us."

He sat back and folded his arms across his chest. His closed expression had her bracing herself. "You walked out without the courtesy of a goodbye. What more do you want to know?"

She flinched.

Jake's gaze dropped to her chest and desire darkened his eyes. His nostrils flared. The contrast between the barely veiled hostility of his words and a look that said he'd seen her naked and would like to again confused her.

She felt her nipples contract and glanced down at the checkbook clenched in her fingers. Only then did she realize her pale-yellow cotton shirt clung damply to her breasts, revealing their areolas and the lace pattern of her thin bra. Adam was quite a splasher, and he must have gotten her wet during his bath.

She folded her arms. But embarrassment wasn't the cause of the heat circulating through her veins. Desire flickered to life deep within her. She tried to ignore it. How could she get turned on by a look from a man she couldn't even remember? Until she recalled everything and everyone she'd forgotten there was no room for passion in her life. No matter how tempting.

"I, um…meant what was my job? And what kinds of things did we do when we were…together?"

The leather chair creaked as he sat back. "You heard the doctor. You need to remember on your own."

"Yes, but—"

"Talia, I'm not playing this game. You managed to fool the doctors, but you haven't fooled me."

Her stomach bottomed out. "Do you think I don't want to remember? Do you think I like not being able to take care of Adam? Or that I like forcing my company on someone who wishes I were anywhere else?"

His lips compressed. "Go to bed. I need to get these plans done."

Stymied, she slowly rose. If she wanted to remember their past, it looked like she was on her own.

"ADAM!"

The cry jolted Jake awake. He blinked in the near darkness and tried to get his bearings. His room. His bed. Talia's voice.

And then he noticed the warmth against his back and turned his head. The boy lay curled in a ball atop Jake's comforter for the second night in a row.

"Adam, where are you?"

"He's in here," he called out. Adam didn't stir.

Talia appeared in his open doorway. The pale moonlight streaming through his window illuminated her nightgown-clad form. Jake never bothered to close the bedroom curtains. No point. An acre of thick pines separated him from his nearest neighbor.

"Thank heavens. I panicked when I couldn't find him." The hand she pressed to her chest accentuated the shape of her breasts as she jerked to a halt just inside his room. He'd once worshipped those breasts. Not anymore. But like a damned teenager, he couldn't keep his eyes off them.

He sat up and the sheet fell to his waist. Talia's gasp rent the air. Even in the near darkness he couldn't miss her gaze raking from his shoulders to the puddle of Egyptian cotton at his hips, and then she knotted her fingers at her waist and averted her face, revealing the bruise and the surgical tape.

You are one sick puppy to be lusting after the walking wounded, Larson.

"I'm sorry. Adam likes to nap with my father. I guess he thought you were a good substitute." Her eyes widened and sought his as if she'd just realized what she said.

She'd certainly snagged Jake's attention with her slip. "You remember your father?"

"Yes." She frowned. "I don't know why I couldn't before."

Yeah, right. "Remember anything else?"

Her teeth worried her bottom lip. "I think I remember his phone number."

He reached for the cordless phone. "Call him."

She looked at his digital alarm clock and then him. "It's three in the morning."

Was he being inconsiderate to wake the man in the middle of the night? "The hospital said they sent the local police to your house to look for next of kin. If your father heard about that he needs to know where you are and that you're safe."

"But the police said my neighbors weren't home. So who would tell my father?"

"Just call him…unless you have a good reason not to."

Jake had to get them out of his house. Sharing dinner with Talia and Adam had brought back too many memories. Listening to the kid's giggles and squeals echoing through the house this evening had been distracting. He had designs to work on and a final episode to refine, damn it. And seeing Talia's damp, clinging T-shirt after Adam's bath had been agonizing for a guy who hadn't gotten laid in months.

He scratched his bristly jaw with his free hand. When had he become too busy for sex? God knows he'd had offers.

Talia approached slowly, stiffly, and he noticed a bruise on her shoulder that he hadn't seen before. She had to be in pain, but she hadn't said anything. "Are you taking the pain pills the doctor prescribed?"

"No. They make me feel foggy and hung over." She took the phone from him. Seconds ticked past. Seconds filled with memories of Talia sharing his bed. Back then when she'd stopped a foot shy of his mattress it had been to do a slow, alluring striptease for him. Her scent filled his nostrils. His body heated at the memories of how she'd driven him insane with her hands and mouth.

Finally, she dialed a number. Even from a yard away he could hear the loud tones bleating through the phone, followed by a recorded voice saying the number had been disconnected.

"Try again. You probably misdialed."

She did with the same results and then stared at the phone with a puzzled expression. "I know I'm dialing the right number. It's the same one he's had for years. I'm sure of it."

Jake took the receiver from her. He'd never met her father. Talia had said Mr. Rivera was too old-fashioned to accept them living together without a commitment, so she'd kept the men in her life apart. "What's his name and where does he live?"

Another hesitation. Was she yanking his chain? Dialing the wrong number on purpose?

"Carlos Rivera. Raleigh, North Carolina."

Jake dialed information, gave the name and city to the operator and received a robotic number no-longer-in-service message. He disconnected. "Would he be listed under anything else?"

Biting her lip, Talia shook her head and winced.

"You should take the pills."

"I can't. I need to be here for Adam."

"I'll cover the kid."

"I— Thank you, but no."

"It's ridiculous to hurt when you don't have to. I'll get you some Tylenol." He cradled the handset, flung back the covers, swung his legs over the side of the mattress and stood.

Talia stumbled back a step. Her rounded eyes examined Jake from his shoulders to his abs, his hips and down his legs. Her lips parted and her chest rose. When her eyes found his again the hunger in the dark depths hit him like a lightning bolt.

She stood within touching distance in his moonlit bedroom and he ached for her. Electricity filled the air between them. Jake reminded himself of the kid behind him and Talia's previous fickle behavior. The combo curbed his urge to reach for her.

Besides, his hunger wasn't because he needed *her.* Any attractive, available, half-naked woman standing within inches of his bed would elicit the same reaction. He could use a good screw right now.

"You've seen me in underwear before, Talia. And out of it."

She swallowed and ducked her chin, but not before he saw the panic flickering to life in her eyes. She wrapped her arms around her ribs, lifting her breasts and drawing the thin cotton fabric taut across her beaded nipples. Her breasts looked larger than before. Had pregnancy changed her body?

What do you care?

"I wish I could remember," she whispered.

If she was faking her faulty memory, and he was certain she was, then she deserved an award for that convincing crack in her voice.

"I'll carry Adam back to bed. The pain pills are in my bathroom cabinet. Help yourself." He scooped up the boy and strode down the darkened hall toward the guest room. The kid was a lightweight, but also a dead weight. Adam didn't even twitch with all the commotion going on around him. Jake remembered his youngest brother and sister sleeping the same comatose way and squelched the memory. No point in looking back.

Jake laid the kid in the middle of the queen-size mattress and covered him. Talia joined him a few moments later. In the absence of a nightlight she had left the adjacent bathroom light on and the door ajar.

"I had to put him in a regular bed when he turned two because he kept climbing out of his crib."

The smile and the love in her voice yanked at a different kind of hunger Jake would just as soon not acknowledge. Had his mother ever cared that much? He couldn't recollect hearing her use that tone or being there to tuck them into bed. She and his father sure as hell hadn't fought to get him back after social services took him away. But his parents hadn't released him for adoption, either. Not that a preteen was high on anybody's wish list.

He looked over his shoulder at Talia. The slash of light behind her clearly outlined her slender figure in the thin gown. Her attire couldn't be called seductive by any stretch of the imagination, but the shadow of her curves jarred him awake below the waist. Intentional? Was she out to resurrect what she'd killed by walking out? Not gonna happen.

He snapped upright as the words she'd just spoken penetrated his lust. "How long ago was that?"

Her soft smile morphed into a frown. “I don’t know.”

“Aw c’mon, Talia.” He couldn’t mask his irritation.

Her brow puckered. “I want to remember. I do. But I can’t.”

“Try harder.”

Grimacing, she lifted a hand to rub her temple. A full minute passed. She crossed the room to tuck the covers around her son and then slowly straightened. “Maybe I’ll wake up tomorrow and remember everything. The doctor said it could happen that way.”

Her wistful tone grated. If Jake had any luck at all, her “lost” memory would return. If not, he’d be stuck with her until he could reach her father and then put Talia and Adam on a train bound for home. As for the amnesia thing, he was a seeing-is-believing kind of guy, and he’d seen nothing to persuade him she wasn’t faking the whole deal. But what did she hope to gain with this farce?

“I have to work tomorrow.” He had a hell of a lot to do. His crew was good, but he was the one who kept the cogs turning, and his was the mug that had to be in front of the camera. He didn’t make the big bucks by sitting back and letting fate play the cards. “You’ll have to keep the rug rat quiet.”

“I will.”

“The doctor said you couldn’t be left alone, so Monday, if you’re still here, you’ll have to go to the shop with me while we shoot.”

"Shoot?" Alarm rounded her eyes and mouth.

"The show."

Looking puzzled, she shrugged and shook her head. The usual flinch followed, as if her head hurt every time she moved it.

"I was in Hollywood signing the contracts for the TV show when you left." No flicker of recognition betrayed her charade.

Was it possible this wasn't a hoax? Nah. Had to be. Amnesia was too hokey to be real.

He massaged the knot in his neck. He'd been flattered and excited when the producer had approached him four-and-a-half years ago. What had started as a simple request to design a car for a movie had evolved into an offer for Jake's own show after Crandall had toured Larson Ltd.'s facility. Discussing the pros and cons with Talia had helped Jake make the decision to accept, and that decision had changed his life. How could she have forgotten the hours they'd lain in the dark talking after making love?

"I'm sorry." Her nails dug into her upper arms. "We weren't married or engaged or anything, were we?"

"I don't do marriage."

"But we were…involved?"

"We were lovers. We lived together almost a year."

Her lashes fluttered. "Why did I leave?"

"You tell me."

She sighed. "I wish I could."

He fisted his hands and fought the urge to reach for

her, to comfort her. *To shake her.* This amnesia business was getting old. "It didn't take you long to replace me."

His bitter words sent her gaze rocketing to the sleeping child and her lips mashed into a thin quivering line. She took a deep breath, squeezed her eyes shut and then whispered, "He—he's not yours then? I mean, I heard what you said about me not calling for four years, but…"

A hesitant question instead of an accusation. If she wanted to milk his assets, wouldn't she have gone with the latter? Or was she more devious than that? "He's not mine if he's two-and-a-half."

"I'm sorry. I had to ask. I can't believe I can't remember who—" She put a fist to her mouth, bowed her head and studied her curled toes with what looked like genuine distress. Her shoulders shook with a ragged inhalation and then squared. "I'm going to remember."

But she didn't look convinced. Either this was the best acting job south of Broadway or Talia really had lost a chunk of her life. At three in the morning he was too tired to make the distinction and too likely to make a mistake if he took her into his arms and offered the comfort she looked like she needed, because for some damned fool reason he still desired her.

"Get some sleep." He turned and headed back toward his room. The more walls between them, the better.

"Jake?" Her voice, barely above a whisper, stopped him at the door. "I'm sorry I can't remember us."

The hell of it? So was he. But he sucked up his regrets and reminded himself she'd replaced him easily enough.

"Don't be. I would never have married you or given you the kid you obviously adore." And he had no right to be irritated that she'd found someone else who would. "Be glad you left, Talia. I am."

Now who was lying?

CHAPTER THREE

JAKE AVOIDED his guests until lunchtime, but that didn't mean he didn't know where they were every second of Sunday morning.

Talia and Adam had played quietly indoors and out, but Jake's radar had honed in on her like a Lo-Jack tracking device. Talia was a distraction. Just one more reason to get rid of her.

After lunch he carried the bag of personal effects he'd retrieved from Talia's car to his den. She perched on the edge of the sofa with a magazine—one containing a big spread on Larson Ltd. "Ready to go through this stuff?"

Talia nodded hesitantly as if she were afraid of what she might discover. Or maybe her head still hurt. She set aside the magazine. "Now's a good time. Adam's down for his nap. Maybe something will trigger my memory and we can…get out of your way."

He bit back a curse. "I don't mean to make you feel unwelcome, but this is a pretty hectic time. I'm trying to finish the show's season plus keep up with my regular workload. After we wrap on Friday I'll have some downtime. If you haven't remembered everything by then or heard from your father or a friend, I'll drive you and Adam home."

And he'd leave them there in the care of anyone other than himself.

"Friday is longer than the two days you offered."

He shrugged his tense shoulders. "You're here. Adam's happy. And I still don't like the idea of you in a hotel room."

Jake upended the bag, pouring everything on the coffee table. The bits and pieces of standard car junk, toys and snacks hadn't told him anything when he'd hastily searched them for names and addresses yesterday. But the navigation system buried beneath the tissue box offered possibilities. He'd been so rattled by Talia's unexpected return and the necessity of bringing her into his home he'd forgotten about it. He picked up the handheld device and hit the on switch. Nothing happened. The batteries were dead.

He pawed through her junk until he located the charger. Just his luck. She had a DC adapter, but no AC. "You keep searching for clues here. I'm going to plug this into my car."

"Why?"

"If you used your navigation system on your trip then I can find out where you were headed, and then I can contact whoever was expecting you." Better yet, he could take them there and dump them.

Problem solved…except for finding out why she'd left him.

He loped outside and hopped into his Escalade. The sooner he had answers, the sooner she'd be gone.

Jake had installed plenty of high-end GPS models on the cars he'd customized, but he wasn't familiar with this particular budget brand. It took him a few minutes to figure out how the gizmo worked. Once he did, the destination on the screen punched the air from his lungs and knocked him back in his seat.

His office address.

Talia had been on her way to see *him.*

But why?

His first thought went to Adam. But the kid couldn't be his. The hospital staff said so. Jake shoved the image of the boy aside. But it nagged him like a loose wire.

Could the doctors and nurses be wrong about the kid's age? Nah. They'd assured him that teeth were a pretty reliable indicator at that age.

Next he considered money, fame or whatever it was women wanted from men with both. He'd never had trouble finding women, but since the show had taken off he'd had more than his share of attention.

Was that why Talia had looked him up now? Had she seen the article in *USA Today* reporting Jake had just inked a new five-year deal?

He grappled for other reasons Talia would look him up and recalled the bruises on her face, shoulder and wrist and the cut on her cheek. A sick feeling entered his stomach, quickly followed by a surge of anger.

The hospital had assumed Talia's cuts and bruises had been caused by the car accident. But what if they hadn't? Could she have been fleeing an abusive relationship?

Whoa, man, you're jumping to some pretty wild conclusions.

But as far as he knew, Talia didn't have any family other than her father, and Jake had been around the block enough times to know the legal system wasn't foolproof in domestic abuse situations. Restraining orders were only as reliable as the one ordered to be restrained, and jackasses who hit women weren't known for their intelligence or law-abiding habits.

Would Talia have considered Jake a safe harbor?

He yanked the GPS cord from his power outlet and headed back into the house. He wanted answers and he wanted them now.

That nagging feeling made him detour up the back stairs to the boy's bedroom. In the dim sunlight seeping through the gap in the closed curtains he examined Adam's face. The kid was pure Talia in the shape of his eyes, nose and mouth. Even his eyebrows arched like hers. Sure, Jake had brown hair and eyes too, but his weren't the same shade as theirs, and his hair was stick-straight, not wavy.

Once in a while something Adam said or did reminded him of his youngest brother, Ricky. But that was just Adam's age.

For the first time Jake wished he had baby pictures of himself to confirm the boy wasn't his and put his mind at rest. But he had none. His parents hadn't taken many pictures and who knew where the ones they had taken were now?

No, Jake decided. The doctors had to be right about Adam's age and that meant the kid wasn't his. He sure as hell didn't want him to be. He jogged down the front stairs to confront Talia. She looked up from the sofa when he entered the den, and the lost look on her face told him she hadn't had any luck with the items from the car.

"None of this triggered anything. Not a person, not a place, not a thing to tell me where I was going or to whom."

"Me. You were coming to see me. My office address was programmed into your navigation system. Why?"

She gasped. "I—I don't know."

The confusion in her eyes combined with the color draining from her face took him aback. No one could fake that pallor. Which meant Talia wasn't lying about the amnesia.

Holy spit.

He crossed the room, sat beside her and grasped her chin, angling her face to inspect the cut and swelling on her cheekbone. A fist could have done this just as easily as an airbag deploying. He ought to know. He'd been punched around by other kids in foster care until he'd learned to fight back.

"The bruises and cuts, are they from your accident or before?"

Her brow puckered. "Before?"

He lowered his hand. "Talia, did someone hit you? A boyfriend? Adam's father? Your father?"

Her fingers flew to the surgical tape on her cheek. "I don't think so. I would remember that. Wouldn't I?" Her hand dropped to her lap and fisted. "Why can't I remember? Adam needs me to remember. If I can't, how can I keep him safe?"

The sharp edge of panic in her voice cut deep. Against his better judgment, Jake pulled her into his arms. "You are safe, and as long as you're here with me, nothing is going to happen to either of you."

Talia hugged his middle, fitting against him just like the old days. Her breasts pressed his chest, her thigh, his leg. Her head tucked beneath his chin and her scent filled his nostrils. Jake's body rumbled to life.

She'd always been physically affectionate, and it had been hard for him to adapt to her frequent hugs after a lifetime without them.

He hissed a breath through clenched teeth and peeled her off one inch at a time. It wasn't easy to do when every cell in his body wanted to cling and his mouth hungered for a taste of her. She might claim she wasn't able to remember how explosive they'd been together, but he hadn't been able to forget. God knows he'd tried.

He shot to his feet. He had to find a way to jar her memories. And the best way to do that was to go back to the beginning.

"I have to get back to work. Come and get me when Adam wakes up. We'll go to the park."

"I'VE BEEN to Tanyard Creek Park before." Talia's eyes didn't stray from Adam on the playground, but she could feel Jake's gaze on her profile as well as she could the hot, humid evening air.

"You remember?"

She turned her head. His assessing expression confirmed her suspicions. "No. But you're watching and waiting as if you expect me to. Did I come here often?"

He exhaled slowly. "We came together. You liked watching people play with their dogs."

She strained for something, *anything,* and found nothing. "I don't think I have a dog."

He shifted on his feet and angled his face toward Adam, who played happily in the sand with the toy truck Jake had retrieved from her wrecked car. Jake's tense muscles practically screamed frustration.

"What do you know?" she prompted, and grasped his bicep. His skin was hot to the touch beneath the cuff of his polo shirt. She let him go. "For pity's sake, Jake, I realize the doctor said to let me remember on my own, but please, tell me if you know something. Do you think I like living in a black hole?"

His gaze hit hers, direct and alert. "You told me your father was allergic to dogs."

She didn't remember, but it sounded…reasonable. A welcome breeze stirred her hair, cooling her overheated skin. She lifted her hair off her nape. "Maybe I'm on vacation. But if I am, I wasn't expecting us to be gone long."

Jake lifted his eyebrow in a silent question.

"There are only a few days' worth of clothing and toiletries for Adam and me in my suitcase."

The dappled shade on the opposite side of the clearing beckoned. A wisp of something too vague to see drifted like a ghost across her consciousness and then evaporated. Keeping an eye on Adam, she strolled around the edge of the play area. Jake followed. When she stopped at a picnic table his posture stiffened and his eyes narrowed.

She dragged her fingertips over the rough wood and sat on the bench. "Tell me why this spot drew me."

His nostrils flared and his pupils expanded. "We shared our first kiss here. At this table. After your office picnic."

Her breath stalled in her chest. She searched his face and dark eyes for answers. Why couldn't she remember? She closed her eyes and tried harder, but it was like trying to catch a cloud.

The bench depressed beneath her and then a warm mouth covered hers. Startled, she opened her eyes. Jake's face was so close to hers he was out of focus. His hands caught her waist, holding her in place while his lips brushed back and forth in slow, gentle sweeps.

Desire, hot, urgent, sensual and familiar, rolled through her. Kissing him felt good. Right. Her lashes drifted shut and a whimper of pleasure bubbled up her throat. She lifted her hand to touch his face, but Jake raised his head abruptly and stood before she made contact.

His gaze probed hers. "Remember now?"

His husky voice made her pulse race. Her lips tingled. But her mind was a blank movie screen—all white space. Disappointment weighted her shoulders. Why couldn't she retrieve memories of the two of them? Jake must have been important to her at one time. "No."

And then a sobering jolt of guilt erased the arousal. Did she even have the right to kiss him? "We can't do that again. Not until I know whether or not I'm committed to someone else."

Jake's eyes tracked her thumb's fidgety sweep over her bare ring finger. He expelled a rough breath.

"I'm not making a pass. I'm trying to prod your memory. Don't attach any significance to the kiss. It meant nothing."

To him, maybe. But to her it meant she'd willingly let go of something good. Why would she have done something so foolish?

JAKE LARSON might be fully clothed, but Talia saw him naked. Blame it on Sunday evening's kiss.

She wrapped her cold hands around her overheated middle and wished the memories of being his lover had stayed lost in the black hole of her brain. No such luck.

Almost as soon as she'd fallen asleep last night

she'd started dreaming, and those Technicolor visions of being Jake's lover had been far too real to be fantasy. She'd awoken this morning hot and bothered, wet and breathless and aching. For Jake. Not a great way to start the week.

She could recall his taste, his scent, the textures of his skin and hair and tongue, and a multitude of other sensory details as vividly as if she'd climbed from his bed hours ago instead of the one in his guest room. She wiped damp palms against her hips.

Why, oh, why had she voluntarily left that passion behind? Had she come to Atlanta to rekindle their affair?

Shoving away the unwanted erotic thoughts, she focused on Jake through the wide office window overlooking the garage area. He looked confident and sexy and right at home in his khaki pants and black polo—apparently his show uniform. From what she could see on the six screens on the console beside her, the camera adored every line of his handsome face and tall, muscled frame, and audio only enhanced the resonance of his deep, magnetic voice.

Falling in love with him would have been all too easy, and she must have loved him or she never would have shared his home or his bed. She knew that much about herself. Or thought she did. The rest…wouldn't come. She stifled a frustrated groan.

"Look, Mommy," Adam said for the umpteenth time. He stood on the leather sofa pushed up against the plate glass, his stubby finger pointing to yet another tool used in supercharging the car Jake worked on. Her son's wide-eyed gaze remained riveted on Jake, his crew and the assortment of cameramen moving around the hoisted coupe with the grace and timing of choreographed dancers.

A wisp of memory teased her, drifting across her brain like a specter. A blue car? But Jake stood beneath a red one. She tried to chase the murky thought, but it vanished.

"See that?"

"I see." She smoothed Adam's hair.

Her son loved anything automotive. But then what boy didn't? There was no genetic link to Jake's passion for cars, just as there was no connection in the similarity of Adam and Jake's hair color. She wished there was, if for no other reason than she hated being adrift. But that would mean she'd kept Jake from his son, and she couldn't bear knowing she'd done something so selfish.

"And cut," the guy beside her said into his microphone headset. "That was great, Jake. We'll break and finish up after lunch."

Jake looked at the window. Adam bounced up and down, waving frantically. Slowly Jake lifted his hand—a hand Talia now knew had touched her intimately, skillfully. As if he read her thoughts, Jake's gaze collided with hers and held. Her pulse and breathing quickened. Her skin tightened. She may have forgotten parts of her life, but she hadn't forgotten what sexual chemistry felt like. And Jake Larson evoked it in spades. She wished he didn't.

But regardless, she couldn't act on the attraction until she knew she wasn't committed to someone else. Did she have someone she loved and shared mornings with the way she had with Jake the past two days?

Adam's father, for example. Was she still involved with him? If so, why wasn't he searching for them? The police knew where to find her if anyone filed a missing-person report. But so far, the police hadn't come knocking. Even if she'd broken up with Adam's father, surely he'd want to keep tabs on his son?

Did he even know about Adam? He must. She wouldn't keep a secret like that. Not unless she had good reason. Like fearing for Adam's safety. She touched her wounded cheek. Could Jake be right? Had she fled an ugly relationship? She didn't think so.

And Adam hadn't asked for his father, not once, a niggling voice reminded her. Wasn't that unusual?

She had too many questions and so few answers.

Jake said something to the man beside him and then strode toward the office. The door opened. Adam scrambled off the sofa and across the room, where he held up his arms in a plea. After a second's hesitation, Jake picked him up and smiled at him.

Talia's heart stuttered. They looked so right together, which made her sudden urge to rip her son from Jake's arms all the more irrational. Apprehension knotted her stomach. What was her brain hiding? And why?

"Let's grab some lunch," Jake said.

"Kin I had 'nother peanut butter sammich?" Adam warbled.

"I don't know if they have peanut butter, kid."

Talia chuckled. "That's his generic phrase to describe anything between two pieces of bread. He'll eat other foods."

Jake's gaze sharpened and probed hers, that lone eyebrow lifting in question. Her breath caught when she realized she'd remembered something else. She waited for more to follow, but nothing did.

How could she remember Adam's food foibles but not his father?

"That's all I recall other than a flash of a blue car earlier." She wasn't about to tell Jake she'd remembered his talent in bed. Her entire body flushed and tingled.

"Your boss's car." Jake shoved open the office door and stalked outside toward his SUV.

Talia raced after him. The sweltering heat and high humidity instantly produced a sheen on her skin. "What do you mean? What boss? You know my boss?"

"Knew," he called over his shoulder as he leaned in and settled Adam in his car seat.

Talia experienced a strange urge to caress his behind. She shoved her hands behind her back. If her dreams were any indication, she'd once had the right to do exactly that to Jake and she'd been bold enough to.

He turned and caught her ogling. Her cheeks caught fire and his eyes narrowed suspiciously before taking in her short-sleeved apricot V-necked top and white linen pants in a slow, pulse-accelerating sweep.

"I knew your boss when you worked in Atlanta. You and I met when I customized his blue Ferrari. He was always in surgery. You handled most of my calls and even some test drives."

"I worked for a surgeon?"

"An orthopedic surgeon." A rapid tapping on the office window drew his attention. He tossed her the keys. "Start the engine and the air conditioning. I'll be right back."

She could cool the car. But what about her memories? Those were hotter than Georgia in July, and judging by Jake's expression, just as unwelcome as a heat wave.

"WHAT do you have?" Jake asked Martha, his office manager.

"I didn't find a phone number or address for Talia's father, but I found this on the Internet." Martha handed him a sheet fresh off the printer.

An obituary column from the Raleigh paper. For Carlos Rivera. Jake scanned the text until he reached the "survived by" part to make sure she had the right Rivera. His gut dropped like a two-ton jack, and he stared out the window at the woman in his car. Talia had been very close to her father and had called him at least twice a week during the time she'd shared Jake's condo.

"Did you show her this?"

"No. You said to give whatever I found to you."

Martha could find a sand flea on a mummy's butt. She was even better at locating obscure car parts.

"Good job." He laid the obit on the desk and dug in his wallet for the business card the doctor had given him flipping open his cell phone. Jake dialed and reached voice mail. After identifying himself he said, "Talia Rivera's father died two weeks ago. Could be that's what she's blocking. I need to know how to break it to her."

He left his number and then looked at Martha. "I'm taking them to lunch and then the cell phone store to see if she can remember which provider she uses. I'll be back to finish up."

Jake strode to the car. He couldn't send Talia back to her father, but if he helped her replace her phone, then maybe one of her friends would call and take her and Adam off his hands.

He had to get rid of them. Because, as attracted as he might be to Talia Rivera, he lived by three firm, fast rules. He didn't do women with children. He didn't repeat his mistakes. And when someone left him he cut them loose. It was easier that way. What good were people who claimed they loved you if you couldn't count on them to stick around?

Like his family. Like his foster parents. Like Talia.

Jake considered last night's kiss in the park to be one of the flat-out dumbest things he'd ever done. Damned if it hadn't revived the craving he'd been certain Talia's cowardly decampment had cured.

He climbed into his SUV. Her scent and her welcoming smile hit him with a flashback of happier times—the nights she'd greeted him at his front door wearing a sinful piece of lingerie or better yet, nothing at all. His entry hall had seen almost as much action as his bedroom.

He crushed the images and debated telling Talia about her father, but the kid in his rearview mirror sealed his lips. Did Adam know his grandfather was dead? Could a two-year-old even fathom death? Probably not. Would Talia have a meltdown? She'd never been the type to get overly emotional before.

But then he'd never thought her the type to bail without explanation, either. Had he known her at all?

Jake's phone rang five minutes later as he opened the door to the restaurant. He checked the number. The doctor's. "Get us a table. I have to take this call."

He answered as soon as the heavy glass door closed between them. "How do I tell her?"

"You don't," the intern said. "The amnesia is a self-protective mechanism. Her body isn't able to handle whatever she's blocking. I can't stress enough that we need to let Talia's memories return spontaneously."

Not what he wanted to hear. "What if I tell her anyway?"

"I'm not sure what will happen. If you're correct and losing her father is what triggered this, then the shock could be traumatic. She could have a more serious breakdown. Has she remembered anything else?"

Frustrated, Jake scrubbed his jaw. "Bits and pieces. Small stuff."

"Then she's making progress. Try to be patient. If she doesn't have a significant amount of recovery before her clinic appointment in two weeks, I'll refer you to a colleague who can try hypnosis. He'll attempt to uncover the memories in a safe, protected setting. In the meantime, you can *gently* evoke memories of innocuous things by serving her favorite foods or buying her favorite flowers. But avoid the big hairy deals."

"Big hairy deals? Is that medical jargon?" Jake couldn't keep the sarcasm and irritation from his voice, and the kid-doc had the nerve to chuckle. "And how am I supposed to know the difference?"

"Go easy on her. Avoid anything that might be painful for her to recall. Focus on the good stuff. Page me if she has problems, but otherwise, take it easy and don't jeopardize her mental health by feeding her information she isn't ready to process."

The good stuff. There'd been a lot of that. Until she left.

The dial tone sounded before Jake could argue he had no intention of keeping Talia around for a couple of weeks. He sure as hell wasn't going to buy her flowers and give her the mistaken impression that he welcomed her back into his life. Maybe reminding her of the couple they used to be would jog her memory of why she'd left and whatever came afterward. But that's what he'd been doing with the trip to the park and that kiss. The one that shouldn't have happened.

He stared across the parking lot at his vehicle, his means of escape, and debated taking the easy way out. But there was a chance that something he'd done had driven Talia away and he wanted to know what it was.

He also had her current safety to consider. He couldn't send her back into a hazardous situation, although now it looked less like domestic abuse and more as if she just didn't want to remember losing her father.

He strode inside, found Talia and Adam's table and sat in an empty chair across from her. She pushed a glass in his direction. Lemonade. How could she remember something as unimportant as his drink preference and not remember her father had died?

The truth hovered on his lips. But as much as he'd cursed and hated Talia for dumping him in such a cowardly manner, he wouldn't risk her well-being. And he sure as hell didn't want to be responsible for her son's. Revealing the truth would have to wait.

But that didn't mean he wouldn't use the week ahead to nudge her memories along.

CHAPTER FOUR

TALIA STARED at the new cell phone on the tabletop and willed it to ring. It stubbornly remained silent.

Why hadn't her father or someone called? It was Monday. She was almost certain she had a job, but she couldn't remember where or for whom she worked. With only three days' worth of clothing in her suitcase, hadn't she expected to be at work today? But she hadn't shown up. Why hadn't someone called to check on her? Didn't she have any friends?

When panic threatened to choke her she tried to comfort herself with the knowledge that she was still making progress. Earlier, Jake had asked for the name of her cellular provider, and the answer had instantly rolled from her tongue. So had her cell number.

But the scanty random fragments weren't enough. She needed more and she needed it *now.*

From her makeshift desk in the corner of Martha's well-appointed domain, Talia glanced through the partially open door of Jake's private office to check on Adam and found him still napping on the black leather sofa. Her child could sleep anywhere. She knew that, but not when or with whom he'd been conceived.

Pushing that disturbing thought aside, she redirected her attention to the job Martha had given her—sorting Jake's mail into two categories: personal letters and requests for car makeovers. Talia knew it was busy work to keep her out of the way, but she didn't mind. It kept her from dwelling on the ether between her ears.

Sorting required reading and the explicit content of several of the personal letters made her blush and gave her indigestion.

A heavily scented letter signed with a red lipstick kiss made her grimace. Jake had quite a fan club. There were offers of sex, marriage proposals and requests for him to father children. And there were pictures. Pictures of scantily clad women who wanted Jake Larson—and not to work on their cars.

Was her stomach churning caused by jealousy? Jealousy implied she still had feelings for Jake beyond lust. If so, then why had she left him? Had he hurt her? His barely suppressed rage when he'd asked her if someone had hit her implied he'd never physically injure a woman, but had he hurt her emotionally? Had she believed leaving him would be less painful than staying with him?

Had Adam's father been a rebound romance?

She shook off her questions, turned to Martha and pointed to the growing stack of personal mail. "Will Jake answer all of these? Some of them are quite… interesting."

Translation: disgusting and desperate.

The office manager nodded. "Every letter gets a reply, but most will only get an autographed photo. Jake will decide who gets what."

Jake. It all came back to Jake. If not for him taking them in, where would she and Adam be right now? She owed him.

The window overlooking the garage drew Talia the way a fresh bloom does bees. Her gaze collided with Jake's and her pulse hiccupped. The call he'd received before lunch had bothered him. He'd been quiet and vigilant ever since, and there was a stiffness in his shoulders this afternoon that hadn't been there earlier.

Had the call been about her? Was that why he looked through the window every time the camera stopped rolling?

What had happened to them four years ago?

If she remembered nothing else before Jake drove her and Adam home on Saturday, she absolutely had to know that. Because the rapid beat of her heart and the warm flush beneath her skin each time their eyes met told her that no matter who or what had come between them, she'd never completely gotten over Jake Larson.

GET HER memory back and get her out of your space before you start breaking rules.

Jake eyed Talia as he loaded the last of the dinner dishes into the dishwasher. The hum of awareness arced between them as it had throughout dinner. His gaze drifted from her face to the curve of her breasts, her waist and hips. Hunger gnawed at him despite his full stomach.

He wanted her. Damn it.

He winched his thoughts back in line. How could he do what the doctor ordered and focus on the good stuff without remembering that one of the best parts of his and Talia's relationship had been the blistering hot anytime/ anywhere sex?

In the twenty-eight hours since Sunday night's kiss he hadn't been able to think about anything else. But unless he broke all three of his rules, a return to the sheets with Talia wasn't in the cards.

He wasn't disappointed. *Liar.*

All right, he was. But he'd get over it.

"Did we prepare meals together in the past like we did tonight?" Talia stood in front of the sink with a cutting board in one hand and a soapy sponge in the other. She looked up at him through her thick lashes and the impact of her gaze siphoned the air from his lungs.

"Dinner. My condo kitchen was about a quarter the size of this one. We did a lot of bumping into each other." And the frequent contact had resulted in them postponing the meal to get naked on more than one occasion. She'd end up naked on the counter or the kitchen table. Hell, they'd even made love on his floor. She'd made him get on the bottom and he hadn't minded the cold tile one bit.

His pulse accelerated. Damn it. He reminded himself of the kid sleeping upstairs—a kid who belonged to someone else. It cooled his blood, but only marginally. "You liked to cook, and you were good at it."

She'd been good at a lot of things.

Like leaving, the voice in his head insisted.

Talia rinsed the cutting board, set it in the drain rack and lifted a chef's knife from the soapy water. She weighed it in her open palm. "This feels comfortable. Familiar."

Go easy on her, the doctor had said. But how could Jake take it easy and get what he needed? If she was blocking her father's death, then prompting her memories of them as a couple shouldn't cause a crisis.

"It ought to. You brought that knife with you the first time you cooked for me. The next day you and your kitchen utensils moved in." Because he hadn't wanted to waste time driving across town to her place when he could come home from work and take her straight to bed.

"Chinese food was your favorite because you claimed it was the only way you could get me to eat my veggies." They'd made beef and vegetable lo mien tonight.

The sponge stilled. Her fingers tightened around it and water streamed into the sink. She stared at the darkened window.

Jake leaned on the counter beside her. "Do you remember?"

A blush climbed her neck and stained her cheeks. The quickening rise and fall of her breasts drew Jake's gaze and his own respiratory rate increased. "Talia?"

She looked at him and the passion smoldering in her eyes knocked him sideways. His hunger swelled. It wasn't the only thing.

Don't do it.

He reached for her.

Don't do it.

Don't—

The familiar taste of her mouth welcomed him, as did the feel of her in his arms and the instantaneous lick of desire. Her lips were as soft and warm as ever, but the superficial kiss wasn't enough. Cradling her uninjured cheek, he plunged his tongue past her lips and delved deeper into the recesses of her mouth, into her slick, satiny heat.

He slid his fingers through her silky hair and gently tugged. Her head tipped back and her tongue twined with his. He vaguely registered dampness on his waist as her arms surrounded him, but he was more interested in the press of her soft flesh to his torso. His blood roared and need clawed through him. He buffed her spine, her waist, and cupped her bottom.

Talia's fingers dug into his back. She shifted restlessly and her belly brushed his groin. His head snapped back. He sucked a sharp breath as a bolt of desire ripped through him, making him grit his teeth. He stared into her flushed face. "How can you forget that?"

Her lids, slumberous and sexy, fluttered open. He couldn't resist another quick sip from her mouth, which only led to a second and a third. He struggled to rein himself in. It wasn't easy. It never had been with Talia.

She spread her palms on his chest and her warmth permeated the thin barrier of his shirt. "Last night I dreamed about…being with you. I remembered your bed and…and a shower, but not cooking dinner."

Snapshots of memories crowded his brain as if she'd called them forth. Memories of hot, wet, slippery sex, tangled sheets, pillows and covers tossed to the floor. His bed and shower had gotten a lot of use and not just the traditional sleeping/bathing variety.

Jake fisted his hands. He could be smart, walk away and gain nothing. Or he could gamble and hope acting on her memories prompted more, which could possibly result in getting her out of his house and exorcising a few of his own ghosts.

But he had rules for a reason, and breaking them could embroil him in something he wanted no part of.

Talia's eyes squeezed shut and the fingers on his chest fisted. "I hate this. I hate not knowing. I hate that I've forgotten the people and places that are important to me."

If she'd been playing the pity card he could have pushed her away. But all he heard was frustration and fear.

"You haven't forgotten Adam. He's the one who matters most." He dragged a knuckle along her uninjured cheek. His pulse throbbed low and heavy.

Aw, hell. He'd never been one to play it safe. "Let me help you remember the rest, Talia."

It took a second for his meaning to sink in and then her eyes widened and her lips parted. "What if…what if there's someone else? At home. Waiting for me."

Her question hit him like a fist in the gut. He'd never been a poacher and he didn't share his women. The idea of her with someone else—

You know she's been with someone else. She had his kid.

But no one had called her and she'd had no voice mails waiting on her cell phone account. "Do you believe there is?"

She briefly closed her eyes and then shook her head. "I don't think I could feel this much with you if I had someone special at home."

He had no explanation for the relief coursing through him, and he sure as hell didn't have the right to feel it.

"Talia, before we do this you need to know nothing has changed. I'm still not interested in marriage or children. Whether your memory returns or not, I'm taking you home the first chance I get. And I'm going to leave you there."

Leaving her first was the only way he could guarantee she wouldn't bail on him again.

SINCE HER brain wouldn't tell her what to do, Talia had to trust her body. Her racing heart, shortened breaths and the fizz of arousal bubbling through her veins told her she might find the answers she craved in Jake's arms.

She took a leap of faith. "I—I'm okay with whatever you can give me, Jake."

Jake traced the bruise on her left upper arm and then skimmed to the one on her wrist with a feather-light touch that plowed goose bumps to the surface. He lifted her hand and brushed a thumb across her empty ring finger. "I don't want to hurt you."

She raised her chin and met his gaze. He cared. No matter what he said, she could see the concern mingling with the desire in his eyes. And right now his caring meant more to her than anything. Jake might push her away with his words, but his protective actions drew her nearer.

"I won't let you hurt me." For Adam's sake, she couldn't afford to. But she needed her memory back and she was convinced Jake held the key. In his touch. In his kisses. In his lovemaking.

Before she could question the wisdom of her decision Jake's mouth covered hers. Though he cradled her waist and nape gently, the raw passion of his kiss held nothing back. His unleashed hunger bent her head back and exhumed an answering response from deep within her. Talia latched on to the familiarity of her response, hoping to uncover more.

When no new memories raced forward to greet her, she mapped his body with her hands, relearning the shape of his muscled chest, the rasp of his evening beard and the texture of his thick hair.

He abruptly lifted his head and glanced at their reflection in the uncurtained window and French doors overlooking his back deck. "Not here."

He laced his fingers through hers and towed her to

the foyer and up the stairs. Each step multiplied her excitement. He didn't turn on a lamp in his bedroom and only the pale moonlight streaming through the windows illuminated the space.

By the time he stopped beside his wide bed and released her, she shook with anticipation. He reached for the hem of his shirt, fisting the fabric and then pulling it over his head in an impressive display of well-defined abs and corded shoulders and arms. Had he always been this muscular?

Talia fingered the top button of her shirt with an unsteady hand.

"Let me." His hands brushed hers aside, skimmed down her torso to tug her shirttails free. His palms slipped beneath the cotton to grip her waist. The contact burned her skin for several heart-pounding seconds before he released her and eased the bottom button free. He slowly worked his way up. Cool air and warm knuckles brushed over her, making her breath hitch with each touch. Finally, he nudged the fabric apart and eased it over her shoulders, being careful not to jar her tender left side.

Her bra wasn't anything special, just basic white cotton with a touch of lace, but that didn't stop Jake from devouring her with his eyes. Her breasts swelled on a shaky indrawn breath. Had she worn sexy lingerie for him in the past? Nothing in her suitcase was remotely alluring. Did she have tantalizing pieces in her drawer at home?

He tossed her shirt aside and hooked two fingers

behind her waistband and reeled her closer. She removed her bra and dropped it. A flick of his thumb and a scrape of a zipper and her pants parted. He eased her pants and panties over her hips and knelt in front of her to remove her sneakers and pull her clothing over her ankles. She braced her arms on his wide shoulders and kneaded his supple skin. His breath dusted her belly, leaving a coating of heat in its wake, and the tickle of his spiky hair against her navel elicited a shiver of desire rather than laughter.

He sat back on his haunches and looked up at her. She felt no shyness, no urge to cover herself. Jake had seen her nude before. Touched her before. Made love to her before. And this felt right.

He rose slowly, his big hands loosening his belt as he backed into the shadows in the corner. The leather chair creaked as he sat and again when he bent to untie, unlace and remove his work boots. She could barely hear the swish of his laces over her pounding heart.

She dampened her dry lips and watched his swift, precise movements. Had they shared this ritual before? They'd lived together, so they must have.

When his boots were out of the way he stood and made quick work of shedding his khakis and underwear. The lean, muscled lines of his body mesmerized her. She must have seen him like this a hundred times, but tonight everything was new and different.

Maybe it was the light and shade cast by the moonlight or the lack of memories, but whatever it was, her fingertips tingled with the need to touch him, trace the dark line of hair bisecting his chest, stroke his thick length, tangle her fingers in the wiry curls at the base of his shaft and cup the tender flesh below. She ached to press herself flush against him, to feel his hair-roughened skin against the smoothness of hers.

He closed the distance between them and pulled her into his arms, granting her unspoken wish. His body blanketed her with heat and his mouth consumed hers. Her belly cradled his erection and his hard thighs flanked hers.

Willing to go wherever this ride took her, she held tight to his waist and kissed him back. And as much as she relished the present and the passion he ignited, she hoped his lovemaking would take her back to the past.

He nudged her toward the bed with the steady press of his hips and she went eagerly. He broke the kiss to sweep back the comforter. Talia climbed onto the cool sheets and scooted to the middle of the mattress without looking away from Jake's intense gaze.

He planted a knee on the bed between her legs. When he leaned forward his erection nudged her intimately, making her core tighten. She arched her back and moved against him. Winding her arms around his torso, she pulled him forward. He planted a hand on either side of her head and lowered ever so slowly until he hovered just above her. She wanted more and tugged. His hot skin seared her.

He stopped an inch shy of her lips. "Remember?"

No!

"I'm trying," she whispered, not wanting to break the spell. But the sensations inundating her didn't allow room for memories.

"See if this works." His elbows bent. He captured a nipple between his teeth and tugged gently. The sharp not-quite-painful nip made her gasp, and then his mouth opened over her and he laved her with the hot, moist stroke of his tongue. The suction of his mouth cast a net of need deep within her, but it didn't drag any memories to the surface. She tangled her fingers in his short hair and whispered words of encouragement.

He shifted to her right side. His hand cupped her other breast, rolled her nipple and made her moan at the twist of sensation low in her abdomen before he caressed his way downward to trace her bikini line and below. He combed through her curls and found her slick flesh deftly, accurately.

The surety and swiftness with which he found her pleasure points attested he'd driven her wild with wanting before. He read her body like an old, familiar book, knowing exactly how to touch her and when to pause to leave her clinging breathlessly to the edge of release. Her hips lifted to meet each stroke, silently begging him to fill the emptiness he created and take her over. But Jake seemed determined to deny her.

When she thought she'd tear his hair out in frustration he rolled to his side and reached for the bedside table. He returned with a condom.

A condom. That didn't feel right. "Did we use condoms before?"

"No." One tightly ground out word. "You were on the pill."

Seconds later he'd sheathed himself and moved above her. At that moment her memory wasn't nearly as important as having him inside her. She opened her arms and legs in welcome and guided him home. His thick tip nudged her and then sank deep, deep enough to force his name from her lungs in a rush of air.

Talia smoothed her hands over his back, savoring his supple skin and shifting muscles. She cupped his bottom and pulled him back each time he withdrew. Her lips found his jaw, his neck, his shoulder. He smelled familiar, tasted familiar.

But the rest of her memories just wouldn't come.

She hugged him tighter and squeezed him with her internal muscles, trying to hold on, trying to reach her past and the peak before he left her again. As if he understood her struggle, Jake's tempo increased. He thrust faster, harder, deeper until Talia tumbled over and over in a breathless whirlwind of sensation.

Before she could recover, the muscles of his face strained. He stiffened, bowed his back and pulsed inside her with a muffled groan. Seconds later his lids lifted, and his gaze locked on hers. That dark brow arched, silently questioning.

Still winded, she reluctantly shook her head.

As an exercise in memory retrieval, making love

had been almost a complete failure. But at the same time it had raised one very important question.

Had she ever stopped loving Jake Larson?

CHAPTER FIVE

MISTAKE. *Big* mistake.

Jake stared into the bathroom mirror. He hadn't exorcised any ghosts. But he had resurrected a few demons he'd just as soon not have riding his back.

He'd never wanted or trusted anybody as much as he had Talia. And she'd let him down. Trusting her again was a bad idea, and if sex hadn't prompted any of her memories, then he had no reason to repeat the exercise.

No matter how much he wanted to.

He was setting himself up for another fall. He had to get Talia home. The sooner the better. If he and his team put in a few extra hours there was a good chance they could wrap the show before Friday. And then he'd get her out of his house and out of his mind.

With that decided he returned to the bedroom and found her asleep in his bed. It had always been that way. Unless he'd kept her awake talking, Talia fell into a deep sleep after sex. Back then he'd jokingly called it her post-coital coma, and he'd lost count of the nights his arm had gone numb with her snoozing on his shoulder. He hadn't minded a single one.

He'd never been one to gab, but talking with Talia in the darkness had seemed safe. Easy. Comfortable. He'd told her things he'd never told anyone else. A hell of a lot more than he'd ever told the counselors the foster care system had assigned to probe his brain.

She knew about his childhood, his overworked, overstressed parents, who no matter how hard they'd tried had never had enough time, energy or money for their kids. He'd told her about ending up in foster care, but not his guilt over how he and his siblings got there. He'd never told anybody that. And never would.

She knew he had two brothers and two sisters, all younger, whom he'd never seen again, and that he'd packed all of his belongings in a duffel bag and left Alabama the day he'd turned eighteen, heading for Mooresville, North Carolina. There he'd scraped up all the grants, scholarships and financial aid he could get to put himself through one of the best auto mechanic technical schools in the country. His next stop had been Atlanta, where he'd busted his knuckles for other shops before he'd saved enough to open his own.

By the time he'd met Talia he'd made a name for himself with his unique customizations and attention to detail. He couldn't think of one other person who knew as much about the real Jake Larson as she did, and she'd never appeared to judge him. She'd seemed to care more about the circumstances he'd made for himself rather than the ones he'd been born to and scraped his way out of.

He'd thought he'd found someone who accepted

him flaws and all. That's why her disappearing act a couple of months after he'd spilled his guts had cut so deep.

Had her supposed acceptance been a lie?

He stood by the bed torn between reason, which told him to get the hell away from her, and the desire to get close to her warm, flushed, sex-scented skin again.

Get in and go to sleep?

Wake her and send her to her room?

Sleep on the sofa in his study?

He couldn't crash in a guest room because each of those was temporarily assigned to Talia and Adam.

He rolled his stiffening shoulders. Climbing between the sheets and holding her was trouble. No doubt about it. His resistance was already shot to hell. Waking her would lead to questions. Questions he didn't want to answer. The leather sofa would be cold. *Cold won't kill you.*

He yanked on his boxers and headed for the hall and almost tripped over Adam. The boy had his blanket fisted in one hand and a trembly bottom lip.

"What's up, kid?"

"I want Pawpaw," Adam said, and punctuated the words with a sniffle. The light seeping from the bathroom caught the gleam of tears on his cheeks.

Jake's heart constricted. It didn't take an Einstein to know the kid meant his grandfather. Jake didn't want to send him back to bed to cry himself to sleep alone, but he couldn't let Adam climb in bed with his naked mother, either. That kind of thing earned therapists the big bucks that paid for Jake to customize their cars.

Now what?

Behind him lay the woman who'd left him and in front of him stood the child she'd had with his replacement. He was stuck between the proverbial rock and a hard place.

But he couldn't walk away from those big, brown, tear-filled eyes. He held out his hand and Adam grabbed his fingers in a snapping-turtle grip. Jake led him back to the guest room, hoisted him onto the bed and tucked him in. He turned to go, but Adam's quivering lip stopped him.

Damn.

"Move over, kid." He'd stay with Adam until the child fell asleep. Jake settled on top of the comforter. Adam wiggled closer and coiled his little toothpick arms around Jake's bicep.

The trust in that gesture clamped a vice around Jake's chest. Kids were so damned innocent. They always put their trust in the wrong people.

He couldn't let Talia or her son come to depend on him. He'd only let them down.

WITH HER heart racing and a scream lodged in her throat, Talia jerked awake to shrieking metal and the jarring impact of her left side against the car door.

Her eyes flew open. Gulping air, she tried to get her bearings. She lay on her side facing an unfamiliar wall on a comfortable mattress and not in a crumpled car.

A dream. Tension drained in a slowly expelled breath. She'd only been dreaming about the accident, not reliving it, but the vividness of the details rattled her. She'd remembered she'd been driving and crying and that she'd reached for a tissue and then looked up and *crash!*

Why had she been crying?

The room slowly came into focus, illuminated by the first rays of sunrise. Jake's room. Jake's bed. She'd slept with him. Her already-pounding heart hammered even faster. Biting her lip, she eased upright. The covers slipped from her bare shoulders. She snatched the sheet up over her breasts and turned her head. The bed was empty.

She brushed a hand over his pillow. Cool. Wherever Jake had gone he'd been gone awhile. He used to sleep later.

She caught her breath and waited for more…but nada. No more memories followed.

Swallowing a frustrated groan, she scanned the room. Her clothing lay in a crumpled pile. And then her gaze landed on Jake's discarded shirt draped across the corner of the dresser. She scooted out of bed, snatched it up and pulled the navy polo he'd changed into before dinner over her head. His scent surrounded her, tweezing a memory just out of reach. She waited for an image to form, but all she got was a smudge of forest-green that made no sense at all. She smoothed the garment over her thighs.

Adam. She needed to check on Adam.

She quickly walked to his room and stopped dead in the doorway. Two dark heads occupied the pillows. Jake, in black knit boxer briefs, lay flat on his back on top of the comforter. Adam lay beside him, a tiny bump beneath the covers with one little hand clutched in Jake's and his beloved blanket clutched in the other.

Suffocating panic assailed her as she stared at the males in her life. She struggled to regulate her breathing. Why would the sight of Jake and Adam together evoke such a strong reaction? She couldn't come up with a reason for her panic other than the obvious fact that her son had needed her and she hadn't heard him, and, oh yeah, she'd been intimate with a man she couldn't remember. A man she might still have feelings for. Why else would she have been coming to see him?

More urgently, what should she do now? She wasn't equipped to face either of the bed's occupants until she figured out what last night meant and if it had been a mistake.

She must have gone terribly wrong somewhere. She'd left Jake, a man who seemed perfect in every way except for his stated aversion to marriage and children, and she'd had a child with someone else.

Just one more person she couldn't remember.

It's only been four days since the crash. Your memory will return.

She sighed and Jake's eyes opened, blinked, zeroed in on her. His gaze raked over her from her tangled hair to her toes curling in the carpet, and her heart skipped beats. He shifted, stilled and turned his head toward Adam. He slowly extricated himself from the boy and the bed.

She didn't remember him leaving his room. But then she'd always slept like the dead after making love. Another memory. But another useless one. Where was the stuff she needed to know? The important stuff?

Jake dipped his head to indicate they leave the room. Talia wanted to escape. She'd prefer to be alone to decode her dream. Did she still have feelings for Jake? Had she been coming to Atlanta to ask him to take her back?

If so, she was out of luck. Sex or no sex, he clearly didn't have the same feelings for her if he couldn't wait to vacate the bed he'd shared with her.

She followed him into the hall, her gaze riveted on the broad, muscled V of his back until he turned, offering an equally tasty view of his powerful chest. She licked her dry lips, but the gesture did nothing to dampen the desire flickering to wakefulness in the pit of her stomach.

"I'm sorry. I didn't hear Adam call."

"He didn't. I found him in the hall. He asked for his Pawpaw." An odd tension flavored Jake's voice and his watchful eyes never left hers.

"My father and Adam are very close. Dad watches Adam while I work. He's my day-care provider." She gasped at the memory. Where had that come from? Where was the rest?

Jake's eyes narrowed. His body stilled and those amazing pectorals and biceps bunched. "Remember anything else?"

"The wreck. I dreamed about it, and it was so real I—" She hugged her middle. "I remembered turning onto the exit ramp and taking my eyes off the road for a second. When I looked up the other car was right in front of me, coming down when it should have been going up. I swerved. But he swerved the same direction and…then it was too late. I—" A chill raced over her. "Oh. My inattention may have contributed to the accident. Adam could have been hurt and it would have been my fault."

She didn't realize she was shaking until Jake wrapped his arms around her and pulled her against the hard wall of his chest. She leaned into him, resting her cheek on his warm flesh, soaking up his strength and stability until a prickle of awareness infiltrated her distress. He rested his jaw on her head in an embrace that felt as comfortable as it was familiar, and she wondered, not for the first time, why had she left this man when they had a connection this strong between them?

She tilted her head back to look at him. Several strands of her hair clung to his morning stubble. She lifted her hand to free them and savored the sensual rasp against her fingertips.

Jake released her abruptly. "The police report says it wasn't your fault. Let's get some coffee."

He sidestepped her and headed downstairs. As rebuffs went, that one hadn't been subtle. She considered detouring by her room to get dressed, but discarded the idea. His shirt covered her. She followed him to the kitchen. The man casually strolling through the house in his underwear cancelled any cooling effects the chilly tile might have had against her bare feet. She willed herself to pull her eyes away from his tight tush and cleared her throat. "I also had a flash of something green earlier…when I put on your shirt."

His hand, holding a scoop of coffee grounds over the basket, stilled. "My favorite shirt was green. It disappeared when you did."

Was she a thief along with who knew what else? "Did…did I take it?"

He shrugged, finished measuring and then shoved the carafe under the faucet.

"Why would I take your shirt?"

His jaw shifted. "If we weren't going to sleep, you used to wear my shirts after sex. You claimed you liked smelling like me—as if I hadn't stamped my scent all over you in bed. I wore the green one the last time we were together."

Was that why she'd reached for his shirt this morning? Out of habit? And was that why she felt so comfortable in his clothing? Had she taken his shirt as a reminder or by accident? Or had he simply lost it? "And if we were going to sleep?"

"You slept naked. We both did. Couldn't stand to have anything between us." Bitterness added a bite to the last phrase.

A frisson danced over her skin. "Did I take anything else?"

Seconds passed while he emptied the carafe into the reservoir. "No."

"I wish I remembered."

The coffeepot hissed to life. "All you need to remember is why you came looking for me and the name of someone who can look out for you when you get home. I'm going to get my shower. We leave for the shop in an hour."

Had she loved him enough to take his favorite shirt? Or was the disappearance merely coincidental? Would she find it when she got home?

Talia sank into a chair and dropped her head into her hands. She *had* to remember why she'd left Jake, but even more important, she had to figure out why she'd come back and why the prospect of seeing him again had made her cry.

A CASE OF déjà vu slammed Jake the second he entered the kitchen twenty minutes later.

He'd provided breakfast for his guests until today. Now Talia stood by the stove cooking. French toast by the smell of it. His favorite. He hadn't had it since she'd left. His mouth watered and his stomach rumbled.

His shirt covered her to midthigh. His gaze coasted down over her wiggling hips and bare legs to the toes tapping out a tune that only she heard.

Oh, yeah, big-time flashback and his body responded with a stepped-up pulse and a burst of heat—the way it always had.

In their past she'd usually been the first to fall asleep and the first to awaken. More often than not back then she'd had breakfast waiting when he stumbled into the kitchen. Some days he'd eaten it hot. Others he'd been so distracted by the chef's seductive private dancing that breakfast had burned or grown cold.

But that was back in the day when he'd thought they'd be together indefinitely. Not married. Just together. A couple for as long as it worked for each of them.

Now he knew better.

But knowing didn't dull the wanting or curb the urge to sneak up behind her and slide his hands beneath the interlock knit and stroke her nipples and damp center the way he used to. His fingers twitched.

A noise halted his forward momentum and yanked his attention to the breakfast nook. His desire ebbed. Adam sat on a stack of phone books at the table, doodling on a piece of paper and munching a banana.

For a second the feeling of rightness at having people in his kitchen enfolded Jake. Breakfast had been the one and only time growing up when his entire family had been in the same place. The one time when his childhood had seemed normal. Whatever the hell normal was.

He shoved the memory aside. This whole scene was a little too homey for comfort and made him want something he'd never risk. He'd had his shot at holding his family together and blown it. He wasn't going there again.

Adam looked up and chirped, "Mornin', Dake."

"Good morning, kid."

Adam slid out of the chair, crossed the room and grabbed Jake's fingers in his little hand. His sticky banana-covered hand.

Jake let himself be towed to the table.

"Sit here."

Jake sat. No reason not to. Adam scrambled back into his chair and started humming. Poor kid. Couldn't carry a tune in a bucket. One of these days somebody would tell him just how bad he sounded. Jake didn't envy him that humiliating moment. Jake had been in third grade when his school music teacher had asked him not to sing at the holiday pageant.

Talia came up behind him. Her silky soft hair brushed his temple as she leaned over his shoulder to put his plate in front of him. Her unique scent combined with the musky aroma of sex enfolded him and his body tightened. He fisted his hands against the urge to spear his fingers in her hair and tug her down for a kiss or into his lap—the way he would have four years ago.

Damn. He hadn't realized how much he'd missed having her around. Kind of ironic that he wanted to forget the past as much as she wanted to remember it.

"Thank you." He forced himself to stay seated when he wanted to get up and get the hell away from temptation.

"You're welcome. Cooking is the least I can do considering all you're doing for us." She set a second plate in front of Adam. The humming stopped and the kid dug in like the reigning champion at a pie-eating contest. "If you could watch him for a few minutes, I'll get dressed."

"Sure."

Talia not joining them was no surprise. Although she used to sit at the table and watch him eat, occasionally stealing a bite from his plate, she'd never been big on breakfast. She headed upstairs, leaving Jake alone with her son.

Her son. Jake still couldn't get over her turning to someone else so soon after leaving him. It left a bitter taste in his mouth and a burn in his gut.

While he ate, Jake studied the boy. Adam was so much like his mother it was eerie, and the more time Jake spent with the kid, the more of Talia he saw in him. If there was any sign of the boy's father in that little energetic package, then Jake didn't see it.

If Jake had been another type of man, Adam could have been his and not some stranger's. But that wasn't the case. Long ago he'd promised himself no ties. No dependents. No pain. And no regrets for what he couldn't change.

He shoved another forkful of French toast into his mouth, but it did nothing to soothe the hunger pains gnawing at him.

Adam's big, sad, brown eyes looked up from his

almost empty plate and nailed Jake. "Pawpaw gone to hebben."

Jake's gut twisted. He glanced over his shoulder to make sure Talia wasn't within hearing range. "Yes, he's gone. I'm sorry."

"He fall down and go to sleep."

Jake's indrawn breath whistled through his teeth. Had Adam been with his grandfather when Rivera had passed?

"Mommy cried and the am'lance came."

The doctor's warning not to force Talia's memories or face a possible breakdown might become an issue if Adam repeated his words in front of his mother. Was Adam old enough to understand if Jake asked him to keep the news to himself? Probably not. But Jake had to try—for Talia's sake.

"Let's not talk to Mommy about Pawpaw. She might cry again." Was that too much pressure to put on Adam? He had no clue. And then Jake realized how odd it was that he wanted to protect Talia when just days ago he couldn't wait to get rid of her.

Only because you don't want to risk her emotional stability and lengthen her stay. No other reason.

"Finish your breakfast, Adam. We're going to the shop."

"To work on cars?"

"Right."

"I draw'd it." Adam abandoned his empty plate, picked up his crayon in one sticky hand and shoved the picture he'd been scribbling in Jake's direction with the other. But the irregularly shaped image on the page wasn't what caught Jake's attention.

Adam held his crayon in his left hand. His *left.*

The back of Jake's neck prickled as unconnected items suddenly coupled like train cars.

Jake was left-handed and his father and grandfather had been lefties.

Jake was tone deaf. Couldn't sing or hum in tune to save his life.

And then there were the times he'd thought Adam reminded him of Ricky at that age.

Two similarities were a coincidence. But three? Denial ricocheted through Jake's skull. But the doctors had said—

Could their guesstimate on Adam's age be off by six months?

Jake shoved his food away only half-eaten. The inferno in his gut had nothing to do with hunger.

He had to get Talia back to North Carolina where she could verify her son's birthdate.

Because her son might also be his.

"I'M SORRY to be taking you away from your show," Talia said to fill the tense silence in the dark car. In the hours since they'd left Atlanta, Jake had been tight-lipped and mostly silent.

"You're not. The torque wrench broke. We can't shoot anything else until the replacement comes in. That'll be Friday at the earliest."

"Do wrenches usually break that easily?"

She was beginning to think he wasn't going to answer when she saw his lips tighten in the headlights of an oncoming car. "They do if I drop them."

Jake had been in the middle of this morning's filming when the wrench had slipped from his hand and hit the floor. She'd known by the expressions on the faces of the men around him that something bad had happened. Seconds later Jake had stormed into the office and ordered Talia to grab her stuff. He'd said he was taking her home early. She'd thought he meant to his house, but the minute they'd arrived he'd ordered her to pack her and Adam's belongings. Within a half hour they'd hit the highway for North Carolina, stopping only for gas, lunch and potty breaks for Adam.

"Will this mess up your schedule much?"

"I build a week in for emergencies. When's his birthday?"

She blinked at the abrupt change in topic. "Whose?"

"Adam's."

She opened her mouth to answer. But the answer wasn't there. She was sure it had been on the tip of her tongue a second ago. "I—I don't remember."

"What time of the year?"

"I don't know."

"Hot or cold when you brought him home from the hospital?"

Why was he so insistent? "Jake, *I don't know.*"

"Is he mine?"

She gasped in surprise. But try as she might to make out Jake's expression, the dashboard lights didn't offer enough illumination. "You said he wasn't."

"Not if he's two and a half." His thumbs tapped the wheel. "He's left-handed and tone deaf."

So was Jake. He couldn't even whistle on key. Her heart thumped. *Hard.*

If Adam was Jake's son, then why had she left Jake? How could she deny father and son the opportunity to know each other? She couldn't believe she'd make such a heartless choice.

"I—we can check his birth certificate when we get home. We should be there soon. My exit is coming up."

How could she remember directions to her house and not her son's paternity?

Did she just not remember or did she really not know who'd fathered Adam? Had she been sleeping with more than one man? Had she cheated on Jake? The possibility made her stomach churn. What kind of person was she? She was almost afraid to find out.

Her dread only increased as they turned through the crape myrtles flanking the entrance to her neighborhood. Apprehension knotted her stomach and tightened her muscles. She glanced over the back of the seat at Adam, now slumped over in his car seat sound asleep. It was after nine, past his bedtime.

Would whatever they discovered change her son's life?

Jake found her street using his GPS—a built-in device far more sophisticated than Talia's portable one, but she'd come to hate the sultry voice giving instructions from the gadget. That disembodied tone was practically the only one talking in the car.

Her house came into view. The white picket fence she'd painted this spring gleamed in the streetlights. Another memory. Little useless facts sprinkled down on her like a shower, when what she needed was a deluge of critical, significant information.

Jake pulled to a stop in her empty driveway. She didn't want to get out of the car. The now-familiar panic gripped her throat. Why?

"Get the door. I'll get Adam."

Jake's words prompted her out of statue mode. She wiped her sweating palms down her pant legs, dug her keys out of her purse and forced her feet to carry her up the sidewalk. The sensor light clicked on, illuminating her path. Her hand shook as she fitted the key into the lock and pushed open the door.

Apprehension crawled over her skin like ants as she flipped the light switch in the foyer and then the den. She turned a slow circle. The house was empty and silent, but everything looked and smelled familiar. She recognized the pictures on the walls, the quilt draped over the back of the sofa and even the orchids and peace lilies blooming on the bookshelf beside the fireplace.

But she didn't remember Adam's father. There was no sign of an adult male sharing her pastel-decorated space.

"Where do you want him?"

She swallowed to ease her dry mouth. Jake stood in her foyer with a still-sleeping Adam cradled in his arms. "His bedroom is upstairs at the end of the hall."

Jake didn't ask how she knew. He just climbed the stairs. Talia strolled through the first level of the house, turning on lights and waiting for something to click and erase the dark spots in her memory. She entered her kitchen with its white cabinets and spotted a folded newspaper on the table. Why hadn't she taken it out for recycling? She always took the paper out as soon as she finished reading it.

She crossed the room and reached for it. Her father's picture stared up at her from the page, stilling her hand. *The obituary page.*

Her father was dead.

Pain speared through her, quickly followed by grief, overwhelming, wrenching waves of grief. A sob rolled up from her chest. She mashed her fingers over her mouth to dam a second one. Her knees buckled, but she caught herself by grabbing the chair.

Memories came rushing back. Memories of going to his house after work to pick up Adam. Having to use her key to get in because her father and Adam hadn't greeted her on the porch the way they usually did. Finding Adam playing with his favorite toy truck on the floor beside her prostrate father.

Adam had looked up and scampered to her. "Pawpaw's takin' a nap," he'd said.

But Talia had known from her father's odd posture

that he wasn't napping. She recalled her terror as she'd sprinted across the room to check for a pulse and hadn't found one. She'd rolled him over, ready to perform CPR, but he'd been gone too long. She'd tried anyway.

"Talia?"

She startled and numbly faced Jake. "He's dead. My father is dead. I called 911. But it was too late."

Sympathy etched lines between his eyes and beside his mouth. His hand grasped her shoulder in a gesture of support. "I'm sorry. I wanted to tell you, but the doctor said not to."

"My father is dead. And I *forgot.* How could I forget that?" And then his words sank in. "Wait. You knew?"

He lowered his hand. "Martha found the obit online Monday. The doctor thinks that's what you're blocking."

Struggling to make sense of the last few weeks, she turned away and hugged herself. Her breaths shuddered in and then back out. Her father was gone—probably instantly from a massive heart attack, the doctors had claimed.

It had been just the two of them ever since her mother had passed away when Talia was fifteen.

And then Adam had made it three.

And now it was back to two. Her and Adam.

And Jake? Was he part of the equation?

"Where's Adam's birth certificate?" Jake's tight voice interrupted her thoughts.

"I'll get it." With anxiety miring every step, she returned to the den, opened the cabinet and the fireproof safe it concealed. *You know where it is but not what it says?*

Her hands shook as she withdrew the folder containing all of Adam's important documents. She couldn't bear to look, but she forced herself.

Father: Jake Larson.

Her heart pounded in panic, in despair. A wave of dizziness swamped her. She stumbled toward the sofa and sank onto the cushion.

What had she done? How could she have kept Jake from knowing his son and her son from his father? What kind of monster was she to deny them both?

Or had she had a very good reason?

Damn her blasted missing memory anyway.

"Talia?" Jake closed the distance between them and plucked the birth certificate from her fingers. She heard his breath hiss. "You have my name on here, but if he's mine, why didn't you tell me you were pregnant when you left me?"

She heard the accusation and implication in his tone and she wanted to give him the answer. She needed to give him one. But she couldn't. "I don't know."

"You claimed you were on the pill. Was that a lie? You wanted kids. Did you deliberately get knocked up?"

She flinched. Could she have done something so heinous? Her mouth worked, but her brain didn't supply any answers and no words emerged.

"Or did you run because you couldn't face me and tell me you'd been with someone else? Maybe that jackass you worked for. He always had the hots for you. Despite his wife."

Her mouth dropped open in horror. Could she have had an affair with her *married* boss? She couldn't even picture his face.

"I—I can't believe I'd do that." But she didn't know. Not for sure.

Jake must have heard the doubt in her voice because his mouth thinned and his eyes hardened. "You knew my rules. No rings. No kids. No forever. Is Adam mine?" he repeated.

"I—" *Don't know.* She bit back the words. He had to be sick of hearing them. She was. A feeling of helplessness overwhelmed her. She shook her head. "I wish I could tell you what you want to know. What we both want to know."

He swore and stomped out of the house. The outside lights flicked on. But Jake didn't get in his car and drive off. He snapped open his cell phone, stabbed out a number and paced back and forth across her lawn like a caged lion while he talked.

She'd never seen Jake this furious. *That* much she knew for sure. Why wouldn't the rest come?

Because she was very afraid that what she didn't know could cost her the most important thing in her life. Her son.

CHAPTER SIX

"YOU NEED a DNA test," Jake's lawyer said over the cell phone.

"If she refuses?"

"Your name on the birth certificate is grounds enough to get a court order. It takes three to five business days to get the test results. That means you could know something before the weekend, but mostly likely it'll be early next week. First thing in the morning I'll find a lab near her place and set up an appointment for tomorrow, and then I'll call you with the time and location. Work for you?"

Less than a week, but it seemed like an eternity. "I'll make it work."

Jake pressed a fist to his stomach. The fast-food burger he'd eaten a couple of hours ago sat like motor sludge in his gut, and fury lit his veins. "If he's mine, where do we go from here?"

"Depends on whether you want to see the boy and how litigious you're willing to get. Has she made any demands yet?"

"No." Talia hadn't asked for anything. She'd even offered to buy his gas for driving them home.

"Do you think she'll hit you up for a chunk of back child support? She's seen your house. She has to have some idea of what you're worth now."

If she cared about his money she hadn't let on. He scanned her compact two-story house in the dark. The place looked well-maintained and it was in a decent neighborhood. If she was hurting for money it didn't show. "Hell if I know."

"What do you want out of this, Jake? Give me a target and I'll hit it."

"I wanted never to be a father. But if I am..." He dropped his head back and stared up at the dark starless sky. "I won't turn my back on any child of mine."

The way his parents had on him.

"First, let's find out if he's yours. Then we'll plan our attack. The fact that she's offered less than full disclosure to this point works in our favor."

Jake ended the call, retrieved Talia's suitcase from the Escalade and returned to the house. He dropped the luggage at the foot of the stairs and found her sitting in the den. She had a large book of some sort opened in her lap. A baby book, he realized as he approached.

"Adam was months behind in cutting most of his baby teeth. The pediatrician was so concerned he had X-rays taken. But my father said I was just as late getting mine." She looked up. Sadness turned down the corners of her mouth. "I didn't remember that on my own. I read it here in my notes. If my father's death is what I'm blocking, then why can't I remember the rest now that I know about Dad?"

"You'll have to ask your doctor."

"What if I never remember? What if this book is all I have of Adam's first three years?"

The emotional quaver in her voice, her vulnerability and her obvious pain dampened his anger, but only slightly. A trapped, backed-into-a-corner feeling took precedence. "I want a DNA test. My attorney is setting up one for tomorrow."

The little color remaining in her cheeks leeched away. "I understand why you don't trust me, but—"

"If you refuse I'll get a court order."

"I'm not refusing, Jake. But this doesn't have to get ugly."

"How can it not? You were pregnant when you left me. You either cheated on me or screwed me over by getting pregnant when I'd specifically told you I didn't want children."

Her spine snapped straight. "I didn't get pregnant by myself."

"Birth control was your issue. You wanted it that way. In fact, you insisted. You claimed stopping for a condom interrupted the romance and kept us from being as close as we could be."

Saying the words out loud made him wince at his stupidity. *Jeezuz.* Had she been setting him up the whole time? Given the way he felt about having kids, he'd been a damned fool to let someone else be in charge of birth control. He should have used a backup method. He had with anyone else. But like he'd said this morning, they'd wanted to be skin to skin with each other.

"No matter what the DNA test shows, I can't trust you, Talia."

The wounded look in her eyes made him feel as though he'd punted a puppy. But he'd only stated the facts.

"I can understand how you'd feel that way. And since I can't remember what happened I can't defend myself or offer an explanation. I'll show you to the guest room."

"I'll stay at a hotel."

She put the book on the coffee table and stood. The record of Adam's life both compelled and repulsed him. He wanted to look. And yet he didn't.

"There's no need. Besides, there aren't any close by. The bed's already made. The sheets are clean. I washed them before leaving for Atlanta." She hesitated and then added, "My father used to stay over quite often. He liked to be around to tuck Adam into bed."

Her eyes shut tightly and she inhaled a long, slow, not-quite-steady breath as if the memory were painful.

He reminded himself she'd just lost her father. For the second time. The urge to take her in his arms and comfort her almost overcame his good sense. He clenched his teeth and shoved his fists in his pockets.

"It's the room next to Adam's. I'll put clean towels in the hall bathroom for you."

If he had an ounce of gray matter between his ears he'd hit the road. "I'll get my bag out of the car."

He took five minutes to do a two-minute job. After retrieving his bag he stood on Talia's front porch, bracing himself before going back inside. The heavy summer-night air reeked of flowers. Not surprising since Talia had always been a plant fanatic. She'd filled his condo and the areas around his front and back doors with blooming plants. The plants had died from neglect after she'd left. His feelings should have done the same.

Why in the hell hadn't they?

Why did he still want her?

She'd lied. Either by omission or commission. And he could not let himself get suckered by those big brown eyes again.

"WHAT HAPPENS when this is…over?" Talia focused on the fingernails digging crescents into her palms rather than the familiar scenery passing outside her car window.

"Depends on the results." Jake's clipped words chilled her. He'd spent the night in her guest room, but he might as well have been back in Atlanta for all the distance between them. Breakfast had been strained. Only Adam had had an appetite.

Jake's anger showed in the hard angle of his freshly shaven jaw, his stiff shoulders and his more aggressive driving style. Not that he was being dangerous, but he accelerated faster than usual at each light, braked harder and turned a little sharper at each corner.

Worry over today had kept her from sleeping well last night, and this morning everything seemed to rub her raw nerves the wrong way. The tape over the cut on her face made her cheek itch. Her head hurt and nausea teased the edges of her consciousness. Any second now, she thought she might burst from the emotions roiling inside her.

To distract herself, she turned and looked at her son. Her world. She hadn't been able to hold Adam close enough this morning. He'd squirmed and squawked a protest until she'd had to let him go. He'd immediately run to Jake, who after a slight hesitation had lifted Adam, carried him to the car and strapped him into his car seat.

Now Adam sat in the back humming off-key, kicking his feet to his self-made music and totally oblivious to the tension between the adults in the car.

If she never remembered another thing, there was one fact she was absolutely certain of. She'd do anything, endure anything for her son. No matter how painful.

She blinked and turned back to Jake's profile. "I mean if he's yours, then what?"

"You'll move to Atlanta."

Test number one, apparently. "What about my job, my house, my—"

"If *your* son is *my* son, then he's going to grow up knowing his father. If you have a problem with that you'd better get an attorney."

The threat sent a tidal wave of panic through her

that made it difficult to fill her lungs. Leaving her friends and a job she loved would be a sacrifice, but one she'd willingly make for Adam to have the opportunity to know Jake. She gasped as the realization sank in. She remembered her job at Adam's pediatrician's office, her friends and her coworkers.

"We'll move closer to you. That's best for Adam."

The stoplight turned green as they approached the intersection. Jake hit the gas. A car coming from the right did the same.

"Look out!" Talia screamed.

Jake threw an arm in front of her, holding her against the seat, and stomped the brake. The Escalade shuddered to a halt, and the car running the light whizzed by, missing their bumper by only inches. To add insult to injury the driver flipped them the bird and blew the horn even though *he* had broken the law.

Talia's heart pounded. She gasped for breath and twisted in her seat to check on Adam. He was fine and seemingly clueless about how close he'd come to being in his second auto accident in less than a week.

"Are you all right?" Jake lowered his arm.

She turned back to Jake, and in that instant, everything was as clear as if her memory had never been gone. Everything. Including the fact that she'd left Jake because she loved him.

Her heart leapt to her throat. "Pull over."

"Are you hurt?" Genuine concern filled his voice.

"No. But I remember. All of it."

"Our appointment—"

"We're only five minutes away. Please, Jake. I know why I left you. And why I came back."

A horn sounded behind them. Jake glared at the rearview mirror and put the SUV into motion. He drove to the next parking lot, turned in and stopped the car. He flicked the key and silenced the engine. Only Adam's humming filled the air.

"I had a stomach flu that I couldn't seem to shake."

His narrowed eyes never strayed from her face. "You never mentioned being sick."

"I didn't want to dampen your excitement. You were in talks with the TV show people." She swallowed to ease the sudden dryness of her mouth. "I went to the doctor. He ran a test and said I was pregnant. He thought I could have been just one of the two-percent-birth-control-pill-failure statistics. I'd known I was a little late, but I never suspected…" She shook her head.

"Why didn't you tell me?"

"I tried. I couldn't make myself come right out and say I was pregnant because I knew how you felt about marriage and children. So I hinted around."

His jaw shifted. "And I made my position clear. No kids. No rings. No commitment."

His adamancy had crushed her. "Yes, you did. But I wanted our baby, Jake. I was afraid you'd tell me to get rid of him, and I loved you so much I was even more afraid I'd let you talk me into it…. So I left."

He clenched his hands into white-knuckled fists. "You had no right to make that decision without me."

"No. I didn't. I realize that now. When I left I never intended to contact you again or ask for anything. But I remembered how miserable you'd been in the foster-care system, and I didn't want that for Adam. That's why I kept your name and picture in my wallet. If anything had ever happened to me, my attorney had instructions to contact you and explain the situation. He's been holding a letter from me to you, explaining how much I loved you and why I did what I did, but that I didn't want to force you to do the one thing you'd always sworn you'd never do. Become a parent."

"Why come after me now? Four years too late."

Too late? She hoped not.

"When my father died I realized that as much as losing him hurt, I was better off for having had him in my life. He was an amazing person and he taught me—and Adam—so much." She closed her eyes and struggled with her grief. When she thought she could speak without her voice breaking, she looked into Jake's dark, wary eyes and willed him to understand.

"I wanted Adam to have that chance with you. How much or how little you want to be involved in his life is up to you. But he deserves to know you, Jake. And you need to know him. He's amazing. Not a day goes by that I don't love him more."

She glanced out the window as comprehension dawned. "It wasn't my father's death I was blocking. It was the prospect of losing my son. That's why I was crying when I took the exit on the way to your house.

And I didn't see the oncoming car because I was digging in my purse for a tissue.

"Adam is all I h-have left. He's my heart, my soul, my reason for being, Jake." Tears burned her eyes and clogged her throat. She searched Jake's hard face, looking for some sign of understanding or forgiveness and found none.

What she'd feared the most could very well come true.

She could lose Adam. At the very least, she'd likely lose Jake again.

And now she knew she'd never stopped loving Jake Larson and she probably never would.

JAKE DIDN'T know what to think.

Should he believe Talia's story? It sounded plausible. But he had enough doubts to want to see the DNA results.

He was a seeing-is-believing kind of guy. He *needed* to see the results.

Mechanically he restarted the car and pulled back onto the road. His eyes kept drifting to the rearview mirror and the boy singing off-key in the backseat.

Is he mine?

And what if Adam *was* his? Jake had had few good examples of parenting and had no clue how to be a father. How could he guarantee he wouldn't fail the kid the way he had his brothers and sisters? What if he turned out to be neglectful like his parents or abusive like more than one of his foster families?

His heart banged like a knocking engine and his mouth dried. He'd never been afraid to take risks. But this one might be more than he could handle.

Thirty minutes and three cheeks swabs later Jake was back in Talia's driveway, clenching the steering wheel until his knuckles ached while Talia unbuckled Adam from his car seat. She turned the boy loose on the lawn. Jake couldn't peel his gaze from the bouncing, running, whooping child.

Adam had been more active and more talkative since waking this morning. And the stuff that came out of the kid's mouth had made Jake laugh out loud more than once.

Is he mine? The question reverberated in his head again.

Talia removed the car seat from the Escalade and set it beside the driveway. She closed the door and walked around to his side. He lowered the window.

"Aren't you coming in?"

"No." He couldn't bear to spend every waking moment over the next few days watching Adam and searching for some small piece of himself in the kid. If he stayed he would. No need to torture himself. The die was cast. Either he was or he wasn't Adam's father.

"But your bag—"

"Is in the back. I brought it out this morning."

Mistake number one: he should have had a vasectomy years ago. But the idea of anybody getting near his goods with a sharp instrument made him cringe.

Mistake number two: he'd let his guard down and trusted Talia.

She'd been young, just twenty-two, when they'd met, fresh out of college and so darned green he'd been afraid someone—like her idiot boss—would take advantage of her. Jake had been thirty-one, bitter and jaded and banged up by the school of hard knocks. He had to admit Talia's rose-colored-glasses outlook had been a big part of her appeal. That and the fact that she overheated his libido from the moment they'd met when she'd delivered her boss's car to his garage.

But she'd left him, pregnant with either his child or someone else's. Could he trust her?

Not a chance he was willing to take.

"I'm sorry I didn't tell you about Adam as soon as I knew. For what it's worth, my father begged me to. He thought you had the right to know."

Small comfort.

"Please give Adam the opportunity to know what a great father he has, Jake." Hugging her arms around her middle, she backed away from the car.

She wouldn't say he was great if she knew he was the reason his family had been torn apart.

The pain in her eyes ripped him wide open. He turned away to look through the windshield instead of at her. "Do you have someone to call who can check in on you and…Adam?"

Why in the hell was saying the kid's name suddenly so hard? But from the moment she'd told him

Adam was his, everything had shifted. Even though he wasn't convinced she was telling the truth, waking up with the kid in his bed again this morning had been different. He must have wasted ten minutes lying there watching the kid breathe.

"I'll call one of my coworkers. They aren't expecting me back at work until next week. I took some time off to deal with my father's estate and get his house ready to put on the market. And I have to make temporary child-care arrangements and tell the office I'm not coming back for long if we're moving to Atlanta. But I'll let them know I'm home."

"Make a follow-up appointment with your doctor."

"I will."

She'd stolen from him, damn it. His peace of mind. His trust. Maybe even his kid. Why did he care about her safety? "You'll hear from me when the lab calls."

"They're supposed to call me, too," she stated unnecessarily. He knew that. "Goodbye, Jake."

He checked to make sure Adam was out of the way and then pulled out of the driveway. He didn't look back.

What was done was done and it couldn't be changed.

And soon he'd know if his greatest fear—becoming a parent—had become a reality. And if it had, he hoped he was man enough to do the job.

HAVING HER memory back was both a blessing and a curse, Talia decided. Because along with the good came the bad.

She moved through the house by rote, cleaning up while Adam napped. She not only recalled and relived the memory of losing her father, she remembered how leaving Jake had torn her heart out. She'd cried the entire eight-hour drive to her father's house. When she'd arrived he'd taken one look at her face, opened his arms and offered her a place to stay for as long as she needed.

For months after returning to Raleigh she'd lived on edge, alternately praying and dreading that Jake would come after her. When she'd finally realized he wasn't coming and that any chance of a happy ending was merely a fantasy, her heart had died a little more.

She shouldn't have expected him to chase her. If nothing else, his late-night, post-lovemaking confessions had taught her that he had a thing about people abandoning him. His family. His foster parents. Her.

Luckily, she'd had their child growing inside her to distract her. For her baby's sake she'd glued the pieces of her heart back together, bought a house and gotten on with her life.

She returned to the den and spotted Adam's baby book on the coffee table where she'd left it last night. She'd filled the album with every memento she could cram between the overstuffed pages. Memories she held in her heart and in her head.

Memories Jake didn't have.

She recalled the way he'd stared at the book last night—as if he wanted to take a look inside the cover but was afraid to. The expression in his eyes had been classic Jake, the man she'd fallen in love with, the one who she suspected yearned to be connected to someone, but because of his unhappy years bouncing through foster care wouldn't allow it.

He'd warned her time and time again during their relationship not to count on him, that he wasn't the kind of man to stick around, but his actions had contradicted his words. He'd shown her he loved her in a dozen different ways. But his words had pushed her away.

And she'd paid attention to the wrong signals.

She caressed the baby book's embossed cover. She had her memories. But she now knew firsthand how empty the lack of them had left her, how unconnected and alone she'd felt.

She'd made a mistake by selfishly denying Jake the chance to see his son born, to see Adam's first years. She should have told Jake about her pregnancy and given him a chance to rise to the occasion. She didn't doubt he would have. Instead she'd taken the easy way out and run home to her daddy.

She could never give back those lost years, but she had it within her power to give Jake the connections he lacked.

And maybe, just maybe she could make him love Adam as much as she did.

CHAPTER SEVEN

"YOU OKAY, man?" Rich, Jake's assistant and right-hand man, asked as soon as the garage emptied for lunch Friday.

Hell, no. "Absolutely."

"You sure? I mean, first you dropped that torque wrench a couple of days ago. I've never known you to drop anything. Steadiest hands I've ever seen whether we're working on a clunker or a three-million-dollar sports car. And now you seem…I don't know…distracted since Talia came back. We've never had to do so many retakes in a shoot."

Jake's neck burned. The valid criticism about his lousy performance today hit home. He wasn't about to admit he'd dropped the fragile tool on purpose Tuesday so he'd have a legitimate excuse to shut down filming for a couple of days and drive to North Carolina and check out Adam's birthdate.

Nor would he admit he was distracted because he kept waiting for the cell phone clipped to his belt to vibrate. The lab had said they probably wouldn't have the results before Monday, but there was a chance they could come through today.

But he could use a sounding board. And Rich knew how to keep his mouth shut. He'd been with Jake since day one. He'd been the first employee hired after Jake had struck out on his own. And he'd known Talia before.

"Adam might be mine."

Bushy eyebrows hiked under the bill of Rich's *Larsonize This!* hat. "Is that good news or bad?"

Good question. "He's a great kid."

"Well, yeah, and his momma's never been hard on the eyes, either. But do you want him to be yours?"

Rich's comment gnawed at Jake's jealous bone. Stupid, because Talia wasn't his. Not anymore. Did he want Adam to be? "Doesn't matter what I want. He either is or he isn't."

"Hey, I'm just saying, it's clear as untinted glass you and Talia still have the hots for each other. You couldn't keep your eyes off the window when she was here. If you wanted to hook up with her, permanent-like, the kid could be yours no matter whose he is biologically. Y'know. You could adopt him or something."

The idea didn't make Jake flinch the way it would have a week ago. A knock on the door saved him from having to come up with an answer. The FedEx guy strolled in. "Package for you, Jake. You gotta sign for this one. Personally."

He received packages all the time. Martha usually signed for them. Some were car parts. Some were gifts of an odd variety from his more ardent female fans. He'd learned to be leery of deliveries that came when he hadn't ordered anything.

"Go eat lunch before the caterers pack up, Rich." Jake always had lunch catered on Fridays as a treat for his crew. He figured it was the least he could do since they were helping him juggle his dual careers, the TV show plus the customizing business.

He signed the electronic keypad and passed it back to Bob, his usual delivery guy, then accepted the box. "They probably have a killer dessert you can take with you if you swing by the canteen."

"I have to admit, I love it when you get packages on Friday. See ya next week, Jake."

Jake carried the box to the office to dump until later, but his gaze fell on the return address. Talia's. His feet and heart and lungs stalled. What could Talia be sending him?

He set the package down on a workbench and reached for a box cutter. One sweep of the blade slit the tape, but Jake hesitated. She couldn't have the results yet, so what was this? Bracing himself, he opened the flaps and folded back the bubble wrap.

His green polo shirt topped the pile.

Talia had taken his shirt when she left. It looked a little more faded than he remembered. Why had she kept it? Unless she hadn't lied about loving him. His heart pounded against his rib cage.

He lifted the shirt and set it aside. A note in Talia's curvy, girly script had been taped to the top of Adam's baby book.

I'd like to share my memories with you. I've enclosed Adam's baby book and two photo albums so you can see your son grow up.
Talia

Your son. Jake's chest tightened. His hands shook as he lifted out the book on top. His skin prickled. Looking at the books meant getting involved. Getting involved meant risking failure. And rejection.

He put the album back in the box and stepped away from the table. Turning on his heel, he hustled toward the canteen. Lunch might ease the burn in his belly.

Running, Larson?

He stopped halfway across the complex and looked back toward the garage. He stood between his present and his past. The past he and Talia had created. The one that wasn't going to go away just because he walked away.

He didn't need a DNA report to tell him Adam was his son. He'd seen the truth in Talia's eyes. A truth he'd been too afraid to believe.

He'd been telling himself all these years that he wasn't afraid to take risks, but he'd been afraid to take the biggest one of all. Letting himself care for someone else. Someone else who might leave him.

Fear of trying is the same as failing.

He'd never looked for his brothers and sisters because he'd been afraid of how their lives had turned out after he'd let them down. He hadn't wanted to know. He hadn't wanted to care.

But he did care, damn it. Twenty-five years later the repercussions of that night still haunted him, crippled him. He just hadn't been willing to own up to it.

Talia had left him.

Because you gave her no choice.

He'd told her in no uncertain terms that he'd never marry her and never give her children. He'd said if she wanted kids she'd better find some other sucker to buy into that happily-ever-after fairy tale.

Except for concealing her pregnancy she'd never been less than honest with him. He couldn't say he'd been the same with her. Or himself. Because while he'd been hurt and pissed off that she'd left him, he'd also been relieved, he realized with twenty-twenty hindsight.

Every night she'd fallen asleep in his arms, he'd wondered if it would be the last. He'd been waiting for her to abandon him from the day she'd moved in. Because everybody else had. But that wall he'd tried so hard to keep between them hadn't kept him from falling in lo—

Love. The realization staggered him. How could he have missed that he'd fallen in love with Talia five years ago?

He'd even built his monstrosity of a house with her in mind, based on a comment she'd made during their last discussion. *Don't you want more than this bachelor lifestyle? Don't you ever want to put down roots and build a home and a family?*

He'd made some asinine comment about liking that he could pack up and move if he got the itch. Looking back, he could see that was the moment he'd lost her. The disappointment on her face wasn't something he'd ever forget.

Had he pushed her away?

No doubt about it. Because he hadn't liked the feeling of waiting for the bad news to hit.

Oh, hell. Now what?

Continue to run like a coward? Or scrounge up the guts to face his fears and risk getting hurt?

TALIA CLOSED the door behind the real-estate agent Saturday afternoon and headed to the kitchen to bake cookies for Adam's afternoon snack. He'd be hungry when he awoke from his nap.

She had to move forward. That meant meeting Jake halfway—more than halfway if necessary. She'd put her father's house and her own on the market today and asked the agent to refer her to a colleague in Atlanta. The lab hadn't called yet, but Talia didn't need to wait for the test results to know she and Adam would be moving.

The doorbell rang. Believing the agent must have forgotten something, Talia returned to the foyer and opened the door. Jake, wearing his favorite green shirt, the one she'd slept in so many nights, stood on her welcome mat.

She gasped and put a hand over her racing heart. "Jake."

"I want to be a part of Adam's life and I want another chance with you. I don't know how to be a father, but I'll learn. You can teach me."

Hope inflated her chest like a balloon.

"I want to marry you and adopt him and be the family you wanted. I'm not afraid to try anymore." He raked a hand through his hair, making the short strands stand in spikes. "Well, hell, yes, I am, but I'm going to do this. And do it right."

Her eyebrows shot up at his vehemence, but happiness filled her heart. In the past she would have just said yes and done whatever Jake asked. And that was why she'd run four years ago. She'd known she wasn't strong enough to stand up to him. But now she was. She had to think of Adam.

"You're going to have to explain this about-face. Come in."

He swept past her, trailing a wave of summer air and a trace of his cologne. She followed him into the den. He kept his back to her with his hands shoved in his pockets and his shoulders stiff.

"I'm the reason my family split up," he said without looking at her. "My parents were at work. They each worked two jobs to keep a roof over our heads and food on the table. I was in charge. My brothers were fighting. Wrestling, like they always did. One went through the storm door."

He paused and Talia wanted to go to him, to wrap her arms around him, but before she could turn thought into action, she remembered that in the past Jake had only opened up to her under the cover of darkness. In bed. After making love.

She stayed put, giving him his space.

"Billy cut his wrist. The blood was spurting out. The girls were screaming and Ricky started howling. Billy was crying because he thought he was going to die. So did I. I couldn't stop the bleeding. I had to call 911. The ambulance came. And then the cops came. They took all of us. And that was it. We were never a family again. Because I wasn't doing my job. I was in charge. I should have stopped their fighting."

The pain in his voice made her eyes burn and her throat clog. He turned then and the agony on his face winded her. "I let them down, Talia. But I won't let you and Adam down."

"I know you won't." That he'd carried this burden so long made her want to cry. "Jake, you were only eleven."

"My parents trusted me. And my brothers and sisters counted on me. When I saw my mother in court, she screamed, 'How could you let this happen?' as they carried us away. She blamed me. My father wouldn't even look at me."

She went to him then and grabbed his biceps. The muscles bunched rock-hard beneath her fingers. "They failed. You didn't. You were a child. Your parents had no right to put that much responsibility on you, then blame you for their neglect."

"They were doing all they could. I needed to do my share."

She cradled his face in her hands. "You kept your brother alive. That's what matters."

He took a deep breath. "There's something else you need to know. I bounced between foster homes because, according to the shrinks, I couldn't bond. I'm going to have to work at this. At us."

Her eyes burned with unshed tears. "Trust has to be earned, Jake. The people who took you in didn't keep you long enough to earn yours. But I will."

She rose on tiptoe and pressed her lips to his. His arms went around her, hugging so tightly she could barely breathe. He opened his mouth and deepened the kiss, plunging his tongue into her mouth and stroking, consuming with an edge of desperation.

Talia reveled in his hunger and her own need rose to meet his. When he finally lifted his head, she sank down onto her heels. "I never stopped loving you, Jake."

The love and tenderness in his smile tilted her world. "Then marry me. I don't want to miss any more of Adam's life. And next time we make a baby," his hand painted a warm swath across her belly, "I'll be there for every milestone."

"You don't want to wait for the paternity test results?"

"Don't need 'em."

That statement proved Jake had come a long way from the scared boy he'd been. "Then yes, Jake, I'll marry you and make a family with you."

"Dake!" Adam shrieked from the door and pelted across the room.

Jake bent and scooped him up. "We already did. We already made a family."

* * * *

Look out for Emilie Rose's glamorous novel,
Wed by Deception, *available from*
Mills & Boon® Desire™ this month!

Trouble in Paradise

JILL MARIE LANDIS

This story is dedicated to my hula sisters one and all, who seem to have no problem getting into trouble in paradise. Dance on, girls, dance on.

"PLEASE FASTEN YOUR SEAT BELTS in preparation for landing. Please remain seated until the captain has unlocked the forward cabin doors and turned off the Fasten Seat Belts sign."

Carrie Evans locked her tray table into position, shifted in her seat and reached up to twist a wayward lock of hair back into the casual upswept knot she'd anchored atop her head with a chopstick. Not just any chopstick—a hand-carved rosewood piece with an enamel design—a new item she was featuring at Time After Time, her upscale, all-things-beautiful eccentricities shop on La Cienega in L.A.

Then she returned to reading a *Spirit of Aloha* complimentary in-flight magazine article that had caught her eye.

Ho'ailona, she read, was the Hawaiian word for signs and symbols, omens sent from the world of spirits to those discerning enough to recognize that they were far from natural occurrences.

"In Hawaii, it's believed that nature provides signs and omens that sound a warning for danger, misfortune, or trouble ahead on one's intended path."

Signs and omens.

Good thing she didn't believe in such nonsense. If she did, she might see the fact that her fiancé, Kurt Rowland, hadn't been able to make the flight for their wedding trip as a very bad sign.

Tossing the colorful airline magazine into her carry-on bag, she left the comfort of her first-class seat behind and smiled at an exotically lovely Hawaiian flight attendant in the doorway. The young woman's makeup was flawless. She wore a vanda orchid tucked behind her ear and both the flight attendant and the orchid looked as fresh as when they took off from L.A. five hours ago.

Carrie wished she could say the same about herself.

The young woman smiled. "Aloha and welcome to Kauai," she said, handing Carrie a map of the island.

"Thanks." Almost in disbelief, Carrie added, "I'm getting married on Saturday. On the beach. At sunset."

"Congratulations." The flight attendant wished her much happiness.

Southern California seemed light-years away as Carrie stepped out of the jetway and into the air-conditioned comfort of the waiting area at the Lihue, Kauai, airport. Exiting the building, she bumped along with the crowd toward the baggage claim, enveloped by the heady scent of plumeria blossoms floating on a blanket of sultry humidity.

Reality hit her as hard as the tropic heat.

I have a wedding to pull off in four days.

A wedding that was taking place two thousand miles from home.

And her groom, who should have been at her side, was still on the other side of the Pacific.

"It's not every day a guy gets the opportunity to be featured on the cover of the *Los Angeles Times* Sunday magazine," she'd reminded him that afternoon as he drove her to Los Angeles International Airport. She was proud and happy that Kurt been chosen for the honor, far more than she was disappointed that they couldn't be on the same flight.

After years of struggling as an unknown artist, Kurt's bold, primitive work was in high demand, but they were both realistic enough to know that fame was fleeting. However, right now he was hot and the *Times* article would really put him on the map. His massive creations graced upscale hotel lobbies and corporate offices all over L.A. Even A-list celebrities were commissioning him to work his magic on their mansion walls.

Carrie made her way to the baggage carousel and edged closer, braced to grab her bag as soon as it trundled past.

Ten minutes later, all but four people had exited the baggage claim area and those left behind were beginning to look forlorn. Carrie's suitcase hadn't come tumbling down the chute onto the carousel as expected. It wasn't oversize. It wasn't overweight. She had the claim tag.

But she had no bag.

Just then, her cell phone rang as if on cue. She glanced at the caller ID and smiled when she saw that it was him.

"You made it." He sounded as if he were right beside her and not an ocean away.

She glanced around at the nearly deserted baggage claim area. Across the carousel, some very pale tourists were helping themselves to complimentary Kona coffee from an air pot on a shelf against the far wall.

"The flight was easy. I took a nap, watched *Spiderman 3* again and went through my folder of wedding plans. Now, here I am."

"Great. The photographer's assistant promised that he'd take care of getting me on the very next plane to Kauai. I'll catch the red-eye and meet you in the morning. Have some champagne on ice and we'll have mimosas and breakfast in bed."

"That sounds fabulous. There's only one little hitch. My bag is missing." She glanced at the ramp that was no longer spewing luggage.

"It'll show up." Kurt's optimism was one of the things she loved most about him.

"I know." She glanced around the baggage claim area. It was only March, but Kauai was extremely hot and muggy. Her parents didn't do hot and muggy well. "I'm beginning to wonder if this was such a good idea after all," she mused aloud.

There was a sudden, ominous silence on the other end of the line. Then Kurt said, "You're not having second thoughts, are you? Look, honey—"

She realized what he was thinking and cut him off. "Oh, no! No. I'm not talking about getting married. I was just wondering if having the wedding all the way over here was such a good idea. I mean, destination weddings are in, but I feel so far away."

Everything was set. Their immediate family and her best friend, the maid of honor, had purchased their airline tickets and reserved rooms. Still, she couldn't help but worry.

"What if my bag doesn't show up? My wedding gown is in it." Simple, elegant ivory silk, her gown was a Vera Wang. It fit her like a glove. "So are the place cards and the photos of arrangements I wanted to show the florist."

"No turning back now. Your bag will get there. Don't worry. You're just exhausted from the long flight. Get some sleep. Things will look better tomorrow."

She sighed. He was always so positive. He made things sound so easy. "You're absolutely right. I love you, Kurt."

"Love you, too, hon. Keep your eye on the goal."

They said their goodbyes. She hung up. She *was* tired. But everything would work out.

She'd never failed at anything in her life and she wasn't about to start now. The sunset wedding on a secluded stretch of beach—the prelude to their marriage—would come off without a hitch. With the help of the Hawaiian event coordinator she'd found on the Internet, she'd planned everything in minute detail.

A destination wedding had been her idea. Having Kurt's bohemian father and brother meet her conservative parents on neutral ground was a far better plan than what would surely become a horrific scene from an unscripted *When Worlds Collide* if she'd opted to hold the reception at her parents' country club outside Chicago.

She didn't have to remind herself that Kurt Rowland was a dream come true. He was not only her fiancé, but her lover, the man of her dreams, her best friend. Just the sound of his voice over the phone had worked its magic.

She was calm. She was refocused now. Everything would be fine.

She'd never believed in love at first sight until the moment her eyes had met Kurt's across a crowded gala in the upscale lobby of L.A.'s latest boutique hotel. The hotelier had ordered gift baskets for VIP guests from Time After Time, and Carrie had received an invitation.

The hotel's automatic door had whisked closed behind her that evening and she'd barely stepped inside the lobby when she'd recognized Kurt, the celebrated artist who had created the floor-to-ceiling mural in the lobby across from the reception desk. His stare was so intent, so sizzling hot, that her high-heeled pumps seemed to have suddenly been Gorilla-glued to the terrazzo marble floor. She couldn't take another step.

It was a second or two more before she even realized he had a woman on each arm, bracketing him like well-placed bookends. One was a striking brunette, the other an icy, glamorous blonde. Both, Kurt explained later, were models. Their attendance was set up by his publicist so that he made a statement walking into the reception.

Barely breathing, she watched as he smoothly left the two women, snagged two glasses of champagne off a passing waiter's tray and carried them across the room to her.

He wore his dark wavy hair long enough to tease the collar of his black Armani T-shirt. He was the only man at the gala in jeans, yet he looked perfectly at ease. He was male-model handsome, but exuded a bad-boy roughness around the edges. Once she got to know him, she found that he laughed easy, loved hard and was a hopeless romantic.

The mural behind him depicted the settlement of L.A., from its early history to the present, the diverse mix of the city's ethnic groups, the grandeur of the miles of sparkling coastline and the lavender, snow-covered mountain peaks that rimmed the L.A. basin.

One glance at his work and she knew they were from two different worlds. She was traditional: classic white on white, vanillas and crèmes, calm on the exterior but a cauldron inside.

He was eclectic: bold colors that bordered on neon, bright blues, reds, sunset oranges and purples, primitive and earthy. He wore black, took chances with his art and his business dealings. Inside, he was as tranquil as a tropical shoreline at sunset.

From that night on, when they weren't hard at work establishing their careers, they were inseparable, forging a relationship that both hoped would last a lifetime.

She learned his parents were back-to-nature hippies from Vermont who'd pledged their undying love to one another while standing naked under the summer solstice moon. Though they'd never bothered with a legal ceremony, Trini and Bogie had devoted their lives to each other and their twin sons until Kurt's mother passed away three years ago.

But unlike his parents, Kurt held traditional beliefs when it came to marriage.

Carrie was the woman he wanted to share his life with—he told her he'd known it from the moment he'd seen her walk into the hotel lobby—and he wanted a legal and binding union.

Two weeks after the gala, they moved in together. A month later, he proposed.

It had taken her nearly two years to say yes. She was fearless on all fronts—except when it came to the idea of marriage. Her parents' marriage had lasted nearly forty years, but only because their mantra was "divorce is not an option."

It wasn't love that frightened Carrie. She knew how much Kurt loved her. It was the notion that marriage would somehow change everything that frightened her. It had taken him over a year and a half to talk her into accepting his proposal and setting a date.

To the casual observer, her parents, Dorothy and Edward Evans, had a marriage as picture-perfect as their privileged lives. But only Carrie knew the truth. Behind closed doors, her parents coexisted in a cocoon of polite, icy exchanges. Any passion, laughter or love had died long ago. As far back as Carrie could recall, they hadn't even shared the same room.

Kurt had finally convinced her that just because her parents hadn't had a loving relationship, that didn't mean their marriage wouldn't be as successful as everything else she'd ever attempted in her life.

Now, as she tried to ignore the humidity in the Lihue airport, she tucked her cell phone back into the outside pocket of her carry-on, looked around and thought, *By week's end, we'll take our vows on a beach on this romantic, magical island.*

But first, she had to track down her bag.

The man behind a Dutch door beneath the Lost Luggage sign wore the placid expression of someone who had heard one too many complaints and was no longer listening.

"Fill this out," he mumbled as he plunked down a form in front of her. "Sign here, and here."

The sheet was covered with drawings of numerous styles and sizes of bags. Many looked exactly alike. Finally she chose what she hoped was her bag type, checked the box, signed and handed back the form. Behind the man in the door, a heavyset woman in a purple- and yellow-flowered muumuu had her back to Carrie as she worked at a computer. Images of bag identification pictures filled the monitor.

"My wedding dress is in that bag." Carrie sighed.

The woman in the muumuu shot her swivel chair around. "Wedding dress, eh? Congratulations, den."

"Thank you. Realistically, how long do you think it will be before my bag arrives?"

The two airline employees exchanged a telling look. Both shrugged.

"Pretty soon. Tomorrow, maybe, at the latest," the woman offered. "Worst case it went to Samoa. Get next week."

"Next *week?*" Carrie gasped. Her fluttering hope began to die. "The wedding is on Saturday night."

Tuesday was nearly gone.

Suddenly what the woman had said dawned on Carrie.

"Samoa?"

The woman burst out laughing and slapped her knees. "Just having some fun wit you. It'll be here… mebbe on da next flight. Somebody will call."

"But it *will* arrive, right?" Carrie glanced between them, seeking reassurance.

"Go get one mai tai. When we find it, we'll call you and have someone deliver it to—" the man paused and glanced down at her form "—to the Hanalei Plantation Hotel."

"Thanks," Carrie mumbled. No way was she having a fruity rum drink with an umbrella stuck in it. It was bad enough Kurt wasn't here. Now her bag was floating somewhere in luggage limbo.

Or, heaven forbid, making its way to Samoa.

RECORDED MUZAK, typical tourist fare, filled the Alamo Rental Car building.

The young Hawaiian female clerk behind the counter couldn't have been nicer, or more apologetic, as she smiled at Carrie.

"Sorry, ma'am, but the Town Car you reserved isn't available. We'll put you in a nice Jeep, though. If you'll just sign here and here. Will you need extra insurance?"

Jeep? There are nice Jeeps?

Carrie shook her head. Hearing herself called ma'am was bad enough.

"I don't need extra insurance. I need the Town Car. We'll be picking up our folks. And my fiancé has an elderly aunt who—"

"Tourists love our Jeep. It has four-wheel drive and the option of a convertible top."

"I really don't think…"

The clerk continued to smile but she tapped her long, bejeweled nails on the counter. Her hair was glossy black and hung loose down her back to her waist. "This is the only car we have available right now. We're completely booked. Take the Jeep and maybe check back in the middle of the week."

"Do you think one of the other rental agencies—"

The young woman shook her head. "Everybody's choke."

Carrie stared, not sure she understood. "Choke?"

"Booked. There are a couple of big conventions on island. Better you take the Jeep and be sure you have a car."

Carrie sighed.

No fiancé beside her. No bag. No dress. No Town Car.

She remembered the in-flight magazine article.

So far, the signs were definitely *not* good.

BY THE TIME she'd pulled out of the Alamo parking lot driving a bright, bumblebee-yellow Jeep that screamed "I'm a tourist, rip me off," the sky began to sprinkle. She ended up circling the small airport twice before she hit the correct exit lane, made it onto the two-lane "highway" and headed north toward her destination at Hanalei.

When the sprinkles escalated to a downpour, she was forced to pull over and deal with the Jeep's zip-on top. It was like wrestling with a vinyl alligator. After fifteen exhausting minutes, she gave up. The rain came in squalls, so between downpours she drove along in a string of traffic at what appeared to be the island's top speed of forty miles an hour. Occasionally she would pull over beneath the biggest tree she could find and wait it out.

She figured she was over halfway there when it began to rain so hard she was forced to stop in the small town of Kilauea. She took refuge in an old stone church built during the town's plantation days. She'd no sooner stepped through the double wooden doors and into the hushed, quiet coolness of the lava-rock walls when her cell phone went off.

She recognized her mother's number.

"Hi, Mom." Carrie didn't dare let her mother hear

the exhaustion or frustration in her voice or Dorothy Evans, whose hobby was making mountains out of molehills, would pounce.

Her mother was a self-described charity fund-raiser who still couldn't hide the fact that she was disappointed Carrie had opted for something other than a traditional church wedding and a five-course dinner at the Willow Creek Country Club. The Evans family had been members for nearly seventy-five years.

Her father, Edward, a conservative stockbroker, had been presented a membership by his father as a wedding gift. Edward had held the office of board president for four years running.

"How is it going, darling?" Her mother wanted to know.

"Great." Soaked to the skin, her crème-colored linen dress looking like something a bag lady would wear, Carrie stood in the open church doorway staring out at the pouring rain. At least she didn't have a suitcase getting soaked in the Jeep. "I'm on the way to Hanalei Plantation."

"Kurt is there, isn't he?" Her mother almost sounded hopeful that Kurt *wasn't* there. She'd been waiting for a crack in Carrie's relationship almost since the beginning.

"The *L.A. Times* called wanting a last-minute interview and photo shoot. He's coming on the next flight."

"Oh, *really?*"

"Yes, really. It's a great opportunity for him. For us," she amended.

"I suppose marrying an *artist,* you'll have to learn to adapt to a more…*fluid*…lifestyle."

Her parents were convinced that marrying an artist was one of the single most foolhardy things Carrie could ever do. What she'd tried to explain to them was that Kurt wasn't a scattered, flaky artist. He was a man with a vision who set goals and didn't lose sight of them until he'd accomplished success. But her parents only believed what they wanted.

She reminded herself that Kurt was *her* choice and this was *her* wedding. Her and Kurt's. She wasn't going to let her mother dampen her spirits. Besides, the rain was doing a great job of that already.

"You know," her mother was saying, "when I went to the Arnold wedding at the club last week, it was just lovely. They served the most wonderful salmon with a creamy artichoke sauce. The bride chose carrot cake. I thought it very untraditional, but then Mary Ellen Franks told me that carrot cake is quite popular at weddings now. Are you having carrot cake? Can they even *get* carrots over there?"

Carrie decided now was not the time to tell her mother that she'd ordered what the event planner had declared an island favorite—a *liliko'i* or passion fruit cake, with white icing smothered in toasted coconut.

"Carrie?"

"I'm here, Mom."

There was a long sigh on the other end of the line and then, "I wish you were getting married here. It would have been so wonderful. Your father always dreamed of walking you down the aisle at St. Augustine's where we were married."

Carrie doubted her parents knew what each others' dreams were anymore.

"Well," Carrie said, trying to stay positive, "the wedding is in four days and I'm here to get the ball rolling, so I'd better get back on the road."

"Call me, dear."

Carrie promised to call again before her parents left Chicago. When the rain let up, she ran back to the car. She tried to ignore the squish of the wet seat beneath her linen skirt as she sat down.

Twenty minutes later she was checking into the Hanalei Plantation Resort high on a bluff above the Hanalei River. The view was spectacular. Feeling like a drowned rat, she was escorted to the private Honeymoon *Hale* Bungalow by a young, dark-eyed bellman attractively wrapped in the male version of a sarong.

He appeared to relish explaining how to correctly pronounce *hale.*

"Hah-lay," he said with a sloe-eyed wink of his bedroom eyes.

"Ha-ha." She rolled her eyes, too exhausted to appreciate his joke.

Once she'd made herself comfortable and helped herself to the complimentary toothpaste and potions in a welcome basket, she ordered breakfast and a bottle of champagne for tomorrow morning, then called and left Kurt a voice mail.

"Aloha, honey. I've got the champagne ordered and I'll see you in the morning. Sweet dreams on the plane."

She walked to the poolside café where she ordered a light salad for dinner. Afterward, a simple pink tank top and khaki shorts, some flip-flops and slip-on rubber reef walkers caught her eye in the hotel gift shop. She bought them, along with a fun, extra-large, men's tank top with a colorful Kauai rooster printed on the back.

As she was about to walk out the door of the shop, she noticed a rack of cards and books on Hawaiian customs and myths. Remembering the interesting in-flight article, she grabbed a few books, too. Since much of Kurt's art incorporated blending the past with the present, she hoped he might find something inspiring in them.

Returning to the cottage, she slipped into the oversize tank top and turned in early. Sometime during the night, her cell rang. The LED numbers on the bedside clock radio glowed 11:00 p.m.

It was Kurt. He should have been in midflight.

"Where are you? Are you all right?" She was drowsy and hot but more concerned about him. Clutching her phone, she wandered across the room in the dark, patting the sliding door to the *lanai* as she searched for the latch in the semidarkness.

"I'm fine. I made the flight…"

"Can you speak up a bit? I can hardly hear you."

"I don't dare." His voice was hushed. "We've been sitting on the runway for two hours…"

"Kurt!" Carrie switched on a light, forgetting about opening the doors. "You haven't been hijacked—"

"Of *course* not."

"Then why are you whispering?"

"There's a lady with a toddler beside me and the little guy *just* stopped screaming. The airport's fogged in. They predict it's going to lift soon, but I wanted you to know I'll be getting in late. How is everything going?"

"Okay." She had a vision of herself navigating the miserable topless Jeep down the highway in the pouring rain.

No Kurt. No bag. No Town Car. No top. No sun. Fog shuts down LAX.

Signs and omens.

"Hon? Carrie? You don't sound okay."

"I'm fine." It was impossible to sound upbeat when it was 2:00 a.m. in her previous time zone. "I'll set the alarm and come pick you up in Lihue."

"There's no guarantee when we'll be taking off. I'll get a cab and meet you at the hotel." He made kissing noises over the phone. "All better?"

She couldn't help but laugh. He was the best.

"Yeah. Thanks, honey. See you tomorrow."

Wide-awake now, she opened the slider and the tropical breeze billowed the sheer white drapes against her bare legs. Somewhere in the distant darkness, drums pounded with a primitive, carnal beat.

Carrie walked back to the bed, picked up the in-flight magazine she'd carried off the plane and slid beneath the crisp sheet. She hoped staring at glossy photos of beaches and endless expanses of ocean would help her drift off again.

Of their own accord, the pages shifted open to the article about the mystical side of island life. Carrie read the first few lines again and then shoved more pillows into place to prop herself up. She glanced toward the wide double doors open to the *lanai,* watching the white sheers dance on the night breeze as she read the article teaser again.

"In Hawaii, it's believed that nature provides signs and omens that sound a warning for danger, misfortune, or trouble ahead on one's intended path."

Exactly what kind of signs and omens? she wondered.

Hurricanes and volcano eruptions? Or simple everyday things like last-minute delays? Lost luggage? The wrong car? Rain? Fog? Tardy fiancés?

Carrie closed the magazine and tossed it on the table. She clicked off the bedside lamp and shut her eyes. The sound of water rushing down the lava-rock waterfall into the pool outside the *hale* was meant to be soothing, but all she could think about was driving around with rain blowing into the Jeep for the next four days. She reached out to Kurt's empty side of the bed and sighed.

He should be here. This was their wedding trip.

So what? She told herself not to sweat it.

After all, she was a doer. An organizer. When *L.A. Magazine* covered the opening of her store they'd called her "one of the sharpest, most inventive and perceptive entrepreneurs to come on the scene in decades."

She'd have no problem pulling off the wedding of their dreams and they'd live happily ever after.

But deep inside that sharp, inventive, perceptive woman, there existed a niggle of doubt when it came to truly believing love could stand the test of time. She knew firsthand about the failure of marriages in today's world, knew the odds weren't good. A niggle of doubt plagued her the way a grain of sand in the wrong part of a sandal could worry itself into a blister.

What if the island is trying to tell me something?

As she lay in the dark, lulled by the sound of gently falling water, caressed by the scent of plumeria on the night wind, her worry mounted.

What if Kurt's last-minute delay, not to mention all the other little setbacks that have occurred since I arrived, are signs and omens foreshadowing disaster ahead?

Ridiculous, she thought as she tossed the magazine back onto the bedside table. *Absolutely crazy.*

She punched her pillow, lay down, closed her eyes.

Ten minutes later she gave up, padded across the room toward the table where she'd left the books on Hawaiian lore and carried them back to the bed.

"ALOHA! You've reached Happily Ever After Events. I'm Rainbow Roberts and I'm not here right now, but wait for the beep, leave a message, and I'll get back to you as soon as possible. Have a sunshine day!"

Carrie waited for the beep. And waited. Finally the recording came on again and this time a generic automated voice announced, "Machine full."

She'd slept fitfully until dawn when she gave up trying and went for a walk along the beach. Afterward, she returned to the gift shop and bought a few more books on Hawaiian myths and legends. Leafing through them over breakfast, she found there was much that was forbidden and mysterious about the islands—and nothing very reassuring.

Back in her room, she checked on Kurt's arrival time only to learn he was going to be far later than he'd estimated. At least he was on the way.

She hadn't gotten where she was in life by assuming everything was under control, so she tried calling the caterer that Rainbow Roberts had booked. When no one answered at Island Grinds Kau Kau Katering, she looked up the address in the phone book and decided to drive to nearby Anahola and take one last look at the menu for herself.

Nearly twenty-five minutes later she was making a third U-turn on a small residential street near the beach. With a map in one hand and the steering wheel in the other, she tried to locate the caterer's headquarters, but the neighborhood of modest dwellings nestled around a bay was clearly residential. She'd passed the same row of houses four times. Kids playing in the yards openly stared as she drove by.

Clearly there was no warehouse, no restaurant, no substantial building that might house Island Grinds Kau Kau Katering. She checked the address again, looked up and finally noticed a small square of worn plywood propped against a rock in the yard in front of a faded green house. The address had been spray painted on the wood with neon orange paint.

Carrie pulled over. According to the map, she was in Anahola and this was the address of Island Grinds. She grabbed her straw bag and stepped out of the Jeep.

The front porch was minuscule and covered with rubber thongs, work boots and tennis shoes of all sizes. She stepped onto the threadbare mat in front of the sagging screen door and knocked.

And waited.

Eventually she heard the sound of heavy footsteps inside. A plus-size elderly woman in yards of ruffled floral fabric opened the door. Silent, she scowled up at Carrie as an episode of *Family Feud* blared out of a television in the background.

"I'm sorry to bother you." Carrie lifted the map and gave it a wave. "But I was looking for…" She suddenly remembered that when Rainbow pronounced *Kau Kau* it had sounded like cow-cow. She wasn't brave enough to give it a try. "I was looking for Island Grinds…" She let the rest of the phrase drift away.

Immediately the woman smiled. "Dis da *kine.*"

"Kine?"

"Place. Da *kine.*" She opened the screen and

stepped outside. "You wanna talk my daughter, Leinani, but she gone *holoholo*."

Carrie had no idea what going *holoholo* meant. Either the woman had left for a place called Holoholo or, for all Carrie knew, she'd gone crazy.

"Has she been *holoholo* long?" she dared.

The woman shook her head and laughed. "Jus' since yesttaday."

"Is she going to be all right?"

"She'll be back couple'a days. Mebbe more. Mebbe not."

"She's not here?"

The woman laughed again and patted Carrie on the shoulder. "No. She gone *holoholo* to Big Island to see her cousin. Took all da *keiki*. Da kids."

Carrie mentally ticked off the days. Today was Wednesday. Three left until the wedding. "My wedding is on Saturday. Rainbow Roberts assured me things were all set—"

The woman cut her off. "Dat one *lolo*. For sure."

"Rainbow is *holoholo,* too?"

"No. Rainbow is *lolo*. Crazy. I don't know if she gone *holoholo,* too, or not."

Carrie knew one thing for certain. If she wasn't off this porch in two seconds she might be going *holo holo lolo* or whatever herself. She pulled out a small notebook and pen, wrote down her name, the name of the hotel and her cell number.

"Have your daughter call me the minute she gets back, okay? Thank you *so* much." She forced a smile and pressed the paper into the woman's hand and bid her goodbye. She was off the porch when the woman called out, "Eh, no worry, yeah?"

Carrie waited until she'd climbed back into the Jeep before she dug her cell out of her purse and dialed Rainbow's number again.

The answering machine was still too full to leave a message.

Carrie started the engine and headed up the hill toward the highway.

The first thing she planned to do when she got back to the hotel was buy a Hawaiian dictionary.

"ELVIS PRESLEY made three films on Kauai, *Blue Hawaii* being the most remembered. Our next stop will be the famous Hanalei Pier where not only *South Pacific* and the *Wackiest Ship in the Army* were filmed, but also *King Kong*. Let's all sing along to the theme song of *Blue Hawaii* as we head to Kauai's lush North Shore…."

There wasn't a cab to be found and all the rental cars were booked when Kurt's flight had finally touched down four hours behind schedule. He walked out to the highway and flagged down a white minivan with a brightly painted sign that read Movie Tours.

The driver was a Hawaiian named Kimo. His dark scowl became all smiles when Kurt offered to pay him and the tour guide, Danny, aka Mr. Perky, the $110 attraction fee just to hitch a ride out to Hanalei.

Kurt figured no amount of money was too much with Carrie waiting for him in bed in the Honeymoon *Hale* she'd described over the phone last night. He would have paid double—until he bumped his way down the narrow aisle to the only empty seat at the back of the luxury van.

There was no place for luggage, so he was forced to sit with his suitcase on his lap. Beside him, a woman with a violent sunburn scooted close to the window. She pulled her straw purse up off the floor, scowled and crossed both arms over her bag.

He nodded in her direction. A tight smile came and went across her lips.

So much for aloha.

As advertised on the side of the van, there was air-conditioning, but comfort was short-lived since Mr. Perky, in baggy shorts and a bright pink and orange aloha shirt, felt obliged to fill every single second with corny banter. When he wasn't talking, he was showing clips from movies filmed on Kauai on a small television mounted at the front of the bus. Between the clips, Danny led the passengers in repetitious choruses of old movie tunes. Just now, they were working their way through the theme from *Gilligan's Island.*

Had he signed on for the entire five-hour tour, Kurt was sure *his* last stop would be the nearest psychiatric ward.

He shifted the suitcase on his lap and stared out the window, ignoring six Texans who had already mutinied and segued from singing "Gilligan's Island" and "Blue Hawaii" to "Hound Dog." They were happily bellowing off-key, ignoring Danny's pleas for them to stop.

Outside, the sky showed intermittent patches of blue between dusty-gray rain clouds that occasionally dropped a gentle mist. Kurt's seat was *maka'i,* the ocean side of the bus. On the other side, the land swept toward towering green mountain peaks.

Kauai, he realized, was a place of majestic views and tropical lushness. It was easy to imagine King Kong stomping his way through the misty fog encircling the tops of the mountains. As the Texans ignored a video clip of *South Pacific* and continued to sing Elvis tunes, Kurt found his attention drawn to a bright yellow Jeep parked on the side of the road beneath the canopy of a huge tree.

It took a second before he realized Carrie was seated behind the wheel of the car holding a map over her head in the drizzling rain.

He reached across the woman beside him and tried to slide the window open. When that didn't work, he gave a shrill whistle, hoping to get Danny's attention, but he couldn't be heard over the Texans.

Trapped in an airtight refrigerated nightmare, Kurt tossed his bag into the aisle and stood up. The woman beside him clutched her purse to her bosom and pressed herself into the corner of the seat.

"You have to sit down, sir," the tour guide bellowed over the microphone.

The Texans stopped singing and swiveled in their seats to stare at Kurt.

"Stop the bus. I want off," he told Kimo.

The van continued to sway down the narrow two-lane highway. Kurt gripped the backs of the seats on either side of him to keep his balance.

"My fiancé is in that yellow Jeep back there. Let me out and I'll walk back." He stooped to glance out the back window as the van rolled on.

"We're not supposed to stop." Mr. Perky had become Mr. Snarly.

Kimo exchanged a telling look with the guide and then backed up Danny.

"No unscheduled stops. Sorry." Kimo shrugged.

"Okay, how much?" Kurt reminded himself it was only money.

Kimo and Danny exchanged another glance.

"Fifty." Kimo had the shoulders of an NFL lineman and was twice as wide around the waist.

"You got it." Kurt reached for his wallet.

Kimo pulled into a turn-out at the top of a hill. The automatic door whooshed open and steamy air was sucked inside. Kurt grabbed his bag, headed up the aisle, and shoved a fifty into Kimo's meaty hand.

"T'anks, bra," Kimo mumbled.

"Buh-bye. Make *every* day a *movie* day!" Danny flung his left arm toward the bus door in a dramatic gesture worthy of Judy Garland.

Kurt hopped out of the van and headed back down the road on foot. The rain was now just a slight mist. The air was warm. He didn't mind getting soaked. Within a few seconds, the rain stopped entirely. He watched the yellow Jeep pull back onto the highway and sat his bag down. Then he started waving his arms over his head.

ONCE THE RAIN ENDED, Carrie swiped her wet hair out of her eyes, started the Jeep and pulled out from beneath the shelter of a huge tree blanketed in red blossoms. She hadn't heard from Kurt, but she hoped he'd be at the hotel when she got back. Her cell hadn't picked up a signal since she entered the Anahola area where Leinani, the caterer, had gone *holoholo*.

Carrie was soaked, her tank top plastered to her skin like a contestant in a wet T-shirt contest. The map she'd picked up at Alamo had almost disintegrated. While fiddling with the air-conditioning control knob, she caught sight of a man in a black shirt standing very close to the edge of the road. He was waving his arms, whistling an ear-piercing whistle. As she drove by, he started running after the Jeep calling, "Carrie! Stop!"

Her heart executed the same flip-flop that it always did whenever she saw Kurt.

She glanced in the rearview mirror. There were no cars immediately behind her, so she braked and pulled over. He came around to the driver's side and reached over the door, laughing and kissing her at the same time.

"I was afraid you weren't going to see me." He wiped a raindrop off the end of her nose.

"What are you doing out here? How did you get

here?" She looked in the rearview mirror and spotted his suitcase standing next to the highway.

"Let's just say I nearly witnessed an Elvis sighting, but I was spared." He glanced around the wet interior of the Jeep. "Why didn't you put up the top?"

"I tried. It has a life of its own." When she noticed his gaze locked on her nipples, she reached down and pulled her sopping wet tank top away from her breasts.

"Wet looks good on you." He winked. "Maybe we should just pull off onto a dirt road and not waste time going back to the hotel."

"Are you kidding? You'd have to be a contortionist to make love in this thing."

"I'm willing to try." After one look at her face he added, "Let's go back to the hotel and get you out of these wet clothes. What do you think?"

"I think I'm really, *really* glad to see you. It doesn't matter how you got here."

"Let me run back and grab my bag. I'll drive to Hanalei."

She watched him jog back down the road a few yards, grab his suitcase and head back to the Jeep. He tossed the bag in back and as if he wrestled vinyl alligators every day of the week, he quickly zipped the top and windows into place. She was happy to relinquish the wheel and climb into the passenger's seat.

"Did you get any sleep on the flight? Are you awake enough to drive?" She reached over and ran her fingertips through his hair where it curled over the collar of his casual polo shirt.

"I'm wide-awake now. I finally got some sleep after the toddler in his terrible twos passed out." He spread his palm possessively over her thigh and began to slide his hand up her leg toward the hem of her shorts. She shivered.

"So why are you driving around in the rain, anyway? I thought you'd be waiting at the hotel."

"It wasn't raining when I left." She sighed and glanced out the window at the endless expanse of ocean. "I don't even know where to start."

"How about with this Jeep?"

"Two big conventions on island. The car companies are choke."

"Choke?" He started laughing and reached up to readjust the rearview mirror.

"Never mind." She waved away the explanation. "They didn't have the Town Car we ordered. The event planner, Rainbow, has an answering machine that's so full it's not taking any more messages. Rather than sit around, I decided to drive to Anahola to talk to the caterer myself."

"What did he say?"

"*She* wasn't there. She went to the Big Island. Actually—" Carrie smiled "—her name is Leinani and her mother told me she had gone *holoholo.* I thought that meant she'd gone crazy, until I found out *lolo* means crazy." She took a deep breath and then said, "Do you believe in signs?"

"What? You mean like stop signs?"

"No, *signs,* as in omens. Warnings."

Kurt stared back at her as if he had serious doubts about her sanity.

He reached over and pressed his palm against her forehead.

"What are you doing?" she asked.

"Checking to see if you have a fever. You sound delirious."

She wished her mounting fear would dissipate like the rain now that he was here, but she still felt edgy. Losing sleep while reading about ancient Hawaiian beliefs and myths hadn't helped at all.

"I'll be okay, now that you're here," she mused aloud.

Kurt squeezed her thigh. "Maybe I should perform a more thorough physical exam." Without warning, he turned down a dirt road that wound its way to a deserted stretch of beach.

"What are you doing?" Carrie grabbed hold of the handle on the door above her as they hit a pothole. To the right, she spied a small stream that tumbled down the hillside to the beach.

"I'm fulfilling a fantasy," he said. "What do you say we see if that stream has a swimming hole?" His heated expression hinted that they wouldn't be doing much swimming.

She could think of a thousand and one things she should be doing in preparation for the wedding, but Kurt was smiling at her in a way that made her heart race and her nerve endings tingle. He drove on until they reached a small, empty field that was obviously a parking area. This afternoon, the Jeep was the only vehicle there.

"Think of this as a prelude to the honeymoon." He opened his door and headed around the car to take her hand.

He led her across the grassy field to where a thick jungle of trees, ferns and vines nearly hid the stream from view. They followed the slow-moving water along the streambed until they could no longer see the parking area. Though the ocean was still out of sight, the sound of the waves crashing on the beach blended with the rush of the stream.

"Here we go." Kurt smiled and waved toward a spot where the rocks formed a natural pool. Though the sky was overcast, the air was warm. "I'll bet on a sunny day this place is crawling with tourists. Lucky for us it's still overcast." He slipped out of his rubber thongs and pulled his shirt over his head. When he reached for the fly of his jeans, he paused and said, "Undress, Carrie. We're going skinny-dipping."

"But—" She glanced around the empty jungle. "What if somebody comes along?"

He walked over to her, ran his hands up and down her arms, took hold of the hem of her top and pulled it over her head. "The water will hide what we don't want seen," he whispered.

"But—"

"The only butt I want to think about right now is yours." He cupped her left cheek and brought her up against him. She felt his erection. He was hard and ready for her. Despite the fact that someone could come along at any moment, she felt herself melting inside, aching for fulfillment.

Within seconds he helped her out of her shorts and stripped off his pants and briefs. It took a moment for them to negotiate the mossy rocks that lined the streambed, and the fresh water cascading toward the ocean was a lot cooler than she expected. To her overly warm skin it felt downright cold.

She let out a squeal when she jumped off the rock and slipped into water up to her neck. Seconds later Kurt took her in his arms and they came together, skin to skin beneath the surface of the water. His hands traced the curves and hollows of her body. Her hands found him unerringly. Within a heartbeat he was pulsing hard and insistent in her hand. He hooked his arm around her waist and lifted her in the water so that she moved against him. She wrapped her legs around his body and felt him slide between them until he sheathed himself inside her.

The sultry air, the chill of the water fresh from the clouds on the mountaintops, the soft sigh of the leaves moving on the breeze, the call of the birds in the trees, all blended together to delight the senses and add to their erotic pleasure.

Carrie lost herself in the moment and let go of all inhibition as Kurt held tight to her waist and she moved up and down his hardened shaft. She clung to him, begging for more and more until she knew that he was near the breaking point. When she could no longer stop the rush of sensation, no longer put off her own release, she pressed her lips to his ear and whispered, "Come with me, Kurt. Come with me *now.*"

He covered her mouth with his. A kiss swallowed her cry of ecstasy. The world disappeared until there was just the two of them climaxing in the stream like primeval forest creatures, panting, sighing, reveling in one another.

Finally, replete, she laid her head on his shoulder. Her heartbeat slowed to a near-normal rate.

"That was wonderful," she sighed, pressing her cheek against his shoulder. She cupped clear water in her hand, lifted it, let it cascade down the back of her neck. She thought about how silly she'd been last night when she'd worried about warning signs and omens.

Now that Kurt was here, now that she was in his arms again, there was no doubt this is where she belonged.

"Carrie?"

"Mmm?"

"Let go, hon."

She wondered why he was whispering.

"What?"

"Let go. Slide down." He was prying her arms from around her neck. "Now."

"What's wrong?"

"Duck down so that your breasts are underwater."

She turned around and there, spread out on the bank above them, was a Cub Scout troop decked out in their navy shorts and shirts with yellow bandanas tied around their necks. Their scout leader was nowhere to be seen.

"Hey, mister," one of the boys yelled. "We know mouth-to-mouth, too, if you need any help."

"Way cool," another chimed in. "He saved her from getting drownded!"

"She sure made a lot of weird noises," added a short kid who was staring at Carrie in amazement.

She was wondering how long she could hold her breath when one of the Cubs yelled, "Mister, if that's your Jeep back there in the field, you forgot to set the parking brake. Our troop master said to tell you it rolled down into a culvert."

A RECORDING OF DON HO'S mellow voice wafted through the hotel boutique the next morning. Since her bag still hadn't arrived, Carrie decided to shop for a few more necessities.

At breakfast on their *lanai,* Kurt tried to assure her that a mini-shopping spree would help her forget about the spectacle they'd made of themselves in front of the Cub Scouts, not to mention the embarrassment of having to climb out of the pool, hurriedly dress and then wait two hours for a tow truck to come and pull the Jeep out of a drainage ditch and back up the hill.

She chose a floral bikini in hot pinks and sunny yellows, some pretty sandals, a sundress and a *pareau,* a piece of colorful rayon fabric that could be tied in numerous ways to create wraparound cover-ups. Kurt waited near the door, chatting on his cell to his father, Bogie, a retired art history teacher.

Carrie changed into the swimsuit in the boutique dressing room and wrapped the *pareau* around her. Tucking her tank top and shorts into the shopping bag, she was ready for the pool, ready to start over on Kauai. Ready to put the past two days behind her.

When she stepped out of the dressing room, Kurt glanced over and gave her a big smile and a thumbs-up. Snapping his phone shut, he waited for her to join him.

"What did your dad say? Shouldn't they be on the flight from Denver already?"

Kurt's father and twin brother, Turk, were traveling together, making the long trek from Vermont to Hawaii.

"They've reached Denver, but their flight is delayed." He looked away a little too quickly for her peace of mind.

She'd only met his brother once. The word eccentric didn't do Turk justice. Their parents, Bogie and Trini, hadn't been expecting twins and had only chosen the one name, Kurt. When their second son was born moments later, they quickly scrambled the same four letters and came up with Turk.

Turk was as handsome as Kurt but not identical in looks. He was also an artist—but instead of choosing a traditional art form, Turk had made a name for himself crafting sculptures out of dryer lint.

When Kurt told her that his brother was one of the

foremost dryer lint artists in the country, Carrie thought he was kidding until she discovered Turk had been awarded a National Endowment Grant for his artistic pursuits. The entire hamlet of Verdant, Vermont, where the Rowland boys grew up, shared in Turk's fame by contributing bushels of colorful dryer lint for his projects.

"Anything wrong?" She had the feeling Kurt was holding something back.

"Everything's fine." He nodded, but only slightly. Just enough *not* to reassure her.

"Kurt, what's going on?"

"The Denver airport is snowed in."

She felt her heart sink to her toes. Snowed in. A natural occurrence, but was it another omen? Turk was Kurt's best man—and now he was stranded in Denver. So was their dad.

"They'll *be* here, Carrie."

"There's something else you're not telling me. I can see it in your eyes."

He ran his hand over the night's growth of dark stubble on his jaw. "I'm not going to tell you unless you promise not to start in with the bad omen thing again."

Last night in bed, she'd tried to tell him a bit about the article she'd read, but his attention kept straying to her breasts and he fell asleep without hearing her out.

"Kurt, please tell me what *else* is going on," she demanded.

"My great-aunt Harriet is missing."

"Missing?"

He nodded, took her hand and led her out of the store. By now both female clerks were not even pretending to ignore them. They'd sidled up closer and were openly listening to the exchange.

He led her down a lava-rock path, through an extensive garden full of dripping crab claw heliconia and overhanging plumeria trees. When they reached a small stone bench beside the pool's cascading waterfall, he sat down and pulled her down beside him.

She stared at their bare toes lined up in their sandals. His great-aunt Harriet was eighty-nine. She lived in a retirement condo in Miami and was to have met up with Bogie and Turk in Denver and travel on to Kauai with them.

Kurt laced his fingers through hers and rubbed the back of her hand with his thumb. "They haven't heard from her since yesterday. She wasn't on her flight from Florida to Denver. They got the airlines to tell them that much. She's not answering her home phone."

"What if..." Carrie hated to say it aloud. Anything could have happened to the woman.

"Dad called her neighbor, Mr. Morganstern, and had him go check the apartment. She's not there. He saw her leave in an airport shuttle."

"You think she could have been kidnapped?"

He laughed and shook his head. "If anyone had kidnapped her, they'd have turned her loose by now. You've never met my great-aunt."

She'd seen photos, though, and Harriet looked harmless enough. "What are we going to do?"

"There's nothing we can do until we hear from her. She'll turn up."

"Aren't you in the least bit worried? She's eighty-nine, Kurt."

"She's always said age is just a number."

"Still, I'm sure your father is worried sick."

"Dad? No way. He believes the universe is in charge."

The universe is in charge. She fell silent, thinking. How could the Rowlands *not* be worried? Is this how Kurt would react if they had a child who was late getting home from school some afternoon? Would he leave it up to the *universe* to take care of Junior?

What if the universe was trying to tell them something right now?

A snowstorm in Denver. Another natural sign. *Ho'ailona.*

She thought, for a moment, she heard the drumbeat of the island echoing inside her—until she realized it was only the pounding of her own heart.

"I'd like to go back to the room," she told him. She didn't dare add that she thought she was having a heart attack.

BY THE TIME THEY reached the door to the Honeymoon *Hale,* Kurt noticed Carrie was more than a little anxious.

"What's wrong?"

She walked inside as if she hadn't heard. The huge cottage was airy, bright and pure luxury. He followed her over to the sliding doors and they walked out onto the balcony. Kurt was still astounded by the breathtaking view of the lush, tropical foliage and the walking paths that meandered past the pool down to the beach. He studied the view with an artist's eye. The colors were magnificent.

He found Carrie in the dressing area, staring at her shopping bags.

"You don't really need to wear anything." He took a step closer, bringing them together, slipped his arms around her waist and brought her against him. He loved that she was tall, that they fit together perfectly. He lowered his lips to hers, tantalized by the same electricity he'd felt the first time he'd kissed her.

She was almost smiling, still distracted. When she pulled out of his arms, alarm bells went off inside him.

"What's wrong, babe?"

She stared down at her hands, refusing to meet his eyes. He placed his hand beneath her chin and gently forced her to look up. "What is it?"

She shrugged. "The signs."

"Not this again." From the look on her face now, he wished he'd paid more attention last night.

Signs and omens, astrological forecasts, mediums and psychics. His mother, Trini, had been a great believer in all things mystical. His twin brother was, too. But Kurt's feet were planted firmly on the ground.

"You're kidding, right? You're not *really* worried," he said.

"I *wish* I was kidding." She crossed over to the table that held a pile of books he hadn't given more than a glance until now. Books on Hawaii, local lore, myths. She shuffled through them until she found the same magazine he'd ignored on his flight. She held it up, tapped the cover.

"Ancient Hawaiians believed that nature sends us signs…*ho'ailona* they called them. The spirit world gives us warnings of troubles to come. Omens. It's up to us to heed them."

He looked at the books. "Where did you get all this stuff?"

"The hotel gift shop."

She had at least ten books on Hawaiian legends, myths, spirits, *kahuna* magic and healing. One of the things he loved about her was that she threw herself into everything, every new interest, with abandon. But all this talk of signs and omens gave him pause—surely she wouldn't resort to such a flimsy excuse to call things off.

He'd dated countless women before Carrie, but from the moment he'd laid eyes on her, he'd known deep in his soul that she was the only one who would ever claim his heart. He wanted her to be his wife. He didn't care how elaborate the ceremony, how many attended, or where it happened. He wanted to stand beside her and officially vow to love, honor and cherish her all the days of his life.

"You aren't having doubts, are you?" He steeled himself for her response.

"What?"

He'd never seen her so distracted. "Doubts. About us. About our marriage." Was she trying to come up with an excuse to cancel the wedding? He couldn't, wouldn't believe it.

She shook her head. "No! No doubts about us, but I'm wondering if this is the right time to get married. Or maybe this just isn't the right place—"

"Everyone's on the way, Carrie. Everything is set."

"I know, but the signs—"

"*What* signs?"

"My lost luggage. I didn't reserve that Jeep and yesterday it rolled into a ditch. Those Cub Scouts—" Her face was flaming with embarrassment. "Your last-minute flight delay—"

"I'm here now." He spread his arms wide. "Hey, I think it's a *good* sign that I was resourceful enough to get here even though there was no transportation available."

"There wasn't?"

"No. I had to bribe a movie-tour van to let me hop a ride."

"You're kidding."

"That's not something I'd kid about. You know what it's like to be cooped up with a bunch of Texans singing Elvis tunes at the tops of their lungs? It was only for a few minutes, but I think I may have irreparable ear damage." He knew a surge of relief when the corner of her mouth lifted in a half smile, but her smile disappeared in an instant.

"But now there's more than just the Jeep incident and my lost bag," she said. "Your dad and brother are stuck on the mainland. Your aunt is *missing.* Our wedding planner and her caterer are MIA, too. If it was just *one* thing, I might not worry, but your family is stranded and no one here returns my calls."

She shook her head, gnawed on her thumbnail for a second and then sighed. "I'm really trying not to turn into Bridezilla here, Kurt, but something *weird* is going on."

"Listen." He reached for her again and started nibbling on the exposed skin of her shoulder. Then he slipped his fingers under the strap of her tank top. "Why don't we get comfortable and discuss this in bed? Afterward, I could really use a nap." He had the strap off her shoulder when he realized her palms were pressed firmly against his chest—and not in a good way.

"Kurt…wait. There's something else I need to talk to you about…"

He pulled back. Stared down into her eyes. "I thought you wanted to—"

"I…it might be bad luck to…you know—" she waved her hand around "—keep this up…" She blushed up to her hairline.

"Bad luck to *keep what up?*"

"To make love anymore before the honeymoon. I mean, it's supposedly bad luck for the groom to see the bride on their wedding day and here we are, *sleeping* together in the same cottage. The *honeymoon* cottage. It's only two days until the wedding. Maybe this isn't such a good idea."

He glanced at the pile of books again. Kahuna *Magic, Myths and Legends of Hawaii.*

"Don't tell me that the ancient Hawaiians thought it was taboo for engaged couples to share a honeymoon cottage before the wedding."

"Are you making fun of me?"

"Certainly not. I'm worried. I put you on the plane and everything was fine. Now, less than twenty hours later, you're getting cold feet."

"I'm not getting anything of the sort. It's just that all these weird things keep happening."

"They aren't weird things. They're just *life.* You're thinking like one of those celebrities who puts a moratorium on sex before the wedding—revirginizing—they call it."

"I'm not revirginizing. I just don't think we should make love before our wedding night. Is that too much to ask?"

"Do you want me to get another room?"

"We can still *sleep* together…" Her words faded away.

"But no lovemaking before the wedding?" It was ridiculous to think they shouldn't make love until the wedding. They'd shared the same living space for two years. "So sleeping side by side is okay? Or do I have to bunk on the floor?" He glanced at the pile of reference books. "Did you read that in an ancient Hawaiian rituals manual somewhere? Sleeping, yes. Hanky-panky, no."

He would have laughed if her eyes weren't so suspiciously bright with unshed tears. She was totally serious.

"I know it sounds ridiculous—" she was clinging to both his hands "—but I don't want any more bad luck. I want our wedding to come off perfectly, so lovemaking is taboo. In Hawaiian the word is *kapu.* It's only for two nights, Kurt."

"What about days?" He tried to kiss her.

"I'm serious."

He shoved his fingers through his hair, paced across the room to put some space between them, walked back and took her hands in his.

"Carrie, honey, you know how much I love you. You know that it doesn't matter to me even if it ends up being just the two of us exchanging our vows on the beach alone. All that's important is that you be my wife. We don't need the luau or the flowers. All we need is each other and the officiate."

"*Kahuna,*" she whispered. "Rainbow said she'd booked a *kahuna.* That's a Hawaiian shaman."

"Whatever. Just so it's legal." He paused, squeezed her hands gently. They were cold as ice. "You know I love you, don't you?"

She nodded. "I do. I don't know what's wrong with me. Ordinarily I wouldn't be frightened of anything…" She let her words drift away.

"Ordinarily you'd be in complete control, just as you are in control of every other aspect of your life. Your career, your shop. You make things happen, Carrie. You're a doer. But you can't control the weather, or the airline luggage department, or the rental company's vehicle availability. Or the Cub Scouts."

When she started to open her mouth in protest, he saw the doubt in her eyes.

"Don't try to tell me a little snow on the mainland is a bad omen. It always snows in Denver in the winter," he said.

"It's almost spring."

"Last year it snowed in Denver in June."

She sighed. Her hands were finally warming up. "You're right. Maybe I am just nervous."

He reached for her, tucked her into his arms as he'd done a million times before and was relieved when her arm slipped around his waist and she melted against him.

"Aren't jitters part of being a bride?" He kissed her, thrilled when she responded like his Carrie, the Carrie who wasn't under the spell of the island lore, signs, omens and a case of nerves.

"Why don't we go for a swim?" He suggested. He needed a plunge into cold water in the worst way. "And I've got another idea. Let's book a couple's massage at the hotel spa. My treat."

"Is that a bribe?"

"You think I'd try to bribe my way into making love to you?"

"Exactly."

SOFT, SOOTHING MUSIC played in the background. The swish of overhead ceiling fans melded with the hush of trade wind breezes gently blowing through bamboo privacy shades that blocked the view of the outdoor massage area at the hotel's spa.

Two massage tables were separated just enough to let the therapists move between them to work on Kurt and Carrie at the same time. She lay there replete, draped in soft batik fabric as the therapist expertly smoothed scented oil down both sides of her spine. Kurt lay on the opposite table.

Bright red cardinals and shama thrush sang in the nearby branches. Carrie opened her eyes and found Kurt staring into them. She smiled. If she'd been a cat, she would have purred. A male therapist was working the muscles across Kurt's shoulders.

At the end of the massage, they showered off in the spa's private couples' shower, an indoor-outdoor grotto complete with a lava-rock wall that offered the experience of showering beneath a faux waterfall without having to go through a strenuous hike to get there.

They returned to the bungalow where Kurt drifted off to take a much-needed nap.

Carrie was just about to call Rainbow again when her cell phone rang. She caught it on the first note and hurried out onto the *lanai,* closing the slider so she wouldn't disturb Kurt.

"Carrie?" It was her mother.

"Hi, Mom."

"Did you see the news? A terrible snowstorm in Denver is headed our way."

"We heard from Kurt's dad. They're waiting for the airport to reopen. You shouldn't have any problem. Storms don't move that quickly."

"What a fiasco. It would have been so much easier if the wedding was in Chicago."

"It's not a fiasco, Mother. It's just a storm. They'll get here. You will, too." Carrie found herself sounding as positive as Kurt and smiled. He was stretched out asleep with his bare feet dangling over the end of the bed. Peering at him through the sliding doors, she was tempted to join him as soon as she hung up. Perhaps wake him with a kiss and—

"It would have been so much nicer if—"

"If I'd gotten married at the club. I know you would have preferred that, Mom, but that's not what we wanted."

"It's not what Kurt wanted, you mean."

"It's not what *I* wanted. Kurt just wants to get married."

"I'll bet he does, now that your shop is doing so well—"

"Mom?" Carrie wasn't in the mood to listen to a lecture on what she had to lose by marrying an artist. Dorothy had no idea that Kurt commanded close to seven figures for most of his murals now. "I've got to go. Someone is coming up the walk."

"Oh, well, goodbye then."

"I love you, Mom. See you day after tomorrow."

"Yes." That sigh again. "Goodbye, dear."

FROM THE *LANAI* Carrie could see a young woman walking up the stone path that led to the *hale.* She hurried through the room to get to the door before the girl knocked and disturbed Kurt.

Carrie stepped outside and quickly closed the door behind her.

"Aloha!" The ethereal-looking blonde was outfitted in a tiered gathered skirt of India gauze. The bright purple fabric was dusted with glittering sequins. Her long, fine hair swirled around her shoulders, which were tan and bare except for the thin spaghetti straps of her satin blouse. There was a ring on every one of her fingers. She didn't look a day over eighteen.

"I'm Oleo. I'm representing Rainbow Roberts of Happily Ever After Events."

Oleo as in margarine? Carrie wondered.

"I'm Carrie Evans." Carrie shook Oleo's hand. Her relief at finally connecting with someone from Happily Ever After was short-lived.

"Rainbow isn't here this month. She's in Bangkok. I'm her assistant and I'll be handling your wedding on Saturday."

"Bangkok?"

Oleo smiled. "She went for liposuction."

"To *Bangkok?*"

"Best cosmetic surgery in the world. A third of the cost." She was carrying a clipboard stuffed with sheets and bits of paper. As Oleo began to riffle through the pile wedged beneath the clip, Carrie didn't know whether to laugh or cry. Her wedding planner was in Bangkok having lipo and left a teenager in charge?

"Do you mind my asking how many weddings you've handled for Rainbow?" Carrie glanced out over the grounds of the hotel. It certainly *looked* like paradise.

Oleo wasn't ruffled in the least. "Oh, I don't know. Five weddings this week alone. I've worked for Rainbow for almost five years. "

"How old are you?" Carrie blurted out the question before she could stop herself.

Oleo blinked. "How *old* am I?"

Carrie shrugged. "I'm just curious."

"Thirty."

"Thirty?" The knot of tension behind Carrie's eyes began to ease.

"I told you they do wonders in Bangkok. Now…" Oleo glanced around. "Is there somewhere we can sit and go over things?"

"My fiancé is asleep inside. How about we go to the poolside tables?"

"Great."

"Let me slip inside and grab my folder."

A few minutes later they were seated beneath an umbrella, poring over Carrie's notes.

"I think photos of you and your husband in the outrigger canoe should be taken after the ceremony. That way if your dress should get wet, it won't matter as much. We've had brides who wanted to arrive at the ceremony by canoe and they've gotten drenched. Far better to exit that way when it won't matter if your dress gets wet afterward."

"Maybe we should cut the canoe ride altogether?"

Oleo waved that idea away with the toss of her beringed fingers. "It'll be a great ending—all the guests watching as you two are paddled off into the night. Tiki torches will be burning on both ends of the canoe. You'll just be paddled a few yards away to another cove and from there, driven back to the hotel."

"It certainly sounds like a dramatic ending."

"Unforgettable, really." Oleo sighed. "Well worth the extra two hundred dollars."

"Here is a photo of what I'd like my bouquet to look like," Carrie held up a magazine shot of ivory roses arranged in an abundant nosegay.

Oleo's lips pursed. Carrie realized Oleo might have been frowning, too, but who could tell with all the Botox injected between her brows?

"Elegra has her own sense of style."

"Elegra?"

"The florist. There's no need to show him, I mean *her,* any photos. Elegra doesn't work that way. He, I mean *she,* works by intuition alone. He…*she* meditates and the image of the arrangement comes to…her."

Carrie couldn't help but notice Oleo was having some gender issues in regard to Elegra.

"Let me guess," Carrie said. "Elegra just returned from Bangkok?"

Oleo's relief was mirrored in her glowing smile.

She nodded. "Exactly. She was Erik before she went to Thailand."

An image of the staid, conservative wedding planner at Willow Creek Country Club flashed across Carrie's mind. The woman was in her fifties, tailored, composed and efficient. She and her staff had coordinated years of tasteful weddings, anniversary and birthday celebrations.

And I have Rainbow, Oleo and Elegra.

A soft hint of the trade winds blew across the poolside courtyard. Somewhere nearby, a wind chime tinkled. A chill ran down Carrie's spine.

What have I done? she wondered. Asking our families to fly thousands of miles to participate in what might very well turn out to be a sideshow. She was tempted to wake Kurt up and tell him to call his dad and brother, have them spend their time tracking down his aunt Harriet and then head back to Vermont. She still had time to stop her parents. And maybe reach Ellen Marshall, her maid of honor.

She and Kurt could fly back to L.A. and marry in a couple of weeks, after things settled down. Everything was fine the way it was anyway. They were happy. They were in love. They were devoted to one another. A promise made under the full moon was binding enough for his parents for over thirty years. Why couldn't that sort of arrangement work for him?

"Carrie?" Oleo was watching her expectantly.

"Excuse me. I was just thinking about something."

"I'm sure there's a lot on your mind."

"You have no idea."

"I was just saying that you're welcome to stop by the wedding reception I'm handling this afternoon on the beach at Kalihiwai here on the North Shore." She slipped a map out from the mass of papers on the clipboard. "The ceremony is at three. The reception is on the beach afterward. Come whenever you like."

"I'm afraid my luggage hasn't arrived yet."

"It's just aloha wear. No worries." Oleo's smile was genuine.

It was too late to cancel and find another wedding coordinator at this point. Besides, Carrie had put down a huge deposit for the flowers, the cake, the luau. Which reminded her, "I tried to find the caterer earlier."

"You did?" Oleo blinked.

Carrie shrugged. "When I couldn't get a hold of Rainbow, I drove to Anahola. The caterer's mother said she's gone *holoholo.* I hope she'll be all right by Saturday."

"That just means she's gone on a pleasurable outing," Oleo explained.

"You speak Hawaiian?"

"Everyone learns a smattering of everyday Hawaiian and a few words of pidgin English if they're here long enough."

"Leinani went all the way to the Big Island. Should I worry?"

Oleo took a deep, calming breath and closed her

eyes. Carrie waited. When Oleo opened her eyes she said, "It's all good."

"The marriage certificate?"

"I have it."

"It'll be legal?"

Oleo laughed. "Perfectly legal in all fifty states. By the way, what time is it?"

Carrie noticed the young woman wasn't wearing a watch. What professional in her right mind didn't wear a watch?

"Eleven-thirty," Carrie said.

Oleo started to gather her things. "I've got to run. Lots to do before this afternoon. I'll see you there."

WHEN CARRIE WALKED BACK into the room, Kurt was awake and watching the news. The minute she crossed the threshold, he hit the power button on the remote and turned off the television, hoping she hadn't seen the screen.

"Hey, babe." He smiled and quickly tossed the remote on the chair he'd vacated. By the time he'd reached her side, he could tell something was wrong and wondered if she'd seen the news while he was sleeping.

"Where have you been?" He tried to sound as if he hadn't a care in the world.

"The wedding planner's assistant dropped by. We chatted out by the pool."

"Feeling better about things?" If anything, she'd lost all the color in her cheeks. He watched her chew on her bottom lip for a second before she finally met his eyes.

"Her name is Oleo."

"Oleo? What happened to Rainbow?" He was proud of himself for remembering the event planner's name. He'd left everything up to Carrie and now he was wondering if he shouldn't have taken a bigger part in the planning. The stress was obviously getting to her.

"Rainbow is in Bangkok getting liposuction. The florist was there recently, too. He was getting… well…let's just say he's not himself anymore."

"I'm sure they do this all the time."

"Go to Bangkok for cosmetic surgery?"

"Coordinate destination weddings."

She walked into his embrace. "Hold me, Kurt. I think I'm going nuts."

"Hey, look at me."

He placed a thumb beneath her chin, tilted her head until she was looking up at him. Her lips were the color of pastel flower petals. Her eyes lush turquoise, outlined with sable lashes. He could see that she was troubled. Her nerves communicated through her touch. It wasn't like Carrie to fall apart and the fact that she was clinging to him now had him worried. He had no idea what she would say or do when she realized what was going on back on the mainland.

"I love you," he reminded her, suddenly hoping his love was enough.

"I love you, too. With all my heart. You know that,

don't you?" She reached up, brushed his hair back, smoothed her fingertips across his brow.

"I know," he said softly.

"Love was enough for your parents, wasn't it? They didn't put themselves through all of this—"

"Six guests and a wedding on the beach is not that much, is it? But it doesn't really matter to me who actually gets here in time. I want you to be my wife. Now and forever, Carrie," he whispered.

"I want you forever, too," she said softly. "I love you. I know I'll always love you. I don't want to risk that love…not now, not ever."

"You really think we'll risk losing our love for one another by taking marriage vows?"

"My parents—"

"We are not your parents. We are not my parents, either."

She sighed. "You're right. I know how much this wedding means to you."

"It should mean everything to you, too."

He wanted her so bad it hurt. He wanted to strip her naked and take her to bed, to make love until dusk crept into the room and the stars came out one by one and filled the tropical night sky like jewels on midnight velvet. He wanted to run his hands over the smooth hills and valleys of the body he knew as well as his own. He wanted his touch to reassure her, to guide her, to encourage her to open her heart and trust in him, to trust in their love and their future together.

But he'd promised not to make love to her until the

official honeymoon. As ridiculous as it seemed, he knew that she was dead serious about the *kapu.*

He had a hard-on that wouldn't quit when he stepped away from her and walked out onto the *lanai*. He hoped the colors and textures of Hanalei Bay and the mountain ridges encircling the valley would take his mind off of making love to Carrie.

But she followed him outside, wrapped her arms around him from behind and laid her cheek against his back. He could feel her warmth through his aloha shirt.

"I'm sorry," she whispered.

He turned and took her in his arms again. "I'm trying to understand."

"I know. I have a feeling Ellen would think I'm nuts. She's always said any woman in her right mind would be dragging *you* to the altar and not the other way around."

"The beach. I'm only dragging you to the beach to get married at sunset."

"Right." She smiled up at him. "By the way, we've been invited to a wedding Oleo is handling this afternoon.

"Great. We have a little time to go sightseeing first. Besides, if I don't get out of this room and away from the bed, I'm going to try to coax you into it."

"I'll get my purse. Speaking of Ellen, I need to call and see if she got away all right."

He wanted to tell her not to bother. The last thing he needed right now was for Carrie to connect with her maid of honor.

"Why don't you call her later?"

"It'll just take a second."

He wished he'd had the presence of mind to hide her cell.

"YOU'VE REACHED Ellen Marshall. Leave a message and I'll get back to you as soon as I can."

Carrie waited until she heard the beep on Ellen's phone, left a message and added, "I can't *wait* to talk to you. I *need* to talk to you. Call me ASAP."

Ellen was pragmatic, funny and had been Carrie's best friend since middle school. When Carrie first told Ellen about Kurt, her friend had flown to L.A. from Chicago to meet him. Later, Ellen told Carrie that Kurt was a keeper and if Carrie didn't marry the man, she was going to steal him for herself.

Carrie knew her friend was kidding, but Ellen's approval was very important to her. They'd been inseparable during their formative teen years and the hours Carrie had spent at the Marshall household had been wonderful reprieves away from her own home where the tension between her parents was so thick you could almost see it.

Ellen would understand her hesitation. She would listen without laughing when Carrie explained about the signs and omens. Well, Ellen might laugh, but she wouldn't make light of Carrie's concerns.

That's what friends were for.

"Ready?" Kurt was waiting by the door looking

like *GQ*-goes-Hawaiian in his bright aloha shirt and *The Ultimate Guide to Kauai* book in hand.

"Ready." She dropped her cell in her purse and followed him out of the Honeymoon *Hale.* She didn't feel nearly as ready as she sounded.

"CLIMB, climb, climb, climb. Then climb some more."

Carrie stared down at the open guidebook in her hands and read the rest of the Hanalei 'Okolehau Trail hike description to Kurt.

"It says 'There are breaks in the vegetation affording grand views, but you couldn't care less because you're puffing so hard.'" She closed the book and handed it back to him.

Her rubber-soled reef walkers were covered with red dirt and mud. Sweat streaked her face as it slipped down from her hairline. Her new shorts had a smear of dirt ground into the seat where she'd hit the steep slope and slid a few inches after tripping over an exposed tree root.

Hands on hips, she shook her head and smiled at Kurt. "This is really no way to win a woman's heart."

Kurt laughed and kissed the tip of her nose. "Hey, admit it. You haven't thought about the wedding for a good thirty minutes."

"How could I? I've been fighting to keep my footing and trying to keep my heart from exploding."

She frowned at the narrow trail through a forest of star pines. It ran straight up along the top of a ridge that rose from the floor of the Hanalei Valley to far beyond the point where they'd stopped at the top of a packed red dirt trail. Beside them power lines from a huge tower swept down toward the watery taro fields below.

"Are we going all the way to the top?" Her legs were aching. She wasn't sure she could make it. In fact, she wasn't sure she wanted to try.

Kurt flipped through the pages of the guidebook. "It says here when you get to the top you'll be 'richly rewarded' with a sweeping view. You can see a fifth of the island from up there."

She didn't want to tell him she'd already seen enough of the island as it was, but just then a cloud slipped across the face of the sun, offering a respite from the heat. She took a deep breath and looked around. The view from where they were was already spectacular.

"How about I sit on that flat rock over there and wait while you go up and enjoy the view? When you come back you can tell me what you saw, okay?"

Kurt hesitated, staring uphill. "No problem. I'm ready to head back if you are."

He loved challenges. She could tell that he really wanted to go on.

"Seriously, I'll be fine. I'll sit and relax. It's so peaceful here." She took a cleansing breath and looked around. Indeed, the spot was magical. The forest floor looked as if a primeval sprite had sprinkled ferns and tiny star-shaped pine trees all over the ground.

"You sure?"

"Positive."

Kurt slipped a small bottled water out of his pack and handed it to her. "It shouldn't take me long," he promised.

"Take your time." They hadn't passed a soul on the trail. Nor had there been any cars parked in the trail-head lot beside the Hanalei River. Carrie made an attempt to brush off the large rock she'd chosen then remembered her pants were already stained. She sat down, stretched out her legs and crossed them at the ankles. She pulled her cell phone out of her pocket. There was no service on the side of the mountain.

A soft, cool breeze started the trees whispering *hush, hush.* Somewhere nearby, a thrush sang a trilling song. She tried whistling in imitation. The thrush stopped singing for a moment, then whistled back.

Carrie closed her eyes and leaned back on her hands, turning her face to the sun until the sound of twigs snapping on the trail below her brought her upright, eyes open, alert.

As if he'd materialized out of nowhere, a tall Hawaiian man with long white hair falling well past his shoulders stood before her. He wore a pair of faded shorts, a T-shirt with the image of a bone fishhook printed on it, and bare feet stained with red dirt. He seemed impervious to the pine twigs and pebbles beneath them. Beside him, a white, mixed-breed shaggy dog sat on its haunches with its tongue lolling.

Startled by the intrusion, street-smart from living in L.A., Carrie immediately got to her feet, ready to run, to scream, to defend herself. She glanced up the hill. Kurt was already out of sight, hidden by the mass of jungle growth.

"Aloha," the man said. His voice was deep, resonant, as if it came from depths outside himself and was channeled through. "Beautiful day, eh?"

"V…very." It took a second to find her voice. She glanced down at the dog then back up at the man. "I…I'm waiting for my fiancé. He's…he's just up there a little way."

She had no idea exactly where Kurt was at this point. Still within shouting distance, she hoped.

"Fiancé."

She nodded. The man hadn't moved an inch. She took a step back and realized there was nowhere to go. If she backed up any farther, she risked sliding down the steep mountainside. "Our wedding is Saturday."

"Congratulations." The man was watching her closely. Too closely. He was silent for a moment or two, his expression serious.

She had the strangest feeling, almost as if he could see into her soul. He closed his eyes, raised his palms and began to chant in a voice that carried on the trades, over the tops of the trees, down into the valley.

"He kau auane'i i ka lae 'a'a."

Goose bumps rose over Carrie's skin. The man's hands dropped to his sides again, he opened his eyes and smiled without explanation.

"Was that a blessing?"

Rainbow Roberts had arranged for a *kahuna* to perform a traditional wedding ceremony. Oleo said it was confirmed.

The man shook his head. "An old Hawaiian proverb. Watch out, lest the canoe land on a rocky reef." He reached down and scratched the dog behind its ear. The animal panted and looked up at him in adoration.

To her relief, the man glanced at the trail ahead and said, "I'd better get going."

Obsessing over the meaning of his words, Carrie barely nodded when he bid her goodbye.

"Aloha," she said, watching him head up the trail. Her knees weak, Carrie sank back down onto the rock.

Watch out lest the canoe land on a rocky reef.

Watch out.

Rocky reef.

The rocky reef of life? The canoe of marriage?

Was it a literal warning?

Is he warning us not to get into the torch-lighted canoe after the ceremony?

Or not to get married at all?

She kept glancing at her watch for another forty minutes before she saw Kurt heading back down the trail and greeted him with questions rather than a kiss.

"Did you see that big Hawaiian man?"

"I didn't see anyone." Kurt wiped his brow with the back of his arm. "The view up there was spectacular. I could see all the way to the Kilauea lighthouse. It was incredible."

"You didn't run into a Hawaiian with long white

hair? And a white dog?" She glanced around him, gazed at the trail. "There must be more than one way up."

"No, and I didn't pass anyone on my way down, either."

"But…" Her heart started to pound. "But there was a man here. He spoke to me. He had a big white dog. He scared the heck out of me. It was almost as if he appeared out of nowhere—and he said something in Hawaiian."

Kurt was digging in his backpack. "There's only one way up and down. I didn't see a man or a dog." He found what he was looking for and pulled out a plastic bottle. "You need some Gatorade. I think you're dehydrated."

"I'm not *de*-anything. I saw a Hawaiian and his dog. He gave me a warning."

Kurt stopped, Gatorade in hand, and stared at her as if he'd just realized what she was saying. His voice dropped an octave. "What *kind* of a warning?"

"Cryptic, that's for sure. Something about the canoe hitting a rocky reef."

"Did he threaten you?"

Suddenly he was all testosterone, ready to defend her, ready to take on an unknown threat. The last thing she needed was him tearing off after some innocent guy who was only trying to impress a tourist.

She laid her hand on his arm. "He didn't threaten me. In fact, I'm sure it was probably nothing."

"What's a canoe got to do with anything?"

"We're leaving the reception luau in a canoe."

"We are?"

She frowned. "Maybe I should cancel it. What do you think?"

"I think you're starting to lose it."

"You're afraid *I'm* starting to *lose* it?" She shook her head. "You don't *believe* I just saw someone standing right *here?*" She pointed to the spot where the man had been. "You think I'm cracking up?" She waved her arms around. "You think maybe this wedding is driving me crazy?"

He tried to put his arm around her shoulders and draw her near.

"It's okay, babe. You've been under a lot of stress."

"Don't *babe* me." She skirted around him and started back down the trail. The slope was steep and slick. The descent was as hard as the climb.

She gave him the silent treatment all the way back to the Jeep. As soon as they were on the road back up the hill to the Hanalei Plantation, she pulled her cell phone out of her pocket. Kurt glanced over for a moment as if about to tell her something, but then turned his attention back to the road.

Three voice mails. Relieved, she saw that one was from Ellen. Two were from her mother. She dialed her maid of honor first.

"HI, CARRIE. It's Ellen. Can you believe this weather? Sheesh. The whole world is shut down. What happened to global warming anyway? I made it to Denver but nothing is moving. Don't worry, though, where there's a will, there's a way. It'll take a national disaster to keep me from getting to Kauai for your wedding."

"Now Ellen is stuck in Denver, too." Carrie stared out the front window. Kurt focused on the narrow road to the hotel.

"Hmm."

"That means your dad and Turk haven't gotten out yet." She was punching in the number to hear the next message.

"Carrie. It's your mother. You must be just frantic by now. Thank heavens we hadn't already left for the airport. O'Hare is shut down. All of the city streets are closed. Give me a call."

"What in the world is going on over there?" She turned to Kurt as he pulled up to the valet parking stand. Her stomach did a backflip as she slid out of the Jeep and waited for him.

"Ready?" He ushered her through the lush tropical garden of the open-air lobby toward the path to their *hale.*

"Both Denver and O'Hare airports are shut down." She glanced up, saw that his expression never changed and realized he wasn't surprised in the least. She stopped dead in her tracks beside a faux waterfall.

"You knew."

When he finally met her eyes, she was certain he'd kept the truth from her.

"You already *knew* both airports are shut down. What's going on, Kurt?"

"Storm of the century."

"What?"

"That's what CNN is calling it. A freak storm of the century. It's moving across the U.S. from the northwest. Ice and snowstorms hitting with unprecedented ferocity. Nothing's moving."

"You knew—"

"Carrie."

"You knew and you didn't even tell me. Why not?"

"I wanted us to have a few hours alone without you worrying about it."

"When did you hear?"

"While you were out at the pool with the wedding coordinator, I woke up and turned on the news."

She remembered how he'd turned the set off the moment she walked in.

None of their guests were on the way. Her parents hadn't even left their house—which in itself was actually a relief. She couldn't imagine her mom and dad camped out in the frequent-flyer lounge. Poor Ellen was no doubt stuck in the airport waiting area with the masses. Turk and Bogie were there somewhere, too.

She pictured Kurt's aunt as a frail eighty-nine-year-old in an airport somewhere, slumped over in a corner with a blanket draped over her shoulders.

Carrie couldn't help it. She moaned.

"What?" Kurt's dark eyes mirrored his concern—not for his stranded guests, but for her sanity.

"Your poor aunt," she mumbled.

"Aunt Harriet is more resourceful than my dad and the dryer lint genius combined."

She almost smiled. "What are we going to do, Kurt?"

"What can we do? I'll call Turk and Bogie and see how they're doing. You call your mom and Ellen. Then we'll change clothes and head up the road to meet Oleo and check out that wedding reception."

"That's *it?* That's your idea of *doing* something?"

"We could stand around and wring our hands, but there's really nothing we can do about the weather, is there?"

He had a point. There wasn't much they could do but wait out the storm on the mainland. *The Storm of the Century.*

Another natural occurrence.

Another omen?

"We can worry just as well on the beach sipping glasses of champagne," Kurt reasoned.

Carrie pictured the Hawaiian on the mountain trail, his piercing dark eyes, his nimbus of white hair. His white dog.

Watch out lest the canoe land on a rocky reef.

Forget about the rocky reef. Things were already bad enough. Standing there beside the faux waterfall with its cool mist on her skin, Carrie shivered. She felt adrift, buffeted by life, as if she were about to capsize.

"What are you thinking?"

She couldn't tell him she was wondering how many more warnings they could ignore before calling off the whole thing.

KURT FLIPPED the plastic key card in the lock, opened the door to the Honeymoon *Hale.* He stood back to let Carrie enter. When she skirted past without a word or a look, his heart sank. All the setbacks were getting to her and he felt helpless.

"I'm going to call Ellen and my mom," she said.

"I'll check in with Bogie and Turk."

His call took less than two minutes. Bogie had managed to nab a table in a pizza and beer bar at the airport and was content watching the sports network. Turk was off trolling for women. Kurt could just see his twin in a casual slouch, hands in his pockets, his long hair artfully falling over his left eye as he flirted with every woman in the place.

Women tended to view Turk as harmless once he started quizzing them on the make and model of their clothes dryers and asking whether or not they used fabric softener or dryer sheets.

When he hung up, Kurt heard Carrie tell Ellen goodbye. Then she tried to call her mother, but gave up.

"The phones must be down. My calls to Chicago aren't going through."

"What about Ellen? Did you reach her?"

She nodded. "She's made her way over to the private jet terminal, hoping to find a way out other than on a commercial airline."

"If anyone can do it, she can." He wished there was something he could do. Wished he'd told Carrie about the storm when he'd learned of it.

She picked up the television remote, muted the sound and flipped through the channels until she found CNN. She stared at the screen for a moment, then turned to him with a disappointed sigh.

He crossed the room, wrapped her in his arms, slipped his hand beneath her tank top, cupped her breast, felt the familiar weight and shape of it against his palm.

She closed her eyes and leaned into him. "Don't tempt me, Kurt. We don't need any more bad luck."

"Run all that by me again. I still don't get how this could be bad luck." She was warm and pliant in his arms and with a little encouragement, he knew she'd be willing.

"Even if it isn't bad luck for the bride and groom to see each other before the wedding, you should have something to look forward to on our wedding night," she whispered.

"Hey, I look forward to this every night. What's that they say about men? We have a sexual thought every twenty seconds?"

"It's more like every two, I think. Especially with you."

"So you can guess what kind of agony I'm in. It's been a hell of a lot of seconds since we made love." He lifted his hips and pressed his erection against her thigh.

She pulled away. She wasn't smiling, but she looked a bit calmer.

"Where are you going?" He watched her long legs and the seductive sway of her hips as she walked across the room.

"To take a shower and change into my new sundress before you succeed in breaking the *kapu* and seducing me. We're going to a wedding reception to see what Oleo can do, remember?"

THEY DROVE TWENTY MINUTES out of their way before they realized they'd missed the road to Kalihiwai Beach. According to KONG radio, the trades were gusting a good twenty-five to thirty knots. Kurt parked as close as he could to where all the wedding guests were huddled inside a huge, white vinyl cabana enclosed on three sides.

The reception tent, complete with see-through plastic windows, had been set up on the sand. Ironwood pines planted on the edge of the roadside shed long, green-gray needles every time the wind blew through them. Wedding guests in colorful attire were huddled inside the tent like garments stuffed in a dry-cleaning bag.

Some gathered near a long buffet table full of appetizer platters and a three-tiered wedding cake on display at one end.

As Carrie and Kurt made their way into the tent, Oleo spotted them and rushed over.

"Aloha, you two." She pressed her palms together

and bowed, her smile wide as the horizon. Apparently she wasn't a bit concerned that the stiff breeze was about to lift one corner of the tent.

Carrie introduced Kurt. He held tight to her hand, almost as if he feared she'd go racing back to the car.

"Let me show you the *pupu* table," Oleo offered.

Kurt leaned close to Carrie's ear and whispered, "The poo poo table?"

Carrie laughed. "Appetizers. *Pupus* are finger food."

"Heavy *pupu*, we like to call this sort of spread," Oleo explained. "This isn't just light finger food. This is enough for a meal." She waved her hand over an array of sushi, delicate lettuce wraps, a mound of stuffed mushrooms, skewers of barbecued chicken strips, fruit and veggie trays.

"Did Kau Kau Katering provide all of this?" Carrie stared at the spread, incredulous that it could have come out of the small house in Anahola.

Oleo shook her head. "No. Leinani does our luau menu, which is what you've chosen. She's still on the Big Island."

Kurt leaned close. "Looks like Oleo can handle our wedding. This is a much bigger event than we've planned."

"Considering there may not be anyone at our wedding at all," Carrie whispered.

Her concern about Oleo's abilities was the least of her worries now. There were at least a hundred guests under the big tent and everything appeared to be well organized, every detail covered. Oleo certainly couldn't be held accountable for the stiff breeze.

As they neared the serving table, Carrie noticed the cake frosting appeared to be coated with a light dusting of sand carried on the wind.

"I see you've noticed the Swarovski crystal bride and groom on top of the cake." Oleo drew them closer to the wedding confection. She pointed to the miniature couple planted atop the cake.

"These were handcrafted from a photo of the couple. Each pair is unique."

The little bride and groom were encrusted with colorful crystal gems, their feet anchored in frosting.

Kurt leaned close and whispered in Carrie's ear. "Please. Tell me you didn't."

She glanced over her shoulder and caught him smiling into her eyes. She couldn't resist a chuckle. "Of course not. We're having flowers on top of the cake. A lei of orchids. Somehow I couldn't imagine us encrusted in crystals."

Outside the tent, the real bride and groom were positioned near the water's edge, posing for photos. They were dressed exactly like their crystal clones. The young woman had chosen a traditional wedding gown with a wide tiered skirt that billowed out like a parachute. The trade wind gusts wreaked havoc with her dress, tipping it up behind her, exposing her backside.

The groom wore long linen pants, a white shirt and a yellow cummerbund that matched his bride's bouquet. He snagged her veil just as it went sailing off her head.

Sand pelted the sides of the tent with each gust. The harried bride and groom gave up on the photo-op, held hands and shielded their eyes as they sprinted toward the shelter.

Just as Carrie looked down at the cake, the crystal bride and groom toppled off and landed facedown at her feet in the sand. A chill ran down her spine.

KURT STARED AT THE FALLEN CAKE topper for a heartbeat before he turned to Carrie. All the color had drained from her face. As signs and omens went, the toppled bride and groom was a biggie. *Huge.*

Drastic times called for drastic measures, he reckoned. He had to act and act fast if there was any hope of salvaging the situation. Before Carrie could utter a word, he took a deep breath and said, "I'm beginning to think you're right."

"What?" She tore her attention away from the unfolding drama playing out in front of them. Oleo was reaching for the bejeweled bride and groom while the newlyweds came reeling into the tent.

Kurt grabbed her by the arm and dragged her across the beach to the car.

"I think the signs and omens are pretty damn clear," he told her.

"What are you saying?"

"I'm finally convinced you're right. *Somebody,* the universe, the island, the ancient spirits, *whatever,* something is trying to warn us not to go through with this. I think the only recourse we have is to call off the wedding until we figure out what's really going on here."

THEY DROVE BACK to the hotel in silence as Carrie wrestled with the realization that Kurt had finally seen the light. When he suggested they have drinks in the hotel lounge, she agreed. They were shown to a table overlooking the magnificent view of Hanalei Bay and Mount Makana in the distance.

On the far side of the open-air room, a trio entertained guests with a medley of Hawaiian songs. Accompanied by the tinkle of ice in glasses and the hushed conversations going on at various tables scattered around the terrace, the singers' mellow voices sometimes faded beneath the occasional whir of the blender behind the bar.

Still adjusting to Kurt's announcement on the beach, Carrie tried to focus on what he was saying.

"I mean, when you first mentioned signs and omens, I have to admit I thought you were just having bridal jitters, but obviously, that's not the case. I see that now. When those figurines fell off the cake, my eyes were opened."

Carrie's stomach was too queasy to enjoy the frothy white *chichi* the waitress set before her. She pulled the violet vanda orchid off the rim of the glass, took a sip of the coconut and vodka whipped drink, then ignored it.

"It's not as if we're going to disappoint our families," Kurt was saying. "They aren't even here. We'll probably lose our deposits for the tables and tent and caterer—" he shrugged "—but I can afford to take the hit." He reached for her hand across the table. "Better safe than sorry, right?"

As she sat listening to this new Kurt, the Kurt who had campaigned for her to say yes for years, the Kurt who wanted to be married more than anything in the world, all she could think of was…*the wedding is off…the wedding is off.*

After everything that had happened, after all the signs and warnings, she should have been relieved, but now all she felt was empty. She'd been planning their wedding for months and now it was suddenly over. To have it end so abruptly—

"I probably should call Oleo and tell her," she said.

"No problem. I'll handle it. You've done all the planning. It's the least I can do."

She listened as he went on about his determination to research Hawaiian lore. There definitely was something going on, he said, and he wanted to learn as much about it as he could.

"I'm so sorry, Carrie. I'm sorry it took me so long to become convinced canceling is for the best." He finished his mai tai in record time and added, "Something bigger than us is at work here." Then he noticed her untouched drink. "Are you going to drink that?"

She shook her head. "No, I…"

He reached for the tall glass and polished off her *chi-chi* in record time. She'd never seen him have more than a couple beers or a minimal amount of wine at dinner.

"Come on," he said, taking the lead and pushing away from the table. "I'll walk you back to the *hale.*"

He walked around her chair, waited for her to stand. His charm, his smile, his old-world manners were part of the reason she fell for him. All the way back to the *hale,* she felt the warmth of his palm as his hand rode possessively at her waist.

When they reached the door, she realized now that the wedding was officially off, it would be safe to lift her self-imposed ban on lovemaking. She needed him more than ever. Needed his reassurance that their love could stand this and any test. She needed to lose herself in him. In their love for each other.

Outside the front door, she turned and wrapped her arms around his neck. He kissed her long and hot and for a moment she forgot she was no longer going to be his bride on Saturday.

Images of Kurt carrying her over the threshold of the Honeymoon *Hale* and then repeating the custom when they returned home to their L.A. loft filled her with melancholy. When the kiss ended, she cupped his cheek and whispered, "I love you."

"I love you, too, babe." Kurt reached around her to open the door. Once inside, he walked straight to the table where she'd left her books.

Kurt riffled through them, picked up three or four and asked, "Mind if I borrow these?"

"Of course not." She watched him head to the closet. He pulled out his travel bag, set it on the bed and then began to take his clothes out of the low chest of drawers.

"What are you doing?" Her heart nearly fell to her toes.

"Packing." He didn't look at her.

"Why?"

The wedding is off.

Could he have *possibly* meant their relationship was over, too?

"The signs were pretty clear, Carrie, and we ignored them. We don't need any more bad luck, do we? Why tempt fate any more than we already have?"

She watched him toss in the last of his things and then he laid the books atop his clothes. He zipped the bag shut, set it on the floor and pulled up the handle.

"You're *leaving* me?"

He walked over and kissed the tip of her nose. "Of course not."

"Then what's going on?" She indicated the bag with a wave of her hand.

"I'm getting my own room. We don't want to upset the Hawaiian spirits any more than we have already, do we?"

IN THE HAZY TWILIGHT of half sleep and the gray hour before dawn, Carrie woke up alone. She lay nestled in bed watching the sunlight gain strength as dawn illuminated the room. Without Kurt beside her, a heavy emptiness pervaded the cottage and she realized his presence filled her life in ways she hadn't realized until now. She felt hollow without him. A future without Kurt was unthinkable.

Just then, her cell phone went off, and she leaped out of bed and tore across the room to grab it. She found her phone on the table near the remaining books. Hoping it was him, her heart faltered when she read Ellen's number on the screen. Still, she needed to talk to her closest friend in the worst way.

"Carrie?" Ellen sounded as if she were right next door. "How are you doing?"

"I'm fine," she lied.

"You sounded down when you answered."

"There's a lot going on here. Everyone is stuck in airports. My parents decided not to even leave the house. I hate to have put you out like this—"

"Oh, Carrie! Don't worry about me. I've met the most fabulous guy. I was trying to pick up any kind of flight the minute this storm lifts—it is moving on by the way—and it just so happens his private jet is headed to Maui. He offered to fly me to Kauai. We got to talking and he's the *greatest* guy. Single. Good-looking. And he flies his own jet! All this has happened because of you, so don't worry about me."

Ellen barely paused to take a breath before she asked, "So what about Saturday? Are you ready?"

Carrie took a deep breath and decided to quickly fill her in on the details. She ran through the events of the past three days, right up to the minute the Swarovski crystal couple took a dive and hit the sand.

Ellen had begun chuckling about the time Carrie mentioned the word *holoholo* and by now she was wheezing with laughter, so much so that she couldn't speak.

Carrie added, "And now the wedding's off."

There was an abrupt, sobering silence on the other end of the connection.

"Kurt agreed to this?" Ellen asked.

"It was his idea."

"You're kidding, right? He's the one who so wanted to get married all along."

"He moved out and got his own room." Carrie still couldn't believe it. She glanced around the silent *hale*. Outside, a lone couple was strolling along the beach. That should be us, she thought.

"He got his own room? So as not to upset the gods, or what?"

"Yeah. Something like that. I'd suggested a ban on sex until the wedding night—"

Ellen started laughing again but not for long. "Possibly one of the dumbest ideas you've ever had, Carrie."

Carrie rolled her eyes. "Oddly enough, it seemed perfectly logical at the time. I was willing to try anything." Even now she wasn't so certain that Kurt's change of heart wasn't the last and final sign.

"What are you going to do?"

"Any suggestions?"

"Where's Kurt right now?"

"In his own cottage."

"Kurt is the best thing that ever happened to you. You make damn sure that wedding comes off on Saturday, Carrie. If I don't get there, we'll all celebrate when you get back. Besides, I might make it for the reception," Ellen said.

"I'm still convinced the wedding was doomed," Carrie admitted.

"Unconvince yourself. Most of all, unconvince him."

"He didn't believe me for days and now, suddenly, he's a complete convert. What if I'm wrong? What if there are no signs, no omens? What if it was just my fear and nerves and now Kurt's called it off."

"Convince him that you should go through with it."

"What if I can't?" Carrie wasn't so sure she was ready to change her mind about things, let alone his.

"Do what comes naturally. Resort to a method as old as time. Seduce him."

S*EDUCE HIM*.

Kurt loved her. The proposal, the wedding, had been his idea from the start. There should be no need to seduce him if it really was safe to hold the ceremony.

What surprised her the most was how very much the idea of putting the wedding off until some unknown date and time depressed her—and how terrible it had been waking up without him this morning.

Carrie slipped into her new swimsuit, tied the bright *pareau* around her waist and paused before the mirror in the dressing area. She left her hair loose, skimming her shoulders. A touch of peach lip gloss and she was ready.

As she walked down the path toward Kurt's smaller cottage, she plucked a plumeria blossom off a nearby tree and tucked it behind her ear.

He was outside on his *lanai,* a cup of coffee on the table. Feet up, casual in a swimsuit and no shirt, he was browsing through one of the mythology books.

Inexplicably nervous, Carrie smoothed down her hair and carefully picked her way across the flat stone path to his *lanai.* When he saw her he looked up and smiled.

When he started to stand, she waved him back into his seat and then bent to kiss him hello.

"Have you been up a while?"

"No, I slept like a baby. Just thought I'd read a bit."

She wished he'd set the book down and hold her. She sat on the arm of his chair, practically draping herself across him as she slipped her arm across his shoulders. Her breast was a fraction of an inch from his cheek. He didn't seem to notice.

Instead he asked, "Remember that guy you saw on the trail? White hair? White dog?"

She nodded. "Of course."

"The one I didn't see," he added.

"You still don't believe me."

He tapped the cover of a book. "Oh, but I do now.

Madam Pele, Goddess of Fire, is known to appear in the form of an old woman with long white hair—"

"But I saw a man—"

"She also appears as...*a white dog.*" His brows went up. "A white *dog,* Carrie. Like the one that apparently appeared to you and then disappeared on the trail."

"But, you surely don't think—"

He set the book aside, spread his hands and shrugged. "What other explanation could there be?"

She frowned, thinking. "Well, the man could have taken another trail."

"I didn't see another trail. You are convinced the island was trying to warn us not to marry. I think you're right."

She thought about the dog, innocent-looking enough, tongue lolling. One would think that Madam Pele, Goddess of Fire, would have more going on behind the eyes—

"I'm pretty sure now that was just a dog," she said. "But...I've been thinking, maybe if we hadn't chosen Kauai, if we'd opted for the country club or L.A. or somewhere else, things might have come off without a hitch."

"Hitch. Glitch. Whatever. We shouldn't chance it. Right?"

She thought about this morning, about waking up alone. Remembered how excited he'd been about the wedding, how anxious he was to be married—which reminded her to ask, "Did you call Oleo and cancel yet?" She held her breath.

"I spoke to her, yes. Last night."

Her voice sank to a near whisper. "Oh."

"Why?"

"I thought maybe I should call myself and explain," Carrie said.

"She completely understood," he added. "And she wished us luck."

When Kurt stood and started gathering up the books, Carrie realized he hadn't given her more than a cursory glance since she arrived. Under normal circumstances, he'd have pulled her into his arms for a welcoming kiss the instant he saw her. She adjusted her *pareau,* shoving it lower on her hips. When that failed to draw his attention, she got up and walked over to the door of his cottage.

"Maybe we should take a walk on the beach," she suggested, leaning provocatively against the wall, her back arched, one arm casually thrown over her head. She hoped he would respond to the invitation in her eyes.

"How about a massage later?" she tempted. "My treat this time."

Kurt glanced at his watch. "Sorry, babe. I went for a run earlier this morning and met a great guy named Gavin Kapono, an art teacher from Kapa'a High School. I saw him outlining a mural on the wall near the luau pavilion and introduced myself. You know something? He even recognized my name.

"Some of his students are going to be here working on a mural this weekend. I told him about the at-risk kids I work with in L.A. and we realized we have a lot in common. Gavin invited me to play a round of golf at Princeville before he meets his students here this afternoon."

Finally he reached for her, but only held her long enough to give her a quick kiss on the cheek. "You don't mind, do you?"

KURT WOULD NEVER FORGET the look on Carrie's face for as long as he lived. Shock, puzzlement, frustration—a stew of emotions clouded her deep blue eyes when he told her that he'd rather play golf than take her up on her massage invitation.

He didn't think turning the tables on her would be this painful, but when she'd perched herself on the arm of his chair and leaned against him, it had taken all his willpower not to pull her across his lap.

He'd been up all night, pacing, hoping he'd done the right thing, wondering how—because of one short article in an in-flight magazine—she'd gone off on such a tangent. After looking through the reading material she'd amassed, he had to admit Hawaiian legend was definitely steeped in mystery, magic and tragedy.

At first he'd worried Carrie was using the signs and omens the article mentioned as an excuse to call off the wedding, but now he saw how it had been fairly easy to become convinced the island spirits were conspiring against them.

It had taken him two years to convince her that he loved her and that they should get married. He'd never lost sight of his goal. All he could do now was hold out until she realized that their love was stronger than any setbacks, that nothing should or could stand in the way of their future happiness together.

"OKAY, KIDS, put your palms together and wiggle your thumbs so it looks like a fish swimming in the water."

Carrie paused near the pool to watch a Hawaiian woman with smiling eyes teach a half dozen tourists' kids a simple hula. A few minutes later she reached her *hale,* opened the door and saw her suitcase sitting in the middle of the floor. A note from the airlines was attached.

Sorry for the delay. Mahalo for your understanding.

The minute she opened the bag, her wedding gown was revealed. She caressed the ivory silk with her fingertips, held it against her and studied herself in the mirror. It was simple, yet as elegant and sophisticated as she remembered. Seeing it against the backdrop of tropical decor and the azure water in view beyond the *lanai,* she realized it wasn't the perfect choice anymore. She sat down on the edge of the bed, holding the gown in her lap.

Kurt was right. Their wedding wasn't about all the trimmings or the party. It wasn't about her gown, or their guests, or the location. It was an outward symbol of their love and it shouldn't matter where or when it took place so long as it did take place. Their wedding was about them. It was the beginning of a lifetime of love and commitment.

She carefully hung the gown in the closet and then her cell rang. Her heart jumped, but it wasn't Kurt calling from the golf course. This time it was her mother.

"We're definitely not going to make it, dear. I'm so sorry." Her mother didn't sound as sorry as Carrie felt. "Has anyone from Kurt's family arrived?"

"As far as we know, his dad and brother are still in Denver."

"I hear Denver might reopen, but nothing is for certain. O'Hare is still closed. I hate to say I told you so, honey—"

Then *don't* say it, Carrie thought.

"—but I was afraid this was a bad idea from the get-go." Then Dorothy added, "I called the club and luckily there's been a reception cancellation in July. I asked them to hold it for you until I could get back to them, but if we're planning to book, they need to know now."

Chicago in July. Carrie pictured herself a melted puddle of ivory silk. A formal reception at the country club was far from the simple sunset-on-the-beach wedding she'd planned.

She glanced across the room at her suitcase. Her mother just said Denver airport was about to reopen. Maybe another bad omen was reversing itself.

"Call and tell them we won't be booking a wedding or a reception at the club."

"Do you plan to go through with this without anyone there?"

Suddenly everything became perfectly clear to Carrie.

"Kurt and I are here. That's what this is all about. Us. Our love for each other." Carrie waited, but her mother was silent on the other end of the line. "I'll call and let you know how things are going on Saturday, Mom. As far as I'm concerned, the wedding is on."

"You're sure about this, dear?"

"I am," she said, amazed and suddenly more certain than she'd ever been about anything. "Everything is going to work out the way it's supposed to."

She hung up, found her wedding folder and called Oleo but was only able to leave a voice mail. She leafed through the notes and numbers and found the name of the *kahuna* scheduled to marry them.

Ekau Ka'awai didn't advertise, but Oleo assured her that all Rainbow's clients raved about him. Carrie found his name listed in the white pages. She took a deep breath and punched in his number.

"Aloha." His voice was deep and sure. She explained that he was supposed to have been officiating at her wedding, but that it had been canceled and she wanted to rebook him.

"I don't have my calendar in front of me," he told her. "Give me your name and I'll see what's up. What happened that you thought you had to cancel?"

"There were just too many things going wrong," she explained.

"You two not getting along?"

"Oh, it's not that. It's just—"

"Jitters?"

"No, at least I don't think so. I don't get jitters. Except—"

"Except what?"

"So many things kept happening over the last few days. Things I took to be omens of bad luck. *Ho... ho'ailona,* I believe you call them."

"*Ho* what?"

"*Ho'ailona?*" She struggled to pronounce the word correctly. "Signs and omens."

She heard a pause and then he said, "*Hua ho'ailona.* Where did you hear this term?"

"I read about it in an in-flight magazine article and started researching—"

"Hawaiian words have more than one meaning. There are hundreds of words for rain alone. *Ho'ailona* not only refers to signs and omens, but it can also stand for a trophy or an emblem of victory."

"But...this past week, it seemed as if nature was transpiring against us. The storm on the mainland. My guests stranded. My fiancé's aunt is missing. I was given the wrong rental car. My bag was lost."

"*Was* lost."

"Yes. They found it."

"And the weather?"

She glanced at the television where the *Weather Channel* was on mute.

"Clearing."

"And the guests? The missing auntie?"

"We haven't heard yet. My parents aren't coming now. And there's a possibility—"

"Anything is possible if you believe in it enough."

"I know." She did know. She had believed in herself enough to make a success of her shop. She believed in Kurt, in his talent. She believed in their love, his commitment to her and hers to him.

"A triumph. A trophy," she whispered. A wedding was certainly the outward symbol of a union that was meant to survive the test of time. Promises made and vows of love that would last for an eternity. *A triumph.*

Suddenly she needed to talk to Kurt in the worst way.

"Thank you so much for your time, Mr. Ka'awai."

"No worries. Get back to me when you're sure."

KURT SHOT THE WORST GOLF round of his life. It was impossible to focus with his future riding on the hope that turning the tables on Carrie would bring her to her senses.

It wasn't until he and Gavin Kapono finished up and stopped by the nineteenth hole for a beer and some chili dogs that he finally called her.

She picked up on his first ring. He tried to sound nonchalant.

"We just finished up," he told her. "What are you doing?"

"Wandering around the hotel shops. How was golf?" She didn't sound at all sad about the canceled wedding.

"Golf was great," he lied.

"Will you be back soon?"

"About an hour, I guess." He wanted to see her right now, but thought he better not rush back yet. "Anything up?"

"I miss you, that's all."

"I miss you, too, Carrie." He noticed Gavin was nodding and smiling his way. "See you in a bit," he added before he hung up.

"What's so funny?" he asked the art teacher.

"You got it bad, man. You got it bad. I hope your plan works."

"If it backfires, I could be flying home without a wife or a fiancée."

"I just hope you're better at convincing your girl to marry you than you are at golf."

"FLIGHTS ARE FINALLY LEAVING Denver airport. The airlines are trying to handle the backup and the backlash from angry customers stranded for more than twenty-four hours…"

After Carrie raced back from the hotel boutique with her hands full of shopping bags, the first thing she did was turn on the *Weather Channel*. When she heard Denver was reopened, she actually laughed out loud and thought, *an omen. A very good omen indeed.*

She started pulling things out of the bags—she'd found just about everything she thought she'd need this afternoon—and ordered the rest from room service. There was a long *pareau* of transparent red fabric shot through with gold thread, a wisp of black thong bikini that was probably illegal on a family-oriented beach, and some Tahitian noni massage oil.

Too modest to wear the thong in public, she slipped into the terry robe provided by the hotel. Then she packed the see-through *pareau* along with the massage lotion in the shopping bag and headed out of the *hale*.

When she arrived at Kurt's room, she thankfully discovered he'd left the door to his *lanai* wide-open. Room service had already delivered the ice bucket and the bottle of champagne she'd ordered along with a tropical fruit platter and an assortment of chocolate brownies and macadamia nuts.

She checked the time then draped herself across Kurt's bed and arranged the crimson fabric across her nearly nude body. She turned on the television and proceeded to wait for him to walk in.

Forty minutes later, the ice in the bucket was nearly melted when she heard Kurt's key card slide into the lock. She had a cramp in her neck from resting her head on her hand while she watched TV, but managed to rearrange herself into a seductive pose.

Kurt stopped just inside the door. His eyes widened. His gaze slid over her body, her barely covered breasts, the rise of her hip, the hint of thong bikini beneath the red and gold fabric.

"What's going on?" He glanced at the table laden with delicacies and swallowed.

"I missed you."

"I wasn't gone *that* long."

"Try that again."

"I missed you, too." He hadn't taken a step toward the bed.

"Make love to me, Kurt."

He swallowed hard. "Taboo, remember? Or *kapu.*" He crossed his forearms in the shape of an X and held them up in front of his face. "*Kapu!* No make love."

She tried not to laugh. "I've done a little reading myself. Since I'm the one who issued the *kapu,* I can lift it."

"You sure you want to? We might be asking for more trouble."

"You haven't seen the news. Denver airport is open. *And,* my bag arrived. Our luck is changing."

He glanced at his watch. "Listen, Gavin wants me to meet the kids working on the mural and give them some advice."

She couldn't believe it. "But—"

Just then, someone started pounding on the door and a high-pitched voice rang out, "Kurt? Kurt, open up!"

"Damn," he mumbled, quickly grabbing the end of the bedspread and tossing it over Carrie, covering all but her head and shoulders.

"Who is it?" She grabbed the bedspread and pressed it to her breasts as she struggled to sit up against the pillows.

"It's my great-aunt Harriet." Kurt shoved his hands through his hair as he headed for the door.

"Kurt, wait!" Carrie called out, but it was too late. He opened the door.

A spark plug of a woman in a pith helmet, khaki jodhpurs and camp shirt came breezing in. She looked as if she'd taken a wrong turn and stepped out of a Victorian novel set in deepest, darkest Africa.

"Aha!" She pointed at Carrie, suddenly sounding like Stanley discovering Livingston. "The blushing bride, I presume!"

Aunt Harriet scanned the room, spotted the champagne and brownies and made her way to the table. Grabbing the biggest brownie on the platter, she plopped into a chair and turned to Kurt.

"Pop the cork on that champagne, dear. Have I got a story for you."

"SO THERE I WAS, in Florida, aware that if I flew to meet your father and Turk in Denver, I'd never get here. I got online, rerouted my trip and went through Dallas and L.A. instead. I decided to spend a night there with an old friend and thus, I had some fun and avoided the *Storm of the Century.*" Harriet shouted "storm of the century" like an overzealous television newscaster.

Kurt jumped up off the end of the bed. "Great story, Aunt Harriet. I told Carrie we didn't have to worry about you."

He glanced at Carrie. She was gaping at his aunt and he was sorry he hadn't told her that his family was a bit more eccentric than he'd led her to believe.

"Well," he said, standing over Harriet as she helped herself to another brownie, "I'm sure you'll want to get settled in your own room."

"I'm fine here," she said, sipping on a glass of champagne. "Like to get to know your bride a bit better."

"Actually I was just telling Carrie that I'm late for an appointment. I'm sure you'd enjoy meeting a local artist and his class, though."

"I am sure I'd like to take off these hiking boots and kick back here with Carrie."

When she refused to budge on her own, Kurt took his aunt by the elbow and hefted her off the chair. He refilled her champagne glass, handed it back and said, "Come along with me, Harriet. Carrie was just saying how tired she is. She's looking forward to a nap."

"Nap? Gave those up years ago. Sleeping is just practicing to die."

He glanced over his shoulder at Carrie and mouthed, "I'll be back in a few minutes. Stay right there."

Carrie nodded. "Nice meeting you, Aunt Harriet. I'll see you in a little while."

She heard Harriet ask as Kurt ushered her out, "Why is she in bed in the middle of the day?"

The door closed behind them with a bang. Sweltering beneath the spread, Carrie threw it off her and got up. She poured a glass of champagne for herself and went into the dressing area to check out her thong in the mirror, wondering how much Harriet had seen before Kurt covered her up. The darn thing was riding up something awful.

Just as she flicked on the light, she noticed a slip of paper lying on the counter. It was written in Kurt's handwriting. The heading at the top immediately drew her attention.

Goal: Wedding by Saturday.
Things to Do:

1. Keep goal in sight.
2. Don't weaken. Prior planning prevents poor performance.
3. Don't give in to temptation until Carrie comes to her senses.

Carrie stared at Kurt's notes to himself. Obviously he hadn't believed they'd been given any signs or omens at all. He'd been humoring her, hoping she would "come to her senses."

Carrie read his note to himself again and realized she'd played right into his hands. At least he didn't yet realize he'd accomplished his goal with such ease.

Two could play at this game, she thought.

She set the paper down exactly where he'd left it. She slipped on her robe, grabbed her shopping bag with the massage oil and *pareau* safely tucked inside, and hurried back to the Honeymoon *Hale*.

Twenty minutes later, Kurt knocked at her door. She took her sweet time answering and effectively blocked the opening with her body.

"Aren't you going to let me in?"

"Actually I really do feel like taking a nap. Power of suggestion, I guess." She shrugged and tossed her hair back over her shoulder.

He reached for her. She let him slip his hand between the lapels of the terry robe, let him run his thumb over the edge of her breast before she pulled back. She heard him groan in frustration.

"You mentioned something about lifting the *kapu,*" he reminded her. His eyes were half lidded, his lashes dark and thick. She took a deep breath and reminded herself that he'd tricked her into thinking that he believed her, that he shared her concerns and that he'd called off the wedding because of them.

She leaned close, ran her finger across his lips and whispered, "I changed my mind."

"But, Aunt Harriet's here. That's a good omen. It's a sign that things are turning in our favor."

She thought of the chubby woman in the pith helmet inhaling brownies and washing them down with champagne. "Possibly, but you've read the Hawaiian lore. I'm just not sure her arrival is proof enough."

"Your luggage has been returned. Denver airport is open."

He looked so darn hopeful she almost gave in.

"Sorry, honey." She reached out to cup his chin, pulled him close and planted a long, slow kiss on his lips. "Why don't you call me later? I'll meet you and Harriet for dinner at the Plantation Café."

"You're sure?"

"Positive."

The minute the door closed, she got on her cell and left a voice mail for Oleo.

Afraid she'd get no response she added, "Call me back. It's a matter of life or death."

Then she changed out of her thong and into a comfortable summer sundress. She found Bogie's and Turk's cell numbers in her wedding folder and left them both voice mails. Then she dialed Ellen and ended up leaving a voice mail for her, too.

Her phone rang a few seconds later.

"Life or *death?* What on earth is happening?" Oleo wanted to know.

"I had to get you to call me back somehow."

"Kurt specifically asked me not to call you. He said he was handling things from now on."

"Actually I'm back in charge, so no need to call him."

"I'm glad you're feeling better. Is the wedding on or off?"

Feeling better? "What did Kurt tell you, exactly?"

"That I wasn't to talk to you at all. He said you ate something that gave you a bad case of King Kamehameha's revenge, that he didn't want you disturbed. I was to put everything on hold and check in with him tomorrow morning."

"Very interesting." Carrie talked to Oleo for a good twenty minutes and then hung up.

SATURDAY MORNING, Carrie skipped breakfast and walked on the beach alone thinking about last night's dinner. She needn't have worried about keeping Kurt at arm's length. Aunt Harriet had talked the whole time, regaling them with details about a recent wine-tasting trip to Italy and France with the Gad-A-Bouts, a group of senior travelers from her condo complex in Miami. By the time Kurt walked Carrie back to the bungalow, she truly did have the headache she claimed was plaguing her.

She almost confessed to having found his note, but decided turnabout was fair play and sent him off with a good-night kiss, although she slipped out onto her *lanai* to watch him walk away.

After a leisurely morning walk on the beach, she returned to the central courtyard area of the hotel where guests were dining on macadamia nut waffles in the open-air restaurant and kids were already splashing in the pool.

She spotted Kurt across the courtyard with Gavin Kapono and his art students, who were working on their mural. She drew close enough to watch, choosing a seat in a shady corner of the outdoor poolside bar that was not yet open. From her vantage point, she could see Kurt, but he couldn't see her.

The mural depicted a scene straight from precontact Hawaii—a traditional Hawaiian village with terraced fields and huts thatched in *pili* grass nestled on the shores of Hanalei Bay. Outrigger sailing canoes sailed into the bay. Waterfalls streamed down the mountainsides. Wisps of clouds wreathed the peaks.

She listened as Kurt spoke to the teens, inspiring them to be great, to dream big dreams. When he told them how important it was to set goals, write them down and never lose sight of them, she couldn't help but smile.

She watched Kurt pick up a brush and begin to sketch a couple standing near the water's edge—a man and woman holding hands, gazing out at the setting sun. The figures were Hawaiian in stature and features, but in her heart she knew without a doubt that he was thinking of the two of them, portraying a timeless scene of a couple committed to one another—a couple whose love would stand the test of time.

As she watched him work his magic with brush and paint, she realized more than ever what she'd known since the night their eyes first met across a crowded hotel lobby. Their love was not about a wedding ceremony, not about gifts or banquets or the guests who would have wished them well.

Their love was not about an hour or a day. It was about a lifetime together.

KURT WATCHED the Kapa'a High School teens paint, offering suggestions when asked. Mostly he enjoyed listening to their easy banter and commenting on the color choices they made.

He'd spent most of the past two days in a cold sweat. He hadn't been able to reach Oleo and finally, her florist phoned him to say that Oleo had to go to the other side of the island and could no longer keep things on hold. She said she was fed up. The wedding was canceled.

He hadn't heard from his dad and brother, and, as

far as he knew, Ellen Marshall hadn't contacted Carrie, either. This morning, when he discovered Carrie wasn't in the *hale,* he spent the early morning hours staring out at the bay convinced he'd handled things in the worst possible way. Around ten, he'd wandered out to the central pool area to join Gavin's class, which was better than moping alone on his *lanai*.

He felt someone come up beside him and knew without looking that it was the woman he loved. He turned to her and his heartbeat spiked as it always did whenever he saw Carrie.

"Hi." He leaned in for a chaste kiss and then introduced her to Gavin and the students. The girls checked out Carrie's capri pants and tank top. The boys simply checked out Carrie until Gavin reminded them all to get back to work. She admired the students' work and then they told the art teacher goodbye. Kurt led her over to the bar where he ordered two mango-guava juice drinks.

"To you," he said, raising his glass in a toast. "I love you."

She took a sip, refused to meet his eyes. "I love you, too."

He slipped his hand beneath her chin, raised her face until their eyes met.

"This was supposed to be our wedding day."

"Yes," she whispered. "It was."

"It's not too late to—"

She cut him off. "I was thinking—"

"What were you thinking?"

"That we should have dinner out on the beach tonight. Right here, at the hotel. They'll set it up for us. Just the two of us. It would be so romantic—"

Romantic. But not a wedding.

He'd played the wrong hand. His heart sank.

"Listen, Carrie, I have a confession to make."

"What could you possibly have to confess?" She reached up and ran her fingers through his hair.

"I wasn't ever really convinced the island was conspiring against us. This whole thing about warning signs and omens is just nuts. I went along with you, hoping that you'd come to realize nothing should stand in our way. Instead I should have persuaded you to marry me in front of a judge before all this escalated. Now I've messed things up with Oleo, and she canceled on me. With any luck, she might be able to pull something together. We'll get married and celebrate back on the mainland. In L.A., in Chicago, in Vermont. All three places if you'd like."

Her eyes widened in shock. "You *never* believed in the signs and omens? You were just *pretending* to go along with me?" She was no longer smiling.

"I thought fighting fire with fire was the way to go. That if I left you alone to really think about it, if I called it off, you'd come around and realize nothing should stand in the way of our future together."

"You thought pretending to go along with me, that letting me believe you were actually sensitive to my fears, would somehow help me ignore the signs and change my mind?"

"I never, ever meant to hurt you."

"But even if your little scheme worked and I *had* changed my mind, it's too late now."

"So you're still convinced we shouldn't go through with the wedding?" He reached for her hand, relieved to see that at least she was still wearing her engagement ring.

"When the time is right, we'll be married." She smiled into his eyes and shrugged. "Will you have dinner with me on the beach tonight?"

"Anything you want." He tried to hide the fact that his heart was breaking. He'd be kicking himself all the way back across the Pacific.

"I'll go talk to the concierge." She finished her juice and smiled up at him sweetly. "At least we'll be alone together on the beach at sunset—unless you want to invite your aunt to join us."

"I'd rather it be just the two of us," he assured her.

As he watched her walk away, his dream of marrying Carrie tonight faded like the fleeting colors of a rainbow, and he knew he had no one but himself to blame.

MUSIC DRIFTED OUT of the lounge and across the hotel terrace. The haunting lyrics of a 1950s love song embraced Carrie and Kurt as they strolled hand in hand down the winding path to the beach below the plantation hotel. He couldn't help but notice that many of the guests dining at the outdoor café watched as they passed by.

When Carrie had opened the door to the Honeymoon *Hale* to greet him, her loveliness took his breath away. She was wearing a long white cotton gown with a deep ruffled hem. The print was a white-on-white hibiscus pattern and unlike a traditional muumuu, the gown was fitted to outline her figure. Her hair was down, the way he liked it.

"You're beautiful," he whispered.

She smiled and lifted her skirt to reveal her white sandals. "Thank you. I found this muumuu in the boutique and couldn't resist taking home a memory."

"If I'd known you were going to wear it, I'd have worn something less casual." He had on swim trunks and an aloha shirt, hoping they might take a moonlit dip after their al fresco dinner. He thought about slipping the white cotton gown off her shoulders and watching her sleek body slip nude through the shimmering water.

"You look great," she told him. "Perfect."

Halfway down the path, the trail curved along the hillside. They'd reached a secluded section where the beach directly below them was still hidden by the overgrown foliage. Carrie stopped walking and Kurt took the opportunity to pull her into his arms.

She melted into his embrace, slipped her arms around his shoulders and kissed him with a searing passion that had nothing to do with the heat of the tropics.

"Sunset is in an hour," she whispered breathlessly when the kiss ended. "The hotel promised tiki torches, white linens, the works for our little dinner. I really think we should be heading down."

He tried to smile. The weather had been clear and sunny all day. There was a light breeze to keep things just cool enough. Sunset promised to be stunning.

Hand in hand, they continued down the path to the beach. When they cleared the final bend, Kurt stopped in his tracks.

A scene reminiscent of a fairy tale appeared on the beach below. A peaked tent, much smaller than the one they'd seen at the disastrous beach wedding, had been set up in the center of the cove. Every tent pole was decorated with a huge spray of tropical blooms. A few round tables draped with white linen were scattered beneath the canopy. Floral centerpieces with tropical flowers in bright yellow, red and orange graced each table. Tiki torches surrounded the area. His heart sank.

"Looks like someone is getting married." Even he could hear how pathetically disappointed he was, but it was his own fault their wedding wasn't happening tonight.

He scanned the rest of the cove, wondering where the hotel might have set up their intimate dinner for two. It was bad enough their wedding had been canceled—now he'd have to watch some other lucky couple celebrate their wedding day.

His gaze swept the beach and trailed back to the center of the reception tent where there was something oddly familiar about a short, stout woman in billowing white linen pants and an oversize shirt standing drinking champagne.

"That looks like Aunt Harriet." It would be just like her to wrangle an invitation to someone else's wedding.

When Carrie didn't respond, he realized her hand was trembling inside his own. He turned to her and noticed bright, unshed tears swimming in her blue eyes.

"Are you all right?" he whispered.

"That *is* your Aunt Harriet."

"Party crashing, no doubt."

"I don't think so." Carrie smiled, blinking back tears.

"What's wrong?"

"Look again."

He did and there, beside his great-aunt, stood his dad, Bogie. Not far away, Turk was chatting with a petite blonde—who just happened to be Oleo. As he watched, dumbfounded, a golf cart equipped with sand tires came rolling down the beach. The Island Grinds Kau Kau Katering logo was painted on the side of the cart.

Two Hawaiian women were seated in front and the back of the cart was piled high with boxes, dishes and serving trays. In the lagoon that fronted the hotel beach, an outrigger canoe decorated with ti leaves and tiki torches was just touching the sand. Five Hawaiian men jumped out and beached the canoe.

"What's going on?" Kurt shook his head in confusion.

Carrie squeezed his hand. "Will you marry me, Kurt? Will you stand beside me as I promise to love and cherish you all the days of my life? Will you make me the same vow?"

For the first time in his life, he found himself close to tears. Suddenly the scene on the beach was forgotten and there was just the two of them.

"Of course, I will. Now and forever."

Someone on the beach shouted, "There they are!"

Everyone started clapping. The outrigger paddlers picked up a ukulele and a guitar and began to sing in Hawaiian. One of the women on the golf cart danced the hula on the sand.

"Looks like they're starting without us." Carrie laughed and clung to his hand as they ran down the path to the beach.

WHEN THEY REACHED the canopy, it was Carrie's turn to be speechless as Ellen Marshall appeared on the arm of a tall, handsome man she introduced as her knight in shining armor. He had whisked her out of the Denver airport on his private jet before the commercial planes were cleared to leave.

"I didn't know you'd be here!" Carrie cried. The last she'd heard from Ellen, her friend was still in Denver.

"I told you I wouldn't miss this for the world," Ellen said.

"I can't believe it." Carrie hugged Ellen again.

"When I checked in, the woman at the front desk

let me in on what was happening and told me I'd better hurry or I'd miss the wedding. We rushed right down," Ellen assured her.

"So everyone knew but me?" Kurt was still beside Carrie, though busy shaking his brother's hand and accepting congratulations from his dad, Turk and Oleo.

Carrie nodded. "Everyone. I'm amazed no one let the cat out of the bag. Oleo was pretty upset about having to pretend to cancel on you."

Just then a woman who had to be six foot four handed her a tropical bridal bouquet made up of pink anthuriums, orchids, touches of tuberose and fern.

"I'm Elegra, the florist. I hope you like it." The woman wore an off-the-shoulder print gown and towered over everyone on the beach.

"It's absolutely stunning. Truly inspired," Carrie told her. "Thank you so much."

Carrie paused to take in the scene again. Her breath caught when she recognized the Hawaiian man she'd seen on the hiking trail. He was standing at the water's edge, same long white hair, same white dog at his side.

"Oh, no. What's he doing here?" she whispered.

Oleo followed her gaze. "Him? That's Ekau Ka'awai, the *kahuna.*"

Carrie turned to Kurt and they both started laughing at the same time.

"I guess it's a sign," she said.

"I guess it's an omen," he added.

Oleo nodded to Turk and suddenly, Kurt's brother

whisked him away from Carrie and led the groom across the sand. Together, they stood beside the *kahuna.*

The musicians started to play the Hawaiian Wedding Song. Elegra handed Ellen a wreath of flowers to place on Carrie's head and then adjusted the hem of her gown. Without urging, everyone fell into place, encircling Ekau, Kurt and Turk near the shoreline. Bogie offered Carrie his arm and escorted her to Kurt. Ellen followed close behind.

Then as the sun began to sink into the turquoise water and the sky fired with a pink and orange glow, Carrie smiled up into Kurt's eyes.

"I promise to love and cherish you all the days of my life," she whispered.

He held her hands in his and vowed the same.

When a wispy passing cloud sprinkled them with a light mist and a rainbow danced on the rays of the setting sun, Ekau Ka'auwai announced, "May you be blessed by *'ehu,* the Hawaiian mist, and *anuenue,* the rainbow, all the days of your lives." Then the *kahuna* winked and told all those gathered around the newlyweds, "In Hawaii, a rainbow is a very, *very* good sign."

Two crowns, two islands, one legacy

Volume 1 – April 2009
BILLIONAIRE PRINCE, PREGNANT MISTRESS
by Sandra Marton

Volume 2 – May 2009
THE SHEIKH'S VIRGIN STABLE-GIRL
by Sharon Kendrick

Volume 3 – June 2009
THE PRINCE'S CAPTIVE WIFE
by Marion Lennox

Volume 4 – July 2009
THE SHEIKH'S FORBIDDEN VIRGIN
by Kate Hewitt

8 VOLUMES IN ALL TO COLLECT!

Two crowns, two islands, one legacy

Volume 5 – August 2009
THE GREEK BILLIONAIRE'S INNOCENT PRINCESS
by Chantelle Shaw

Volume 6 – September 2009
THE FUTURE KING'S LOVE-CHILD
by Melanie Milburne

Volume 7 – October 2009
RUTHLESS BOSS, ROYAL MISTRESS
by Natalie Anderson

Volume 8 – November 2009
THE DESERT KING'S HOUSEKEEPER BRIDE
by Carol Marinelli

8 VOLUMES IN ALL TO COLLECT!